TALES
of
TERROR

DICK DONOVAN

Annotations by George Cavendish

Solis Press

MORE HORROR FROM SOLIS PRESS:

Horror Tales: "The Vampyre", "Carmilla", and "Olalla" edited by George Cavendish

A Book of Bargains by Vincent O'Sullivan

The Hound of the Baskervilles: Illustrated Edition by Arthur Conan Doyle
and Sidney Paget

First published in 1899. This edition has minor spelling changes and
has been completely reset and published in 2018 by Solis Press

Typographical arrangement copyright © 2018 Solis Press

Annotations copyright © 2018 George Cavendish

ISBN: 978-1-910146-36-1

Published by Solis Press, PO Box 482,
Tunbridge Wells TN2 9QT, Kent, England

Web: www.solispress.com | *Twitter*: @SolisPress

Contents

About the Author

DICK DONOVAN WAS THE *nom de plume* of James Edward Preston Muddock (1843–1934), also known as Joyce Emmerson Preston Muddock.

Muddock was a prolific British journalist and author of mystery and horror fiction. Between 1889 and 1922 he published nearly 300 detective and mystery stories and, for a time, his detective stories were as popular as those of Arthur Conan Doyle.

Muddock travelled to India when he was fourteen years of age and his later career as a journalist allowed him to travel to China, the USA and Australia. He used his extensive knowledge of the world to good effect in the short stories collected in this volume.

One of the characters in Muddock's detective fiction was the Glaswegian detective, Dick Donovan. This character became so popular and well known, that Muddock started publishing stories using Dick Donovan as his pen name. Muddock also wrote true crime stories, horror, and thirty-seven novels, mostly as Dick Donovan.

Despite his prolific output, Muddock had few publications after about 1920 and died in 1934, relying on his daughters to support him at the end of his life.

This new edition of *Tales of Terror* from Solis Press features short annotations as footnotes that explain some aspects of the stories that nowadays might be less well understood.

I

The Woman with the 'Oily Eyes'

THE STORY AS TOLD BY DR. PETER HASLAR, F.R.C.S.LOND.[1]

ALTHOUGH OFTEN URGED TO put into print the remarkable story which follows I have always strenuously refused to do so, partly on account of personal reasons and partly out of respect for the feelings of the relatives of those concerned. But after much consideration I have come to the conclusion that my original objections can no longer be urged. The principal actors are dead. I myself am well stricken in years, and before very long must pay the debt of nature which is exacted from everything that lives.

Although so long a time has elapsed since the grim tragedy I am about to record, I cannot think of it even now without a shudder. The story of the life of every man and woman is probably more or less a tragedy, but nothing I have ever heard of can compare in ghastly, weird horror with all the peculiar circumstances of the case in point. Most certainly I would never have put pen to paper to record it had it not been from a sense of duty. Long years ago certain garbled versions crept into the public journals, and though at the time I did not consider it desirable to contradict them, I do think now that the moment has come when I, the only living being fully acquainted with the facts, should make them known, otherwise lies will become history, and posterity will accept it as truth. But there is still another reason I may venture to advance for breaking the silence of years. I think in the interest of science the case should be recorded. I have not always held this view, but when a man bends under the weight of years, and he sniffs the mould of his grave, his ideas undergo a complete change, and the opinions of his youth are not the opinions of his old age. There may be exceptions to this, but I fancy they must be very few. With these preliminary remarks I will plunge at once into my story.

It was the end of August 1857 that I acted as best man at the wedding of my friend Jack Redcar, C.E.[2] It was a memorable year, for our

---

1 Fellow of the Royal College of Surgeons, i.e. he was a qualified surgeon. He, perhaps unusually, uses the title doctor rather than the traditional mister.

2 Civil engineer.

TALES OF TERROR *Dick Donovan*

hold on our magnificent Indian Empire had nearly been shaken loose by a mutiny which had threatened to spread throughout the whole of India.[3] At the beginning of 1856 I had returned home from India after a three years' spell. I had gone out as a young medico in the service of the H.E.I.C.,[4] but my health broke down and I was compelled to resign my appointment. A year later my friend Redcar, who had also been in the Company's service as a civil engineer, came back to England, as his father had recently died and left him a modest fortune. Jack was not only my senior in years, but I had always considered him my superior in every respect. We were at a public school together, and both went up to Oxford, though not together, for he was finishing his final year when I was a freshman.

Although erratic and a bit wild he was a brilliant fellow; and while I was considered dull and plodding, and found some difficulty in mastering my subjects, there was nothing he tackled that he failed to succeed in, and come out with flying colours. In the early stage of our acquaintance he made me his fag,[5] and patronized me, but that did not last long. A friendship sprang up. He took a great liking to me, why I know not; but it was reciprocated, and when he got his Indian appointment I resolved to follow, and by dint of hard work, and having a friend at court, I succeeded in obtaining my commission in John Company's[6] service. Jack married Maude Vane Tremlett, as sweet a woman as ever drew God's breath of life. If I attempted to describe her in detail I am afraid it might be considered that I was exaggerating, but briefly I may say she was the perfection of physical beauty. Jack himself was an exceptionally fine fellow. A brawny giant with a singularly handsome face. At the time of his wedding he was thirty or thereabouts, while Maude was in her twenty-fifth year. There was a universal opinion that a better matched couple had never been brought together. He had a masterful nature; nevertheless was kind, gentle, and manly to a degree.

---

3 This rebellion was against the British East India Company that controlled India. The company at its peak had a military force of about 260,000, which was twice the size of the British Army.

4 The Honourable East India Company (another name used for the British East India Company).

5 To act as an unofficial servant to senior students.

6 John Company was an informal name of the British East India Company. Perhaps after Sir John Watts, one of the founders.

It may be thought that I speak with some bias and prejudice in Jack's favour, but I can honestly say that at the time I refer to he was as fine a fellow as ever figured as hero in song or story. He was the pink of honour, and few who really knew him but would have trusted him with their honour, their fortunes, their lives. This may be strong, but I declare it's true, and I am the more anxious to emphasize it because his after life was in such marked contrast, and he presents a study in psychology that is not only deeply interesting, but extraordinary.

The wedding was a really brilliant affair, for Jack had troops of friends, who vied with each other in marking the event in a becoming manner, while his bride was idolized by a doting household. Father and mother, sisters and brothers, worshipped her. She was exceedingly well connected. Her father held an important Government appointment, and her mother came from the somewhat celebrated Yorkshire family of the Kingscotes. Students of history will remember that a Colonel Kingscote figured prominently and honourably as a royalist during the reign of the unfortunate Charles I.

No one who was present on that brilliant August morning of 1857, when Jack Redcar was united in the bonds of wedlock to beautiful Maude Tremlett, would have believed it possible that such grim and tragic events would so speedily follow. The newly-married pair left in the course of the day for the Continent, and during their honeymoon I received several charming letters from Jack, who was not only a diligent correspondent, but he possessed a power of description and a literary style that made his letters delightful reading. Another thing that marked this particular correspondence was the unstinted—I may almost say florid—praise he bestowed upon his wife. To illustrate what I mean, here is a passage from one of his letters:—

I wish I had command of language sufficiently eloquent to speak of my darling Maude as she should be spoken of. She has a perfectly angelic nature; and though it may be true that never a human being was yet born without faults, for the life of me I can find none in my sweet wife. Of course you will say, old chap, that this is honeymoon gush, but, upon my soul, it isn't. I am only doing scant justice to the dear woman who has linked her fate with mine. I have sometimes wondered what I have done that the gods should have blest me in such a manner. For my own part, I don't think I was deserving of so much happiness, and I assure you I am happy—perfectly, deliciously happy. Will it last? Yes, I am sure it will. Maude will always be to me what she is now, a flawless woman; a woman with all the virtues that turn women into angels, and without one of the weaknesses or one of the vices which too often mar an otherwise perfect feminine character. I hope, old boy, that if ever you marry, the woman you choose will be only half as good as mine.

Had such language been used by anyone else I might have been disposed to add a good deal more than the proverbial pinch of salt before swallowing it. But, as a matter of fact, Jack was not a mere gusher. He had a thoroughly practical, as distinguished from a sentimental, mind, and he was endowed with exceptionally keen powers of observation. And so, making all the allowances for the honeymoon romance, I was prepared to accept my friend's statement as to the merits of his wife without a quibble. Indeed, I knew her to be a most charming lady, endowed with many of the qualities which give the feminine nature its charm. But I would even go a step farther than that, and declare that Mrs. Redcar was a woman in ten thousand. At that time I hadn't a doubt that the young couple were splendidly matched, and it seemed to me probable that the future that stretched before them was not likely to be disturbed by any of the commonplace incidents which seem inseparable from most lives. I regarded Jack as a man of such high moral worth that his wife's happiness was safe in his keeping. I pictured them leading an ideal, poetical life—a life freed from all the vulgar details which blight the careers of so many people—a life which would prove a blessing to themselves as well as a joy to all with whom they had to deal.

When they started on their tour Mr. and Mrs. Redcar anticipated being absent from England for five or six weeks only, but for several reasons they were induced to prolong their travels, and thus it chanced I was away when they returned shortly before Christmas of the year of their marriage. My own private affairs took me to America. As a matter of fact a relative had died leaving me a small property in that country, which required my personal attention; the consequence was I remained out of England for nearly three years.

For the first year or so Jack Redcar wrote to me with commendable regularity. I was duly apprised of the birth of a son and heir. This event seemed to put the crown upon their happiness; but three months later came the first note of sorrow. The baby died, and the doting parents were distracted. Jack wrote:—

My poor little woman is absolutely prostrated, but I tell her we were getting too happy, and this blow has been dealt to remind us that human existence must be chequered in order that we may appreciate more fully the supreme joy of that after-life which we are told we may gain for the striving. This, of course, is a pretty sentiment, but the loss of the baby mite has hit me hard. Still, Maude is left to me, and she is such a splendid woman, that I ought to feel I am more than blest.

This was the last letter I ever received from Jack, but his wife wrote at odd times. Hers were merely gossipy little chronicles of passing events, and singularly enough she never alluded to her husband, although she wrote in a light, happy vein. This set me wondering, and when I answered her I never failed to inquire about her husband. I continued to receive letters from her, though at long intervals, down to the month of my departure from America, two years later.

I arrived in London in the winter, and an awful winter. London was indeed a city of dreadful night. Gloom and fog were everywhere. Everybody one met looked miserable and despondent. Into the public houses and gin palaces such of the poor as could scratch a few pence together crowded for the sake of the warmth and light. But in the streets sights were to be seen which made one doubt if civilization is the blessing we are asked to believe it. Starving men, women and children, soaked and sodden with the soot-laden fog, prowled about in the vain hope of finding food and shelter. But the well-to-do passed them with indifference, too intent on their own affairs, and too wrapped in self-interests to bestow thought upon the great city's pariahs.

Immediately after my arrival I penned a brief note to Jack Redcar, giving him my address, and saying I would take an early opportunity of calling, as I was longing to feel once more the hearty, honest grip of his handshake. A week later a note was put into my hand as I was in the very act of going out to keep an appointment in the city. Recognizing Mrs. Redcar's handwriting I tore open the envelope, and read, with what feelings may be best imagined, the following lines:—

> For God's sake, come and see me at once. I am heart broken and am going mad. You are the only friend in the world to whom I feel I can appeal. Come to me, in the name of pity.
>
> MAUDE REDCAR.

I absolutely staggered as I read these brief lines, which were so pregnant with mystery, sorrow, and hopelessness. What did it all mean? To me it was like a burst of thunder from a cloudless summer sky. Something was wrong, that was certain; what that something was I could only vaguely guess at. But I resolved not to remain long in suspense. I put off my engagement, important as it was, and hailing a hansom directed the driver to go to Hampstead, where the Redcars had their residence.

The house was detached and stood in about two acres of ground, and I could imagine it being a little Paradise in brilliant summer weather; but it seemed now in the winter murk, as if a heavy pall of sorrow and anguish enveloped it.

I was shown into an exquisitely furnished drawing room by an old and ill-favoured woman, who answered my knock at the door. She gave me the impression that she was a sullen, deceptive creature, and I was at a loss to understand how such a woman could have found service with my friends—the bright and happy friends of three years ago. When I handed her my card to convey to Mrs. Redcar she impertinently turned it over, and scrutinized it, and fixed her cold bleared grey eyes on me, so that I was induced to say peremptorily, 'Will you be good enough to go to your mistress at once and announce my arrival?'

'I ain't got no mistress,' she growled. 'I've got a master'; and with this cryptic utterance she left the room.

I waited a quarter of an hour, then the door was abruptly opened, and there stood before me Mrs. Redcar, but not the bright, sweet, radiant little woman of old. A look of premature age was in her face. Her eyes were red with weeping, and had a frightened, hunted expression. I was so astounded that I stood for a moment like one dumbfounded; but as Mrs. Redcar seized my hand and shook it, she gasped in a nervous, spasmodic way:

'Thank God, you have come! My last hope is in you.'

Then, completely overcome by emotion, she burst into hysterical sobbing, and covered her face with her handkerchief.

My astonishment was still so great, the unexpected had so completely paralysed me for the moment, that I seemed incapable of action. But of course this spell quickly passed, and I regained my self-possession.

'How is it I find this change?' I asked. It was a natural question, and the first my brain shaped.

'It's the work of a malignant fiend,' she sobbed.

This answer only deepened the mystery, and I began to think that perhaps she was literally mad. Then suddenly, as if she divined my thoughts, she drew her handkerchief from her face, motioned me to be seated, and literally flung herself on to a couch.

'It's an awful story,' she said, in a hoarse, hollow voice, 'and I look to you, and appeal to you, and pray to you to help me.'

'You can rely upon my doing anything that lies in my power,' I answered. 'But tell me your trouble. How is Jack? Where is he?'

'In her arms, probably,' she exclaimed between her teeth; and she twisted her handkerchief up, rope-wise and dragged it backward and forward through her hand with an excess of desperate, nervous energy. Her answer gave me a keynote. She had become a jealous and embittered woman. Jack had swerved from the path of honour, and allowed himself to be charmed by other eyes to the neglect of this woman whom he had described to me as being angelic. Although her beauty was now a little marred by tears and sorrow, she was still very beautiful and attractive, and had she been so disposed she might have taken an army of men captive. She saw by the expression on my face that her remark was not an enigma to me, and she added quickly: 'Oh, yes, it's true, and I look to you, doctor, to help me. It is an awful, dreadful story, but, mind you, I don't blame Jack so much; he is not master of himself. This diabolical creature has enslaved him. She is like the creatures of old that one reads about. She is in possession of some devilish power which enables her to destroy men body and soul.'

'Good God! this is awful,' I involuntarily ejaculated; for I was aghast and horror-stricken at the revelation. Could it be possible that my brilliant friend, who had won golden opinions from all sorts and conditions of men, had fallen from his pedestal to wallow in the mire of sinfulness and deception?

'It is awful,' answered Mrs. Redcar. 'I tell you, doctor, there is something uncanny about the whole business. The woman is an unnatural woman. She is a she-devil. And from my heart I pity and sorrow for my poor boy.'

'Where is he now?' I asked.

'In Paris with her.'

'How long has this been going on!'

'Since a few weeks after our marriage.'

'Good heavens, you don't say so!'

'You may well look surprised, but it's true. Three weeks after our marriage Jack and I were at Wiesbaden. As we were going downstairs to dinner one evening, we met this woman coming up. A shudder of horror came over me as I looked at her, for she had the most extraordinary eyes I have ever seen. I clung to my husband in sheer fright, and I noted that he turned and looked at her, and she also turned and looked at him.

'"What a remarkable woman," he muttered strangely, so strangely that it was as if some other voice was using his lips. Then he broke into a laugh, and, passing his arm round my waist, said: "Why, my dear little woman, I believe you are frightened."

'"I am," I said; "that dreadful creature has startled me more than an Indian cobra would have done."

' "Well, upon my word," said Jack, "I must confess she is a strange-looking being. Did ever you see such eyes? Why, they make one think of the fairy-books and the mythical beings who flit through their pages."

'During the whole of the dinner-time that woman's face haunted me. It was a strong, hard-featured, almost masculine face, every line of which indicated a nature that was base, cruel, and treacherous. The thin lips, the drawn nostrils, the retreating chin, could never be associated with anything that was soft, gentle, or womanly. But it was the eyes that were the wonderful feature—they absolutely seemed to exercise some magic influence; they were oily eyes that gleamed and glistened, and they seemed to have in them that sinister light which is peculiar to the cobra, and other poisonous snakes. You may imagine the spell and influence they exerted over me when, on the following day, I urged my husband to leave Wiesbaden at once, notwithstanding that the place was glorious in its early autumn dress, and was filled with a fashionable and light-hearted crowd. But my lightest wish then was law to Jack, so that very afternoon we were on our way to Homburg, and it was only when Wiesbaden was miles behind me that I began to breathe freely again.

'We had been in Homburg a fortnight, and the incident of Wiesbaden had passed from my mind, when one morning, as Jack and I were on our way from the Springs, we came face to face with the woman with the oily eyes. I nearly fainted, but she smiled a hideous, cunning, cruel smile, inclined her head slightly in token of recognition, and passed on. I looked at my husband. It seemed to me that he was unusually pale, and I was surprised to see him turn and gaze after her, and she had also turned and was gazing at us. Not a word was uttered by either of us, but I pressed my husband's arm and we walked rapidly away to our apartments.

' "It's strange," I remarked to Jack as we sat at break fast, "that we should meet that awful woman again."

' "Oh, not at all," he laughed. "You know at this time of the year people move about from place to place, and it's wonderful how you keep rubbing shoulders with the same set."

'It was quite true what Jack said, nevertheless, I could not help the feeling that the woman with the oily eyes had followed us to Homburg. If I had mentioned this then it would have been considered ridiculous, for we had only met her once, and had never spoken a word to her. What earthly interest, therefore, could she possibly take in us who were utter strangers to her. But, looked at by the light of after events, my surmise was true. The creature had marked Jack for her victim from the moment we unhappily met on the stairs at Wiesbaden. I tell you, doctor, that that woman is a human ghoul, a vampire, who lives not only by sucking the blood of men, but by destroying their souls.'

Mrs. Redcar broke down again at this stage of her narrative, and I endeavoured to comfort her; but she quickly mastered her feelings sufficiently to continue her remarkable story.

'Some days later my husband and I moved along with the throng that drifted up and down the promenade listening to the band, when we met a lady whom I had known as a neighbour when I was at home with my parents. We stopped and chatted with her for some time, until Jack asked us to excuse him while he went to purchase some matches at a kiosk; he said he would be by the fountain in ten minutes, and I was to wait for him.

'My lady friend and I moved along and chatted as women will, and then she bade me good-night as she had to rejoin her friends. I at once hurried to the rendezvous at the fountain, but Jack wasn't there. I waited some time, but still he came not. I walked about impatiently and half frightened, and when nearly three-quarters of an hour had passed I felt sure Jack had gone home, so with all haste I went to our apartments close by, but he was not in, and had not been in. Half distracted, I flew back to the promenade. It was nearly deserted, for the band had gone. As I hurried along, not knowing where to go to, and scarcely knowing what I was doing, I was attracted by a laugh—a laugh I knew. It was Jack's, and proceeding a few yards further I found him sitting on a seat under a linden tree with the woman with the oily eyes.

'"Why, my dear Maude," he exclaimed, "wherever have you been to? I've hunted everywhere for you."

'A great lump came in my throat, for I felt that Jack was lying to me. I really don't know what I said or what I did, but I am conscious in a vague way that he introduced me to the woman, but the only name I caught was that of Annette. It burnt itself into my brain; it has haunted me ever since.

'Annette put out her white hand veiled by a silk net glove through which diamond rings sparkled. I believe I did touch the proffered fingers, and I shuddered, and I heard her say in a silvery voice that was quite out of keeping with her appearance:

'"If I were your husband I should take you to task. Beauty like yours, you know, ought not to go unattended in a place like this."

'Perhaps she thought this was funny, for she laughed, and then patted me on the shoulder with her fan. But I hated her from that moment— hated her with a hatred I did not deem myself capable of.

'We continued to sit there, how long I don't know. It seemed to me a very long time, but perhaps it wasn't long. When we rose to go the promenade was nearly deserted, only two or three couples remained. The moon was shining brilliantly; the night wind sighed pleasantly in the trees; but the beauty of the night was lost upon me. I felt ill at ease, and, for the first time in my life, unhappy. Annette walked with us nearly to our door. When the moment for parting came she again offered me the tips of her fingers, but I merely bowed frigidly, and shrank from her as I saw her oily eyes fixed upon me.

'"Ta, ta!" she said in her fatal silvery voice; "keep a watchful guard over your husband, my dear; and you, sir, don't let your beautiful little lady stray from you again, or there will be grief between you."

'Those wicked words, every one of which was meant to have its effect, was like the poison of asps to me; you may imagine how they stung me when I tell you I was seized with an almost irresistible desire to hurl the full weight of my body at her, and, having thrown her down, trample upon her. She had aroused in me such a feeling of horror that very little more would have begotten in me the desperation of madness, and I might have committed some act which I should have regretted all my life. But bestowing another glance of her basilisk eyes upon me she moved off, and I felt relieved; though, when I reached my room, I burst into hysterical weeping. Jack took me in his arms, and kissed and comforted me, and all my love for him was strong again; as I lay with my head pillowed on his breast I felt once more supremely happy.

'The next day, on thinking the matter over, I came to the conclusion that my suspicions were unjust, my fears groundless, my jealousy stupid, and that my conduct had been rude in the extreme. I resolved, therefore, to be more amiable and polite to Annette when I again met her. But, strangely enough, though we remained in Homburg a fortnight longer we did not meet; but I know now my husband saw her several times.

'Of course, if it had not been for subsequent events, it would have been said that I was a victim of strong hysteria on that memorable night. Men are so ready to accuse women of hysteria because they are more sensitive, and see deeper than men do themselves. But my aversion to Annette from the instant I set eyes upon her, and the inferences I drew, were not due to hysteria, but to that eighth sense possessed by women, which has no name, and of which men know nothing. At least, I mean to say that they cannot understand it.'

Again Mrs. Redcar broke off in her narrative, for emotion had got the better of her. I deemed it advisable to wait. Her remarkable story had aroused all my interest, and I was anxious not to lose any connecting link of it, for from the psychological point of view it was a study.

'Of course, as I have begun the story I must finish it to its bitter end,' she went on. 'As I have told you, I did not see Annette again in Homburg, and when we left all my confidence in Jack was restored, and my love for him was stronger than ever if that were possible. Happiness came back to me. Oh! I was so happy, and thinking I had done a cruel, bitter wrong to Jack in even supposing for a moment that he would be unfaithful to me, I tried by every little artifice a woman is capable of to prove my devotion to him.

'Well, to make a long story short, we continued to travel about for some time, and finally returned home, and my baby was born. It seemed to me then as if God was really too good to me. I had everything in the world that a human being can reasonably want. An angel baby, a brave, handsome husband, ample means, hosts of friends. I was supremely happy. I thanked my Maker for it all every hour of my life. But suddenly amongst the roses the hiss of the serpent sounded. One day a carriage drove up to our door. It brought a lady visitor. She was shown into our drawing-room, and when asked for her name made some excuse to the servant. Of course, I hurried down to see who my caller was, and imagine my horror when on entering the room I beheld Annette.'

'"My dear Mrs. Redcar," she gushingly exclaimed, emphasizing every word, "I am so delighted to see you again. Being in London, I could not resist the temptation to call and renew acquaintances."

'The voice was as silvery as ever, and her awful eyes seemed more oily. In my confusion and astonishment I did not inquire how she had got our address; but I know that I refused her proffered hand, and by my manner gave her unmistakably to understand that I did not regard her as a welcome visitor. But she seemed perfectly indifferent. She talked gaily, flippantly. She threw her fatal spell about me. She fascinated me, so that when she asked to see my baby I mechanically rang the bell, and as mechanically told the servant to send the nurse and baby in. When she came, the damnable woman took the child from the nurse and danced him, but he suddenly broke into a scream of terror, so that I rushed forward; but the silvery voice said:

'"Oh, you silly little mother. The baby is all right. Look how quiet he is now."

'She was holding him at arm's length, and gazing at him with her basilisk eyes, and he was silent. Then she hugged I him, and fondled him, and kissed him, and all the while I felt as if my brain was on fire, but I could neither speak nor move a hand to save my precious little baby.

'At last she returned him to his nurse, who at once left the room by my orders, and then Annette kept up a cackle of conversation. Although it did not strike me then as peculiar, for I was too confused to have any clear thought about anything—it did afterwards—she never once inquired about Jack. It happened that he was out. He had gone away early that morning to the city on some important business in which he was engaged.

'At last Annette took herself off, to my intense relief. She said nothing about calling again; she gave no address, and made no request for me to call on her. Even had she done so I should not have called. I was only too thankful she had gone, and I fervently hoped I should never see her again.

'As soon as she had departed I rushed upstairs, for baby was screaming violently. I found him in the nurse's arms, and she was doing her utmost to comfort him. But he refused to be comforted, and I took him and put him to my breast, but he still fought, and struggled, and screamed, and his baby eyes seemed to me to be bulging with horror. From that moment the darling little creature began to sicken. He gradually pined and wasted, and in a few weeks was lying like a beautiful waxen doll in a bed of flowers. He was stiff, and cold, and dead.

'When Jack came home in the evening of the day of Annette's call, and I told him she had been, he did not seem in the least surprised, but merely remarked:

'"I hope you were hospitable to her."

'I did not answer him, for I had been anything but hospitable. I had not even invited her to partake of the conventional cup of tea.

'As our baby boy faded day by day, Jack seemed to change, and the child's death overwhelmed him. He was never absolutely unkind to me at that period, but he seemed to have entirely altered. He became sullen, silent, even morose, and he spent the whole of his days away from me. When I gently chided him, he replied that his work absorbed all his attention. And so things went on until another thunderbolt fell at my feet.

'One afternoon Jack returned home and brought Annette. He told me that he had invited her to spend a few days with us. When I urged an objection he was angry with me for the first time in our married life. I was at once silenced, for his influence over me was still great, and I thought I would try and overcome my prejudice for Annette. At any rate, as Jack's wife I resolved to be hospitable, and play the hostess with grace. But I soon found that I was regarded as of very little consequence. Annette ruled Jack, she ruled me, she ruled the household.

'You will perhaps ask why I did not rise up in wrath, and, asserting my position and dignity, drive the wicked creature out of my home. But I tell you, doctor, I was utterly powerless. She worked some devil's spell upon me, and I was entirely under the influence of her will.

'Her visit stretched into weeks. Our well-tried and faithful servants left. Others came, but their stay was brief; and at last the old woman who opened the door to you was installed. She is a creature of Annette's, and is a spy upon my movements.

'All this time Jack was under the spell of the charmer, as I was. Over and over again I resolved to go to my friends, appeal to them, tell them everything, and ask them to protect me; but my will failed, and I bore and suffered in silence. And my husband neglected me; he seemed to find pleasure only in Annette's company. Oh, how I fretted and gnawed my heart, and yet I could not break away from the awful life. I tell you, doctor, that that woman possessed some strange, devilish, supernatural power over me and Jack. When she looked at me I shrivelled up. When she spoke, her silvery voice seemed to sting every nerve and fibre in my body, and he was like wax in her hands. To me he became positively brutal, and he told me over and over again that I was spoiling his life. But, though she was a repulsive, mysterious, crafty, cruel woman, he seemed to find his happiness in her company.

'One morning, after a restless, horrible, feverish night, I arose, feeling strangely ill, and as if I were going mad. I worked myself up almost to a pitch of frenzy, and, spurred by desperation, I rushed into the drawing-room, where my husband and Annette were together, and exclaimed to her:

'"Woman, do you not see that you are killing me? Why have you come here? Why do you persecute me with your devilish wiles? You must know you are not welcome. You must feel you are an intruder."

'Overcome by the effort this had cost me, I sank down on the floor on my knees, and wept passionately. Then I heard the silvery voice say, in tones of surprise and injured innocence:

'"Well, upon my word, Mrs. Redcar, this is an extraordinary way to treat your husband's guest. I really thought I was a welcome visitor instead of an intruder; but, since I am mistaken, I will go at once."

'I looked at her through a blinding mist of tears. I met the gaze of her oily eyes, but only for a moment, as I cowered before her, shrank within myself, and felt powerless again. I glanced at my husband. He was standing with his head bowed, and, as it seemed to me, in a pose of shame and humiliation. But suddenly he darted at me, and I heard him say: "What do you mean by creating such a scene as this? You must understand I am master here." Then he struck me a violent blow on the head, and there was a long blank.

'When I came to my senses I was in bed, and the hideous old hag who opened the door to you was bending over me. It was some little time before I could realize what had occurred. When I did, I asked the woman where Mr. Redcar was, and she answered sullenly:

'"Gone."

'"And the —— Annette; where is she?" I asked.

'"Gone, too," was the answer.

'Another blank ensued. I fell very ill, and when my brain was capable of coherent thought again I learnt that I had passed through a crisis, and my life had been in jeopardy. A doctor had been attending me, and there was a professional nurse in the house; but she was a hard, dry, unsympathetic woman, and I came to the conclusion—wrongly so, probably—she, too, was one of Annette's creatures.

'I was naturally puzzled to understand why none of my relatives and friends had been to see me, but I was to learn later that many had called, but had been informed I was abroad with my husband, who had been summoned away suddenly in connection with some professional matters. And I also know now that all letters coming for me were at once forwarded to him, and that any requiring answers he answered.

'As I grew stronger I made up my mind to keep my own counsel, and not let any of my friends know of what I had gone through and suffered; for I still loved my husband, and looked upon him as a victim to be pitied and rescued from the infernal wiles of the she-demon. When I heard of your arrival in England, I felt you were the one person in the wide world I could appeal to with safety, for you can understand how anxious I am to avoid a scandal. Will you help me? Will you save your old friend Jack? Restore him to sanity, doctor, and bring him back to my arms again, which will be wide open to receive him.'

I listened to poor Mrs. Redcar's story patiently, and at first was disposed to look upon it as a too common tale of human weakness. Jack Redcar had fallen into the power of an adventuress, and had been unable to resist her influence. Such things had happened before, such things will happen again, I argued with myself. There are certain women who seem capable of making men mad for a brief space; but under proper treatment they come to their senses quickly, and blush with shame as they think of their foolishness. At any rate, for the sake of my old friend, and for the sake of his poor suffering little wife, I was prepared to do anything in reason to bring back the erring husband to his right senses.

I told Mrs. Redcar this. I told her I would redress her wrongs if I could, and fight her battle to the death. She almost threw herself at my feet in her gratitude. But when I suggested that I should acquaint her family with the facts, she begged of me passionately not to do so. Her one great anxiety was to screen her husband. One thing, however, I insisted upon. That was, the old woman should be sent away, the house shut up, and that Mrs. Redcar should take apartments in an hotel, so that I might be in touch with her. She demurred to this at first, but ultimately yielded to my persuasion.

Next I went to the old woman. She was a German Suisse—her name was Grebert. I told her to pack up her things and clear out at once. She laughed in my face, and impertinently told me to mind my own business. I took out my watch and said, 'I give you half an hour. If you are not off the premises then, I will call in the police and have you turned out. Any claim you have on Mrs. Redcar, who is the mistress here—shall be settled at once.'

She replied that she did not recognize my authority, that she had been placed there by Mr. Redcar, who was her master, and unless he told her to go she should remain. I made it plain to her that I was determined and would stand no nonsense. Mr. Redcar had taken himself off, I said; Mrs. Redcar was his lawful wife, and I was acting for her and on her behalf.

My arguments prevailed, and after some wrangling the hag came to the conclusion that discretion was the better part of valour, and consented to go providing we paid her twenty pounds. This we decided to do rather than have a scene, but three hours passed before we saw the last of the creature. Mrs. Redcar had already packed up such things as she required, and when I had seen the house securely fastened up I procured a cab, and conveyed the poor little lady to a quiet West-end hotel, close to my own residence, so that I could keep a watchful eye upon her.

Of course, this was only the beginning of the task I had set myself, which was to woo back the erring husband, if possible, to his wife's side, and to restore him to the position of happiness, honour, and dignity from which he had fallen. I thought this might be comparatively easy, and little dreamed of the grim events that were to follow my interference.

Three weeks later I was in Paris, and proceeded to the Hotel de l'Univers, where Mrs. Redcar had ascertained through his bankers her husband was staying. But to my chagrin, I found he had departed with his companion, and the address he had given for his letters at the post-office was Potes, in Spain. As I had taken up the running I had no alternative but to face the long, dreary journey in pursuit of the fugitives, or confess defeat at the start.

It is not necessary for me to dwell upon that awful journey in the winter time. Suffice to say I reached my destination in due course.

Potes, it is necessary to explain, is a small town magnificently situated in the Liebana Valley, in the Asturian Pyrenees, under the shadow of Pico de Europa. Now, what struck me as peculiar was the fugitives coming to such a place at that time of the year. Snow lay heavily everywhere. The cold was intense. For what reason had such a spot been chosen? It was a mystery I could not hope to solve just then. There was only one small hotel in the village, and there Annette and Redcar were staying. My first impulse was not to let them know of my presence, but to keep them under observation for a time. I dismissed that thought as soon as formed, for I was not a detective, and did not like the idea of playing the spy. But even had I been so disposed, there would have been a difficulty about finding accommodation. Moreover, it was a small place, and the presence of a foreigner at that time of year must necessarily have caused a good deal of gossip. The result was I went boldly to the hotel, engaged a room, and then inquired for Redcar. I was directed to a private room, where I found him alone. My unexpected appearance startled him, and when he realized who I was, he swore at me, and demanded to know my business.

He had altered so much that in a crowd I really might have had some difficulty in recognizing him. His face wore a drawn, anxious, nervous look, and his eyes had acquired a restless, shifty motion, while his hair was already streaked with grey.

I began to reason with him. I reminded him of our old friendship, and I drew a harrowing picture of the sufferings of his dear, devoted, beautiful little wife.

At first he seemed callous; but presently he grew interested, and when I referred to his wife he burst into tears. Then suddenly he grasped my wrist with a powerful grip, and said:

'Hush! Annette mustn't know this—mustn't hear. I tell you, Peter, she is a ghoul. She sucks my blood. She has woven a mighty spell about me, and I am powerless. Take me away; take me to dear little Maude.'

I looked at him for some moments with a keen professional scrutiny, for his manner and strange words were not those of sanity. I determined to take him at his word, and, if possible, remove him from the influence of the wicked syren who had so fatally lured him.

'Yes,' I said, 'we will go without a moment's unnecessary delay. I will see if a carriage and post-horses are to be had, so that we can drive to the nearest railway station.'

He assented languidly to this, and I rose with the intention of making inquiries of the hotel people; but simultaneously with my action the door opened and Annette appeared. Up to that moment I thought that Mrs. Redcar had exaggerated in describing her, therefore I was hardly prepared to find that so far from the description being an exaggeration, it had fallen short of the fact, Annette was slightly above the medium height, with a well-developed figure, but a face that to me was absolutely repellent. There was not a single line of beauty nor a trace of womanliness in it. It was hard, coarse, cruel, with thin lips drawn tightly over even white teeth. And the eyes were the most wonderful eyes I have ever seen in a human being. Maude was right when she spoke of them as 'oily eyes.' They literally shone with a strange, greasy lustre, and were capable of such a marvellous expression that I felt myself falling under their peculiar fascination. I am honest and frank enough to say that, had it been her pleasure, I believe she could have lured me to destruction as she had lured my poor friend. But I was forearmed, because forewarned. Moreover, I fancy I had a much stronger will than Redcar. Any way, I braced myself up to conquer and crush this human serpent, for such I felt her to be.

Before I could speak, her melodious voice rang out with the query, addressed to Jack:

'Who is this gentleman? Is he a friend of yours?'

'Yes, yes,' gasped Jack, like one who spoke under the influence of a nightmare.

She bowed and smiled, revealing all her white teeth, and she held forth her hand to me, a delicately shaped hand, with clear, transparent skin, and her long lithe fingers were bejewelled with diamonds.

I drew myself up, as one does when a desperate effort is needed, and, refusing the proffered hand, I said:

'Madame, hypocrisy and deceit are useless. I am a medical man, my name is Peter Haslar, and Mr. Redcar and I have been friends from youth. I've come here to separate him from your baneful influence and carry him back to his broken-hearted wife. That is my mission. I hope I have made it clear to you?'

She showed not the slightest sign of being disturbed, but smiled on me again, and bowed gracefully and with the most perfect self-possession. And speaking in a soft gentle manner, which was in such startling contrast to the woman's appearance, she said:

'Oh, yes; thank you. But, like the majority of your countrymen, you display a tendency to arrogate too much to yourself. I am a Spaniard myself, by birth, but cosmopolitan by inclination, and, believe me, I do not speak with any prejudice against your nationality, but I have yet to learn, sir, that you have any right to constitute yourself Mr. Redcar's keeper.'

Her English was perfect, though she pronounced it with just a slight foreign accent. There was no anger in her tones, no defiance. She spoke softly, silvery, persuasively.

'I do not pretend to be his keeper, madame; I am his sincere friend,' I answered. 'And surely I need not remind you that he owes a duty to his lawful wife.'

During this short conversation Jack had sat motionless on the edge of a couch, his chin resting on his hands, and apparently absorbed with some conflicting thoughts. But Annette turned to him, and, still smiling, said:

'I think Mr. Redcar is quite capable of answering for himself. Stand up, Jack, and speak your thoughts like a man.'

Although she spoke in her oily, insidious way, her request was a peremptory command. I realized that at once, and I saw as Jack rose he gazed at her, and her lustrous eyes fixed him. Then he turned upon me with a furious gesture and exclaimed, with a violence of expression that startled me:

'Yes, Annette is right. I am my own master. What the devil do you mean by following me, like the sneak and cur that you are? Go back to Maude, and tell her that I loathe her. Go; relieve me of your presence, or I may forget myself and injure you.'

Annette, still smiling and still perfectly self-possessed, said:

'You hear what your friend says, doctor. Need I say that if you are a gentleman you will respect his wishes?'

I could no longer control myself. Her calm, defiant, icy manner maddened me, and her silvery voice seemed to cut down on to my most sensitive nerves, for it was so suggestive of the devilish nature of the creature. It was so incongruous when contrasted with her harsh, horribly cruel face. I placed myself between Jack and her, and meeting her weird gaze, I said, hotly:

'Leave this room. You are an outrage on your sex; a shame and a disgrace to the very name of woman. Go, and leave me with my friend, whose reason you have stolen away.'

She still smiled and was still unmoved, and suddenly I felt myself gripped in a grip of iron, and with terrific force I was hurled into a corner of the room, where, huddled up in a heap, I lay stunned for some moments. But as my senses returned I saw the awful woman smiling still, and she was waving her long white bejewelled hand before the infuriated Jack, as if she were mesmerizing him; and I saw him sink on to the sofa subdued and calmed. Then addressing me she said:

'That is a curious way for your friend to display his friendship. I may be wrong, but perhaps as a medical man you will recognize that your presence has an irritating effect on Mr. Redcar, and if I may suggest it, I think it desirable that you should depart at once and see him no more.'

'Devil!' I shouted at her. 'You have bewitched him, and made him forgetful of his honour and of what he owes to those who are dear to him. But I will defeat you yet.'

She merely bowed and smiled, but deigned no reply; and holding her arm to Jack, he took it, and they passed out of the room. She was elegantly attired. Her raven hair was fascinatingly dressed in wavy bands. There was some thing regal in her carriage, and gracefulness in her every movement; and yet she filled me with a sense of indefinable horror; a dread to which I should have been ashamed to own to a little while ago.

I tried to spring up and go after them, but my body seemed a mass of pain, and my left arm hung limp and powerless. It was fractured below the elbow. There was no bell in the room, and I limped out in search of assistance. I made my way painfully along a gloomy corridor, and hearing a male voice speaking Spanish, I knocked at a door, which was opened by the landlord. I addressed him, but he shook his head and gave me to understand that he spoke no English. Unhappily I spoke no Spanish. Then he smiled as some idea flitted through his mind, and bowing me into the room he motioned me to be seated, and hurried away. He returned in about five minutes accompanied by Annette, whom he had brought to act as interpreter. I was almost tempted to fly at her and strangle her where she stood. She was undisturbed, calm, and still smiled. She spoke to the man in Spanish, then she explained to me that she had told him I had slipped on the polished floor, and falling over a chair had injured myself, and she had requested him to summon the village surgeon if need be.

Without waiting for me to reply she swept gracefully out of the room. Indeed, I could not reply, for I felt as if I were choking with suppressed rage. The landlord rendered me physical assistance and took me to my bedroom, where I lay down on the bed, feeling mortified, ill, and crushed. Half an hour later a queer-looking old man, with long hair twisted into ringlets, was ushered into my room, and I soon gathered that he was the village surgeon. He spoke no English, but I explained my injury by signs, and he went away, returning in a little while with the necessary bandages and splints, and he proceeded rather clumsily to bandage my broken arm. I passed a cruel and wretched night. My physical pain was great, but my mental pain was greater. The thought forced itself upon me that I had been defeated, and that the fiendish, cunning woman was too much for me. I felt no resentment against Jack. His act of violence was the act of a madman, and I pitied him. For hours I lay revolving all sorts of schemes to try and get him away from the diabolical influence of Annette. But though I could hit upon nothing, I firmly resolved that while my life lasted I would make every effort to save my old friend, and if possible restore him to the bosom of his distracted wife.

The case altogether was a very remarkable one, and the question naturally arose, why did a man so highly gifted and so intelligent as Jack Redcar desert his charming, devoted, and beautiful wife, to follow an adventuress who entirely lacked physical beauty. Theories without number might have been suggested to account for the phenomenon, but not one would have been correct. The true answer is, Annette was not a natural being. In the ordinary way she might be described as a woman of perverted moral character, or as a physiological freak, but that would have been rather a misleading way of putting it. She was, in short, a human monstrosity. By that I do not mean to say her body was contorted, twisted, or deformed. But into her human composition had entered a strain of the fiend; and I might go even further than this and say she was more animal than human. Though in whatever way she may be described, it is certain she was an anomaly—a human riddle.

The morning following the outrage upon me found me prostrated and ill. A night of racking pain and mental distress had told even upon my good constitution. The situation in which I found myself was a singularly unfortunate one. I was a foreigner in an out-of-the-way place, and my want of knowledge of Spanish, of course, placed me at a tremendous disadvantage.

The landlord came to me and brought his wife, and between them they attended to my wants, and did what they could for my comfort. But they were ignorant, uncultivated people, only one remove from the peasant class, and I realized that they could be of little use to me. Now the nearest important town to this Alpine village was Santander, but that was nearly a hundred miles away. As everyone knows who has been in Spain, a hundred miles, even on a railway, is a considerable journey; but there was no railway between Santander and Potes. An old ramshackle vehicle, called a diligence, ran between the two places every day in the summer and twice a week in the winter, and it took fourteen hours to do the journey. Even a well-appointed carriage and pair could not cover the distance under eight hours, as the road was infamous, and in parts was little better than a mule track. I knew that there was a British Consul in Santander, and I was hopeful that if I could communicate with him he might be able to render me some assistance. In the meantime I had to devise some scheme for holding Annette in check and saving my friend. But in my crippled and prostrate condition I could not do much. While lying in my bed, and thus revolving all these things in my mind, the door gently opened and Annette glided in— 'glided' best expresses her movement, for she seemed to put forth no effort. She sat down beside the bed and laid her hand on mine.

'You are ill this morning,' she said softly. 'This is regrettable, but you have only yourself to blame. It is dangerous to interfere in matters in which you have no concern. My business is mine, Mr. Redcar's is his, and yours is your own, but the three won't amalgamate. Jack and I came here for the sake of the peace and quietness of these solitudes; unhappily you intrude yourself and disaster follows.'

Her voice was as silvery as ever. The same calm self-possessed air characterized her; but in her oily eyes was a peculiar light, and I had to turn away, for they exerted a sort of mesmeric influence over me, and I am convinced that had I not exerted all my will power I should have thrown myself into the creature's arms. This is a fact which I have no hesitation in stating, as it serves better than any other illustration to show what a wonderful power of fascination the remarkable woman possessed. Naturally I felt disgusted and enraged, but I fully recognized that I could not fight the woman openly; I must to some extent meet her with her own weapons. She was cunning, artful, insidious, pitiless, and the basilisk-like power she possessed not only gave her a great advantage but made her a very dangerous opponent. At any rate, having regard to all the circumstances and my crippled condition, I saw that my only chance was in temporizing with her. So I tried to reason with her, and I pointed out that Redcar had been guilty of baseness in leaving his wife, who was devoted to him.

At this point of my argument Annette interrupted me, and for the first time she displayed something like passion, and her voice became hard and raucous.

'His wife,' she said with a sneer of supreme contempt. 'A poor fool, a fleshly doll. At the precise instant I set my eyes upon her for the first time I felt that I should like to destroy her, because she is a type of woman who make the world common-place and reduce all men to a common level. She hated me from the first and I hated her. She would have crushed me if she could, but she was too insignificant a worm to do that, and I crushed her.'

This cold, brutal callousness enraged me; I turned fiercely upon her and exclaimed:

'Leave me, you are a more infamous and heartless wretch than I believed you to be. You are absolutely unworthy the name of woman, and if you irritate me much more I may even forget that you have a woman's shape.'

She spoke again. All trace of passion had disappeared. She smiled the wicked insidious smile which made her so dangerous, and her voice resumed its liquid, silvery tones:

'You are very violent,' she said gently, 'and it will do you harm in your condition. But you see violence can be met with violence. The gentleman you are pleased to call your friend afforded you painful evidence last night that he knows how to resent unjustifiable interference, and to take care of himself. I am under his protection, and there is no doubt he will protect me.'

'For God's sake, leave me!' I cried, tortured beyond endurance by her hypocrisy and wickedness.

'Oh, certainly, if you desire it,' she answered, as she rose from her seat. 'But I thought I might be of use. It is useless your trying to influence Mr. Redcar—absolutely useless. His destiny is linked with mine, and the human being doesn't exist who can sunder us. With this knowledge, you will do well to retrace your steps; and, if you like, I will arrange to have you comfortably conveyed to Santander, where you can get a vessel. Anyway, you will waste your time and retard your recovery by remaining here.'

'I intend to remain here, nevertheless,' I said, with set teeth. 'And, what is more, madame, when I go my friend Redcar will accompany me.'

She laughed. She patted my head as a mother might pat the head of her child. She spoke in her most insidious, silvery tones.

'We shall see, *mon cher*—we shall see. You will be better to-morrow. *Adieu!*'

That was all she said, and she was gone. She glided out of the room as she had glided in.

I felt irritated almost into madness for some little time; but as I reflected, it was forced upon me that I had to deal with a monster of iniquity, who had so subdued the will of her victim, Redcar, that he was a mere wooden puppet in her hand. Force in such a case was worse than useless. What I had to do was to try and circumvent her, and I tried to think out some plan of action.

All that day I was compelled to keep my bed, and, owing to the clumsy way in which my arm had been bandaged, I suffered intolerable pain, and had to send for the old surgeon again to come and help me to reset the fracture. I got some ease after that, and a dose of chloral sent me to sleep, which continued for many hours. When I awoke I managed to summon the landlord, and he brought me food, and a lantern containing a candle so that I might have light. And, in compliance with my request, he made me a large jug of lemonade, in order that I could have a drink in the night, for I was feverish, and my throat was parched. He had no sooner left the room than Annette entered to inquire if she could do anything for me. I told her that I had made the landlord understand all that I desired, and he would look after me, so she wished me good-night and left. Knowing as I did that sleep was very essential in my case, I swallowed another, though smaller, dose of chloral, and then there was a blank.

How long I slept I really don't know; but suddenly, in a dazed sort of way, I saw a strange sight. The room I occupied was a long, somewhat meagrely furnished, one. The entrance door was at the extreme end, opposite the bed. Over the doorway hung a faded curtain of green velvet. By the feeble light of the candle lantern I saw this curtain slowly pulled on one side by a white hand; then a face peered in; next Annette entered. Her long hair was hanging down her back, and she wore a nightdress a soft, clinging substance, which outlined her figure. With never a sound she moved lightly towards the bed, and waved her hand two or three times over my face. I tried to move, to utter a sound, but couldn't; and yet what I am describing was no dream, but a reality. Slightly bending over me, she poured from a tiny phial she carried in the palm of her hand a few drops of a slightly acrid, burning liquid right into my mouth, and at that instant, as I believe, it seemed to me as if a thick, heavy pall fell over my eyes, for all was darkness.

I awoke hours later. The winter sun was shining brightly into my room. I felt strangely languid, and had a hot, stinging sensation in my throat. I felt my pulse, and found it was only beating at the rate of fifty-eight beats in the minute. Then I recalled the extraordinary incident of the previous night, which, had it not been for my sensations, I might have regarded as a bad dream, the outcome of a disturbed state of the brain. But as it was, I hadn't a doubt that Annette had administered some subtle and slow poison to me. My medical knowledge enabled me to diagnose my own case so far, that I was convinced I was suffering from the effects of a potent poisonous drug, the action of which was to lower the action of the vital forces and weaken the heart. Being probably cumulative, a few doses more or less, according to the strength of the subject, and the action of the heart would be so impeded that the organ would cease to beat. Although all this passed through my brain, I felt so weak and languid that I had neither energy nor strength to arouse myself, and when the landlord brought me in some food I took no notice of him. I knew that this symptom of languor and indifference was very characteristic of certain vegetable poisons, though what it was Annette had administered to me I could not determine.

Throughout that day I lay in a drowsy, dreamy state. At times my brain was clear enough, and I was able to think and reason; but there were blanks, marked, no doubt, by periods of sleep.

When night came I felt a little better, and I found that the heart's action had improved. It was steadier, firmer, and the pulse indicated sixty-two beats. Now I had no doubt that if it was Annette's intention to bring about my death slowly she would come again that night, and arousing myself as well as I could, and summoning all my will power, I resolved to be on the watch. During the afternoon I had drunk milk freely, regarding it as an antidote, and when the landlord visited me for the last time that evening I made him understand that I wanted a large jug of milk fresh from the cow, if he could get it. He kept cows of his own; they were confined in a chalet on the mountain side, not far from his house, so that he was able to comply with my request. I took a long draught of this hot milk, which revived my energies wonderfully, and then I waited for developments. I had allowed my watch to run down, consequently I had no means of knowing the time. It was a weary vigil, lying there lonely and ill, and struggling against the desire for sleep.

By-and-by I saw the white hand lift the curtain again, and Annette entered, clad as she was on the previous night. When she came within reach of me I sprang up in the bed and seized her wrist.

'What do you want here?' I demanded angrily. 'Do you mean to murder me?'

Her imperturbability was exasperating. She neither winced nor cried out, nor displayed the slightest sign of surprise. She merely remarked in her soft cooing voice, her white teeth showing as her thin lips parted in a smile:

'You are evidently restless and excited to-night, and it is hardly generous of you to treat my kindly interest in such a way.'

'Kindly interest!' I echoed with a sneer, as, releasing her wrist, I fell back on the bed.

'Yes; you haven't treated me well, and you are an intruder here. Nevertheless, as you are a stranger amongst strangers, and cannot speak the language of the country, I would be of service to you if I could. I have come to see if you have everything you require for the night.'

'And you did the same last night,' I cried in hot anger, for, knowing her infamy and wickedness, I could not keep my temper.

'Certainly,' she answered coolly; 'and I found you calmly dozing, so left you.'

'Yes—after you had poured poison down my throat,' I replied.

She broke into a laugh—a rippling laugh, with the tinkle of silver in it—and she seemed hugely amused.

'Well, well,' she said; 'it is obvious, sir, you are not in a fit state to be left alone. Your nerves are evidently unstrung, and you are either the victim of a bad dream or some strange delusion. But there, there; I will pardon you. You are not responsible just at present for your language.'

As she spoke she passed her soft white hand over my forehead. There was magic in her touch, and it seemed as if all my will had left me, and there stole over me a delightful sense of dreamy languor. I looked at her, and I saw her strange eyes change colour. They became illumined, as it were, by a violet light that fascinated me so that I could not turn from her. Indeed, I was absolutely subdued to her will now. Everything in the room faded, and I saw nothing but those marvellous eyes glowing with violet light which seemed to fill me with a feeling of ecstacy. I have a vague idea that she kept passing her hand over my face and forehead; that she breathed upon my face; then that she pressed her face to mine, and I felt her hot breath in my neck.

Perhaps it will be said that I dreamed all this. I don't believe it was a dream. I firmly and honestly believe that every word I have written is true.

Hours afterwards my dulled brain began to awake to things mundane. The morning sun was flooding the room, and I was conscious that somebody stood over me, and soon I recognized the old surgeon, who had come to see that the splints and bandages had not shifted. I felt extraordinarily weak, and I found that my pulse was beating very slowly and feebly. Again I had the burning feeling in the throat and a strange and absolutely indescribable sensation at the side of the neck. The old doctor must have recognized that I was unusually feeble, for he went to the landlord, and returned presently with some cognac which he made me swallow, and it picked me up considerably.

After his departure I lay for some time, and tried to give definite shape to vague and dreadful thoughts that haunted me, and filled me with a shrinking horror. That Annette was a monster in human form I hadn't a doubt, and I felt equally certain that she had designs upon my life. That she had now administered poison to me on two occasions seemed to me beyond question, but I hesitated to believe that she was guilty of the unspeakable crime which my sensations suggested.

At last, unable longer to endure the tumult in my brain, I sprang out of bed, rushed to the looking-glass, and examined my neck. I literally staggered back, and fell prostrate on the bed, overcome by the hideous discovery I had made. It had the effect, however, of calling me back to life and energy, and I made a mental resolution that I would, at all hazards, save my friend, though I clearly recognized how powerless I was to cope with the awful creature single-handed.

I managed to dress myself, not without some difficulty; then I summoned the landlord, and made him understand that I must go immediately to Santander at any cost. My intention was to invoke the aid of the consul there. But the more I insisted, the more the old landlord shook his head. At length, in desperation, I rushed from the house, hoping to find somebody who understood French or English. As I almost ran up the village street I came face to face with a priest. I asked him in English if he spoke my language, but he shook his head. Then I tried him with French, and to my joy he answered me that he understood a little French. I told him of my desire to start for Santander that very day, but he said that it was impossible, as, owing to the unusual hot sun in the daytime there had been a great melting of snow, with the result that a flooded river had destroyed a portion of the road; and though a gang of men had been set to repair it, it would be two or three days before it was passable.

'But is there no other way of going?' I asked.

'Only by a very hazardous route over the mountains,' he answered. And he added that the risk was so great it was doubtful if anyone could be found who would act as guide. 'Besides,' he went on, 'you seem very ill and weak. Even a strong man might fail, but you would be certain to perish from exhaustion and exposure.'

I was bound to recognize the force of his argument. It was a maddening disappointment, but there was no help for it. Then it occurred to me to take the old priest into my confidence and invoke his aid. Though, on second thoughts, I hesitated, for was it not possible—nay, highly probable—that if I told the horrible story he and others would think I was mad? Annette was a Spanish woman, and it was feasible to suppose she would secure the ear of those ignorant villagers sooner than I should. No, I would keep the ghastly business to myself for the present at any rate, and wait with such patience as I could command until I could make the journey to Santander. The priest promised me that on the morrow he would let me know if the road was passable, and, if so, he would procure me a carriage and make all the preparations for the journey. So, thanking him for his kindly services, I turned towards the hotel again. As I neared the house I observed two persons on the mountain path that went up among the pine trees. The sun was shining brilliantly; the sky was cloudless, the air crisp and keen. The two persons were Annette and Redcar. I watched them for some minutes until they were lost to sight amongst the trees.

Suddenly an irresistible impulse to follow them seized me. Why I know not. Indeed, had I paused to reason with myself it would have seemed to me then a mad act, and that I was risking my life to no purpose. But I did not reason. I yielded to the impulse, though first of all I went to my room, put on a thicker pair of boots, and armed myself with a revolver which I had brought with me. During my extensive travelling about America a revolver was a necessity, and by force of habit I put it up with my clothes when packing my things in London for my Continental journey.

Holding the weapon between my knees, I put a cartridge in each barrel, and, providing myself with a stick in addition, I went forth again and began to climb the mountain path. I was by no means a sanguinary man; even my pugnacity could only be aroused after much irritation. Nevertheless, I knew how to defend myself, and in this instance, knowing that I had to deal with a woman who was capable of any crime, and who, I felt sure, would not hesitate to take my life if she got the chance, I deemed it advisable to be on my guard against any emergency that might arise. As regards Redcar, he had already given me forcible and painful evidence that he could be dangerous; but I did not hold him responsible for his actions. I regarded him as being temporarily insane owing to the infernal influence the awful woman exercised over him. Therefore it would only have been in the very last extremity that I should have resorted to lethal weapons as a defence against him. My one sole aim, hope, desire, prayer, was to rescue him from the spell that held him in thrall and restore him to his wife, his honour, his sanity. With respect to Annette, it was different. She was a blot on nature, a disgrace to humankind, and, rather than let her gain complete ascendency over me and my friend, I would have shot her if I had reason to believe she contemplated taking my life. It might have involved me in serious trouble with the authorities at first, for in Spain the foreigner can hope but for little justice. I was convinced, however, that ultimately I should be exonerated.

Such were the thoughts that filled my mind as I painfully made my way up the steep mountain side. My fractured arm was exceedingly painful. Every limb in my body ached, and I was so languid, so weak that it was with difficulty I dragged myself along. But worse than all this was an all but irresistible desire to sleep, the result, I was certain, of the poison that had been administered to me. But it would have been fatal to have slept. I knew that, and so I fought against the inclination with all my might and main, and allowed my thoughts to dwell on poor little Maude Redcar, waiting desolate and heartbroken in London for news. This supplied me with the necessary spur and kept me going.

The trees were nearly all entirely bare of snow. It had, I was informed, been an unusually mild season, and at that time the sun's rays were very powerful. The path I was pursuing was nothing more than a rough track worn by the peasants passing between the valley and their hay chalets dotted about the mountain. Snow lay on the path where it was screened from the sun by the trees. I heard no sound, saw no sign of those I was seeking save here and there footprints in the snow. I frequently paused and listened, but the stillness was unbroken save for the subdued murmur of falling water afar off.

In my weakened condition the exertion I had endured had greatly distressed me; my heart beat tumultuously, my pulses throbbed violently, and my breathing was stertorous. I was compelled at last to sit down and rest. I was far above the valley now, and the pine trees were straggling and sparse. The track had become very indistinct, but I still detected the footsteps of the people I was following. Above the trees I could discern the snow-capped Pico de Europa glittering in the brilliant sun. It was a perfect Alpine scene, which, under other circumstances, I might have revelled in. But I felt strangely ill, weak, and miserable, and drowsiness began to steal upon me, so that I made a sudden effort of will and sprang up again, and resumed the ascent.

In a little time the forest ended, and before me stretched a sloping plateau which, owing to its being exposed to the full glare of the sun, as well as to all the winds that blew, was bare of snow. The plateau sloped down for probably four hundred feet, then ended abruptly at the edge of a precipice. How far the precipice descended I could not tell from where I was, but far far below I could see a stream meandering through a thickly wooded gorge. I took the details of the scene in with a sudden glance of the eye, for another sight attracted and riveted my attention, and froze me with horror to the spot. Beneath a huge boulder which had fallen from the mountain above, and lodged on the slope, were Annette and Redcar. He was lying on his back, she was stretched out beside him, and her face was buried in his neck. Even from where I stood I could see that he was ghastly pale, his features drawn and pinched, his eyes closed. Incredible as it may seem, horrible as it sounds, it is nevertheless true that that hellish woman was sucking away his life blood. She was a human vampire, and my worst fears were confirmed.

I am aware that an astounding statement of this kind should not be made lightly by a man in my position. But I take all the responsibility of it, and I declare solemnly that it is true. Moreover, the sequel which I am able to give to this story more than corroborates me, and proves Annette to have been one of those human problems which, happily for the world, are very rare, but of which there are several well authenticated cases.

As soon as I fully realized what was happening I drew my revolver from the side pocket of my jacket and fired, not at Annette, but in the air; my object being to startle her so that she would release her victim. It had the desired effect. She sprang up, livid with rage. Blood—his blood—was oozing from the sides of her mouth. Her extraordinary eyes had assumed that strange violet appearance which I had seen once before. Her whole aspect was repulsive, revolting, horrible beyond words. Rooted to the spot I stood and gazed at her, fascinated by the weird, ghastly sight. In my hand I still held the smoking revolver, levelled at her now, and resolved if she rushed towards me to shoot her, for I felt that the world would be well rid of such a hideous monster. But suddenly she stooped, seized her unfortunate victim in her arms, and tore down the slope, and when the edge of the precipice was reached they both disappeared into space.

The whole of this remarkable scene was enacted in the course of a few seconds. It was to me a maddening nightmare. I fell where I stood, and remembered no more until, hours afterwards, I found myself lying in bed at the hotel, and the old surgeon and the priest sitting beside me. Gradually I learnt that the sound of the shot from the revolver, echoing and re-echoing in that Alpine region, had been heard in the village, and some peasants had set off for the mountain to ascertain the cause of the firing. They found me lying on the ground still grasping the weapon, and thinking I had shot myself they carried me down to the hotel.

Naturally I was asked for explanations when I was able to talk, and I recounted the whole of the ghastly story. At first my listeners, the priest and the doctor, seemed to think I was raving in delirium, as well they might, but I persisted in my statements, and I urged the sending out of a party to search for the bodies. If they were found my story would be corroborated.

In a short time a party of peasants started for the gorge, which was a wild, almost inaccessible, ravine through which flowed a mountain torrent amongst the debris and boulders that from time to time had fallen from the rocky heights. After some hours of searching the party discovered the crushed remains of Jack Redcar. His head had been battered to pieces against the rocks as he fell, and every bone in his body was broken. The precipice over which he had fallen was a jagged, scarred, and irregular wall of rock at least four thousand feet in height. The search for Annette's body was continued until darkness compelled the searchers to return to the village, which they did bringing with them my poor friend's remains. Next day the search was resumed, and the day after, and for many days, but with no result. The woman's corpse was never found. The theory was that somewhere on that frightful rock face she had been caught by a projecting pinnacle, or had got jammed in a crevice, where her unhallowed remains would moulder into dust. It was a fitting end for so frightful a life.

Of course an official inquiry was held—and officialism in Spain is appalling. It was weeks and weeks before the inevitable conclusion of the tribunal was arrived at, and I was exonerated from all blame. In the meantime Redcar's remains were committed to their eternal rest in the picturesque little Alpine village churchyard, and for all time Potes will be associated with that grim and awful tragedy. Why Annette took her victim to that out of the way spot can only be guessed at. She knew that the death of her victim was only a question of weeks, and in that primitive and secluded hamlet it would arouse no suspicion, she being a native of Spain. It would be easy for her to say that she had taken her invalid husband there for the benefit of his health, but unhappily the splendid and bracing air had failed to save his life. In this instance, as in many others, her fiendish cunning would have enabled her to score another triumph had not destiny made me its instrument to encompass her destruction.

For long after my return to England I was very ill. The fearful ordeal I had gone through, coupled with the poison which Annette had administered to me, shattered my health; but the unremitting care and attention bestowed upon me by my old friend's widow pulled me through. And when at last I was restored to strength and vigour, beautiful Maude Redcar became my wife.

NOTE BY THE AUTHOR.—The foregoing story was suggested by a tradition current in the Pyrenees, where a belief in ghouls and vampires is still common. The same belief is no less common throughout Styria,[7] in some parts of Turkey, in Russia, and in India. Sir Richard Burton deals with the subject in his *Vikram and the Vampire*. Years ago, when the author was in India, a poor woman was beaten to death one night in the village by a number of young men armed with cudgels. Their excuse for the crime was that the woman was a vampire, and had sucked the blood of many of their companions, whom she had first lured to her by depriving them of their will power by mesmeric influence.

---

7 The south-eastern province of Austria, which borders Slovenia.

II

Sequel to the Woman with the 'Oily Eyes'

AT THE TIME THE inquiry was held into the circumstances of Jack Redcar's death, the authorities deemed it their duty to find out something of Annette's past history. In this they were aided by certain documents discovered amongst her belongings, and, by dint of astute and patient investigation, they elicited the following remarkable facts. Her real name was Isabella Ribera, and she was born in a little village in the Sierra Nevada, of Andalusia. Her mother was a highly respectable peasant-woman, of a peculiarly romantic disposition, and fond of listening to and reading weird and supernatural stories. Her father was also a peasant, but intellectual beyond his class. By dint of hard work, he acquired a considerable amount of land and large numbers of cattle, and ultimately became the mayor of his village.

There were two peculiarities noticed about Isabella Ribera when she was born. She had an extraordinary amount of back hair, and the lids of her eyes remained fast sealed until she was a year old. An operation was at first talked about, but the child was examined by a doctor of some repute in the nearest town, and he advised against the operation, saying that it was better to let nature take her course. When the girl was in her thirteenth month she one day suddenly opened her eyes, and those who saw them were frightened. Some people said that they were seal's eyes, others that they were the eyes of a snake, and others, again, that 'the devil looked through them.' The superstitious people in the village urged the parents to consult the priest, and this was done, with the result that the infant was subjected to a religious ceremony, with a view to exorcising the demon which was supposed to have taken possession of her.

As the girl grew she displayed amazing precocity. When she was only four she was more like a grown woman in her acts and ways than a child, and the intuitive knowledge she exhibited only served to increase the superstitious dread with which she inspired people. One day, when she was nearly five, her father had a pig killed. The girl witnessed the operation, and seemed to go almost mad with delight. And suddenly, to the horror and consternation of those looking on, she threw herself on the dying animal and began to drink the blood that flowed from the cut throat. Somebody snatched her up and ran screaming with her to her mother, who was distracted when she heard the story.

The incident, of course, soon became known all over the village, and indeed far beyond it, and a fierce hatred of the child seized upon the people. The consequence was, the parents had to keep a very watchful eye over her. They were seriously advised to have the girl strangled, and her body burnt to ashes with wood that had been blessed and conse-crated by the priests. Fearing that an attempt would be made upon her life by the villagers, Isabella's parents secretly conveyed her away and took her to Córdoba, where she was placed in the care of the mother superior of a convent.

At this place she was carefully trained and taught, but was regarded as an unnatural child. She seemed to be without heart, feeling, or senti-ment. Her aptitude for learning was looked upon as miraculous, and a tale of horror or bloodshed afforded her an infinite amount of enjoy-ment. When she was a little more than twelve she escaped from her guardians and disappeared.

For a long time no trace of her was forthcoming, then it became known that she had joined a band of gipsies, and gained such a domi-nating influence and power over them, that she was made a queen and married a young man of the tribe. A month afterwards he was found dead one morning in his tent. The cause of his death remained a mys-tery, but it was noticed that there was a peculiar blue mark at the side of his neck, from which a drop or two of blood still oozed.

A few weeks after her husband's death, Isabella, queen of the gipsies, announced to her tribe that she was going to sever herself from them for a time and travel all over Europe. Where she went to during the succeeding two years will never be known; but she was next heard of in Paris, where she was put upon her trial, charged with having caused the death of a man whom she alleged was her husband. She was then known as Madame Ducoudert. The husband had died in a very myste-rious manner. He seemed to grow bloodless, and gradually faded away. And after his death certain signs suggested poison. An autopsy, howev-er, failed to reveal any indications of recognized poisons. Nevertheless madame was tried, but no evidence was forthcoming to convict her, and she was acquitted.

Almost immediately afterwards she quitted Paris with plenty of money, her husband, who was well off, having left her all his property. The Paris police, through their agents and spies, ascertained that she proceeded direct to Bordeaux, where, in a very short time, she unit-ed herself to a handsome young man, the only son of an exceedingly wealthy Bordeaux wine merchant. She had changed her name at this stage to Marie Tailleux. She had a well-developed figure, an enormous quantity of jet black hair, and perfect teeth. In other respects she was considered to be ugly, by some even repulsive. And yet she exercised a fatal fascination over men, though women feared and hated her.

She went from Bordeaux to London with the wine merchant's son, and six months later the English people were treated to a sensation. 'Madame and Monsieur Tailleux' travelled extensively about England and Scotland. Monsieur fell ill, soon after arriving, of some nameless disease. His illness was characterized by prostration, languor, bloodlessness. He consulted several doctors, who prescribed for him without effect.

The pair at last took up their residence at a very well-known metropolitan hotel, where they lived in great style, spent money lavishly, and were supposed to be people of note. But one morning monsieur was found dead in bed, and as no doctor had been treating him for some time, and the cause of death could not be certified, an inquest was ordered and a post-mortem became necessary. Those who made the examination had their suspicions aroused. They believed there had been foul play—at any rate, the man had died of poison. The police were communicated with: result, the arrest of madame, and columns and columns of sensational reports in the papers.

Amongst madame's belongings was found a little carved ebony box containing twelve receptacles for twelve tiny phials. Some of these phials were empty, others full of liquid that varied in colour; that is, in one phial it was yellow, in another red, in another green, in another blue, and yet another held what seemed to be clear water.

The chemical analysis of the contents of the stomach quite failed to justify the suspicions of poison. But the blood had a peculiar, watery appearance; the heart was flabby and weak. Madame accounted for possession of the phials by saying they contained gipsy medicine of great efficacy in certain diseases. There was such a small quantity in each phial as to make analysis practically impossible. Certain animals, however, were treated with some of the contents, and seemed actually to improve under the treatment. Under the circumstances, of course, there was nothing for it but to release madame, as the magistrate said there was no case to go before a jury.

It is worth while to quote the following description of the woman at this time. It appeared in a report in *The Times*.

The prisoner is a most extraordinary looking woman, and appears to be possessed of some wonderful magnetic power, which half fascinates one. It is difficult to say wherein this power lies, unless it be in her eyes. They are certainly remarkable eyes, that have a peculiar, glistening appearance like oil. Then her voice is a revelation. Until she speaks one would be disposed to say the voice of such a harsh-featured woman would be hard, raucous, and raspy. But its tones are those of a silver bell, or a sweet-toned flute. Her self-possession is also marvellous, and she smiles sweetly and fascinatingly. Somehow or another she gives one the impression that she has some of the attributes of the sirens of old, who were said to lure men to their destruction. Possibly this is doing the woman an injustice; but it is difficult to resist the idea. Her hands, too, are in striking contrast to her general physique. They are long, thin, lithe, and white. Taken altogether, she cannot certainly be described as an ordinary type of woman, and we should be disposed to say that, allied to great intelligence, was a subtle cunning and a cruelty of disposition that might make her dangerous.

This description was written during the time the woman was a prisoner. The writer showed that he had a keen insight, and had he but known some of her past history he would probably have written in a much more pronounced way.

'Madame Tailleux' was discharged for the want of legal evidence, and Madame Tailleux soon afterwards left England and went to America, where she became 'Miss Anna Clarkson'; and though nobody knew anything at all about her, she had no difficulty in making her way into so-called Society; but not as an associate and companion of women, who shunned and hated her as she hated them; but men followed her, as men are alleged to have followed Circe.[8]

Indeed, in some respects, the classical description of Circe with her magic and potions might apply to Isabella Ribera, with the many aliases.

In a very little while Phineas Miller fell a victim to her potent spells. Phineas was a young man, a stockbroker, and rich. The twain journeyed to Florida, from whence Phineas wrote to an intimate friend that he was strangely ill, and he believed the climate was affecting him. He looked like a corpse, he said. He was languid. He took no interest in anything. He suffered from a peculiar prostration, and found a difficulty in moving about. Yet he experienced no pain, and at times sank into a dreamy state that was pleasant. He thought, however, as soon as he left that part of the country he would be all right.

---

8 The Ancient Greek goddess of magic who was also an enchantress. She had the power to drug animals, such as lions and wolves, to become docile.

He was doomed, however, never to leave that part of the country. He went out one day with Miss Anna Clarkson, and an old negro, to shoot in the swamps. They had a boat which was in charge of the negro. That evening, Miss Clarkson returned alone. She was drenched and covered with slime and mud. There had been an accident. The boat had capsized by striking against a sunken tree. They were all thrown into the water. She managed to cling to the boat, and ultimately to right it, but her companions disappeared. The negro, she thought, was taken by a crocodile.

A search-party went out to try and recover the bodies. The negro was never found, Miller was. He presented an extraordinary appearance, and those who examined him said he had not died by drowning. This theory, however, found no favour. Men were often drowned in the swamps, which swarmed with alligators and crocodiles, huge snakes, and other repulsive things. When a man once got into the water he had no chance. It was a perfect miracle how Miss Clarkson escaped. 'Poor thing, she must have had an awful time of it.'

It is true that crocodiles, alligators, and snakes did swarm in the swamps, and the remarkable thing was that Miller's body was recovered. Much sympathy was shown for Miss Clarkson; Miller was duly buried and forgotten in a week.

Amongst the lady's most pronounced sympathizers was a Mr. Lambert Lennox, an Englishman engaged in fruit farming. He was about forty-five, a widower with two daughters and a son. It was generally agreed that he was one of the finest men in Florida. He was an athlete. He stood six feet two in his stockings. His health was perfect. It was his boast that he had never been laid up a day with illness.

Mr. Lennox had some business to transact in Jamaica, West Indies, and sailed for that island in one of the trading vessels. In the same vessel went 'poor' Miss Clarkson. A month or two later Mr. Lennox, Jun., received from Mr. Lennox, Sen., a letter dated from Jamaica, in the West Indies. Amongst much other news the writer told his son that he had not been well. He had a strange anaemic appearance, felt weak and languid, had no energy, suffered from unquenchable thirst, and was constantly falling asleep suddenly, often at the most inopportune moments. He had consulted a doctor, who was of opinion that the climate of Jamaica didn't suit him, and he advised him to get away as soon as possible. 'I shall therefore be home in about six weeks,' Mr. Lennox added.

But in the meantime he departed for his long home. Mr. Lambert Lennox died somewhat suddenly one morning, and was buried in the evening. The doctor who had been attending him certified that he had succumbed to low fever. The next mail that went out bore the sad intelligence to his family, and people marvelled much when they heard that handsome Lambert Lennox, the man with the iron constitution, had slipped away so quickly, more particularly as long residence in Florida had inured him to a hot climate and miasma.

It was found difficult to trace Miss Clarkson's movements during the next two or three years, but there were grounds for believing that she travelled extensively, and amongst other places visited India, and in this connection there was a somewhat vague and legendary story told. At a hill station a strange and mysterious woman put in an appearance. She was thought to be either a Spaniard or a Portuguese. She was known as Mademoiselle Sassetti, though why 'Mademoiselle,' if Spanish or Portuguese, was not explained. But that is a detail.

This mysterious lady claimed to have occult powers. She could read anyone's future. She could perform miracles. The women kept away from her because they were afraid of her, though there was no definite statement as to how this fear arose. But the men showed no fear, as became them, and amongst others who consulted her was a handsome, much beloved young military officer. His frequent visits to the sorceress caused a good deal of talk, as it was bound to do in an Indian hill station. Grey-bearded men shook their heads sadly, and wise and virtuous women turned up their noses and muttered mysterious interjections such as 'Ah!' 'Oh!' 'Umph.'

One day the station was startled by a report that the young officer had been found dead in a jungle in one of the valleys. He had been bitten by a cobra, so the report said, for there was a peculiar little blue mark at the side of his neck. If the virtuous ones didn't actually say it served him right, they thought it; and the grey beards looked more knowing than ever, and mumbled that the young officer had been dining somewhere not wisely but too well, and had mistaken the jungle for his bedroom, and gone to sleep, otherwise how did the cobra manage to bite him in the neck.

It seemed a plausible theory. Anyway it got over a difficulty, and it brought an unpleasant little scandal to a tragic and abrupt end. So the virtuous ones went about their many occupations again, and the atmosphere was purer when it was known that the sorceress had disappeared as mysteriously as she had come.

The next direct evidence we got was that under the name of Isabella Rodino the adventuress turned up in Rome, where she rented a small but expensive villa in the fashionable Via Porta Pia. Everyone who knows Rome knows how exclusive society is, but while Isabella Rodino made no attempt to be received by Roman society she attracted to her villa some of the male representatives of the best families in the city. Amongst these gentlemen was the scion of one of the oldest Roman houses.

Now it may be said boldly here, and that without any reflections, that the young gentlemen of Rome, as of most other continental cities, are allowed a good deal more latitude than would be accorded to the same class in, say, cold blooded, unromantic, prosaic, and common-place London, whose soot and grime, somehow, seem to grind their way into people's brains and hearts. Anyway the young gentleman referred to, whose baptismal name was Basta, did not at first provoke any very severe criticism, but he was destined ultimately to give the Romans a sensation to talk about for the proverbial nine days, for one Sunday morning a humble fisherman, having some business on the Tiber, fished out of that classic river the stark body of the scion. Over Rome flew the news, and those who loved him, and looked to him to uphold the honour and dignity of his family, were horror stricken.

Now, it's a very curious thing that his distracted relatives firmly believed that the young prodigal had in a moment of remorse, after a night's debauch, flung himself into eternity *via* the Tiber, and so mighty was their pride that they used their wealth, their influence, and their power to stifle inquiry, and caused a report to be circulated that Basta had met his end through accident. It is no less curious that the family doctor who examined the body was of opinion that there was something mysterious about the lad's death, for he certainly had not died by drowning, and on one side of the neck was a peculiar little bluish puncture. But as the family persisted in *their* view, the doctor, not wishing to lose their influential patronage, observed a discreet silence.

A week later, however, an agent of the police called on Isabella Rodino, and did something more than hint that it was desirable that within twenty-four hours she should leave Rome as quietly and unobtrusively as possible. The result of this functionary's call was that Isabella Rodino journeyed to Florence by that night's mail train. It was known that she only sojourned two days in the fair city on the Arno.

After that there is another hiatus of something like two years in her known career, and it is not easy to fill it up. And this brings us to that fatal night at Wiesbaden, when ill-starred Jack Redcar met the enchantress on the hotel stairs. From that point to the moment when, her role being finished, she disappeared for ever from the ken of men, the reader of the story can fill in for himself. She played out her last act under the name of Annette. In selecting her many names she seemed actuated by a fine sense of poetic euphony, and in selecting her victims she was guided by a 'damnable' discrimination.

'Annette,' as we will now call her, was a human riddle, and she illustrates for the millionth time the trite adage that 'Truth is stranger than Fiction,' besides which she presents the world with an object lesson in the study of the occult.

III

The Corpse Light

MY NAME IS JOHN Patmore Lindsay. By profession I am a medical man, and a Fellow of the Royal College of Surgeons, and Member of the Royal College of Physicians, London. I am also the author of numerous medical works, the best known, perhaps, being *How to Keep in Good Health and Live Long*. I was educated at one of the large public schools, and took my degree at Oxford. I have generally been regarded as 'a hard-headed man,' and sceptical about all phenomena that were not capable of being explained by rational and known laws. Mysticism, occultism, spiritualism, and the like only served to excite my ridicule; and I entertained anything but a flattering opinion of those people who professed belief in such things. I was pleased to think it argued a weakness of mind.

I have referred to the few foregoing facts about myself because I wish to make it clear that I do not belong to that class of nervous and excitable people who fall a prey to their own fancies; conjure up shapes and scenes out of their imaginings, and then vow and declare that they have been confronted with stern realities. What I am about to relate is so marvellous, so weird and startling, that I am fain to begin my story in a half apologetic way; and even now, as I dwell upon it all, I wonder why I of all men should have been subjected to the unnatural and unearthly influence. But so it is, and though in a sense I am only half convinced, I no longer scoff when somebody reminds me that there is more in heaven and earth than is dreamt of in our philosophy.

But to my story, and when it is told the reader can judge for himself how powerful must have been the effect of what I witnessed, when it could induce a man of my mental fibre to commit to paper so astounding a narrative as the one I now pen. It is about twenty years ago that I took up a practice in the old-fashioned and picturesque little town of Brinton-on-Sea. At that time there was no railway into Brinton, the nearest station being some seven or eight miles away. The result was, the town still retained a delightful old-time air, while the people were as primitive and old-fashioned as their town. Nevertheless, Brinton was far ahead of its neighbours, and, though in a purely agricultural district, was enterprising and business-like, while its weekly Tuesday market brought an enormous influx of the population of the district for miles around, and very large sums of money changed hands. Being the chief town of the parish, and boasting of a very curious and ancient church, and a still more ancient market cross, to say nothing of several delightful old hostelries, and a small though excellent museum of local curiosities, consisting principally of Roman remains and fossils, for which the district was renowned, it attracted not only the antiquary and the gourmand, but artists, tourists, and lovers of the picturesque, as well as those in search of quietude and repose. The nearest village was High Lea, about three miles away. Between the two places was a wide sweep of magnificent rolling down, delightful at all times, but especially so in the summer. Many an ancient farmhouse was dotted about, with here and there a windmill. The down on the seaside terminated in a high headland, from which a splendid lighthouse sent forth its warning beams over the fierce North Sea. Second only in conspicuousness to this lighthouse was an old and half ruined windmill, known all over the country side as 'The Haunted Mill.'

When I first went to live in Brinton this mill early attracted my attention, for it was one of the most picturesque old places of its kind I had ever seen; and as I had some artistic instincts, and could sketch with, as my too flattering friends said, 'no mean ability,' the haunted mill appealed to me. It stood on rising ground, close to the high-road that ran between Brinton and High Lea. I gathered that there had been some dispute about the ownership, and, as is usually the case, the suckers of the harpies of the law had fastened upon it, so to speak, and drained all its vitality away after the manner of lawyers generally. The old-fashioned, legal luminaries of the country were a slow-going set, and for over a quarter of a century that disputed claim had remained unsettled; and during that long period the old mill had been gradually falling into ruin. The foundations had from some cause sunk, throwing the main building out of the perpendicular. Part of the roof had fallen in, and the fierce gales of a quarter of a century had battered the sails pretty well to match-wood. A long flight of wooden steps led up to the principal door, but these steps had rotted away in places, and the door itself had partly fallen inwards. Needless to say, this mill had become the home of bats and owls, and, according to the yokels, of something more fearsome than either. It was a forlorn and mournful-looking place, any way, even in the full blaze of sunshine; but seen in moonlight its appearance was singularly weird, and well calculated to beget in the rustic mind a feeling of horror, and to produce a creepy and uncanny sensation in anyone susceptible to the influence of *outré* appearances. To me it did not appeal in any of these aspects. I saw in it only subject matter for an exceedingly effective picture, and yet I am bound to confess that even when transferred to board or canvas there was a certain grim suggestiveness of things uncanny, and I easily understood how the superstitious and unreasoning rustic mind was awed into a belief that this mouldering old mill was haunted by something more creepy and harrowing than bats and owls. Any way, I heard wonderful tales, at which I laughed, and when I learned that the country people generally gave the mill a wide berth at night, blamed them for their stupidity. But it was a fact that worthy, and in other respects intelligent, farmers and market folk coming or going between Brinton and High Lea after dark preferred the much longer and dangerous route by the sea cliffs, even in the wildest weather.

I have dwelt thus long on the 'Haunted Mill' because it bulks largely in my story, as will presently be seen, and I came in time to regard it with scarcely less awe than the rustics did.

It was during the second year of my residence in Brinton that a young man named Charles Royce came home after having been absent at sea for three years. Royce's people occupied Gorse Hill Farm, about two miles to the south of Brinton. Young Charley, a fine, handsome, but rather wild youngster, had, it appears, fallen desperately in love with Hannah Trowzell, who was a domestic in the employ of the Rector of the parish. But Charley's people did not approve of his choice, and, thinking to cure him, packed him off to sea, and after an absence of three years and a month the young fellow, bronzed, hearty, more rollicking and handsome than ever, returned to his native village. I had known nothing of Charles Royce or his history up to the day of his return; but it chanced on that very day I had to pay a professional visit to the Rectory, and the Rector pressed me to lunch with him. Greatly interested in all his parishioners, and knowing something of the private history of most of the families in his district, the rev. gentleman very naturally fell to talking about young Royce, and he told me the story, adding, 'Hannah is a good girl, and I think it's rather a pity Charley's people objected to his courting her. I believe she would have made him a capital wife.'

'Has she given him up entirely?' I asked.

'Oh, yes, and is engaged to Silas Hartrop, whose father owns the fishing smack the *North Sea Beauty*. I've never had a very high opinion of Silas. I'm afraid he is a little too fond of skittles and beer. However, Hannah seems determined to have him in spite of anything I can say, so she must take her course. But I hope she will be able to reform him, and that the marriage will be a happy one. I really shouldn't be a bit surprised, however, if the girl took up with her old lover again, for I have reason to know she was much attached to him, and I fancy Charley, if he were so minded, could easily influence her to throw Silas overboard.'

This little story of love and disappointment naturally interested me, for in a country town the affairs of one's neighbours are matter of greater moment than is the case in a big city.

So it came to pass that a few weeks after Charley's return it was pretty generally known that, even as the Rector had suggested it might be, young Royce and pretty Hannah Trowzell were spooning again, and Silas had virtually been told to go about his business. It was further known that Silas had taken his dismissal so much to heart that he had been seeking consolation in the beer-pot. Of course, folk talked a good deal, and most of them sympathized with Silas, and blamed Hannah. Very soon it began to be bruited about that Royce's people no longer opposed any objections to the wooing, and that in consequence Hannah and Charley were to become husband and wife at Christmas, that was in about seven weeks' time. A month of the time had passed, and the 'askings'⁹ were up in the parish church, when one day there went forth a rumour that Charles Royce was missing. Rumour took a more definite shape a few hours later when it was positively stated that two nights previously Charles had left his father's house in high spirits and the best of health to visit Hannah, and walk with her, as she was going into the town to make some purchases. On his way he called at the 'Two Waggoners,' a wayside inn, where he had a pint of beer and purchased an ounce of tobacco. From the time he left the inn, all trace of him was lost, and he was seen no more. Hannah waited his coming until long past the appointed hour, and when he failed to put in an appearance, she became angry and went off to the town by herself. Next day her anger gave place to anxiety when she learnt that he had left his home to visit her, and had not since returned; and anxiety became alarm when two and three days slipped by without bringing any tidings of the truant. On the night that he left his home, the weather was very tempestuous, and it had been wild and stormy since. It was therefore suggested that on leaving the 'Two Waggoners' he might have got confused when he reached the common, which he had to cross to get to the Rectory; and as there were several pools and treacherous hollows on the common, it was thought he had come to grief, but the most diligent search failed to justify the surmise.

---

9 More commonly called marriage banns nowadays.

Such an event as this was well calculated to cause a sensation, not only in Brinton and its neighbourhood, but throughout the county. Indeed, for many days it was a common topic of conversation, and at the Brinton weekly market the farmers and the rustics dwelt upon it to the exclusion of other things; and, of course, everybody, or nearly everybody, had some wonderful theory of his or her own to account for the missing man's disappearance. One old lady, who every week for twenty years had trudged in from a village five miles off with poultry and eggs for the Brinton market, declared her belief that young Royce had been spirited away, and she recommended an appeal to a wondrous wise woman, locally known as 'Cracked Moll,' but whose reputation for solving mysteries and discovering lost persons and things was very great. Ultimately Royce's people did call in the services of this ancient fraud, but without any result. And despite of wide publicity and every effort on the part of the rural and county police, to say nothing of a hundred and one amateur detectives, the mystery remained unsolved. Charles Royce had apparently disappeared from off the face of the earth, leaving not a trace behind.

In the process of time the nine days' wonder gave place to something else, and excepting by those directly interested in him, Charles Royce was forgotten. Hannah took the matter very seriously to heart, and for a while lay dangerously ill. Silas Hartrop, who was much affected by his disappointment with regard to Hannah, went to the dogs, as the saying is, and drank so heavily that it ended in an attack of delirium tremens. I was called in to attend him, and had hard work to pull him through. On his recovery his father sent him to an uncle at Yarmouth, who was in the fishing trade, and soon afterwards news came that young Hartrop had been drowned at sea. He was out in the North Sea in his uncle's fishing smack, and, though nobody saw him go, it was supposed that he fell overboard in the night. This set the local tongues wagging again for a time, but even the affairs of Brinton could not stand still because the ne'er-do-well Silas Hartrop was drowned. So sympathy was expressed with his people, and then the affair was dismissed.

About two years later I received an urgent message late one afternoon to hasten with all speed to High Lea, to attend to the Squire there, who had been taken suddenly and, as report said, seriously ill. I had had rather a heavy day of it, as there had been a good deal of sickness about for some time past, and it had taken me several hours to get through my list of patients. I had just refreshed myself with a cup of tea and was about to enjoy a cigar when the messenger came. Telling him to ride back as quickly as possible and say that I was coming, I busied myself with a few important matters which had to be attended to, as I might be absent for some hours, and then I ordered my favourite mare, Princess, to be saddled.

I set off from Brinton soon after seven. It was a November night, bitterly cold, dark as Erebus,[10] while every now and then violent squalls swept the land from seaward. Princess knew the road well, so I gave the mare her head, and she went splendidly until we reached the ruined mill, when suddenly she wheeled round with such abruptness that, though I was a good horseman, I was nearly pitched from the saddle. At the same moment I was struck in the face by something that seemed cold and clammy. I thought at first it was a bat, but remembered that bats do not fly in November; an owl, but an owl would not have felt cold and clammy. However, I had little time for thought, as my attention had to be given to the mare. She seemed disposed to bolt, and was trembling with fear. Then, to my intense astonishment, I noticed what seemed to be a large luminous body lying on the roadway. It had the appearance of a corpse illuminated in some wonderful and mysterious manner. Had it not been for the fright of my mare I should have thought I was the victim of some optical delusion; but Princess evidently saw the weird object, and refused to pass it. So impressed was I with the idea that a real and substantial body was lying on the road, notwithstanding the strange unearthly light, that I slipped from the saddle, intending to investigate the matter, when suddenly it disappeared, and the cold and clammy *something* again struck me in the face.

I confess that for the first time in my life I felt a strange, nervous, unaccountable fear. I say 'unaccountable,' because it would have been difficult for me to have given any explanation of my fear. Why and of what was I afraid? Now, whatever the phenomenon was, there was the hard, stern fact to face that my horse had seen what I had seen, and was terrified. There was something strangely uncanny about the whole business, and when a terrific squall, bringing with it sleet and rain, came howling from the sea, it seemed to emphasize the uncanniness, and the ruined mill, looming gaunt and grim in the darkness, caused me to shake with an involuntary shudder. The next moment I was trying to laugh myself out of my nervousness. 'Princess and I,' I mentally argued, 'have been the victims of some atmospheric delusion.' That was all very well, but the *something* cold and clammy that struck me in the face, and which *may* have struck the mare in the face also, was no

---

10 In Greek mythology Erebus was the personification of darkness.

atmospheric delusion. With an alacrity I did not often display, I sprang into the saddle, spoke some encouraging words to the mare, for she was still trembling, and when she bounded forward, and the haunted mill was behind me, I experienced a positive sense or relief.

I found my patient at High Lea in a very bad way. He was suffering from an attack of apoplexy,[11] and though I used all my skill on his behalf he passed away towards midnight. His wife very kindly offered me a bed for the night, but as I had important matters to attend to early in the morning I declined the hospitality, though I was thankful for a glass or two of generous port wine and some sandwiches. It was half-past twelve when I left the house on my return journey. The incident by the haunted mill had been put out of my head by the case I had been called upon to attend, but as I mounted my mare the groom, who had brought her round from the stable, said, 'It be a bad night, doctor, for riding; the kind o' night when dead things come out o' their graves.'

I laughed, and replied:

'Tom, lad, I am surprised to hear you talk such rubbish. I thought you had more sense than that.'

'Well, I tell 'ee what, doctor; if I had to ride to Brinton to-night I'd go by the cliffs and chance being drowned, rather than pass yon old mill.'

These words for the moment unnerved me, and I honestly confess that I resolved to go by the cliffs, dangerous as the road was in the dark. Nevertheless, I laughed at Tom's fears, and ridiculed him, though when I left the squire's grounds I turned the mare's head towards the cliffs. In a few minutes I was ridiculing myself.

'John Patmore Lindsay,' I mentally exclaimed, 'you are a fool. All your life you have been ridiculing stories of the supernatural, and now, at your time of life, are you going to allow yourself to be frightened by a bogey? Shame on you.'

I bucked up, grew bold, and thereupon altered my course, and got into the high road again.

There had been a slight improvement in the weather. It had ceased to rain, but the wind had settled down into a steady gale, and screeched and screamed over the moorland with a demoniacal fury. The darkness, however, was not so intense as it was, and a star here and there was visible through the torn clouds. But it was an eerie sort of night, and I was strangely impressed with a sense of my loneliness. It was absolutely unusual for me to feel like this, and I suggested to myself

---

11 A stroke or cerebral haemorrhage.

that my nerves were a little unstrung by overwork and the anxiety the squire's illness had caused me. And so I rode on, bowing my head to the storm, while the mare stepped out well, and I anticipated that in little more than half an hour I should be snug in bed. As we got abreast of the haunted mill the mare once more gibbed, and all but threw me, and again I was struck in the face by the cold clammy *something*.

I have generally prided myself on being a bold man, but my boldness had evaporated now, and I almost think my hair rose on end as I observed that the illuminated corpse was lying in the roadway again; but now it appeared to be surrounded by a lake of blood. It was the most horrible, weird, marrow-curdling sight that ever human eyes looked upon. I tried to urge Princess forward, but she was stricken with terror, and, wheeling right round, was setting off towards High Lea again. But once more I was struck in the face by the invisible *something*, and its coldness and clamminess made me shudder, while there in front of us lay the corpse in the pool of blood. The mare reared and plunged, but I got her head round, determining to make a wild gallop for Brinton and leave the horrors of the haunted mill behind. But the corpse was again in front of us, and I shrank back almost appalled as the *something* once more touched my face.

I cannot hope to describe what my feelings were at this supreme moment. I don't believe anything human could have daunted me; but I was confronted by a supernatural mystery that not only terrified me but the mare I was riding. Whichever way I turned, that awful, ghastly object confronted me, and the blow in the face was repeated again and again.

How long I endured the unutterable horrors of the situation I really don't know. Possibly the time was measured by brief minutes. It seemed to me hours. At last my presence of mind returned. I dismounted, and reasoned with myself that, whatever the apparition was, it had some import. I soothed the mare by patting her neck and talking to her, and I determined then to try and find a solution of the mystery. But now a more wonderful thing happened. The corpse, which was still made visible by the unearthly light, rose straight up, and as it did so the blood seemed to flow away from it in great, gurgling streams, for I solemnly declare that I distinctly heard gurgling sounds. The figure glided past me, and a sense of extraordinary coldness made me shiver. Slowly and gracefully the shining corpse glided up the rotting steps of the old mill, and disappeared through the doorway. No sooner had it gone than the mill itself seemed to glow with phosphorescent light, and to become transparent, and I beheld a sight that took my breath away. I am disposed to think that for some moments my brain became so numbed that insensibility ensued, for I am conscious of a blank. When the power of thought returned, I was still holding the bridle of the mare, and she was cropping the grass at her feet. The mill loomed blackly against the night sky. It had resumed its normal appearance again. The wind shrieked about it. The ragged scud raced through the heavens, and the air was filled with the sounds of the raging wind. At first I was inclined to doubt the evidence of my own senses. I tried to reason myself into a belief that my imagination had played me a trick; but I didn't succeed, although the mystery was too profound for my fathoming. So I mounted the mare, urged her to her fastest pace, galloped into Brinton, and entered my house with a feeling of intense relief.

Thoroughly exhausted by the prolonged physical and mental strain I had endured, I speedily sank into a deep though troubled slumber as soon as I got into bed. I was unusually late in rising the next day. I found that I had no appetite for breakfast. Indeed, I felt ill and out or sorts; and, though I busied myself with my professional duties, I was haunted by the strange incidents of the preceding night. Never before in the whole course of my career had I been so impressed, so unnerved, and so dispirited. I wanted to believe that I was still as sceptical as ever, but it was no use. What I had seen might have been unearthly; but I *had seen it*, and it was no use trying to argue myself out of that fact. The result was, in the course of the afternoon I called on my old friend, Mr. Goodyear, who was chief of the county constabulary. He was a strong-minded man, and, like myself, a hardened sceptic about all things that smacked of the supernatural.

'Goodyear,' I said, 'I'm out of sorts, and I want you to humour a strange fancy I have. Bring one of your best men, and come with me to the haunted mill. But first let me exact from you a pledge of honour that, if our journey should result in nothing, you will keep the matter secret, as I am very sensitive to ridicule.'

He looked at me in amazement, and then, as he burst into a hearty laugh, exclaimed:

'I say, my friend, you are over-working yourself. It's time you got a *locum tenens*,[12] and took a holiday.'

I told him that I agreed with him; nevertheless, I begged him to humour me, and accompany me to the mill. At last he reluctantly consented to do so, and an hour later we drove out of the town in my dog-

---

12 Latin for 'someone to hold your place'.

cart. There were four of us, as I took Peter, my groom, with me. We had provided ourselves with lanterns, but Goodyear's man and Peter knew nothing of the object of our journey.

When we got abreast of the mill I drew up, and giving the reins to Peter, I alighted, and Goodyear did the same. Taking him on one side, I said, 'I have had a vision, and unless I am the victim of incipient madness we shall find a dead body in the mill.'

The light of the dog-cart was shining full on his face, and I saw the expression of alarm that my words brought.

'Look here, old chap,' he said in a cheery, kindly way, as he put his arm through mine, 'you are not going into that mill, but straight home again. Come, now, get into the cart, and don't let's have any more of this nonsense.'

I felt disposed to yield to him, and had actually placed my foot on the step to mount, when I staggered back and exclaimed——

'My God! am I going mad, or is this a reality?'

Once again I had been struck in the face by the cold clammy *something*; and I saw Goodyear suddenly clap his hand to his face as he cried out—'Hullo, what the deuce is that?'

'Aha,' I exclaimed exultantly, for I no longer thought my brain was giving way, 'you have felt it too?'

'Well, something cold and nasty-like struck me in the face. A bat, I expect. Confound 'em.'

'Bats don't fly at this time of the year,' I replied.

'By Jove, no more they do.'

I approached him, and said in a low tone—'Goodyear, this is a mystery beyond our solving. I am resolved to go into that mill.'

He was a brave man, though for a moment or two he hesitated; but on my insisting he consented to humour me, and so we lit the lantern, and leaving the groom in charge of the horse and trap, I, Goodyear, and his man made our way with difficulty up the rotting steps, which were slimy and sodden with wet. As we entered the mill an extraordinary scene of desolation and ruin met our gaze as we flashed the light of the lantern about. In places the floor had broken away, leaving yawning chasms of blackness. From the mouldering rafters huge festoons of cobwebs hung. The accumulated dust and dampness of years had given them the appearance of cords. And oh, how the wind moaned eerily through the rifts and crannies and broken windows! If ever there was a place on this earth where evil spirits might dwell it was surely that ghoul-haunted old mill. The startling aspect of the place impressed us all, perhaps me more than the other two. We advanced gingerly, for the floor was so rotten we were afraid it would crumble beneath our feet.

My companions were a little bewildered, I think, and were evidently at a loss to know what we had come there for. But some strange feeling impelled me to seek for something; though if I had been asked to define that something, for the life of me I could not have done it. Forward I went, however, taking the lead, and holding the lantern above my head so that its rays might fall afar. But they revealed nothing save the rotting floor and slimy walls. A ladder led to the upper storey, and I expressed my intention of mounting it. Goodyear tried to dissuade me, but I was resolute, and led the way. The ladder was so creaky and fragile that it was not safe for more than one to be on it at a time. When I reached the second floor and drew myself up through the trap, I am absolutely certain I heard a sigh. You may say it was the wind. I swear it was not. The wind was moaning drearily enough, but the sigh was a distinctive note, and unmistakable. As I turned the lantern round so that its light might sweep every hole and corner of the place, I noticed what seemed to be a sack full of something lying in a corner. I approached and touched it with my foot, and drew back in alarm, for touch and sound told me it contained neither corn nor chaff. I waited until my companions had joined me. Then I said to Goodyear, 'Unless I am mistaken there is something dreadful in that sack.'

He stooped and placed his hand on the sack, and I saw him start back. In another moment he recovered himself, and whipping out his knife cut the string which fastened up the mouth of the sack, and revealed a human skull with the hair and shrivelled mummified flesh still adhering to it.

'Great heavens!' he exclaimed, 'here is a human body.'

We held a hurried conversation, and decided to leave the ghastly thing undisturbed until the morrow. So we scuttled down as fast as we could, and went home. I did not return to the mill again myself. My part had been played. Investigation made it absolutely certain that the mouldering remains were those of poor Charley Royce, and it was no less absolutely certain that he had been foully murdered. For not only was there a bullet-hole in the skull, and a bullet inside, but his throat had been cut. It was murder horrible and damnable. The verdict of the coroner's jury pronounced it murder, but there was no evidence to prove who had done the deed. Circumstances, however, pointed to Charley's rival, Silas Hartrop. Was it a guilty conscience that drove him to drink? And did the Furies[13] who avenge such deeds impel him on that dark and stormy night in the North Sea to end the torture of his accursed earthly life? Who can tell? The sea holds its secrets, and not a scrap of legal evidence could be obtained. But though the law declined the responsibility of fixing the guilt of the dark deed on Silas, there was a consensus of opinion that he was the guilty party. It was a mystery, but the greatest mystery of all was that I, the sceptic, should have been selected by some supernatural power to be the instrument for bringing the foul crime to light. For myself, I attempt no explanation. I have told a true story. Let those who can explain it. I admit now that 'there are more things in heaven and earth than are dreamt of in our philosophy.'

---

13 In Greek mythology, the three Furies are deities of vengeance.

IV

'Red Lily'

ON ONE OF THE wildest nights for which the Bay of Biscay is notorious, the sailing ship *Sirocco* was ploughing her way under close-reefed topsails across that stormy sea. The *Sirocco* was a large, full-rigged vessel, bound from Bombay towards England, her destination being London. She had a mixed cargo, though a large percentage of it was composed of jute. Four months had passed since she cleared from her port of lading, and was towed out of the beautiful harbour of Bombay in a dead calm. For many days after the tug left her the *Sirocco* did nothing but drift with the current. She was as 'a painted ship upon a painted ocean.' No breath came out of the sultry heavens to waft her towards her haven in far away England. It was a bad beginning to the voyage. The time was about the middle of August, and all on board were anxiously looking forward to reaching their destination in time to spend Christmas at home. But as August wore out and September came in, and still the horrid calms continued, pleasant anticipations gave place to despair, for many a thousand leagues of watery wastes had to be sailed before the white cliffs of Albion would gladden the eyes of the wanderers.

The crew of the vessel numbered sixty hands all told, and in addition there were twenty saloon passengers. With two of these passengers we have now to deal. The one is a fair young girl, slender, tall, and delicate. She is exceedingly pretty. Her features are regular and delicately chiselled. Her hair is a soft, wavy, golden brown, and her brown eyes are as liquid and gentle as a fawn's. The pure whiteness of her neck and temples is contrasted by the most exquisite tinge of rose colour in the cheeks, which puts, as it were, a finish upon a perfect picture. The whiteness of her skin, the delicate flush in the face, the brown, flossy hair, the tall, slender, graceful figure were all so suggestive of the purest of flowers that her friends for many years had called her 'Red Lily.' Her name was Lily Hetherington, and she yet wanted some months to the completion of her twenty-first birthday. Lily was the daughter of an officer of the Hon. East India Company's Service—his only daughter, and by him worshipped. For many years he had been stationed in India, and at last, seeing no chance of returning to his wife and family, which consisted of two sons in addition to the girl, he requested them to join him in the East. This request was quickly and gladly complied with, and Mrs. Hetherington and her children started on their journey. Mr. Hetherington at that time was well off, for he had invested all his savings in the Agra & Masterman Bank, and held shares to a large amount in the concern, the stability of which, at that period, no one would have dared to have doubted. Indian officers throughout India swore by it, and they congratulated themselves, as they entrusted their hard won money to the Bank, that they were making splendid provision for their wives and children when those wives and children should become widows and orphans.

As Mr. Hetherington possessed considerable influence he had no difficulty in quickly procuring his sons suitable appointments. Fond as he was of his lads, who were aged respectively twenty-two and twenty-four, his love for them was as nothing when compared with that he bore for his beautiful daughter, his 'Bonnie Red Lily,' as he called her. Nor was Lily less fond of her father. She was a mere child when he left England, but she had never forgotten him, and never a mail left but it bore from Lily a long and loving epistle to the lonely officer, who was bravely doing his duty in the distant eastern land.

One day, soon after her arrival, Mr. Hetherington said to his daughter as they sat in the verandah of the bungalow, 'Lily, my pet, I have got a little surprise for you.'

'Have you, pa dear; and pray what is it?' she answered. 'You are such a dear, good kind papa that you are always giving me pleasant surprises.'

'Well, yes, of course, I like to give you pleasant surprises, but this one is different from any of the others,' he returned with a smile, at the same time stroking her soft brown hair, and looking proudly into her beautiful face.

'Oh, do tell me what it is,' she exclaimed, as he paused in a tantalizing way; 'do you hear, pa? Don't keep me in suspense.'

'Restrain that woman's curiosity of yours, my darling, and don't be impatient.'

'I declare you are awfully wicked, papa,' she returned, with a pretty pout of her red lips. 'Tell me instantly what it is. I demand to know.'

'And so you shall,' he answered, as he kissed her fondly and patted her head. 'To-morrow, then, I have a visitor coming to stay with us for a week or two.'

'Indeed. Is it a lady or gentleman?'

'A gentleman.'

'Oh, do tell me what he's like.'

'Well, well, you are a little Miss Curious,' Mr. Hetherington laughed heartily as he blew a cloud of blue smoke from his cigar into the stagnant air. 'Not to keep you in suspense any longer, then, the name of my visitor is Dick Fenton, Richard Cronmire Joyce Fenton, to give him his full name. He is a year or two your senior, and a fine, handsome, manly young fellow to boot.'

'Indeed,' muttered Lily, thoughtfully, as she fancied that her father's words had a hidden meaning.

'Yes. His father was a very old friend of mine, and we saw long service together. He died some four or five years ago, but before dying he made me promise I would look after his boy, who was an only child and motherless. Of course, I gladly gave this promise, and have sacredly carried it out.'

'Ah, what a good, kind, generous man you are,' Lily said, as she nestled closer to him, and tightened her little white fingers round his brown, hairy hand.

'I saw there was stuff in the lad, and I took to him almost as if he had been my own son. Unfortunately, my good friend Fenton died poor, and was only enabled to leave three thousand pounds, for which he had insured his life, for his son's education. I succeeded in getting Dick into one of the Company's training establishments, and the marked ability he displayed very soon pushed him forward, and having gone through his cadetship with honour and credit, he was appointed a year ago to what in time will be a most lucrative post. I have watched the lad closely, and seen with pride the many noble qualities he possesses, and I have no doubt at all he will distinguish himself. During the years that he has been my *protégé* I have constantly said to myself, "If my Lily should like Dick, and Dick should like my Lily, they shall be man and wife."'

'Oh, papa!' exclaimed Lily, as the beautiful tinge in her face deepened to scarlet, that spread to her neck and temples.

'Why, my darling, why do you blush so? It is surely every honest woman's desire to become a wife, and I am very anxious to see you comfortably married before I die. Men go off very suddenly in this treacherous country, and I am well worn with service, and cannot hope to last much longer. But, understand me, Lily, pet, your own will and womanly instincts must guide you in this matter. I shall not seek to influence you in any way, and if you have already given your heart to another, if he is an honest and worthy man, even though he be poor as a church mouse, I shall not offer the slightest opposition to your wishes. It is your future happiness I study, and I am not selfish enough to attempt to coerce you into an objectionable union.'

Lily rose and twined her arms round her father's neck, and pressing her soft, white face to his bronzed cheeks, said:

'My dear, dear father, I have not given my heart to any one, and your wishes are mine.'

On the morrow Fenton duly arrived at Mr. Hetherington's bungalow. He had travelled by dawk[14] from a station near Calcutta; and when he had refreshed himself with a bath, and made himself presentable, Hetherington took him on one side, and said:

'Dick, lad, I have repeatedly spoken to you about my daughter, and before I introduce you to her, let me say that I shall be proud to have you as a son-in-law, providing that there is the most perfect reciprocal feeling between you and my Lily. I am not a man of many words, and I will content myself with remarking that your father was the very soul of honour. Never disgrace him, and never betray the confidence I repose in you.'

'Do not doubt me, sir,' said Dick. 'I am indebted to you for everything, and I should be base if I did anything that could inflict pain upon you or yours.'

'Bravely said, my boy. God prosper you. Win Lily if you can; but win her as a man should.'

Hetherington had previously made known his wishes to his wife, and she had readily acquiesced in them.

Fenton was, as his guardian had described him, a fine, manly, handsome young fellow. His frank, open hearing was well calculated to find favour with women, even if he had not been possessed of good looks.

Hetherington and his wife watched the young people narrowly, and they soon saw that a mutual liking for each other was springing up, and before Dick's leave of two months had expired he and Lily were betrothed, while the bond between them was that of the most perfect love.

Dick returned to his station, and Mr. and Mrs. Hetherington congratulated themselves on having, so far as they were able, provided for their daughter's future, a future that seemed likely to be one of unclouded happiness.

'*L'homme propose, et Dieu dispose,*'[15] says the French proverb, and never was the proverb more fully borne out than in this case. Within

---

14 A word associated with India: a relay system for bringing goods and post. Derived from the Hindi word *dak* meaning post.

15 'Man proposes, God disposes.' Perhaps meaning humans want one thing but God has other plans.

six months of Dick's return to his duties, all civilized India was shocked to its inmost heart by a terrific commercial convulsion—for so only can it be described. Through the length and breadth of the land, the fearful rumour spread on the wings of the wind that the great bank of Agra & Masterman had broken. Men stood aghast, and women paled with fright, for, to hundreds and thousands of households in all parts of the world, it meant utter ruin, as many and many a one at the present day knows to his bitter cost. Many a widow living in poverty now might have reposed in the lap of luxury, and many a young man and woman, now in ignorance and want, might have been otherwise but for this cruel collapse of the great banking firm. It was so essentially an Indian bank, a depository for the earnings of Indian servants of the Company,[16] that it affected a class of people who for the most part had been tenderly nurtured and led to believe that they occupied, and were destined to occupy so long as they might live, a good position in life, and to take their stand among the great middle class of society.

At first men doubted the rumour, but soon the awful truth became too apparent to be longer questioned, and those who had grown grey and feeble beneath the burning Indian sun saw now that their few remaining days must be passed in poverty and misery. It was bitter, very bitter, but it was fate, and could not be averted.

Amongst the greatest sufferers was Mr. Hetherington. He had invested, one way and another, nearly one hundred thousand pounds in that bank, and now every penny piece was gone. The shock came upon him with great severity. His health had long been failing, and he had looked forward with great eagerness to retiring from the service in another year and 'going home' with his family. But that was never to be now. For a time he was stunned. He tried to bear up against the blow, but he was only human; his brain gave way, and in a moment of temporary aberration he shot himself.

This new grief almost crushed the unhappy widow and her family. Fortunately 'the boys' had good appointments that held out every promise of improvement, but their incomes at that time were scarcely sufficient for their own needs, though they generously curtailed their expenses in every way in order to contribute towards the support of their sister and mother.

The shock of her father's death threw Lily into a dangerous illness, and for some time her life was threatened; but there was one who never

---

16 The East India Company.

lost an opportunity of cheering her with his love, and that was Dick Fenton.

When she was convalescent she one day said to him:

'Dick, I have something to say to you.'

'Nothing very serious, darling,' he answered, laughingly.

'Yes, very serious. When I was first engaged to you my father was considered to be a wealthy man, and I understand that he promised you that my dowry should be something handsome. That is all changed now. We are ruined, and my dear father is in his grave. Under these circumstances I can no longer hold you to your engagement, and therefore release you from every promise. You must give me up and seek for someone better suited for you than I am.'

She fairly broke down here, and burst into violent weeping. Dick's arm stole around her waist, he pressed her head to his breast, and, whispering softly to her said, with deep earnestness:

'Lily, there is one thing, and only one thing, that shall break our engagement.'

'What is that?' she stammered between her sobs.

'The death of one of us!' he answered, with strong emphasis.

She needed no further assurance. There was that in his manner and tone that convinced more than words could possibly have done. And so, save for the shadow which hung over the little household, she would have been perfectly happy.

A year went by and Mrs. Hetherington still lingered in India, for she did not like to leave her sons; but failing health at length rendered it necessary that she should return to England. At this time Dick had just been granted two years' leave of absence, and he urged Lily to become his wife before they left India, as he too was going home. She had asked him, however, to postpone the event, and made a solemn promise that the wedding should take place on Christmas Day, adding:

'It is not long to wait, dear. It is now the middle of July, and, as we sail in a fortnight, the vessel is sure to be home by that time. Besides, I am so fond of Christmas. It is so full of solemn and purifying associations, and a fitting season for a man and woman to take upon themselves the responsibility of the marriage state. A wedding on Christmas Day brings good luck. Of course you will say this is stupid superstition. So it may be, but I am a woman, and you must let me have my way.'

Pressing his lips to hers, he made answer:

'And so you shall, my own Red Lily; but, remember, come what may, you'll be my wife on Christmas Day.'

'Come what may, I will be your wife on Christmas Day,' she returned solemnly.

August arrived, and Dick, Lily, and Mrs. Hetherington were passengers on board the good ship *Sirocco*. Their fellow-passengers were a miscellaneous lot, and included several Indian officers, a planter or two, a clergyman, and some merchants, who, having amassed fortunes, were going home to end their days.

The second officer of the *Sirocco* was a young man, of about eight- or nine-and-twenty, Alfred Cornell. He was a wild, reckless, daring fellow, with a splendid physique. His hair was almost black, his eyes the very darkest shade of brown, and small, keen, and piercing as a hawk's. In those eyes the character of the man was written. For somehow they seemed to suggest a vain, heartless, selfish, vindictive nature, and the firm lips told of an iron will. He was every inch a sailor, bold as a lion, and a magnificent swimmer. The crew, however, hated him, for he was the hardest of task masters, but was an especial favourite with the captain, as such men generally are, for he was perfect in every department of his profession, and the sailors under his control were kept to their duties with an iron hand.

About this man—Alfred Cornell—there was something that amounted almost to weirdness. The strange, keen eyes exercised a sort of fascination over some people. This was especially the case with women. In fact, he made a boast that he had never yet seen the woman he could not subdue. From the moment that he and Dick Fenton stood face to face a mutual dislike sprang up in their hearts for each other. Dick could not exactly tell why he did not take to the man, but he had an instinctive dislike for him. The fact was there, the cause was not easy to determine, but instincts are seldom wrong. The moment that Alfred Cornell and Lily Hetherington met each other a shadow fell upon her, and a devil came into his heart. She had an instinctive dread of him, and yet felt fascinated. He thought to himself:

'By heavens, that's a splendid girl, and I'll win her if I die for it.'

For the first week or two he paid her no more than the most ordinary attentions, and the dread she at first felt for him began to wear off; she could not help admitting to herself that he was certainly handsome and attractive. The pet name by which she was known amongst her family—the Red Lily—soon leaked out on board, as such things will, and the passengers with whom she was most intimate frequently addressed her in this style by way of compliment, for she was a favourite with them all, and her beauty was a theme of admiration amongst the men—even the ladies could not help but admit that she *was* 'good looking,' though they said spiteful things about her, as women will say of each other. Alfred Cornell had never addressed her in any other way but as 'Miss Hetherington'; but one morning, when the ship was in the tropics, she had gone on deck very early to see the sun rise. The heat in the cabins was so great that she could not sleep, and as the sailors had just finished holy-stoning[17] and washing down she had thrown a loose robe over her shoulders and gone quietly on to the poop. It was Cornell's watch, but in all probability she did not know that at the time. It was a very long poop, and save for the man at the wheel not a soul was to be seen. The sea was oily in its calmness, and the sky was aflame with the most gorgeous colours, such colours as can be nowhere seen save in the tropics, and only then when the sun with regal pomp and splendour commences to rise. The sails hung in heavy folds against the masts, and there was a rhythmical kind of motion in the ship as she rose and fell ever so gently to the light swell which even in the calmest ocean is never absent. Lily leaned pensively against the mizzen rigging, gazing thoughtfully across the sleeping sea to where the gold, and amethyst, and purples, and scarlets were blended together in one blaze of dazzling colour. Suddenly she was startled by a voice speaking in a subdued tone close to her ear, and which said:

'The Red Lily is up early this morning.'

She recognized the voice as that of Cornell, and turning quickly round said, with much dignity:

'Excuse me, sir, I am Miss Hetherington to you.'

'Miss Hetherington,' he answered, strongly emphasizing the words. 'I beg your pardon, but the pretty name so fits you that I made bold to use it. I trust I have not offended you.'

'Oh, no,' she said, as she averted her gaze from his piercing eyes, for she felt like a bird before the fabled basilisk.[18] She would have rushed away, but was spellbound. The strange man held her in a thrall.

'How charming you look this morning,' he remarked. 'Why, you put even the glory of the sunrise to shame.'

'Really, Mr. Cornell,' she exclaimed indignantly, and blushing to the very roots of her hair, 'you insult me by such extravagant and stupid compliments. I don't like men who talk nonsense, and think that all a

17 Washing the decks using a Bible-shaped sandstone.
18 The basilisk was the legendary serpent king, which could cause death with a single glance.

girl wants is to be flattered. Of course plenty of empty headed girls do, but I'm not one of them.'

'Don't be angry with me, please; I am sincere. Can the wretched moth that flutters into the flame of the candle help itself? Not a bit of it. You would pity the moth; why not pity me?'

'This is audacity, Mr. Cornell, and I will complain to the captain about you,' she exclaimed as she made a movement to go. But ever so lightly, and without any effort, he touched her hand. What was the fearful magic of that touch that she should thrill so? What was the power in his voice that held her in a spell? She did not go, but stood there. Her left hand resting on one of the rattlings of the rigging, her right hanging down by her side, his large powerful fingers touching hers, her head averted, for she felt as if she dare not look at him.

'It is not in your nature to be cruel, Miss Hetherington'—he spoke low, so that there should be no possibility of the man at the wheel catching his words, though he was so far off there was not much fear of that—'why, then, should you be cruel with me?'

'I am not cruel, but you are rude, very rude,' she answered with a voice that trembled from suppressed emotion.

'I am *not* rude, and you *are* cruel,' he returned, dwelling deliberately on every word. 'You are a beautiful young woman, and I am a man. Surely I should be less than a man if I failed to admire you? Do you not admire the beauty of the sky there? why, then, should I do less than you, though in your face I find more to admire than in those glowing colours.'

'If you do not instantly leave me I will call out for assistance,' she said. She felt faint and powerless, and as though she would certainly fall down on the deck if she let go her hold of the rigging.

'No, you must not do that,' he answered, coolly. 'How can I possibly help feeling for you what I do feel. I am not a stone statue, but a man with a heart, and though a bolt from heaven should strike me into the sea for speaking the words, I tell you now, though I never utter another syllable to you, *that I love you.*'

He had never taken his fingers from hers, and now he pressed her hand. The sea seemed to be going round and round before her eyes. The wonderful colours in the sky were all blended in one confused mass. The ship appeared to be sinking beneath her feet, and yet she managed to murmur in a low, weak voice:

'For God's sake leave me!'

Without another word he walked away, and then she seemed to breathe more freely, and in a few minutes had quite recovered herself.

She turned and went towards the companion way, and as she did so she saw Cornell talking to the captain, who had just come on deck. The captain bade her good morning, but Cornell was as immovable and impassive as a piece of sculpture.

Oh! what a sense of relief she experienced when she got down to her cabin. The spell seemed to be lifted at last, and, closing the door, she threw herself into the bunk and wept passionately. When the hysterical fit had passed she was relieved, and she determined to tell her mother what had happened, but this determination only lasted for a few minutes, as on reflection she thought that it could but lead to unpleasantness, and in a little floating world such as a ship is the slightest things are looked upon as legitimate food for scandal to batten upon. Therefore, her second thoughts were to keep the matter to herself. Still she was very unhappy, and Dick noticed it. He naturally asked her the cause, but she made an excuse by saying that she was a little out of sorts. She was strongly tempted to tell him all, but was restrained by a fear that it might lead to a quarrel between him and the second mate.

For several days after the unpleasant incident with Cornell she studiously avoided going on deck alone for fear of meeting him, but whenever he had occasion to pass her she would shudder, for his strange eyes seemed to exercise a power over her which was simply marvellous. She felt, in fact, when he was looking at her that she could grovel at his feet at his mere bidding. It was a dreadful feeling, and her health naturally suffered. Her mother and lover were both concerned about her, but she endeavoured to remove any anxiety they might have had by saying that her indisposition was of a very trivial character.

One evening she had been sitting on the poop with Fenton. The weather was fine, but a strong breeze was blowing, and the vessel was tearing through the water. The daylight had almost faded out, and it was impossible to distinguish people who were standing or sitting only a few yards away. Fenton left her for a few minutes to go down to his cabin for some cigars, and scarcely had he disappeared when she was startled by the sudden appearance of Cornell. It seemed almost as though he had risen up out of the deck. She was seated on a camp stool, and he bent his head low until she could feel his hot breath on her cheek. He whispered to her in a voice that could not possibly have been heard by anyone else, however near they might have been; but she heard every word, every syllable, as it was poured into her ear, and it seemed to burn into her brain.

'Lily, you are cruel,' he said; 'I love you madly, and yet you avoid me. You must give me some encouragement, or I will drown myself; and if you breathe a word of what I have said to you to any living soul, I tell you in God's name that I will throw myself overboard, and my death will lie at your door. Remember what I say. I am a determined man, and nothing on earth will stop me carrying out my will.'

Once again his fingers touched her hand; then in a moment he was gone as suddenly as he had appeared. He seemed to fade away into the darkness like a spectre, but almost immediately afterwards she heard him bawling some orders in stentorian tones to the watch.

When Fenton came back she was trembling and faint, and though she struggled hard to conceal from him that she was agitated, he could not fail to observe it, and in a tone of alarm asked the cause.

'Oh, nothing, dear—nothing,' she answered; 'at least, nothing of any consequence. A slight feeling of faintness has come over me; but really it is not worth bothering about.'

Oh, how she longed to tell him all; but the words of the strange man who was exercising such a powerful influence over her were still ringing in her ears, and she was silent.

Fenton did not make any further remark then on the subject, but he felt uneasy. He was convinced that there was some mystery, but what it was he could not for the life of him determine. The thought did flash through his brain that she was deceiving him, but instantly he put it away as unworthy of him. It seemed so preposterous to associate deceit with the Red Lily, who was as pure as the beautiful flower after which she was called.

When he escorted her down to the cabin a little later, he said:

'Darling, I am uneasy about you. Something is wrong, I am sure, but your gentle heart prompts you to keep it from me for fear of giving me pain. Do be good to yourself for my sake. Why don't you take your mother into your confidence, and tell her if you have any trouble, since you do not apparently care to confide it to me.'

'Do not be uneasy,' she answered. 'Believe me, oh, do believe me, when I say that my indisposition is of a very trifling character. I have nothing to tell my mother, and you know perfectly well, Dick, you have my full confidence.'

She felt a little guilty as she said this, for she knew that she ought to have told him at once of Cornell's conduct. But, firstly, the strange fascination he exercised over her kept her silent; and, secondly, she was really afraid of causing a scene between the two men. Besides, she comforted herself with the thought that the voyage would soon be over, and once clear of the ship it would be good-bye to Cornell for ever. She regarded him as a vain, presumptuous fellow, who imagined that every girl he looked at must be in love with him.

As soon as her lover had left her, and she had been to wish her mother good-night, the Red Lily once again gave unrestrained vent to her feelings, and wept passionately. She could not help it. She felt almost as if she would die if she did not weep, and weep she did bitterly until she fretted herself to sleep.

The following morning she was weak and pale, and did not put in an appearance at breakfast. The beautiful pink had faded from her face, and she had the look of one who was jaded and unhappy. Mrs. Hetherington visited her daughter, and naturally felt alarmed. There was a doctor on board, and Mrs. Hetherington expressed a determination to consult him; but Lily pleaded with such earnestness, and at last expressed such a strong determination not to see him, that her mother yielded, and Lily kept in her cabin all that day.

On the following day she was better. Cornell's influence had passed away, and she had to a considerable extent regained her spirits.

The weather was now very chilly, and unfortunately the wind was unfavourable, so that the ship had to sail on long and short tacks. It was worse than tantalizing to those who had looked forward so eagerly to spending Christmas with their friends in the dear old country. The hope of doing that was now past, for the distance was too great to cover in the time that intervened between them and the great Christian Festival. Well wrapped in rugs, Lily was once more seated on deck in company with Dick. She had been doing some fancy needlework, and he had been sketching a large vessel that had been in company with them two or three days. Presently he laid down his sketching block on the deck, and looking up into the fair face of his companion, he said:

'Lily, pet, do you remember the promise you made to me before we left India?'

'What was that, Dick?' she asked.

'That you would become my wife on Christmas Day.'

'Oh, yes,' she said quickly, and with some slight agitation; 'but we shall not be home by that time.'

'That is true; but it need not affect your promise.'

'I don't understand you,' she answered.

'You are surely aware, Lily, that a marriage on board of a ship is perfectly legal. Even a captain has the power to marry people; but it fortunately happens, as you know, that we have a Church of England clergyman amongst us, and therefore I claim the fulfilment of your promise.'

'Oh, Dick, it cannot be.'

TALES OF TERROR *Dick Donovan*

'Cannot be!' he echoed in some astonishment. 'Were your words, then, *only* words after all?'

'Ah, love, do not be harsh with me. I should so much prefer that our wedding took place in the regular way on shore, and it is to be hoped that we shall arrive in England by the New Year.'

'I am far from being harsh with you, Lily,' answered Dick, a little sadly; 'but you yourself expressed a wish to be married on the Christmas morning, even saying that you were superstitious about it. Although there is every prospect now that we shall be at sea on that day, there is no reason at all why we should not be married on board; and if you like we will go through the ceremony again when we reach England. The mere circumstance of being married in or out of a church cannot possibly affect our union, and I am sure you have too much good sense to be influenced by the stupid idea which possesses some small brained people—that a marriage performed out of a church cannot be sanctified.'

'I have no such idea,' she said. 'I should be ashamed of myself if I had.'

'Very well, then, Lily, say that you will be my wife on Christmas morning, even though we are at sea.'

'How long does it want to Christmas, Dick?'

'Three weeks exactly.'

'Then I promise you that if mamma offers no objection I will gratify your wish.'

'I am perfectly satisfied that your mother will willingly let us have our own way, so on Christmas Day we will become man and wife, if we are both living.'

'On Christmas Day we will become man and wife if we are both living,' she repeated solemnly, but the words had scarcely left her lips when she almost uttered a scream, for close beside her stood Cornell. He had his sextant in his hand, and had come up the companion way near which Dick and Lily were sitting with the captain to take the sun.

'Make eight bells,' said the captain, 'we shall get no sun to-day.'

'Eight bells,' roared out Cornell.

'Come, dear, let us go down to luncheon,' said Dick as he rose, gathered up the wraps, and offered his arm to his *fiancée*.

She had to pass Cornell to reach the companion way, and she saw his hawk-like eyes fixed upon her, although he pretended to be examining the figures on his sextant.

Those eyes burned into her soul, as it were, and the strange hysterical feeling came back again so that she felt as if she must weep, but by a powerful effort she controlled herself, and Dick did not notice how she was affected.

The question of the marriage being put to Mrs. Hetherington, that lady said that she should offer no objection to the wishes of the young people. Consequently it was soon understood that the monotony of the voyage would be relieved by a wedding on Christmas morning. In which case there would be a double occasion for rejoicing and festivities.

Christmas at sea is always a festive time, but this particular one on board the *Sirocco* promised to be unusually lively. The captain gave orders to the steward that he was to reserve a good supply of his best champagne for the occasion, and the cook was ordered to make plenty of cakes and fancy things; while the butcher was instructed to kill the fattest geese of the few that remained, and the last pig was to be slaughtered in order to add to the feast. The lady and gentlemen passengers rummaged amongst their boxes to try and fish out suitable little presents to give to the young couple, and there was much fun and laughter as all sorts of odd suggestions were made; while the ladies further busied themselves in improvising suitable decorations for the saloon. In fact, this coming marriage was looked upon as a blessing almost, for the voyage had been so long and tedious, that the little excitement caused by the prospective union of the Red Lily and Dick Fenton was most welcome.

As the second mate seemed to purposely avoid Lily now, she recovered her spirits; in fact, several days passed without her seeing him, and she began to laugh at her stupidity in allowing him to have such an influence over her. Dick could not fail to notice the change, and, attributing it to the pleasure she anticipated at the near prospect of their union, he was delighted also.

Christmas Day was now anxiously looked forward to by all the passengers, and as it only wanted eight days to the time great preparations were going on, and ladies busied themselves in stoning raisins and performing other incidental necessaries in connection with the concoction of those mysteries—Christmas puddings. The gentlemen found occupation in dressing the saloon with flags, and decorations ingeniously constructed by the fair sex out of the most likely and unlikely things. No one who has not been a long voyage in a passenger ship can imagine with what avidity every little incident calculated to relieve the monotony of life at sea—if it can truthfully be said to be monotonous—is seized upon. Therefore, Christmas tide and a marriage in the bargain were such important events, that the little floating world which the *Sirocco* represented was agitated to its very centre, and the excitement rose to fever heat.

Life at sea, however, is influenced by laws which do not affect it on land. Changes in the weather; changes from calm to rough weather have a marked effect on a floating community, and a few hours often produce the most extraordinary transformations. An oily sea may become raging mountains of water, and the steadiness of a ship is turned into violent pitching and tossing that renders walking to all but the most experienced a matter of great difficulty. At such times soup plates will perform somersaults into your lap, and joints of meat evince a decided objection to remain in their proper positions. While, as for poultry, wine bottles, &c., they suddenly acquire an agility for flying through the air, so that what with dodging these missiles, and holding on like grim death to the table or the back of the settee, one's life at meal time on board of a ship in stormy weather is by no means as comfortable as it might be in a well appointed dining room on shore.

Within a week of Christmas it became manifest that the *Sirocco* was destined to encounter some bad weather. There had been sullen calms succeeded by fitful bursts of storm, but the good ship had crept on and on until she had reached the verge of the Bay of Biscay. The bay, although it bears such a bad character, is suggestive of nearing home to those who come from afar, and consequently the passengers were high-spirited, notwithstanding that it was pretty certain that a good deal of knocking about was in store for them.

One night during the middle watch a furious squall suddenly burst upon the vessel, and as she had all sail set she heeled over almost on to her beam ends. Several sails were rent to fragments by the force of the wind, and the long strips flying out in the tempest made a tremendous cracking like the cracking of stock whips. 'All hands' were called on deck, and there were all the noise, and shouting, and uproar incidental to a sudden squall in the dead of night. To the timid and the inexperienced this is particularly alarming, for as the ship flies along on her side the waters hiss in a strange manner, the shouting and tramp of the sailors, the orders given hastily and in stentorian tones, the cracker-like reports of the torn sails, the groaning and creaking of the rudder chains, the indescribable howling of the wind, and the extreme angle of the vessel, are sufficiently alarming to produce nervousness even in those whose acquaintance with the sea is not of recent date. And this is more particularly the case when such a squall occurs at night; then the sky is inky in its blackness, and nothing can be seen save the spectral-like outlines of the rigging and the masts, and such objects as are immediately near the spectator. When this particular squall struck the ship it happened that the Red Lily's cabin was on the weather side, and so suddenly did the ship heel over that Lily narrowly escaped being thrown from her bunk. Although this was not her first experience of a squall at night she felt unusually alarmed, for the vessel was lying over at such an unusual angle, and there was so much noise on deck.

Hastily throwing on a few articles of clothing, and covering them with a dressing gown, she encased her feet in slippers, and rushed over to her mother's cabin, which was on the lee side. Undisturbed by the shock Mrs. Hetherington was sleeping soundly, and so, not wishing to wake her, the first impression of alarm having passed away, Lily closed the cabin door gently, and then went up the companion way and peeped out into the darkness. The white waters were flying past, and the vessel was lying over almost to her lee scuppers. Lily stepped on to the deck, holding on to the handle of the companion way door. There was a babel of mingled sounds, and the wind was blowing a perfect hurricane. She had stood there but a few minutes when suddenly she became aware that Cornell was standing beside her. He was superintending the stowing of the mizen to'gallant sail. He was evidently surprised to see her there. She was about to descend again, for his presence brought back all her old fears, when he caught her arm, and with gentle force restrained her.

'This is fortunate,' he said. 'The opportunity I have longed for this squall has at last given me.'

'Let me go,' she exclaimed, 'or I will scream.' She was trembling with fear and excitement, but he still held her.

'You dare not,' he answered in a strange tone. Then, after a pause, he added, 'You have been cruel to me, but you must be so no longer or I shall die. I cannot live without you.'

'Are you mad?' she said with a shudder.

'Perhaps I am. If I am you have made me so.' He passed his arm round her waist and held her closely.

She struggled to free herself, but she was powerless in his strong grasp. The mysterious influence he exercised over her now kept her tongue tied so that she could not scream, could not cry out. He bent low and pressed his lips to hers, and yet that did not break the spell which bound her.

'You are to be married on Christmas Day,' he said in a whisper. 'I hope before then *he* or I will be dead. If I live you shall become *my* wife. Do you hear? my wife. You may think I am talking mere words, but you will see.'

He released her and she found herself in her cabin. How she got down she did not know. She was burning with indignation and shame. His polluting lips had touched hers, and she shivered as she thought of it. She rubbed her lips with her handkerchief as though he had left some stain which she was trying to wipe away. She yearned to go at once to Fenton's cabin and tell him all, but a deadly fear of Cornell withheld her, the spell of his extraordinary power was upon her, and she felt that she *dare not* open her mouth to tell aught of what had occurred. The man's influence, whatever it was, was paramount. She feared and hated him, and yet dare not denounce him. Of course she was weak, but then he was no ordinary man. His strength of will was enormous, and subdued her.

During the rest of the night she could not sleep, and she longed for Christmas Day to come, so that, as Dick's wife, she might be free from the persecutions of the mysterious Cornell.

When the morning broke the storm had died away, leaving a gentle wind that wafted the ship along at about eight knots an hour.

'We shall have steady weather now,' the captain observed at breakfast time, as he examined the barometer that swung over the cabin table.

His prognostication proved correct. The wind increased day by day until it was blowing a strong gale, but as it was favourable a large spread of canvas was carried upon the ship.

The day preceding Christmas Day arrived; the *Sirocco* was in the Bay of Biscay, off the inhospitable Cape Finisterre. By Christmas Eve the wind had increased very much, so that the ship was 'snugged down.' Extra look outs were kept, for a great number of outward and home-ward bound vessels were in the Bay. The night promised to be a very 'dirty one,' but there was merriment on board, and many a toast to 'Sweethearts and Wives' was drunk, both in the cabin and in the fore-castle, for a liberal allowance of grog had been served out to the crew.

The preparations for the wedding were all complete. The saloon was gaily decorated, and it was arranged that the marriage ceremony was to be performed at eleven o'clock in the morning. But before eleven o'clock strange things were to happen.

The night waned, and as eight bells sounded Dick Fenton went on deck to smoke a cigar before turning in. The ladies had all retired, and only a single night lamp burned in the saloon. The wind had drawn ahead a good deal, and the vessel could only carry close-reefed main-top sail and fore-topsail, so that she was making very little way, simply 'forging,' as sailors say, at the rate of about two knots an hour. A favour-ite seat with Dick when he went on deck to smoke his cigar was on the rail near the mizzen shrouds. There he was under the shelter of the captain's gig, which was slung outside on davits, and his feet rested on a hen coop that ran along the poop. Sitting there now pensively dreaming of his Red Lily, and the happiness that awaited him on the morrow when she would become his wife, he had no thought of danger. There was music in the rush of the wild waters and the screaming sweep of the wind. The vessel had that short, jerky motion which a ship has in a rough sea when under reefed topsails.

Suddenly there rose up before Dick's vision the dark figure of a man.

'Hallo! is that you, captain?' exclaimed Dick.

'No,' was the answer, and in the gruff voice Dick recognized the second mate.

'Oh, it's you, Cornell,' he said. 'This is a wild night. Do you think the wind will free at all before the morning?'

'It may, and may not,' was the somewhat surly answer, and in the husky tones Cornell betrayed that he was the worse for liquor. 'I suppose you were thinking of the Red Lily,' he remarked.

'Really, Mr. Cornell, you are a little familiar,' Dick said, not unkindly, for he was willing to make every allowance at such a time.

'Bah, why am I familiar?' sneered the second mate. 'I suppose the night before his marriage every man thinks of the woman who is to be his wife.'

'I suppose he does,' Dick answered curtly, for he was not anxious to prolong the conversation seeing the strange humour Cornell was in.

'You have quite made up your mind that she is to be your wife?' asked Cornell.

'Well, please God that nothing happens between now and the morning, Miss Hetherington will certainly become Mrs. Fenton.'

'But it is destined that *something* shall happen,' Cornell exclaimed, 'and you will never see the morrow.'

The words were spoken rapidly, and with a lightning like movement he threw the whole weight of his body against Dick, who, unprepared for such an assault, was pressed backwards, and falling between the boat and the side of the vessel was lost in the dark, hissing waters.

'A man overboard!' cried the second mate with all the power of his lusty lungs, and instantly the dreadful cry was taken up, and the watch came rushing aft. The captain, who was in his cabin, tore on deck, and in a moment all was confusion.

'Who is it, who is it?' exclaimed the captain.

'Mr. Fenton, I think, for I saw him sitting on the rail a few minutes before,' said Cornell.

'Clear away the boat, men, quick!" cried the captain.

Then he and Cornell cut away life buoys and cast them into the sea.

'I will try and save him, sir,' said Cornell, as he divested himself of his heavy sea boots and his oil skins.

Divining his motives the captain laid hold of his arm and said:

'Are you mad, man! It is enough that one life should be sacrificed.' But Cornell, making no reply, shook himself free, mounted the rail, and dived headlong into the black waters.

The excitement was now intense. Everyone on board knew what had happened, but everyone did not know that it was Dick who had gone. The Red Lily was in this state of blissful ignorance, though she with the other ladies crowded up the companion way, and waited in breathless and painful anxiety.

The boat was manned and lowered. Lamps were brought and held up so as to throw a light as far as possible over the sea. The boat was away about an hour. It was a fearful agony of suspense that hour. The ship was hove to, and everything done that could be done. The searchers returned at last, bringing with them the second mate in an exhausted condition, but not Dick; he had gone, and as nothing more could be done, sail was again set, and the *Sirocco* went upon her way with one soul less.

Christmas morning dawned. The gaiety was changed to sorrow, and the marriage decorations were taken down and signs of mourning appeared.

Tenderly and gently the sad news was broken to the Red Lily, and those who told her did not fail to tell how 'nobly' the second mate had risked his life to try and save that of her lover. Tenderly as the news was broken, the shock stunned her, and for days she lay in a state of partial coma. But there were loving hands to tend, and loving voices to soothe, and gradually she came round. All the sunshine, however, seemed to have gone out of her nature, and she was a crushed woman.

For the first time for many days she went on deck, and was propped with pillows in a sofa-chair, and for the first time since that terrible night she saw Cornell. All her feeling of revulsion for him had changed, and, stretching forth her white hand to him, she said in her loving, sweet voice:

'Mr. Cornell, I have been unjust to you. You must forgive me. You are a brave and generous man.'

He took her hand and answered:

'I grieve with you, Miss Hetherington. I did my best to save him, but it was not to be. No man can prevent his fate. It is not for me to say why, at such a moment, your lover should have met his doom. It was Destiny; but, though I battled with the waves and the darkness of the night, it was not my destiny to drown.'

Lily shuddered. The man spoke so strangely. There was such a weird appearance about him, and his influence over her was as strong as ever. And yet a fearful thought came to her. Was it not probable that Cornell had hurled her lover into the sea, and then, seized with sudden remorse, had dived after him?

Oh, how that dreadful thought troubled and pained her! She struggled with it for days, and wept and wept and wept again. At one moment she resolved to take her mother into her confidence, and tell her all. But whenever this feeling came upon her the mysterious Cornell seemed to be at her side, and then all her will power went again. She felt that she hated him one moment, but the next she could and would have grovelled at his feet, overcome by a curious fascination, mingled with a sort of admiration, for the daring, reckless, wicked, iron-willed fellow.

$$\sim$$

A week later the ship was in the London docks.

Lily and her mother went on shore at Gravesend. The poor girl was bowed with sorrow, and she felt as though she would never again hold up her head. Before she left the ship Cornell begged hard to be allowed to call upon her. She wanted to refuse him, but could not, and, with the consent of her mother, she gave him permission to do so, for the mother felt she was indebted to him.

Lily and Mrs. Hetherington went to reside in the west end of London, and Cornell, availing himself of their permission, was almost a daily visitor. He announced his intention of not going to sea again for some time, and the old fascination he had exercised over Lily was exerted now to a greater degree; and though she was sure she possessed no love for him, she felt drawn towards him in a strange manner. One day, four months after their arrival home, he pressed her to become his wife, and she reluctantly gave her consent. She would have said 'No' if she could, but she was powerless; and believing that she had previously misjudged him and done him a wrong, she said:

'I will be a dutiful and faithful wife to you, but you must never hope to win my love. *That* is buried in the cruel sea.'

It was arranged that the wedding was to take place in a few months' time. 'He objected to the delay, but she was firm on the point, for she felt that it would not be respectful to her dead love to marry so soon after the calamity. Many a girl who knew Lily and her lover envied her. Cornell was so 'handsome,' so 'fascinating,' so 'manly,' 'such a splendid type of a sailor'; but when her friends congratulated her she only sighed. She felt as if she were sacrificing herself; but then her affianced husband had so nobly risked his life for her lover's sake, notwithstanding his previous strange conduct, and on that account alone she was going to give him her hand. She little dreamed that his jumping overboard was only part of his diabolical plan, and was meant to avert suspicion—which it did most effectually. So far as the risk to himself was concerned, it was reduced to a minimum, for he was a magnificent and powerful swimmer, and before he took the leap he was careful to see that plenty of lifebuoys had been dropped over, and that the boat was all ready for lowering. In the course of the next few months Mrs. Hetherington and her daughter removed to the village of Bowness, on the banks of Windermere, as they had friends living there; and it was arranged that the marriage should take place in the parish church of that place.

The wedding day came. It was a glorious summer's morning, and the air was filled with the music of birds and the scent of flowers. The wedding was to be very quiet, and but few guests had been invited. Those who knew Lily well said that the 'Red Lily had drooped.' All the brightness was out of her life, for she felt that her heart was beneath the waves of the Bay of Biscay.

The wedding party had assembled in the church, and the ceremony had commenced. When the grey-haired clergyman asked if any one knew any just cause or impediment why the man and woman should not be joined together in the bonds of holy matrimony, there rose up a man in the body of the church, and in a loud and steady voice exclaimed:

'I forbid this marriage.'

Had a thunderbolt fallen through the roof the consternation and confusion could not have been greater. With a great cry the Red Lily threw up her arms, and then fell forward on her face in a swoon. For a few moments Cornell stood as if petrified. His face was ghastly pale. By this time the man had come forward to the altar rails, and then Cornell found tongue.

'Good God!' he exclaimed, 'is it possible that the dead can come to life?'

'No; but the living can thwart the machinations of a villain, and I am here to do that,' said Dick Fenton, for he it was. 'This man,' continued Dick, addressing the astonished spectators, 'attempted to murder me.'

No one moved. They were dumb with amazement, for they naturally thought a madman was amongst them. Dick himself stooped and lifted up the inanimate form of the Lily, and bore her into the vestry. Taking advantage of the confusion—for everyone seemed bewildered—Cornell stole from the church, got clear away, and was never heard of more.

It was some time before Lily recovered consciousness.

It is better to leave the reunion of the lovers to the imagination of the reader, for words always fail to convey anything like an adequate notion of such a scene. The news of the affair had rapidly spread over the village; an enormous crowd had gathered about the church, and the uproar was immense. The wedding party had to wait a considerable time before they could get back to their homes; then explanations were given.

On that dreadful night in the Bay of Biscay Dick had escaped death almost by a miracle, as it were. He was a good swimmer, but was a little stunned by striking his head against the side of the vessel in his descent. He had a recollection, however, of making a powerful effort to swim, and in a little while he felt something touch his hand, and found it was a lifebuoy. On this he supported himself for a long time—it seemed to him two or three hours. Then he saw the outlines of a vessel, which he took to be the *Sirocco*, and he shouted with all his might, and presently had the satisfaction to hear the plash of oars. He had only a faint recollection of hearing a human voice, and feeling the grasp of hands about him. Then ensued a blank. When next he opened his eyes he found himself in a comfortable cabin, and he soon learnt that it was not the *Sirocco* that had picked him up, but an outward bound ship, called the *Golden Fleece*. She was bound for the Cape, and so Dick was mortified to find that he must accompany her there, unless a homeward bounder should be fallen in with, and he could get on board. This chance did not occur, and so to the Cape he went, but the vessel made a long voyage. As soon after arrival as possible he took ship for England, and on reaching there he soon discovered to his amazement that the Red Lily was on the eve of being married to Cornell. He hurried down to the Lake District, and was there a whole week determining not to declare himself until the last moment, so that the discomfiture of his enemy might be the more complete.

For some months after this strange and startling incident Lily remained in such delicate health that grave fears were at one time entertained. Sudden joy is almost as bad as great sorrow at times, and the unexpected return of her lost lover had been too great a shock. Care, attention, and change of air, however, gradually restored her, and again she made preparations for her marriage, which was to take place on Christmas Day, twelve months after the terrible scene in the Bay of Biscay, when Dick was hurled into the sea.

The day came at last—cold, crisp, and bright. The earth was wrapped in a robe of spotless white, and the church was decorated with holly and winter flowers. As the bells pealed forth merrily, and the winter sun shone out from the dull sky, Dick Fenton led his bride down the pathway to the carriage that waited them at the gate, and the crowd of villagers that had gathered in the old churchyard declared that no bonnier bride had ever been seen than the Red Lily.

V

The Pirate's Treasure

A TRUE AND DRAMATIC STORY OF THE SEA

AT THE TIME THE startling events I am about to relate occurred, I had but recently passed my final examination in medicine, after what I may modestly say was a successful course of study in Glasgow, of which city I am a native. For some time I had been anxiously expecting my diploma, which would give me the right to practise my profession, and I was trying to obtain an appointment as surgeon on board a splendid East Indiaman, known as the *Clydesdale*. Singularly enough, on the very day that I received the intimation that my application had been favourably considered, I was placed in possession of a letter from a dear friend in London, asking me if I would proceed on his behalf with all possible speed to Surinam,[19] on a very delicate and important mission. For an hour or two I was exercised in my mind as to the proper course I ought to pursue in my own interests; that is, whether I should accept the *Clydesdale* appointment, or undertake my friend's commission. Something prompted me to choose the latter, and I immediately communicated my decision to London. In a post or two I received my instructions, with a bank draft for my expenses, and I was told to secure a berth in a vessel if possible proceeding direct to the place where my business was to be transacted. I therefore lost no time in making inquiries about a ship, and at last heard of one called the *Ariadne*. She had been chartered by a Glasgow company, and was then loading up at the West Quay, and was to sail in a few days. I at once secured a passage in her, and went down to see the vessel for the first time the very day she was to leave. Little did I dream then how strangely my destiny was to be affected by the fact of my having undertaken my friend's commission. While I stood examining her from the pier, two sailors, who seemed to be roaming idly about, stopped and began to converse by my side.

'Has the *Ariadne* shipped all her hands, Jack?' asked the one; 'I see she has the Blue Peter flying. Somebody told me she has been sold to a Dutch firm now. How would you like to sail in her?'

---

19 A Dutch colony in South America.

'Not me, mate,' replied the other; 'I know too much about her. I made a voyage in her four years ago, and a cleaner or livelier craft is not on the sea! But there is a limb of the devil in her as skipper that is enough to cause her to sink to the bottom. It was in my voyage that he did for Bill Burnett with the pump-sounding rod, because the little fellow snivelled a bit, and was not handy to jump when he was ordered aloft to set the fore-royal. It was his first voyage, and the boy was mortal afraid to venture; but the captain swore he would make him, and in his passion hit him a rap with the iron rod and killed him. When he saw what he had done he lifted the body while it was still quivering and hove it over the side; and many a long day the men wondered what had become of little Bill, for they were all below at dinner, and none but myself saw the bloody deed. It was needless for me to complain and get him overhauled, as there were no witnesses; but I left the ship, and berths would be scarce before I would sail with him again or put my foot on the deck of his ship. I tell you, mate, there's a curse on her, and them as sails in her will come to grief.'

Knowing what tyrants shipmasters are in general, and how much their passengers' comfort depends on them, I was somewhat startled by this piece of information respecting the temper of the man I purposed to sail with. But necessity has no law! The circumstance was probably much misrepresented, I thought, and, from a simple act of discipline, exaggerated to an act of wanton cruelty. But be that as it might—my affairs were urgent. There was no other vessel for the same port—I must either take my passage or run the risk of being superseded. The thing was not to be thought of, so I went and secured my berth. As my preparations were few and trifling, I had everything arranged and on board just as the vessel was unmooring from the quay. During the night we got down to the Clock Lighthouse, and stood off and on, waiting for the captain, who had remained behind to get the ship cleared out at the Custom House. Soon afterwards he joined us, and, the pilot leaving us in the return-boat, we stood down the Forth under all our canvas. Her beloved Majesty Queen Victoria[20] had not long been on the throne, and piracy on the high seas was still a lucrative pursuit. Every merchantman, therefore, generally carried a fair amount of armament, and our vessel was no exception, although I, for one, certainly never anticipated any adventure.

For four weeks we had a quick and pleasant passage. The *Ariadne* was a good sailor; for, being American built, and originally intended

---

20 Reigned 1837–1901.

for a privateer, she sailed uncommonly fast, generally running at the rate of twelve knots an hour in a good wind.

As I expected, Captain Mahone, an Irishman by birth, proved to be, in point of acquirements, not at all above the common run of skippers in command of sailing ships at that period. He was haughty and overbearing, and domineered over the crew with a high hand; in return for which he was evidently feared and detested by them all. He had been many years in the West Indies, and during most of that time had commanded a local trader, and had, between the fervid suns of such high latitudes and the copious use of grog, become of a rich mahogany colour, or something between vermilion and the tint of a sheet of new copper. He was a middle-sized man, square built, with a powerful and muscular frame. His aspect, naturally harsh and forbidding, was rendered more so by the sinister expression of his left eye, which had been nearly forced out by some accident, and the lineaments of his countenance expressed plainly that he was passionate and furious in the extreme. In consequence of this I kept rather distant and aloof; and, except at meals, we seldom exchanged more than ordinary civilities.

By our reckoning, our ship had now got into the latitude of the Bermudas, when one evening at sunset the wind, which had hitherto been favourable, fell at once into a dead calm. The day had been clear and bright; but now huge masses of dark and conical-shaped clouds began to tower over each other in the western horizon, which, being tinged with the rays of the sun, displayed that lurid and deep brassy tint so well known to mariners as the token of an approaching storm. All the sailors were of opinion that we should have a coarse night, and every precaution that good seamanship could suggest was taken to make the vessel snug before the gale came on. The oldest boys were sent up to hand and send down the royal and top-gallant sails and strike the yards, while the topsails and staysails were close-reefed. These preparations were hardly accomplished when the wind shifted, and took us aback with such violence as nearly to capsize the vessel. The ship was put round as soon as possible, and lay to, while all hands remained on deck in case of any emergency.

About ten, in the interval of a squall, we heard a gun fired as a signal of distress. The night was as black as pitch, but the flash showed us that the stranger was not far to leeward; so, to avoid drifting on the wreck during the darkness, the main topsail was braced round and filled, and the ship hauled to windward. In this manner we kept alternately beating or heaving-to as the gale rose or fell till the morning broke, when, through the haze, we perceived a small vessel with her masts carried away. As the wind had dropped, the captain had gone to bed; so it was the mate's watch on deck. The steersman, an old grey-headed seaman, named James Gemmel, proposed to bear down and save the people, saying he had been twice wrecked himself, and knew what it was to be in such a situation. Owing to the captain being below, the mate was irresolute what to do, being aware that the success of the speculation depended on their getting to Surinam with all possible speed; however, he was at length persuaded—the helm was put up, and the ship bore away.

As we neared the wreck, and were standing by the mizen shrouds with our glasses, the captain came up from the cabin. He looked up with astonishment to the sails and the direction of the vessel's head, and in a voice of suppressed passion said, as he turned to the mate, 'What is the meaning of this, Mr. Wyllie? Who has dared to alter the ship's course without my leave, when you knew very well that we shall hardly be in time for the market, use what expedition we may?' The young man was confused by this unexpected challenge, and stammered out something about Gemmel having persuaded him. 'It was me, sir,' respectfully answered the old sailor, wishing to avert the storm from the mate; 'I thought you wouldn't have the heart to leave the wreck, and these people to perish, without lending a hand to save them! We should be neither Christians nor true seamen to desert her, and——'

'Damn you and the wreck, you old canting rascal! Do you dare to stand there and preach to me?' thundered the captain, his fury breaking out. 'I'll teach you to disobey my orders! I'll give you something to think of!' and seizing a capstan-bar which lay near him he hurled it at the steersman with all his might. The blow was effectual—one end of it struck him across the head with such force as to sweep him in an instant from his station at the wheel, and to dash him with violence against the lee bulwarks, where he lay bleeding and motionless. 'Take that, and be damned to you!' exclaimed the wretch, as he seized the helm and sang out to the men: 'Stand by sheets and braces—hard a-lee—let go!' In a twinkling the yards were braced round, and the ship, laid between six points to the wind, was flying through the water.

Meanwhile Gemmel was lying without anyone daring to assist him, for the crew were so confounded that they seemed quite undetermined how to act. I stepped to him, therefore, and the mate following my example, we lifted him up. As there was no appearance of respiration, I placed my hand to his heart, but pulsation had entirely ceased—the old man was dead! The bar had struck him directly on the temporal bone, and had completely fractured that part of the skull.

'He is a murdered man, Captain Mahone!' said I, laying down the body, 'murdered without cause or provocation.'

'None of your remarks, sir!' he retorted; 'what the devil have you to do with it? Do you mean to stir up my men to mutiny? Or do you call disobeying my orders no provocation? I'll answer it to those who have a right to ask; but till then, let me see the man who dare open his mouth to me in this ship.'

'I promise you,' returned I, 'that though you rule and tyrannize here at present, your power shall have a termination, and you shall be called to account for your conduct in this day's work. Rest assured that this blood shall be required at your hands, though you have hitherto escaped punishment for what has stained them already.' This allusion to the murder of little Bill Burnett seemed to stagger him considerably; he stopped short before me, and, while his face grew black with suppressed wrath and fury, whispered:

'I warn you again, young man, to busy yourself with your own matters. Meddle not with what does not concern you; and belay your slack jaw, or, by ——! Rink Mahone will find a way to make it fast for you!' He then turned round, and walked forward to the forecastle.

During this incident no attention had been paid to the wreck, though the crew had set up a yell of despair on seeing us leave them. Signals and shouts were still repeated, and a voice, louder in agony than the rest, implored our help for the love of the blessed Virgin, and offered riches and absolution to the whole ship's company if they would but come back. The captain was pacing fore and aft without appearing to mind them, when, as if struck with some sudden thought, he lifted his glass to his eye—seemed to hesitate—walked on—and then, all at once changing his mind, he ordered the vessel again before the wind.

On speaking the wreck, she proved to be a Spanish felucca[21] from the island of Cuba, bound for Curaçao,[22] on the coast of the Curaccas. As all the boats had been lost in the storm, the people could not leave their vessel, which had sprung a leak badly and was sinking fast; so our captain lowered and manned our jolly-boat, and went off to them.

After an absence of a couple of hours he returned with the passengers, consisting of an elderly person in the garb of a Catholic priest, a sick gentleman, a young lady, apparently daughter of the latter, and a

---

21 A small boat with one or two triangular sails. More often used in the Red Sea, Mediterranean Sea or the Nile.

22 An island about 40 miles north of Venezuela's coast. Still a part of the Netherlands.

female servant. With the utmost difficulty, and writhing under some excruciating pain, the invalid was got on board, and carried down to the cabin, where he was laid on a bed on the floor. To the tender of my professional services the suffering man returned his thanks, and would have declined them, expressing his conviction of being past human aid, but the young lady, eagerly catching at even a remote hope of success, implored him with tears to accept my offer. On examination I found his fears were but too well grounded. In his endeavours to assist the crew during the gale he had been standing near the mast, part of which, or the rigging, having fallen on him, had dislocated several of his ribs and injured his spine beyond remedy. All that could now be done was to afford a little temporary relief from pain, which I did; and, leaving him to the care of the young lady and the priest, I left the cabin.

On deck I found all bustle and confusion. The ship was still lying-to, and the boats employed in bringing the goods out of the felucca, both of which were the property of the wounded gentleman. The body of the old man, Gemmel, had been removed somewhere out of sight; no trace of blood was visible, and Captain Mahone seemed desirous to banish all recollections both of our quarrel and its origin.

As the invalid was lying in the cabin, and my stateroom occupied by the lady and her female attendant, I got a temporary berth in the steerage made up for myself for the night. I had not long thrown myself down on the cot, which was only divided from the main cabin by a bulkhead, when I was awakened by the deep groans of the Spaniard. The violence of his pain had again returned, and between the spasms I heard the weeping and gentle voice of the lady soothing his agony, and trying to impart hope—prospects to him which her own hysterical sobs told plainly she did not herself feel. The priest also frequently joined, and urged him to confess. To this advice he remained silent for a while, but at length he addressed the lady:

'The Padre says true, Isabella. Time wears apace, and I feel that I shall soon be beyond its limits and above its concerns. But ere I go I would say that which it would impart peace to my mind to disclose— I would seek to leave you at least one human being to befriend and protect you in your utter helplessness. Alas! that Diego di Montaldo's daughter should ever be thus destitute! Go, my love! I would be alone a little while with the father.'

An agony of tears and sobs was the only return made by the poor girl, while the priest with gentle violence led her into the stateroom.

'Now,' continued the dying man, 'listen to me while I have strength. You have only known me as a merchant in Cuba; but such I have not always been. Mine is an ancient and noble family in Catalonia; though I unhappily disgraced it, and have been estranged from it long. I had the misfortune to have weak and indulgent parents, who idolized me as the heir of their house, and did not possess resolution enough to thwart me in any of my wishes or desires, however unreasonable. My boyhood being thus spoiled, it is no matter of wonder that my youth should have proved wild and dissolute. My companions were as dissolute as myself, and much of my time was spent in gambling and other extravagances. One evening at play I quarrelled with a young nobleman of high rank and influence. We were both of us hot and passionate, so we drew on the spot and fought, and I had the misfortune to run him through the heart, and leave him dead. Not daring to remain longer at home, I fled in disguise to Barcelona, where I procured a passage in a vessel for the Spanish Main. On our voyage we were captured by Moorish pirates; and the roving and adventurous mode of life of these bold and daring men suiting both my inclinations and finances, I agreed to make one of their number. For many months we were successful in our enterprises; we ranged the whole of these seas, and made a number of prizes, some of which were rich ships of our own colonies. In course of time we amassed such a quantity of specie as to make us unwilling to venture it in one bottom; so we agreed to hide it ashore, and divide it on our return from our next expedition. But our good fortune forsook us this time. During a calm the boats of the Guarda-costa came on us, overpowered the ship, and made all the crew, except myself and two others, prisoners. We escaped with our boat, and succeeded in gaining the island of Cuba, where both of my comrades died of fever. Subsequent events induced me to settle at St. Juan de Buenavista, where I married, and as a merchant prospered and became a rich man. But my happiness lasted not! My wife caught the yellow fever and died, leaving me only this one child. I now loathed the scene of my departed happiness, and felt all the longings of an exile to revisit my native country. For this purpose I converted all my effects into money, and am thus far on my way to the hidden treasure with which I intended to return to Spain. But the green hills of Catalonia will never more gladden mine eyes! My hopes and wishes were only for my poor girl. Holy father! you know not a parent's feelings—its anxiety and its fears. The thoughts of leaving my child to the mercy of strangers—or, it may be, to their barbarities—is far more dreadful than the anguish of my personal sufferings. With you rests my only hope. Promise me your protection for her, and the half of all my wealth is yours.'

'Earthly treasures,' replied the priest, 'avail not with one whose desires are fixed beyond the little handful of dust which perisheth. My life is devoted to the service of my Creator, and the conversion of ignorant men—men who have never heard of His salvation. I was bound on an errand of mercy, and if the heathen receive the light of truth, how much more a daughter of our most holy Church? I, therefore, on behalf of our community, accept of your offer, and swear on this blessed emblem to fulfil all your wishes to the best of my poor abilities.'

'Enough; enough!' said Montaldo. 'I am satisfied. Among that archipelago of desert islands, known by the name of the Roccas, situated on the coast of the province of Venezuela, in New Grenada, there is one called the Wolf Rock; it is the longest and most northern of the group, and lies the most to seaward. At the eastern point, which runs a little way into the sea, there stands an old vanilla tree, blasted and withered, and retaining but a single solitary branch. On the eve of the Festival of St. Jago the moon will be at her full in the west. At twenty minutes past midnight she will attain to her highest altitude in the heavens, and then the shadow of the tree will be thrown due east. Watch till the branch and stem of the tree unite and form only one line of shade. Mark its extremity; for there, ten feet below the surface, the cask containing the gold is buried. The gold, father, was sinfully got; but fasts and penances have been done, masses without number have been said, and I trust that the blessed Virgin has interceded for the forgiveness of that great wickedness! I have now confessed all, and confide in your promise; and as you perform your oath, so will the blessing or curse of a dying man abide with you. I feel faint—dying. Oh! let me clasp my child once more to my heart before I——'

Here the rest of the sentence became indistinct from the death-rattle in his throat. I leaped off my cot and sprang up the hatchway, and had my foot on the top of the companion ladder when a piercing shriek from below making me quicken my steps I missed my hold, and fell against some person crouching on the outside of the cabin door. It was pitch dark, so that I could not see. 'Who is that?' I demanded, but there was no answer, and the person with whom I had collided rose and, without uttering a single word, softly ascended the companion way ladder; but as he emerged into the faint light which still lingered in the horizon I fancied that I could distinguish him to be the captain.

On my entering the cabin I found the Spaniard dead, and his daughter lying in a state of insensibility by his side; while the black servant was howling and tearing her hair like one in a frenzy. The priest was entirely absorbed in his devotions, so, without disturbing him, I lifted the lady and bore her into the stateroom. The greater part of the night was passed in trying to restore her to sensation. Fit after fit followed each other in such quick succession that I began to have fears for the result; but at length the hysterical paroxysm subsided, and tears coming to her relief she grew somewhat composed, when I left her in charge of her attendant.

The next day was spent in taking out the remainder of the felucca's cargo. There seemed now no anxiety on the captain's part to proceed on his voyage. He appeared to have forgotten the necessity, expressed on a former occasion, of being in port within a limited time. During the days that followed he was often in a state of inebriety, for the wine and spirits of the Spaniards were lavishly served out to the whole ship's company, with whom he also mixed more, and he changed that haughtiness of bearing which had marked his conduct hitherto.

Yielding to the passionate entreaties of Isabella, the old Spaniard's body was kept for several days, but at last she grew reconciled to her father's remains being committed to the deep, and one evening as the sun was setting the body was brought on deck swathed in canvas, and the priest conducted a mass, and solemnly intoned the following prayer:— 'May the angels conduct thee into Paradise; may the martyrs receive thee at thy coming; and mayst thou have eternal rest with Lazarus, who was formerly poor!' He then sprinkled the body with holy water, and continued:—'As it hath pleased God to take the soul of our dear brother here departed unto Himself, we therefore commit his body to the deep, in the sure and certain hope of a joyful resurrection on that day when the sea shall give up its dead. Let him rest in peace!' The Spaniards present responded 'Amen!' and the priest repeating 'May his soul, and the souls of all the faithful departed, through the mercy of God, rest in peace. Amen!' he made the sign of the Cross, the end of the grating was gently elevated, and the corpse heavily plunged into the water. The waves parted, heaving and foaming round the body as it disappeared, when, to our horror and astonishment, we beheld it the next minute slowly return to the surface deprived of the canvas covering in which it had been sewed. The dead man came up as he had gone down, in an upright position, and floated a little time with his back to the vessel, but the motion of the water turned him round by degrees till we distinctly saw his face. The head was thrown back, and the eyes wide open, and under the strong stream of light poured on them from the setting sun they seemed to glare ghastly and fearfully upwards. His grey hair, long and dishevelled, floated about his face, at times partially obscuring it; and one arm, stretched forth and agitated by the action of the waves, appeared as if in the act of threatening us. When the first burst of horror had subsided, I caught hold of Isabella to prevent her seeing the body, and was leading her off when some of our sailors whispered that it was the murdered man, old James Gemmel. The captain had been hitherto looking on with the rest without having apparently recognized him, but when the name struck his ear he shrank back and involuntarily exclaimed, 'It's a lie! It's an infamous lie! Who dares to say he was murdered? But don't let him come on board; for God's sake keep him down, or he'll take us with him to the bottom! Will nobody keep him down? Will nobody shove him off? Helm a-lee!' he bawled out, waving his hand to the man at the wheel; but the man had deserted his post, eager to see what was going on; the skipper, therefore, ran to the wheel himself, and again issued his commands, 'Let go the main topsail weather-braces, and bring round the yard! Let them go, I say!' His orders were speedily executed. The vessel gathered way, and we quickly shot past the body of the old man.

For several days after this we pursued our course with a favourable wind, which drove us swiftly forward on our voyage. The captain now kept himself constantly intoxicated, seldom made his appearance in the cabin, but left us altogether to the care of the steward. All subordination was now at an end; his whole time was spent among the seamen, with whom he mixed familiarly, and was addressed by them without the slightest portion of that respect or deference commonly paid to the captain of a vessel. The appearance of the men also was much altered. From the careless mirth and gaiety, and the characteristic good humour of sailors, there was now a sullenness and gloom only visible. A constant whispering, a constant caballing was going on, a perpetual discussion, as if some design of moment was in agitation, or some step of deep importance was about to be taken. All sociality and confidence towards each other were banished. In place of conversing together in a body as formerly, they now walked about in detached parties, and among them the boatswain and carpenter seemed to take an active lead. Yet, in the midst of all this disorder, a few of the crew kept themselves separate, taking no share in the general consultation, but from the anxiety expressed in their countenances, as well as in that of the mate, I foresaw some storm was brewing, and about to burst on our heads.

Since Montaldo's death Isabella had been in the habit of leaving her cabin after sunset to enjoy the coolness of the evening breeze, and in this she was sometimes joined by the priest, but more frequently was only attended by her woman. One evening she came up as usual, and after walking backward and forward on deck with me till the dews began to fall, she turned to go below, but just as she approached the companion way one of the sailors, whom we had rescued from the felucca, who now, in the absence of all discipline, lounged about the quarter-

THE PIRATE'S TREASURE

deck without rebuke, shut down the head, and throwing himself on it, declared that none should make him rise without the reward of a kiss. This piece of insolence was received with an encouraging laugh by his fellows, and several slang expressions of wit were uttered, which were loudly applauded by those around. Without a word of remonstrance, Isabella timidly stooped, and would have attempted getting down the ladder without disturbing the men, when, burning with indignation, I seized the rascal by the collar, and pitched him head foremost along the deck. In an instant he got on his legs, and pulling a long clasp-knife out of his pocket, with a loud imprecation made towards me. All the other sailors likewise made a motion to assist him, and I expected to be assailed on all hands, when the mate interfered, and laying hold of the marline-spike which I had caught up wherewith to defend myself, pushed me back as he whispered:

'Are you mad that you interfere? For heaven's sake keep quiet, for I have no authority over the crew now!'

And he spoke the truth, for the negro, brandishing his knife, and supported by his comrades, was again advancing, when the hoarse voice of the boatswain, as he ran to the scene of the action, arrested his progress.

'Hollo! you there; what's the squall for? Avast! Avast! Mingo. Off hands is fair play. Ship that blade of yours, or I'll send my fist through your ribs, and make daylight shine through them in a minute.'

I related the behaviour of the fellow, and was requesting him to order the others forward, when I was cut short by his exclaiming, to my astonishment:

'We shall do as we like here, young man! We are all alike free in a British ship. But damn his eyes for an insolent son of a sea cook. He wants to kiss this pretty lady! I'll let him know she belongs to his betters! The black wench is good enough for him any day. Come, my dear!' he continued, turning to Isabella; 'give me the same fee, and I'll undertake to clear the way for you myself.'

He made as if he meant to approach her, when, careless of what the consequences might be to myself, I hastily stepped forward, and, lifting up the head of the companion, allowed Isabella to run below.

'This lady is no fit subject for either wit or insolence,' said I, shutting the doors, 'and he is less than man who would insult an unprotected female.'

For a little while he stood eyeing me, as if hesitating whether he should resent my interference or remain passive. At length he turned slowly and doggedly away, as he uttered:

89

'You ruffle big, and crow with a brisk note, sir. But I've seen me do as wonderful a thing as twist your wind pipe, and send you over the side to cool yourself a bit; and so I would serve you in the turning of a wave, if it wasn't that we may have use for you yet! I see in what quarter the wind sets; but mind your eye! for sink me if I don't keep a sharp look out ahead over you.'

I now saw that things had come to a crisis—that the crew meant to turn pirates, and I was going to be detained among them for the sake of my professional services. I could not without a shudder reflect on what must be the fate of Isabella among such a gang of reckless villains; but I firmly resolved that, come what might, my protection and care over her should cease but with my life.

To be prepared for the worst, I immediately went below, loaded two pistols which I had brought on board with me, and concealed them in my breast, securing at the same time all my money and papers about my person.

While thus employed, one of the cabin boys came down for a telescope, saying that a sail had hove in sight to windward. Upon this I followed him up, and found the crew collected together in a clamorous consultation as to the course they should follow. Some were for laying to till she came near enough, and seizing her if a merchantman; and if not, they could easily sheer off. But this motion was overruled by the majority, who judged it best to keep clear for fear of accidents. Accordingly, all the spare canvas was set, and we were soon gaining large before the wind. But the *Ariadne*, though reckoned the fastest vessel that ever left the Clyde when close hauled on a wind, was by no means so fleet when squared and going free. She had now met with her match, for the stranger was evidently gaining rapidly on us, and in two hours we saw it was impossible for us to escape. The priest and I were ordered down, with a threat of instant death if we offered to come on deck, or made any attempt to attract observation.

I now communicated to Isabella my apprehensions with respect to the crew, along with my resolution to leave the vessel if the other proved a man-of-war, and earnestly advised both her and the priest to take advantage of it also. She thanked me with a look and a smile that told me how sensible she was of the interest I took in her welfare, and expressed her willingness to be guided by me in whatever way I thought best.

Shortly after this we heard a gun fired to bring us to, and the *Ariadne* hailed and questioned as to her port and destination. The answers, it appeared, were thought evasive and unsatisfactory, for we were ordered to come close under the lee quarter of her Majesty's sloop-of-war *Tartar*, while an officer was sent to examine our papers, for it appeared the *Tartar* had been specially detailed to keep a look out in those waters for a notorious pirate, who had committed some extraordinary deeds of daring while flying the English flag, and pretending to be a peaceful trader. This was now our only chance, and I resolved that if the officer did not come below I would force the companion door, and claim his protection. But I was not put to this alternative. As soon as he arrived, I heard him desire the hatches to be taken off, so that he could examine the hold. The inspection did not satisfy him, for he hailed the sloop, and reported that there were Spanish goods on board, which did not appear in the manifest.

'Then remain on board, and keep stern lights burning all night, and take charge of the ship,' was the reply. In a state of irksome suspense we remained nearly two hours, expecting every moment to hear the officer descending. At length, to our relief, the companion doors were unlocked, and a young man, attended by our captain, entered the cabin. He looked surprised on seeing us, and, bowing to Isabella, apologized for intruding at such an unseasonable hour.

'But I was not given to understand,' he added, 'that there were passengers in the ship—prisoners I should rather pronounce it, Captain Mahone, for you seem to have had them under lock and key, which is rather an unusual mode of treating ladies, at least in a vessel supposed to be bound on a trading voyage. No wine, sir,' he continued, motioning away the bottle which the captain was hastily placing on the table, 'no wine, but be pleased to show me your register and bill of lading.'

He had not been long seated to inspect them when a shuffling and hurried sound of feet was heard overhead, and a voice calling on 'Mr. Wright' for assistance showed that some scuffle had taken place above. Instantaneously we all started to our feet, and the lieutenant was in the act of drawing his sword, when, accidentally looking round, I observed Mahone presenting a pistol behind. With a cry of warning, I threw myself forward, and had just time to strike the weapon slightly aside, when it went off. The ball narrowly missed the head of Wright, for whom it had been aimed, but struck the priest over the right eye, and the unfortunate man, making one desperate and convulsive leap as high as the ceiling, sunk down dead, and before the captain could fire again I discharged the contents of my pistol into his breast. We then rushed up on deck, but it was only to find that the boat's crew had been mastered, and to behold the last of the men tumbled overboard. The pirates then dispersed, and exerted themselves to get the ship speedily under way, while the boatswain sang out to extinguish the stern lights that the *Tartar* might not be guided by them.

'It is all over with us!' exclaimed my companion, 'but follow me; we have one chance for our lives yet. Our boat is still towing astern. You throw yourself overboard and swim till I slide down the painter, and cut her adrift. Come, bear a hand, and jump. Don't you see them hastening aft?' and in an instant he pitched himself off the taffrail, slid down the rope which held the boat, and cast her loose. But this advice, however judicious, it was impossible for me to follow, for at that moment repeated shrieks from Isabella put to flight all thoughts for my own individual safety. I, therefore, hurried back to the cabin, determined that if I could not rescue her along with myself, to remain and protect her with my life. And in the nick of time I arrived. The candles were still burning on the table, and through the smoke of the pistols, which still filled the cabin, I beheld her struggling in the arms of a Spanish sailor—the identical fellow who had displayed such insolence in the early part of the evening. With one stroke of the butt end of my pistol I fractured the cursed villain's skull, caught up Isabella in my arms, ran up the ladder, and had nearly gained the side when the boatswain, attracted by her white garments, left the helm to intercept me, and I saw the gleam of a dagger or knife of some sort on the point of descending, when he was suddenly struck down by some person from behind. I did not stop to discover who had done me this good office, but hailing Wright, and clasping Isabella firmly in my arms, I plunged into the water, followed by, at that moment, an unknown ally. With the aid of my companion, whom I now found to be John Wyllie, the mate, we easily managed to support our charge till the boat reached us, when we found that the greater part of the *Tartar*'s men, who also jumped overboard, had been rescued in a similar manner.

When the morning dawned we perceived the *Ariadne*, like a speck in the horizon, and the sloop of war in close chase. Our attention was next turned to our own situation, which was by no means enviable. We had escaped, it is true, with our lives, for the present, but without a morsel of food, or a single drop of fresh water with us in the boat. We could at best only expect to protract existence for a few days longer, and then yield them up ultimately in horror and misery. By an observation taken the day before, on board the *Tartar'* Mr. Wright informed us we were to the north-east of the Bahamas, and distant about one hundred and seventy miles from Walling's Island, which was the nearest land. This was a long distance, but as despair never enters the breast of a British sailor, even in situations of the utmost extremity, we cheered up each other, and, as no other resource was left us, we manned our oars, and pulled away with life, trusting to the chance of meeting with some vessel, of which there was a strong probability, as this was the common course of our leeward traders. And our hopes were not disappointed, for next day we fortunately fell in with a brig from the Azores, bound for Porto Rico, on board of which we were received with much kindness, and in five days we found ourselves safely moored in Porto-Real harbour.

My first step on landing was to inquire for a boarding house for Isabella, and I had the good luck to be directed to one kept by a respectable English family in Orange Terrace, and to this I conducted her. My next transaction was to charter a small cutter, and to communicate to Wright the secret of the hidden treasure, at the same time asking him to adventure himself and his men on its recovery. I also gave him to understand the probability of a rencontre[23] with the pirates, in the event of their having escaped the sloop, for I was aware that Mahone had overheard the whole confession from my finding him listening at the cabin door. Without hesitation the lieutenant at once agreed to accompany me, and engaging some hands out of a vessel newly arrived, we soon mustered a party of fourteen men, and we hired a cutter. As it wanted only six days to the Festival of St. Jago, and the distance across the Caribbean Sea was great enough to require all our exertions to be there in time, we embarked and sailed that very night.

Our cutter proved a very fast vessel, and though the winds were light and variable we made the Roccas on the evening of the sixth day. As the Spaniard had foretold, the moon was climbing the western sky, and pouring the fullness of her splendour with a mild and beautiful effulgence on the untroubled deep as we slowly drifted with the current between the Wolf Rock and the adjacent isle. All was silent and calm over the whole desert archipelago and the vast surrounding waters, save now and then the flight of a sea fowl awakening from its slumbers as we passed, or the occasional roar of the jaguar faintly wafted from the mainland. We ran the cutter into a deep and narrow creek, moored her safe, and proceeded, well-armed, to the eastern extremity. There we found the projecting point of land, and the old vanilla tree exactly in the situation described—its huge, twisted trunk was still entire, and from the end of its solitary branch, which was graced by a few scattered leaves, the body of a man in the garb of a sailor hung

---

23 French for 'meet'.

suspended in irons. The clothes had preserved the body from the birds of prey, but the head was picked clean and bare, leaving the eyeless and bleached skull to glitter white in the moonlight. In perfect silence, and with something of awe on our spirits, impressed by the solitude and dreariness of the scene, we seated ourselves on the rocks, and, with my watch in my hand, I began to mark the progress of the shadow. For nearly three hours we watched in this manner, listening attentively for the slightest sound from seaward; but everything continued hushed and still, except the creaking of the chain as the dead man swung to and fro in the breeze. Midnight was now drawing near, the moon, radiant and full, was careering high through the deep blue of heaven, and the shadows of the branch and stem were approaching each other, and towards the desired point. At length the hand of my watch pointed to within one minute of the time. It passed over. The branch and stem now merged into one, and threw their shadow due east, and the first spadeful of earth had been thrown out when the man who had been stationed to keep a look-out came running to inform us that a boat was rapidly approaching from the east.

We immediately concluded that they must be some of the *Ariadne's* crew; and their long and vigorous strokes, as they stretched out to the full extent of their oars, showed that they knew the importance of every minute that elapsed. Our implements for digging were hastily laid aside, and we concealed ourselves among the rocks till the pirates came within reach. In a short time the boat was run ashore, and eight armed men came forward, partly Spaniards and partly the ship's crew, among whom I recognized the boatswain, and, to my surprise, Mahone, whom I had shot and left for dead in the cabin. Without giving them time to prepare for the assault we quitted our shelter, and sprung among them at once, laying about with the short swords we had provided ourselves with. For a little space the skirmish was toughly and hotly contested, for the pirates were resolute and reckless, and fought with the desperation of men who knew that the only chance for their lives lay in their own exertions. In the confusion of the fray I had lost sight of Wright, and was closely engaged with one of the Spaniards, when the voice of the boatswain, shouting forth a horrible imprecation, sounded immediately behind me. I turned round, and sprang aside from the sweep of his cutlass, and, as my pistols were both empty, retreated, acting upon the defensive, when he pulled out his, fired, and hurled the weapon at my head. The shot passed without injuring me, but the pistol, aimed with better effect, struck me full on the forehead. A thousand sparks of light flashed from my eyes, I felt myself reeling, and on the point of falling, when a cut across the shoulder stretched me at once on the ground. When I recovered from my stupor and opened my eyes, the morning was far advanced, the sun was shining bright overhead, and I found myself at sea, lying on the deck of the cutter, and Wright busily engaged in examining my wounds. From him I learned that the pirates had been mastered after a severe conflict, in which four had been slain and left on the island, two had escaped unobserved during the fight, and made off with their boat, and two had been wounded, and were prisoners on board, one of whom was Mahone. On our arrival at Porto Rico we delivered them over to the civil power, and soon afterwards Mahone was tried for the murder of the priest, when he was convicted on our evidence, condemned, and executed.

Under good nursing and care I gradually recovered, and by the fall of the season, without any further adventures, I once more landed safe in Scotland.

Isabella is not now that destitute and unprotected orphan whom I first saw on the middle of the western ocean, but the happy mistress of a happy home, diffusing life and gladness on all around her. My friend Wright has lately been placed on the list of post-captains, and is anxiously waiting for more bustling times, when there will be more knocking about and more hard blows and quicker promotion than can be hoped for in piping times of peace. John Wyllie, too, has had advancement in his line, being now master of one of the finest ships sailing out of the Clyde, and I have the additional satisfaction of knowing that none of the crew of the cutter have had reason to regret their having jeopardized their lives in fighting for the 'Pirate's Treasure,' which proved to be of far greater value than the confession of the dying Spaniard had led me to believe. Altogether that voyage was an extraordinary one, and at this period I can look back and feel the truths of the saying that 'Some men are born to strange destinies.'

In this present day we have become more prosaic, and true romances of the sea such as I have described will soon be things of the past.

VI
The Legend of Wolfspring

A STORY OF THE BLACK FOREST

WOLFSPRING CASTLE STOOD IN the very heart of the Black Forest, and for centuries had been in possession of the Barons of Wolfspring, one of the most powerful German families of the Middle Ages, and who, even at the present day, although living on the wreck of their former greatness only, still keep up a semblance of dignity.

The seat of these territorial lords was a castellated Gothic mansion built for strength and defence. It was a massive and imposing pile, gloomy and forbidding as to its external aspects, but designed internally with an eye to the comfort and luxury of its occupants. Nevertheless, there were many dark, tortuous corridors and vaulted tapestry rooms, in which there were ghostly echoes. There were also secret stairways, concealed spring doors, and deep down in the basement a number of gloomy dungeons, in which many a ghastly tragedy had been enacted.

A dark grove of pine and mountain ash encompassed the castle on every side, and threw an aspect of weirdness around the scene, and even shut out the sunshine, which failed to penetrate to that part of the forest's dark depths.

The extraordinary and astounding events that are now about to be related occurred long ago, but incredible as they may seem to the modern sceptic, are still vouched for by those who have their homes in the Black Forest at the present time.

At the period referred to the then Baron of Wolfspring had an only daughter, whose ravishing beauty had caused her to become the talk of Germany, and suitors from all parts had sought her hand. As she was the apple of her father's eye, however, he had carefully guarded her, in the hope that she would remain with him, as he could not bear the idea of her parting from him. Nevertheless, he surrounded her with nearly everything she desired, and was constantly devising new plans for her amusement. On reaching her twenty-first year her father made it the occasion for a fête, such as was rarely seen even in Germany, and preparations were made for it months before the time. Invitations were sent out lavishly, and it was calculated that the Black Forest would witness a gathering of beauty and bravery which would pass down to posterity as an historical event. The lady's birthday fell in the winter time, but that did not prevent the invited guests from assembling in great numbers.

The castle bells rang out a merry peal at the approach of a winter twilight, and the warder was stationed with his retinue on the battlements, to announce the arrival of the company who were invited to share the amusements that reigned within the walls. The Lady Marguerite, the baron's only daughter, never looked more ravishing than on this occasion. The large vaulted apartments were thrown open for the reception of the numerous guests, and by midnight the castle was a scene of gaiety and brilliancy, and the greatest good humour prevailed.

Suddenly it was noted that amongst the guests in the ballroom was a very remarkable-looking man, who had not been noticed before, and who was an utter stranger to every one present. He attracted attention by his dignified bearing, his handsome features, and the magnificence of his dress. The baron was appealed to, but had to confess that he did not know the stranger, who, on being asked for his name and rank, politely asked that he might be allowed to remain incognito, but he hinted that his lineage was perhaps superior to any else present, and his wishing to remain unknown for a time was a mere whim; but, for convenience sake, he requested that he might be addressed as the count. As may be supposed this mysterious stranger aroused no little curiosity, and his boast of superiority engendered some amount of ill-feeling. It would have been contrary to all traditions of Wolfspring hospitality for the baron to request his strange guest to retire, especially on such an occasion, and although he had come without retinue or following of any kind, and not one of the retainers could give any information as to when or how he arrived, he was treated by the host with every consideration and respect.

It soon became only too obvious, however, that the stranger's presence was likely to be productive of much heart-burning, if not of actual mischief, for he bestowed all his attentions on the beautiful Marguerite, and quite ignored the other ladies. This would probably have led to a speedy open rupture, as some or other of the jealous men would have been sure to have insulted him, and in that age insult was quickly followed by blows and bloodshed. But somehow or other it began to be whispered that the proud and uninvited guest was none other than the king's brother, who for certain family reasons had long lived abroad, but his wealth, power, and possible succession to the throne had caused him to be a very-much-talked-of personage in Germany, although no one seemed to know anything about him. But there had been stories of his handsome appearance and his eccentricity. As may be supposed the mere suggestion that the unbidden guest was the mysterious brother of the king at once silenced criticism, and there was a general desire to pay him homage and treat him with respect.

All these flattering attentions he acknowledged with lofty dignity, and it was obvious that he was bent on winning the good opinion of the host's fair daughter, and equally obvious that she was fascinated by his brilliancy and wit; and when he casually remarked, with a sigh, that in another half-hour he must tear himself from her, and leave the fair scene to ride forth again on his journey, she flew to her father and begged of him to press the count to prolong his stay for a few days. Not wishing to deny his daughter anything, the baron approached the count, who, however, did not seem disposed to yield, until beautiful Marguerite herself added her persuasions to those of her father, and then, with a gracious bow, the count expressed his intention of accepting the invitation.

The festivities were prolonged far into the night. Outside the elements waged war, for a terrific gale swept through the forest, bringing with it the heaviest fall of snow that had been experienced for many years. But the storm did not interfere with the comfort of the revellers, who began to disperse to their respective rooms as the castle bell tolled the hour of five.

The day had far advanced when the guests reassembled for the morning meal. Then experiences were exchanged, and strange stories told. One averred that he had been the victim of remarkable phenomena in his room, another that he had heard the flapping of wings at his window, and when, out of a kindly feeling, he arose and opened the window, thinking that some poor storm-beaten bird was in distress, he was greeted with eldrich[24] laughter and shrill screams that pealed through the forest. Others, again, said that they had heard heavenly music; but several, who occupied apartments near those in which the count had been placed, affirmed that they were startled by awful and unearthly sounds proceeding from his room, and yet they were unable to define those sounds. The more level-headed guests smiled as they heard these fantastic stories, and were disposed to attribute them to the figments of wine-heated brains. The mysterious count was almost the last to put in an appearance at the breakfast table, and when he gathered the subject of the conversation a dark smile of unutterable meaning played round his saturnine features, which then relapsed into an

---

24 An archaic form of eldritch, which means unearthly or supernatural.

expression of the deepest melancholy. He addressed his conversation principally to Marguerite, and talked enthusiastically of the different climes he had visited, of the sunny regions of Italy, where the very air breathes the fragrance of flowers, and the summer breeze sighs over a land of sweets. When he spoke to her of those delicious countries where the smile of the day sinks into the softer beauty of the night, and the loveliness of heaven is never for an instant obscured, he drew sighs of regret from the bosom of his fair auditor, and for the first time in her life she longed to leave her home and wander in the lands of delight of which the count drew such graphic pictures.

It soon became evident that the count was bent upon making an impression upon the heart of Marguerite, and when a week had elapsed he still lingered at the castle, although most of the guests had departed, but he begged his host's permission to be allowed to prolong his stay, as he had never before experienced so much happiness. As the baron had now quite come to believe he was entertaining the king's brother, and the probable future king, he was nothing loth that the stranger should stay, and he even began to think that he could now reconcile himself to the loss of his daughter, so long as there was a prospect of her becoming a queen. For that high honour he was prepared to sacrifice even his own feelings.

Days rolled on, and every moment increased the fervour of the inexpressible sentiments with which the stranger had inspired Marguerite. He never discoursed of love, but he looked it in his language, in his manner, in the insinuating tones of his voice, and in the slumbering softness of his smile; and when he found that he had succeeded in impressing her, a sneer of the most diabolical meaning spoke for an instant, and died again on his dark-featured countenance. When he met her in the company of her father he was at once respectful and submissive, and it was only when alone with her, in her rambles through the forest with her favourite hounds, that he assumed the guise of the more impassioned admirer.

As he was sitting one evening with the baron in a wainscoted apartment of the library, the conversation happened to turn upon supernatural agency. The stranger remained reserved and mysterious during the discussion, but when the baron in a sneering manner denied the existence of spirits, and satirically invoked their appearance, if there was any truth in the many stories he had heard, the count's eyes seemed to glow with unearthly lustre, and his form to dilate to more than its natural dimensions. When the conversation had ceased, to the astonishment of every one a chorus of celestial harmony was heard pealing through the dark forest glade. The stranger was disturbed and gloomy; he looked at his noble host with compassion, and something like a tear swam in his dark eyes. After the lapse of a few seconds the music died gently in the distance, and all was hushed as before. The baron soon after quitted the apartment, and was followed almost immediately by the stranger. He had not long been absent from the room when harrowing groans were heard, as if some person was suffering the agonies of an unusually painful death, and when the attendants and others rushed out to ascertain the cause the baron was discovered stretched dead in the corridor. His countenance was convulsed with pain, and the grip of a human hand was clearly visible on his blackened throat. The alarm was instantly given, the castle searched in every direction, and, to the alarm and consternation of everyone, it was found that the count had disappeared. Guests and servants alike mounted their horses and scoured the forest in every direction, but not a trace of the stranger could be discovered, and it was noted that the many paths diverging from the castle were covered with the unsullied and untrodden snow. There was no sign of either man or horse having passed. How, then, had the count gone away! The mystery was profound, and a strange fear fell upon the assembly.

In due course the body of the baron was committed to the earth with all the pomp and ceremony befitting the burial of a person of his high rank, and then those who had remained behind to pay their last respects to the dead host dispersed to their homes, and the remembrance of the dreadful transaction was recalled but as a thing that should be spoken of with bated breath. Men shuddered as they referred to it, and women became hysterical. What was the awful mystery? Would it ever be cleared up? Who was the strange count, and how had he disappeared? He had gone as he came; no one knew how.

After the disappearance of the stranger who had fascinated her and won her love, the spirits of the gentle Marguerite declined. The loss of her lover and the awfully mysterious death of her father threw the girl into a profound melancholy, and she refused to be comforted. She would walk early and late in the walks that he had once frequented so that she might recall his last words, dwell on his honeyed smile, and wander to the spot where she had once discoursed with him of love. She avoided all society, and when alone in the solitude of her chamber she gave vent to her affliction in tears, and the love that the pride of maiden modesty concealed in public burst forth in the hours of privacy. So beauteous, yet so resigned, was the fair mourner that she seemed already an angel freed from the trammels of the world and prepared to take her flight to heaven.

The winter slowly passed. It lingered unusually long that year, but at length the snow melted under the warm rays of the spring sunshine, and in a little while thereafter summer burst in all its glory, and the great forest was resonant with a thousand glad voices of revivified nature. Marguerite had had a seat erected in a spot commanding a magnificent view which had more than once called forth the admiration of the count, although he had only seen it under its winter aspects. Here one summer day she sat wrapped in thought, when she was suddenly startled by someone approaching. She turned round quickly, and to her infinite surprise beheld the count, looking even handsomer and more fascinating than when she last beheld him. He stepped gaily to her side, and commenced an animated conversation.

'You left me,' exclaimed the delighted girl, 'and I thought all happiness was fled from me for ever; but you return, and shall we not be happy?'

'Happy,' replied the stranger with a scornful burst of derision, 'can I ever be happy again! Can the—— but excuse the agitation, my love, and impute it to the pleasure I experience at our meeting. Oh! I have many things to tell you; aye! and many kind words to receive. Is it not so, sweet one? Come, tell me truly, have you been happy during my absence? No! I see in that sunken eye, in that pallid check, that the poor wanderer has at least gained some slight interest in the heart of his beloved. I have roamed to other climes, I have seen other nations, I have met with other women, beautiful and accomplished, but I have met with but one angel, and she is here before me. Accept this simple offering of my affection, dearest,' continued the stranger, plucking a heath-rose from its stem; 'it is beautiful as yourself, and sweet as is the love I bear thee.'

'It is sweet, indeed,' replied Marguerite, 'but its sweetness must wither ere night closes around. It is beautiful, but its beauty is short-lived, as the love evinced by man. Let not this, then, be the type of your attachment. Bring me the delicate evergreen, the sweet flower that blossoms throughout the year, and I will say, as I wreathe it in my hair, "The violets have bloomed and died, the roses have flourished and decayed, but the evergreen is still young, and so is the love of my wanderer." Ah, don't think me immodest if I confess my love for you. You taught me love, why then should I conceal my feelings? You will not—cannot desert me again. I live but in you; you are my hope, my thoughts, my existence itself, and if I lose you I lose my all. I was but a solitary wild flower in the wilderness of nature, and can you now break the fond heart you first taught to glow with passion?'

'Speak not thus,' returned the stranger, suddenly changing his manner; 'it rends my very soul to hear you. Leave me, forget me, avoid me forever, or your eternal ruin must ensue. I am a thing abandoned of God and man, and did you but see the seared heart that scarcely beats within this moving mass of deformity you would flee me as you would an adder in your path. Here is my heart, love, feel how cold it is. There is no pulse that betrays its emotion, for all is chilled and dead as the friends I once knew.'

Marguerite was alarmed. 'You are unhappy, love,' she exclaimed; 'but do not think I am capable of abandoning you in your misfortunes. No! I will wander with you through the wide world, and be your servant, your slave, if you will have it so. I will be true to you, and though the cold world may scorn you, though friends fall off and associates wither in the grave, there shall be one fond heart who will love you better in your misfortune, and cherish you, bless you still.'

She ceased, and her blue eyes swam in tears as she turned them glistening with affection towards the stranger. He averted his head from her gaze, and a scornful sneer of the darkest, the deadliest malice passed over his fine countenance. In an instant the expression subsided, his fixed glassy eye resumed its unearthly chillness, and he turned once again to his companion.

'It is the hour of sunset,' he exclaimed; 'the soft, the beauteous hour, when the hearts of lovers are happy, and Nature smiles in unison with their feelings; but to me it will smile no longer. Ere the morrow dawns I shall be far, very far, from the house of my beloved, from the scenes where my heart is enshrined, as in a sepulchre. Must I leave you, sweetest flower of the wilderness, to be the sport of the whirlwind, the prey of the mountain blast?'

'No, we will not part,' replied the impassioned girl: 'where thou goest will I go; thy home shall be my home, and thy God shall be my God.'

'Swear it, swear it,' resumed the stranger, wildly grasping her by the hand; 'swear to the oath I shall dictate.' He then desired her to kneel, and holding his right hand in a menacing attitude towards heaven, and throwing back his dark raven locks, he exclaimed with the ghastly smile of an incarnate fiend, 'May the curses of an offended God haunt you, cling to you for ever, in the tempest and in the calm, in the day and in the night, in sickness and in sorrow, in life and in death, should you swerve from the promise you have made to be mine. May the dark spirits of the damned howl in your ears the accursed chorus of fiends; may despair rack your bosom with the quenchless flames of hell! May your soul be as the lazar-house of corruption, where the ghost of departed pleasure sits enshrined, as in a grave, where the hundred-headed worm never dies, where the fire is never extinguished. May a spirit of evil lord it over your brow, and proclaim as you pass by, "This is the abandoned of God and man"; may fearful spectres haunt you in the night season; may your dearest friends drop day by day into the grave, and curse you with their dying breath; may all that is most horrible in human nature, more solemn than language can frame or lips can utter, may this, and more than this, be your eternal portion should you violate the oath you have taken.' He ceased, and hardly knowing what she did, the terrified girl acceded to the awful adjuration, and promised eternal fidelity to him who was henceforth to be her lord.

'Spirits of the damned, I thank you for your assistance,' exclaimed the count, as if he had become suddenly frenzied. 'I have wooed my fair bride bravely. She is mine—mine for ever. Aye, body and soul, both mine; mine in life, and mine in death. What, in tears, my sweet one, ere yet the honeymoon is past? Why! indeed, you have cause for weeping; but when next we meet we shall meet to sign the nuptial bond.' He then imprinted a cold salute on the cheek of his young bride, and softening down the unutterable horrors of his countenance, requested her to meet him at eight o'clock on the ensuing evening in the chapel adjoining the castle of Wolfspring. She turned round to him with a passionate cry of pain, and as if to implore him to release her from her rash vow, but he had gone—disappeared as suddenly as if the earth had opened and swallowed him.

Marguerite arose with a sense of unutterable horror weighing her down. On entering the castle she was observed to be weeping, and her relations vainly endeavoured to ascertain the cause of her uneasiness; but the tremendous oath she had sworn completely paralysed her faculties, and she was fearful of betraying herself by even the slightest intonation of her voice or the least variable expression of her countenance. When the evening was concluded the family retired to rest; but Marguerite, who was unable to sleep, owing to the troubled state of her mind, requested to be allowed to remain alone in the library that adjoined her apartment.

Midnight came; every domestic had long since retired to rest, and the only sound that could be distinguished was the sullen howl of the bandog[25] as he bayed the waning moon. Marguerite remained in the

---

25 A dog for guarding or protection.

library in an attitude of deep meditation. The lamp that burnt on the table where she sat was dying away, and the lower end of the apartment was already more than half obscured. The clock from the northern angle of the castle tolled out the hour of twelve, and the sound echoed dismally in the solemn stillness of the night. Suddenly the oaken door at the farther end of the room was gently lifted on its latch, and a bloodless figure, apparelled in the habiliments of the grave, advanced slowly up the apartment. No sound heralded its approach, as it moved with noiseless steps to the table where the lady was stationed. She did not at first perceive it, till she felt a death-cold hand fast grasped in her own, and heard a solemn voice whisper in her ear, 'Marguerite.' She looked up; a dark figure was standing beside her. She endeavoured to scream, but her voice was unequal to the exertion; her eyes were fixed, as if by magic, on the form, which slowly removed the garb that concealed its countenance, and disclosed the livid eyes and skeleton shape of her father. It seemed to gaze on her with pity and regret, and mournfully exclaimed, 'Marguerite, the dresses and the servants are ready, the church bell has tolled, and the priest is at the altar, but where is the affianced bride? There is room for her in the grave, and to-morrow shall she be with me.'

'To-morrow?' faltered out the distracted girl.

'The spirits of hell shall have registered it,' answered the spirit, 'and to-morrow must the bond be cancelled.'

The figure ceased, slowly retired, and disappeared.

The morning—evening—arrived; and already, as the clock struck eight, Marguerite was on her road to the chapel. It was a dark, gloomy night; thick masses of dun clouds sailed across the firmament; and the roar of the winter wind echoed awfully through the forest trees. She reached the appointed place; a figure was in waiting for her; it advanced, and disclosed the features of the count. 'Why! this is well, my bride,' he exclaimed, with a sneer; 'and well will I repay your fondness. Follow me.' They proceeded together in silence through the winding avenues of the chapel, until they reached the adjoining cemetery. Here they paused for an instant; and the count, in a softened tone, said, 'But one hour more, and the struggle will be over. And yet this heart of incarnate malice can feel when it devotes so young, so pure a spirit to the grave. But it must—it must be,' he proceeded, as the memory of her love for him rushed through his mind; 'for the fiend whom I obey has so willed it. Poor girl, I am leading you indeed to our nuptials; but the priest will be death, thy parents the mouldering skeletons that rot in heaps around, and the witnesses of our union the lazy worms that revel on the rotting bones of the dead. Come, my young bride, the priest is impatient for his victim.' As they proceeded a dim blue light moved swiftly before them, and displayed at the extremity of the churchyard the portals of a vault. It was open, and they entered it in silence. The hollow wind came rushing through the gloomy abode of the dead; and on every side were piled the mouldering remnants of coffins, which dropped piece by piece upon the damp earth. Every step they took was on a dead body, and the bleached bones rattled horribly beneath their feet. In the centre of the vault rose a heap of unburied skeletons, whereon was seated a figure too awful even for the darkest imagination to conceive. As they approached it the hollow vault rung with a hellish peal of laughter; and every mouldering corpse seemed endued with unearthly life. The count paused, and as be grasped his victim in one hand, one sigh burst from his heart—one tear glistened in his eye. It was but for an instant; the figure frowned awfully at his vacillation, and waved his gaunt hand.

The count advanced; he made certain mystic circles in the air, uttered unearthly words, and paused in excess of terror. On a sudden he raised his voice, and wildly exclaimed, 'Spouse of the spirit of darkness, a few moments are yet yours; you may know to whom you have consigned yourself. I am the undying spirit of the wretch who cursed his Saviour on the Cross. He looked at me in the closing hour of His existence, and that look has not yet passed away, for I am cursed above all on earth. I am eternally condemned to hell, and must cater for my master's taste till the world is parched as is a scroll, and the heavens and the earth have passed away. I am he of whom you may have read, and of whose feats you may have heard. A million souls has my master condemned me to ensnare, and then my penance is accomplished, and I may know the repose of the grave. You are the thousandth soul that I have damned. I saw you in your hour of purity, and I marked you at once for my own. Your father I killed for his temerity, and permitted him to warn you of your fate; and yourself have I beguiled for your simplicity. Ha! the spell works bravely, and you shall soon see, my sweet one, to whom you have linked your undying fortunes, for as long as the seasons shall move on their course of nature—as long as the lightning shall flash, and the thunders roll—your penance shall be eternal. Look below and see to what you are destined.'

She looked, with a sense of unutterable horror freezing the very blood in her veins. The vault split in a thousand different directions; the earth yawned asunder; and the roar of mighty waters was heard. A living ocean of molten fire glowed in the abyss beneath her, and blending with the shrieks of the damned and the triumphant shouts of the fiends, rendered horror more horrible than imagination. Ten millions of souls were writhing in the fiery flames, and as the boiling billows dashed them against the blackened rocks of adamant, they cursed with the blasphemies of despair, and each curse echoed in thunder across the wave. The count rushed towards his victim. For an instant he held her over the burning lake, looked fondly in her face, and wept as if he were a child. This was but the impulse of a moment; again he grasped her in his arms, strained her to his bosom passionately, as if some finer emotion had overcome him; then, with a wild and sudden movement, he dashed her from him to the ground, and as she fell, paralysed and dying at his feet, he exclaimed fiercely, 'Not mine is the crime, but the religion you profess; for is it not said in that religion that there is a fire of eternity prepared for the souls of the wicked, and have you not deserved its torments? Had you spurned me at the first hour we met, when I sought your destruction, you would have been saved. But you were weak, and though good men and true sought to woo you, you would not listen to them, but threw yourself into my arms, stranger though I was.'

Stooping with these words he raised her insensible form as easily as if she had been a child, poised her for an instant above his head, and then, with an awful imprecation, he hurled her from him. Her delicate form bounded from rock to rock, and the chorus of a thousand voices seemed to shake the very earth in a fierce exultant cry. Then the tomb closed. A darkness as of death fell, and a strange silence followed. For a few minutes the count stood like a statue, a pale blue lambent flame playing about him, until suddenly he turned, the light faded, he drew his cloak about him, and went forth into the darkness, and was seen no more.

From that day the inhabitants of Wolfspring fled in horror from the accursed spot, and the castle gradually crumbled into ruins. Nothing now remains but a heap of grass-grown stones, where in summer time the forest adder glides. The peasant passes the place with a shudder; and around the wood fires on a winter night the humble forest folk will recall the story, current for generations, of the Fair Maid of Wolfspring and the Mysterious Count.

VII

The White Raven

THE STORY AS TOLD BY LYDIA STAINSBY

IT WAS GENERALLY SAID of my father—who was a son of the late Sir John Mark Stainsby—that he was somewhat of an oddity. He certainly had original ideas, and it was a favourite remark of his that he did not care to baa, because the great family of human sheep baaed in chorus. It was due, no doubt, to this faculty of originality that he became the owner of Moorland Grange, which was situated on the edge of wild Dartmoor. My father was a widower; I was his only daughter, but I had four brothers, and I doubt if any girl's brothers were more devoted to her than mine were to me. We were a very united family, and had for many years resided in London, and as my father had ample means we found life very enjoyable. I was considered to be an exceedingly fortunate young woman. My friends all too flatteringly told me I was beautiful, and I know that when I looked into my mirror the reflection that met my gaze was certainly not one to make me shudder. Of course this was vanity, but then that is a woman's especial privilege, and so I don't intend to make any apology for the remark, for I am quite sure that I never was a plain-looking girl.

When my father purchased Moorland Grange I was just turned twenty years of age, and was looking forward with eager pleasure—what girl does not?—to my marriage with one of the dearest and most devoted of men. His name was Herbert Wilton. By profession he was a civil engineer, and for some time he had been in the Brazils, surveying for a new line of railroad which an English company had undertaken to construct. Herbert's engagement had nearly expired, and we were to be married on the New Year's Day following his return.

My father had some relatives in Devonshire; he was exceedingly fond of that part of the country. And on one occasion, after having been on a visit there, he said:

'Lydia, how would you like to go and live in Devonshire?' I told him that hardly anything could give me greater pleasure, and then he astonished me by telling me that he had bought one of the 'queerest, tumble-down, romantic, ghost-haunted old houses imaginable.' It was known as 'Moorland Grange,' and he had got it for, as he said, 'an old song,' as it had been without a tenant for twenty-five years. The cause of this was, as I learnt, mainly attributable to an evil reputation it had acquired, owing to a remarkable murder that had been committed in the house at some remote period. That at least was the current legend, and it certainly affected the interests of the owners of the property. It was another instance of the truth of the adage about giving a dog a bad name. This house had got a bad name, and people shunned it as they might have shunned a leper. For some time the estate had been in Chancery,[26] and as no purchaser could be found for it, my father had been able to secure it at a ridiculously low figure, and he intended—as he told me cheerfully—to purge it of its evil reputation.

At this time only my two younger brothers—who were mere boys—were at home, the others being in India; and so they, my father and I, with three servants, started for Moorland Grange, so as to get it in order, as we intended to reside there permanently.

The time of year was April, and the nearest station to the Grange was Tavistock, where we arrived about five in the afternoon, on as wild, bleak, and windy a day as our fickle and varying climate is capable of giving us even in tearful April. From the station we had a drive of over three miles. My father had deputed an old man named Jack Bewdley to meet us with a trap. Jack had been promised work on our new estate as handy man, woodcutter, or anything else in which he could be useful. He had nearly reached the allotted span, and was gnarled and twisted like an ancient oak. Born and bred in the neighbourhood of Dartmoor, he had never been fifty miles away from his native place in his life. He was a blunt, rugged, honest rustic, very superstitious and very simple: and as soon as he saw me he exclaimed, as he opened his bleared old eyes to their fullest capacity:

'By goom, miss, but you be powerful handsome! I hope as how you won't be a seeing of the White Raven in th' owd Grange.'

This compliment made me blush, and I asked him what the White Raven was, whereupon he looked very melancholy, and answered:

'Ah, I woan't be the chap to make your pretty face white wi' fright, so doan't ye ask me, please.' As I was in no way a nervous or superstitious girl, I was amused rather than otherwise at old Jack's mysterious air, and I did not question him further then, as I felt pretty sure when we had become better acquainted he would be more communicative. We reached the Grange after a very cold and windy drive. The day was done, but there was just light enough lingering in the angry

---

26 The Court of Chancery would administer unclaimed estates.

sky to outline the place in ghostly silhouette. It was a house of many gables, with all sorts of angles and projecting eaves, and a grotesque gothic porch that was approached by a flight of steps with stone balustrades. The whole building was covered with a mantling of dense ivy, which obscured the windows and hung down in ragged streamers, that swayed and rasped mournfully in the chill wind. All around were gloomy woods, and the garden was a forlorn wilderness of rank weeds. Old Jack's wife had got a few of the rooms cleaned out for our immediate use, and some furniture had been sent in, so that we were enabled to make ourselves tolerably comfortable on this the first night in our strange abode.

The next day I set to work with my brothers to explore the house, and soon I was quite able to endorse my father's opinion that it was the queerest, oddest, most romantic and ghostly place imaginable. I have already said that I was neither nervous nor superstitious, but I honestly confess that the rambling, draughty, echoing building quite depressed me. The Grange was said to be over 400 years old, though in some respects it had been modernized; nevertheless it was full of surprises in the shape of nooks and corners, deep, dark recesses, strange angles, dimly-lighted passages, winding staircases, and wainscoted and raftered rooms. One of these rooms was long and narrow, tapering away at one end almost to a point. The walls were wainscoted right to the ceiling, and the ceiling itself panelled with oak. There was a wide open fireplace, and a very massive carved mantel. Two diamond-paned windows lighted the room, one of the windows being filled in with blue and red glass. But at this time the windows were so obscured by the hanging ivy that we had to cut it away to let in the light. I became greatly interested in this antique chamber, and in a spirit of fun and ridicule I at once dubbed it 'the haunted chamber,' and declared I would use it as my bedroom. Afterwards, when talking about it to my father, I said laughingly:

'If that room, pa, hasn't got a ghost, it will have to have one, and we must invent one for it.'

'Oh,' he added, 'according to old Jack Bewdley that's the room where the White Raven shows itself.'

A little later I went to Jack, who was busy trying to clear some of the weeds away from the long-neglected grounds, and I said to him:

'Look here, Bewdley, what's this story about the White Raven? Come, now, you must tell me.'

He paused in his work, leaned his grizzled chin on the handle of his spade, and as a scared look spread itself over his shrivelled face, he answered me thus:

'There be zum foak in these parts, miss, as vow they've seen th' White Raven, and they doa say as, how them as sees it dies within th' week. But I doan't know if them as said they've seen it died or not.'

'Have you seen it, Jack?' I asked, trying to look very serious, though I could scarcely keep from laughing.

'Noa, noa, thank God, noa!' he exclaimed with startling earnestness, and mopping his bald head with his red handkerchief, although the weather was cold, while his tanned and weather-beaten cheeks seemed to me to become pale. Then he asked, 'Have you been in what we foak call the oak chamber?'

Guessing what room he referred to I told him that I had, and he at once said that it was in that chamber that the mysterious White Raven always showed itself to the doomed person.

Of course I was incredulous, and ridiculed the whole idea; nor can I say I was more deeply impressed when on a subsequent and more critical examination of the chamber I found the following doggerel carved in old English on one of the panels—

The stranger who beneath this roof shall lie,
And sees the White Raven is sure to die;
For a curse rests on the unhallowed place,
And the blood that was shed you here may trace.
So, stranger, beware, sleep not in the room,
Lest you should meet with a terrible doom.

From people in the neighbouring villages I learned that in this very room, which I had been prompted to call the haunted chamber, tradition said that at some distant period a very beautiful lady had been brutally done to death by a jealous and dissipated husband, who gave out that she had eloped. He allowed her body to fester and moulder away in the room, and many years afterwards her skeleton was found, and that since then she had haunted the place in the shape of a white raven, while to anyone to whom she appeared it was a fatal sign. But why that should have been so nobody attempted to explain.

Now I will honestly confess that the gruesomeness of the story— which, however, I did not believe in its entirety—so far affected me that I changed my mind about occupying the room myself, and my father said he would take it for his own bedroom. But he also, for some reason or other, did not occupy it, although it was made into a most luxurious sleeping apartment. In the course of a few weeks the Grange began to present a very different appearance, and where gloom and melancholy had reigned, cheerfulness and light spread themselves. Under the fostering care of three or four gardeners the gardens blazed with flowers; some of the timber that encroached too much on the house was cut away, and the windows of the building were cleared of the ivy. I came at last to love the old place, for it was so bizarre, so unlike anything else I had ever seen: and in spite of all the predictions and croakings of the ignorant peasantry round about, who declared that sooner or later the curse which had affected everyone who had ever lived there since the poor lady was murdered would affect us, we were very comfortable and very happy. The summer lingered long that year, but the autumn was short, and winter set in with quite startling suddenness; by the end of the first week in December snow began to fall, and it continued snowing more or less for several days until the country round about was buried.

During all the year I had been pining for my love, who came not, although I knew that he was on his way home. But he had remained in Brazil longer than he intended, owing to the death from yellow fever of one of the surveying party, so that Herbert had been induced to renew his engagement for another six months, to do the dead man's work. With painful suspense and anxiety I had for days been scanning the papers for a report of the vessel which was bearing him to me, for she was overdue, but the weather at sea had been fearful, and old seamen said that vessels making for the Channel would have a hard time of it. As she was to call at Plymouth I persuaded my father to take me there in order that we might welcome Herbert as soon as ever he touched English soil again. As papa denied me nothing, he readily consented to this, but it was not until three days before Christmas that the welcome news came to me that the vessel had entered the Sound.

Need I dwell upon the joy I experienced when, after our long separation, I felt Herbert's dear arms around me once more? How handsome and manly he looked! The sun had tanned him brown, the fine sea voyage home had braced him up after the enervating Brazilian climate, and he declared that he had never been in better health in his life. He was possessed of a wonderful constitution, and during the whole time he had been in Brazil had never had a day's illness.

Of course I told him that, selfish as it seemed, I was going to keep him for Christmas Day, and on New Year's Day I was to become his bride, according to the long prior arrangement. He said that it was necessary for him to go to London to see his friends and to make some preparations, but he promised that he would be with me again on Christmas Eve. And so I parted from him, and as we were to meet again so soon, and in less than a fortnight he was to be my husband, I was verily at that moment one of the happiest girls alive.

As my father was thoroughly imbued with the spirit of old-fashioned English hospitality he generally kept open house at Christmas time, and this being our first Christmas at the Grange we had a large number of visitors, so that the house was quite full. In order that Herbert, when he came, might be fittingly bestowed as the bridegroom-elect, we decided that he should occupy the haunted chamber, for it certainly was the best sleeping room in the house; and though some silly and unusual nervousness—as I believed then—had prevented my occupying it as I intended, neither I nor my father attached the slightest importance to the supernatural stories current in the district. With my own hands I arranged the room for Herbert, filling it with knick-knacks and odds and ends, and everything I could think of that was likely to give him pleasure or add to his comfort.

Christmas Eve of that year was marked by a snowstorm such as, the country people said, had not been known for forty years. The train that brought my love from London was very late, and I had become quite anxious, but all anxiety was forgotten when I helped him to divest himself of his snow-laden topcoat in the hall, and taking me in his arms he kissed me in his hearty, cheery way. We were a very jovial party, and that night was a happy, gladsome night, the memory of which will never leave me. Nor shall I ever forget dear Herbert's words, as he kissed me good-night on the stairs as the great hall clock struck one.

'Darling little woman,' he whispered, 'what joy, what happiness, what ecstasy, to think that in a week's time you will belong to me!'

I had no words. I could only sigh in token of the supreme happiness that filled my heart to overflowing.

Christmas morning broke bright, clear, and beautiful. The snow had ceased to fall, and a hard frost had set in. It was veritable Canadian weather—crisp, crystalline, and invigorating. As soon as breakfast was over Herbert took me on one side and said:

'You know, Lydia, I am about one of the most practical men that you could find in a day's march, and hitherto I have been without, as I believe, a scrap of superstition in my composition. But, by jove! after last night's experience I'll be hanged if I don't believe with Shakespeare that there are more things in heaven and earth than are dreamt of in our philosophy.'

At these words I turned deadly pale. I scarcely knew why, but such was the case, and I gasped out:

'What—what do you mean?'

'Well,' he answered, with a laugh that wasn't sincere, for it was obviously forced, 'I believe that room in which I slept is positively haunted.'

Now, I may state here that not a word of any kind had been mentioned to Herbert about the stories that were current with regard to the house. Both my father and I had resolved that the subject should be strictly avoided, so that none of our lady guests might be alarmed. As he spoke, I looked up into his brown face, and I saw that it was filled with a puzzled and troubled expression, while his splendid eyes had an unusual expression in them.

'Tell me,' I said quickly, 'what did you see or hear?'

'Oh, don't let us talk about it,' he answered lightly. 'Perhaps, after all, I have simply been dreaming.'

'Yes, yes—tell me—you must tell me, Herbert,' I exclaimed. 'You know that I am strong-nerved.'

He seemed to hesitate; but laughing again, though it was the same forced laugh, he said:

'Well, the fact is, if ever I saw a raven in my life, I saw one last night, only it was white.'

At this I almost fainted, and he caught me by the arm. I made a desperate effort, however, and recovered myself.

'Go on; tell me all about it,' I said peremptorily.

And the sum and substance of what he told me was this. He had seen a white raven, or what appeared to be a white raven, flying round and round the room. It made no noise, which amazed him and, as he confessed, startled him. He tried to catch this mysterious and noiseless bird, but it had no substantiality—it was an airy phantom; but once or twice, when he appeared to grasp it, a deep groan and sigh broke upon his ears.

Although a strange fear seemed to turn my heart cold, I endeavoured not to show it, nor could I bring myself to tell my lover of the tradition so common all over the countryside about the murdered lady and the White Raven.

If the extraordinary apparition had any real effect on Herbert, he soon shook it off, and his hearty ringing laughter made music in the house, and his eyes were filled again with the old look of love with which they always greeted me. It had been arranged that the gentlemen were to form a shooting party, to go out on to the moor and try and bag some wild ducks. At first I was disposed to dissuade Herbert from going—ah, would that I had done so!—but it seemed to me weak and foolish. Moreover, he was so anxious to go for the novelty of the thing, and so I whispered in his ear as he was standing on the steps:

'Take care of yourself, love, for my sake.'

'Of course I will, darling; and you do the same,' he answered cheerily.

I watched his manly form until he was hidden from my sight by the trees. He looked splendid in his perfect health, and his magnificent physique was set off to every possible advantage by the superb coat of Russian sable that he wore. How proud I felt of him! for truly be was a man to be proud of.

Three hours later the party returned, minus Herbert. They said he had got separated from them in some way, and they quite thought he had come back. Although a sense of something being wrong overcame me for the moment, I tried to think that it was simply nervousness. Of course, the gentlemen at once hurried back to the moor, and when they came again they brought my lover mangled and shattered, and, as it seemed then, in the agony of death. Oh, my God! how awful it was! I thought I should have gone raving mad. It appears that Herbert had been found in a hollow, whither he had fallen by the breaking away of the snow under his feet. In his fall he had not only fractured an arm and some of his ribs, but his gun had gone off full in his face, and, besides disfiguring him frightfully, had destroyed both his eyes.

It can be imagined what a terrible shock it was to the household, and how the joy and mirth were turned to lamentations and moaning. Doctors were procured, but they pronounced the sufferer's condition as critical; they left us no room to hope that the sight would be restored under any circumstances.

Ah, what a fearful dark Christmas that became to me! I think in my agony of mind I cursed my fate, my God; and how I hated the house, and shuddered as I thought of the horrible room where my beloved had seen the strange apparition of the White Raven.

Up to a short time previously, it would have been difficult to have found a girl more sceptical than I was about anything that savoured of superstition; but now I was filled with a strange dread, and feared my own shadow.

When I saw old Jack for the first time after the accident, he said to me:

'Is it true, miss, that Meester Wilton's been asleeping in the haunted room?'

'Yes, Jack; it is,' I answered, in heartbroken tones.

'Then, maybe, he's seen the White Raven?'

'He has,' I replied; whereupon I thought the old man would have fallen down in a fit, so scared did he seem; and he mumbled out:

'God bless us and preserve us all! I wouldn't sleep in that room, miss, not if Queen Victoriey was to give me her golden crown. That there room, miss, ought to be shut up, and no one ever allowed to go anigh it agen.'

The shadow that had so suddenly and cruelly fallen upon us rendered the Christmas festivities out of the question, and most of the guests sorrowfully departed the following day. Many long weeks ensued—dark, torturing weeks to me, for my loved one was suspended, as it were, by a single hair over that profound abyss into which all living atoms finally fall, and from which no sound ever comes to break the mystery. But if they were dark weeks to me, how much, how infinitely, how unspeakably darker to him who, in the pride of his manhood, had been deprived of the power of ever again beholding the wonders of God's creation. And yet he murmured not, nor uttered complaint nor groan. To me the one consolation I had in this hideous calamity was being near him, being able to tend him, and hear his voice, which had lost none of its old cheerfulness. Slowly, very slowly, as the summer drifted by, he began to regain some of his lost strength, and we led him out beneath the trees and into the sunlight, though it was ever, ever night to him, for not a glimmer of vision remained. And as I looked at his sightless orbs and his maimed and torn face, from which no human power could banish the cruel and ghastly scars, I hated the Grange with a hate that hath no words.

One day he asked to be taken to where my father was, and, putting his arm in mine, we entered my father's presence.

'Mr. Stainsby,' he began, with an attempt at a smile, 'I am not quite the same man I was when I came here last Christmas. But in my misfortune an angel has watched over me in the person of your daughter, who, but for this mishap, would now have been my wife. She has brought me out of the shadow of the grave, and I owe a duty to her no less than to you. That duty is to release her from all promises and vows, and leave her perfectly free to bestow her heart on some one who is whole and sound. I am now but a battered wreck, and all I can hope for is to break up soon and drift away into the great and mysterious ocean of eternal silence. But let me ask you, sir, to see to it that the man upon whom you bestow your daughter is as near perfection as a man may come; for no more perfect woman than she is walks the world. I have nothing more to add further than, in such poor words as well up from my stricken heart, to thank you for your hospitality.'

He had tried so hard to be strong and collected, and show no sign of the awful despair that was crushing him. But is the man born who could go through such an ordeal unmoved? His lips quivered, his voice grew weak, and something like a spasm caught his breath.

My own eyes were filled with blinding, scalding tears, and my heart fluttered like the wing of a bird in pain. Gliding over to where he stood, I placed my arms about his neck, and laying my cheek against his scarred face, I found voice to say to my father, who was also deeply affected and moved:

'Father, the man whom Herbert would have you choose for me need be sought no further than this room. He is here. My heart beats to his heart; my face is pressed to his.'

My father came to us. He laid one hand on Herbert's shoulder, and the other on my head; and thus he spoke:

'A woman's love that clings not to a man when calamity overtakes him is worthless. Freely do I bestow her upon you, Herbert, if it is her wish and your wish that you should be united.'

'My husband,' I murmured, as I clung closer to him, and it was my only answer. Herbert tried to persuade me that it was to my happiness and my interest to abandon him; but he might as well have tried to convince the winds of heaven that they should not blow. Externally the Herbert as I had first known him had changed. His handsome face was handsome no longer, and his wondrous eyes were sightless forever. But his heart was the same. What could change that—the bravest, truest, tenderest that ever beat in man's breast? And so ere the next Christmas had dawned I was Herbert's wife, and soon after that my father abandoned the accursed Grange to the gloom and the silence and the melancholy from which he had reclaimed it, and a little later it was burned to the ground. We never knew how the fire originated; but it was generally supposed that some of the superstitious people in the neighbourhood wilfully set it alight, under the impression that a place that was accursed by the spilling of human blood should no longer be allowed to encumber the earth. When I heard of its destruction I confess that I rejoiced, and I said to myself:

'Never again will the White Raven bring calamity to a household as it has brought to ours.'

For five years I walked with my husband in his darkness, and let him see the world through my eyes. Two children blessed—literally blessed—our union, a girl and a boy. But my beloved husband never fully recovered from the shock of the awful accident on that dark and memorable Christmas Day; and, though he uttered no moan, his blindness preyed upon his mind, and a short, brief illness took him from me.

For long years the grass has waved over his grave. Other men have praised my face and sought my hand; but to all I have turned a deaf ear, for my love was buried in Herbert's grave. But in my son the father lives again, and when I gaze upon his handsome face and splendid figure, I feel that God is very good, and that He chastens us to make us more perfect in His sight.

VIII
With Fire and Death

A STORY OF A GREAT DEED

What though the field be lost?
All is not lost; th' unconquerable will,
And study of revenge, immortal hate,
And courage never to submit or yield.

THE SCENE OF THIS story is Meerut, the time May Day, 1857, a
year in which England's hold on India was well nigh shaken off.[27]
Meerut is situated on a plain, and lies forty miles or so to the north and
east of Delhi. It is bounded on the east by the Ganges and on the west
by the Jumna, and covers an area of, roughly speaking, about five miles
in circumference. In the fateful '57 it was one of the most important
military stations, and the largest cantonment in British India. A great
wall, or esplanade, which in its turn was cut in two by a deep nullah,[28]
divided the town into two separate parallelograms, one of which was
occupied by the European force, the other by the natives.

The hot day—and Meerut is hot—had closed, and the short Indian
twilight had given place to a night of exceeding beauty. A refreshing
breeze was blowing from the east, and the moon burnished with a sheen
that was almost dazzling the domes of the numerous mosques, and
threw into silhouette relief the palms and cocoa trees, and the masses
of native huts. The majority of the European population were taking
their airing as was customary after the sun had set, and the 'Park Road'
was a scene of gaiety. Strings of vehicles, numberless horsemen, and
crowds of natives moved to and fro. The air was filled with the murmur
of many voices; the laughter of women, the sweet prattle of children,
and wafted on the breeze came the monotonous sounds of tom-toms,
and the wail-like singing of groups of natives as they prepared their
suppers over the open braziers of charcoal that scented the atmosphere
with its fumes. Abutting on the Park Road, and commanding a wide
and extensive view, was a handsome bungalow surrounded with a well-

---

27 The Indian rebellion of that year was the first major uprising against the rule of the
British East India Company.
28 A ravine.

kept garden. On the verandah were a party of ladies and gentlemen. The men were military men, and the ladies were their relatives, and playing about on the verandah, under the care of an old ayah,[29] was a sweet English child, fragile, and white of face, as most English children are who are born in India, but of an exquisite beauty that promised a magnificent womanhood. But though well and hearty then, that dear child was in a few days to be lying dead, gashed and hacked almost beyond recognition. From the roof of the verandah a swinging lamp threw a soft light over the little group seated in a semicircle, with small tables before them, on which were glasses and the inevitable brandy pawnee.[30] Two silent khidmutgars[31] stood like dusky statues ready to obey the slightest order given by their master or mistress.

This bungalow was the home of an officer whom it is only necessary to refer to as the colonel. The sweet child playing there was his only daughter, and one of the ladies, whose beautiful face was clouded with an expression that might be described as half fear, half anxiety, was his wife. All the colonel's male companions were officers, one of them being Lieutenant George Willoughby, of the Ordnance Commissariat Department. He was a young man, but was the officer in charge of the great Delhi magazine. He looked every inch a soldier, and his face expressed determination and force of character. Lounging there in a large chair, toying with a fragrant cigar, and apparently deeply interested in watching the little volumes of smoke curl upward as he puffed them from under his moustache, his legs crossed, his head thrown back, and one arm hanging listlessly over the rail of the chair, he was the picture of a quiet, unobtrusive English gentleman. But a slight study of the face would have convinced anyone that beneath that calm exterior lay a tremendous latent power that once aroused could be terrible and deadly to his enemies, and that this was really the case was soon to be amply proved.

Another of the group was a still younger man, handsome as Apollo, and with a frame that seemed to be knit with steel. Although younger his military rank was equal to Willoughby's, for he too was a lieutenant of the Bengal Artillery, and was also stationed at Delhi. His name was Richard Shelton, and, like his friend and colleague, he had a pronounced soldierly bearing, and his fine bright blue eyes, of the true

---

29 A local woman employed as a nanny.
30 Brandy and water.
31 Local men employed as servants.

English type, and his clear cut features and firm mouth, spoke of a frank, open, loyal, and brave nature.

These two officers and friends had ridden over that afternoon from Delhi on a visit to their friend, the colonel, with the object of discussing the portentous signs of the times, for the air was filled with rumours, and mutiny had displayed itself. Discontent was rampant in the native regiments, and the question was to what extent would it go? If there were those amongst the British who read the handwriting on the wall with ill-concealed alarm, it is none the less true that the majority of the officers in Upper India were rather disposed to laugh these fears to scorn. For with the almost fatuous self-reliance peculiar to the English, they believed they were powerful enough to hold their own against any number of natives. With one exception, perhaps, all the gentlemen there belonged to the first category. The exception was Richard Shelton. He was young, and had but recently received his promotion, and not only was he endowed with an unusual share of animal spirits, but he was of a sanguine, almost enthusiastic temperament, and moreover he was in love. On the first blush that may seem a reason why he should have been more anxious, but love is ever hopeful, and indisposed to look on the gloomy side of things. At any rate, being full of the fire of youth, and not having yet acquired the staid wisdom of his elders, young Shelton did not trouble himself much about what the morrow or the next week might bring forth. Very likely, if somebody had said to him—

'I say, Shelton, old fellow, if the natives were to rise what would you do?' This answer would have come with a ringing laugh—'Why, go for them, and smash them. What else would you have me do?'

The young lady with whom Shelton was in love was the colonel's niece, Blanche Merton, an orphan girl of great beauty, and the colonel's ward. She had only come out to India a year before as governess to her cousin—the colonel's daughter. Blanche had been born and had spent most of her life in one of the sweetest and breeziest of Hampshire villages, and she had not resided long enough in India to become jaded and enervated by the climate, which, in course of time, insidiously undermines the constitutions of white women. A handsomer couple, and a couple more suited to each other than Lieutenant Shelton and Blanche Merton, could not have been found in the whole of British India. They had known each other eight months, and been desperately in love nearly the whole time. The conversation of the little party had flagged somewhat, but suddenly Willoughby asked in a preoccupied way:

'What is going to be the upshot of matters, colonel, do you think?'

This question had reference to the mutinous spirit that had shown itself. There had been a parade on the 24th of April, when eighty-five out of ninety men had mutinied, and that very week, beginning with the 1st of May, they were to be tried, and the cantonment was accordingly greatly excited.

'Well,' answered the colonel, thoughtfully, as he stroked his moustache and twirled his cigar between his long white fingers, 'the prisoners will be convicted on the clearest of evidence, and exemplary punishment meted out to them.'

'And what after that?' asked Willoughby, significantly.

'Ah, that remains to be seen. I think and hope we are strong enough to hold our own, but if there was a general rising, that is about all we could do, and might succumb unless succour was speedily sent to us.'

This remark had rather a depressing effect, and there was silence again; but Blanche had gone into the house for something, and Shelton, thinking only of her, and how entrancingly beautiful she looked in her white gauze dress, and with the bunch of Indian roses in her dark hair, had slipped away after her.

Presently Willoughby said: 'Yes, we might hold our own for a time— a short time, but it's no use blinking the fact, we are weak in numbers.'

'It seems to me,' returned the colonel, with the same thoughtful air, 'that you in Delhi are worse off than we are.'

'True,' said Willoughby, with a bitter little laugh, 'for the first thing the mutineers would do if they got the upper hand would be to endeavour to loot the magazine to obtain the vast supplies of the munitions of war that we've got there.'

'It would be a terrible thing if they should succeed in doing that,' put in the colonel's wife, and shuddering as she spoke.

'It would,' answered Willoughby, quietly.

'And there are such a few of you to guard the magazine,' added the lady.

'Very few,' said Willoughby in the same quiet way. Then, after a pause, he continued with a significant emphasis, 'But, nevertheless, I don't think if all the regiments here and in Delhi were to mutiny they would obtain possession of the magazine while I am in charge.'

'Why not?' asked the colonel's wife.

'Because I would blow it up if I found that I couldn't hold the place,' was the quiet but impressively emphatic answer.

'Well, well,' said the colonel, wishing to change the subject, for he saw that it was affecting the ladies, 'it won't come to that. We may have a little trouble, but we shall get over it. Any mutinous spirit will be put down with an iron hand. Besides, I really don't think the natives generally have any bad feeling for us.'

Backwards and forwards along the road went a continuous stream of natives—Hindoos[32] and Brahmins, high caste and low caste—mingling freely with the Europeans. And could the colonel at that moment have read the hearts that beat beneath those dusky skins he would have seen how grievously in error he was, for the hatred and loathing for the feringhees[33] were all but universal. And, though 'white robed peace' seemed to smile on all that fair scene, there was beneath a seething mass of discontent, only wanting a tiny vent as a beginning, when the whole mine might explode and spread desolation and ruin throughout India. But little did any of those ladies and gentlemen sitting on that verandah that hot May night dream of the volcano beneath their feet, and least of all did Shelton and Blanche trouble themselves with the portents in the air. These two young people, so full of life and health and hope, were building castles in the air and dreaming of the day that should see them united.

There was a considerable pause again in the conversation, and then Willoughby, in that quiet, emphatic way of his which was well calculated to carry conviction, remarked in answer to what the colonel had just said:

'I don't altogether agree with you, colonel. My impression is the natives hate us heartily, and if they can but get the chance will sweep us out of the land.'

'Ah, yes, if they can but get the chance,' replied his host. 'But there's the point. They will not get the chance.'

In a few minutes a khidmutgar came to announce that tea was served, and the ladies and gentlemen went into the house, but the child still played about, and the ayah remained. She was squatted down in one corner of the verandah enjoying a few draws of a bubble-bubble. The khidmutgars who had been waiting on the colonel and his party commenced to clear the tables of the glasses and bottles; and one of the men, a stern, sullen-looking fellow, said to the other:

'Heard you, Jewan, what these feringhee dogs said?'

'Some of it, Meerza,' returned the man addressed. 'But I understand not so much of their hateful language as you.'

---

32 An archaic spelling of Hindus.
33 An Indian and Asian derogatory term for a white person.

'Well, the colonel sahib says we don't hate his countrymen.'

Here the two men broke into a scornful laugh, and Jewan remarked:

'Poor fool. Ere the moon has waned he may have learnt differently. If all goes well, the blood of all the white devils in Meerut shall dye the streets, and even the Gunga[34] over there shall run red with it. Shiva the Destroyer has willed it, and it will be as I say.'

'What is that you say, Jewan?' asked the little girl, who had been arrested in her play by the words that fell from the man's lips. Her question caused him to turn upon her with a look so wild and so full of fierce hatred that she screamed and rushed towards her nurse. The ayah sprang up and caught her in her arms, saying soothingly:

'What is it, Missy Baba? What has frightened the pet lamb?'

'Oh! ayah, Jewan looks so dreadful he has frightened me.'

Alarmed by the scream of the child the colonel ran from the house, asking excitedly what was the matter.

'Oh, papa, papa!' exclaimed his daughter, as she flew to him, 'I heard Jewan say such dreadful things; and when I asked him what it was he had said, he frightened me by the way he glared at me.'

'What does this mean, you rascal?' demanded the colonel, angrily, and speaking in Hindostanee.[35] 'I am tempted to horsewhip your hide, you black dog.'

The man drew himself up to every inch of his height. He was a tall, commanding-looking man with a mobile face, and eyes that seemed to burn like glowing coals.

'Sahib,' he said, proudly and scornfully, 'I am no dog.'

Then, without another word, he marched down the steps of the verandah into the garden and disappeared into the darkness.

The colonel was much distressed. It was another sign of the times. A few months before no servant would have dared to have answered his master in such a way.

The other ladies and gentlemen had by this time appeared on the scene, and many were the anxious inquiries as to the cause of the disturbance. But for the sake of the ladies the colonel gave an evasive answer, and, re-entering the house, leading his daughter by the hand, the others followed all but two—Shelton and Blanche. They lingered. With the artfulness of a lover he detained her by saying, 'Oh, I say, Blanche, isn't this a splendid night? How brilliant the moon is.'

---

34 The Ganges River.

35 Hindi.

'Yes,' she answered, linking her hands in his arm, and turning her own beautiful face up to his. 'But I wish, dear, we were under an English sky instead of this Indian one.'

'Why?'

'I—I hardly know. I don't like this country. If the fears that I have heard expressed that the natives may rise are realized how dreadful it will be.'

'Tut—little woman,' answered the brave lad cheerily. 'Don't let any gloomy forebodings trouble you. There is discontent, it is true, but we shall calm it down.'

'I hope so—I hope so,' said Blanche, with an unusually thoughtful air.

'It will be so, my pet. But come, let us go in, for I heard the colonel suggest cards.'

'But shall I not have you to myself for a few minutes again this evening? Remember that as you leave so early in the morning I shall not see you before you go.'

'Of course, darling, we shall have another spoon to-night,' he said in his hearty manner, and letting his lips come into contact with hers, to which she made no objection. 'You see Willoughby and I must report ourselves in Delhi by eight o'clock, but I intend to come over next Sunday and see you.'

'Oh, you love,' she murmured, allowing him to embrace her still more closely, until they were suddenly startled by the voice of the colonel, who, coming on to the verandah, said:

'I say, you young people, we want you, you know. You can surely manage to tear yourselves from each other's arms for a little while.'

'Certainly, certainly, colonel,' answered Shelton in an embarrassed way. 'But I was just drawing Blanche's attention to that group of stars, and——'

'Ah, how very funny,' interrupted the colonel with a laugh. 'It seemed to me you were trying to smother her, and I wasn't sure which was your head and which was hers. But come now, get in. We want to make up some whist parties.'

A little later on Blanche did manage to get another few minutes alone with her lover, and with many warm embraces they separated—not for ever, for they were to meet again, but under circumstances that neither dreamed of then. His promise to see her again on the Sunday remained unfulfilled. Not from any fault of his, but for reasons that were not explained an order was issued of a peremptory character which prevented any officer or private going outside of Delhi.

On the following Saturday, that is on May 9, there was enacted in Meerut an extraordinarily dramatic scene, that was the prelude, though the white people knew it not, of a ghastly drama such as India had never before witnessed during the rule of the British.

In the interval between the 1st and the 9th the mutineers had been tried by a court-martial composed of native and British officers, and sentenced to ten years' hard labour. The first part of the sentence—that of stripping them of their uniform in the presence of all the regiment—was to be carried out, and on that eventful Saturday morning, under a strong guard of rifles and carabineers, the disgraced eighty-five were marched to the parade-ground to be still further disgraced.

It was a stirring scene, for when the *reveille* had sounded long lines of troops, mounted and on foot, marched towards the plain that forever afterwards was to be historic ground. The clattering of horses' hoofs and the rumbling of artillery added to the general commotion, and soon the plain was swarming with armed men. It was no dress or drill parade, but a terribly stern display of authority and power, that it was firmly believed would overawe the mutinous spirit. Heavily shotted field guns were placed in position, while the drawn sabres of the dragoons flashed blindingly in the blazing sunlight. On three sides of the plain were bodies of troops armed with the new grooved rifle, and were ready, should the signal be given, to belch forth fire and send their rotary messengers of death into the surging masses of natives.

The mutineers belonged to the 3rd Native Cavalry, and their commanding officer was Colonel Carmichael-Smyth. All being ready, he stepped forward, and in a loud, clear voice, that was not altogether free from emotion, however, he read the sentence of the court-martial. That formality ended, the accoutrements were taken from the mutineers, and their uniforms stripped from their backs. Then came the armourers and smiths with their shackles and tools, and, in the presence of that great concourse of spectators, civilian and military, the disgraced men were made to wear the chains of felons. They raised their arms and cried aloud to their general to save them from such ignominy, but the fiat[36] had gone forth. They were doomed. There was not a sepoy[37] or native civilian present but gasped for breath as he felt the rising indignation in his throat. But what could they do in the presence of those stern white soldiers, those shotted guns, those grooved rifles, and the

---

36 Order or command.
37 A local man serving with the British forces.

drawn sabres? Yes, they could do something—they could endure and wait.

When, after some hours, the ceremony was completed, the manacled felons were consigned to the gaol, and over them was placed a native guard only. Oh, fatuous act of folly! Who was responsible for it? History is silent, and he or they who made the blunder have long since mouldered to the dust from whence they sprang.

The anxious and eventful day ended. The Europeans took their airing as usual, and met each other at the dinner tables hopeful and cheerful. They had struck such terror into the hearts of the natives, by the stern and terrible act, that all fear of a rising had passed. Such was the general feeling amongst the whites, but during the hours of the short Indian night there was an unusual movement amongst the natives. In the lines of the native soldiery, through the surrounding villages and amongst the crowded bazaars, a fatal sign was passing. Fleet-footed natives sped from place to place and put into the hands of the principal men a small cake. It was a chupatty,[38] and by prearrangement was the signal for a rising. The broiling sun rose on the Sunday morning, and the Europeans, having no thought of coming danger, wended their way to the station church. Amongst them were the colonel and his family, including his sweet little daughter and her pretty governess Blanche, who looked prettier than ever, and was radiant with a sense of happiness that found no expression in words, but showed itself in her beaming eyes and flushed cheeks. And the cause of this was a letter from her lover in Delhi, brought to her that morning by a coolie. In it Shelton expressed his joy that the great 'disarming and felon-marking act' of the day before had passed off so quietly; and he expressed a belief that the lesson thus taught to the natives would be lasting, and there would be no more mutinous conduct. But what had excited in Blanche such a sense of joy was this line: 'And now, sweetest of women, to-morrow I shall hold you in my arms again, for I have got two days' leave, and am going to spend them in Meerut. You may look for me about tiffin time.'[39]

Full of the expectation that this great joy would be realized, how eagerly did she look forward to the morrow. But, had she been gifted with the power of prescience, and could have foreseen the events that

---

38 Chapatti: a pancake-shaped unleavened bread.
39 Tiffin in India is a light snack, so this would have been tea time.

were to happen in a few hours, she would have shrunk with curdling horror, and have cried aloud to God for protection.

Divine service ended, and homeward the people returned again, laughing and chatting and hand-shaking as friends met friends. And tiffin was partaken of, and the siesta indulged in without a single thought of insecurity. Alas, what fatal blindness! Was it not a cruel fate that dulled the senses of every white man in the cantonment on that awful Sunday! Had someone only suspected and been able to arouse the officers to a sense of their danger, in all human probability history would never have been called upon to record the ghastly horrors of the Indian Mutiny. While the white people slept through the sweltering heat of that May afternoon there was unusual stir in the native lines and in the bazaars, and down the Ganges, as well as down the Jumna,[40] a budgerow[41] slowly drifted, and at intervals of about five minutes on board of that budgerow there were sounded three distinct and emphasized strokes on a large tom-tom. That beating of the tom-tom was a signal to the villagers and fishermen who dwelt on the banks of the rivers to repair with all speed to the city in readiness for the great event.

Still the white men slept! A fatuous belief in their might had lulled them to a fatal slumber. Shiva, the Destroyer—the God of the natives—had spoken, but the God of the Christians gave no sign.

The white men slept!

The afternoon waned. The evening breeze set in, and the Christians rose and prepared for evening worship; and as they wended their way to church they saw for the first time sights and sounds that paled the faces of the women, and begot anxiety in the men. Columns of illuminated smoke were rising to the darkening sky; and from afar off came the sound of bugles calling to arms, and mingling with it was the roll of musketry. Service in the church did not take place, and, the scared people hurried back; for now from lip to lip flew the news—'The native soldiers have risen!' It had a dreadful sound, for under any circumstances it meant a tremendous struggle, and many a brave man would bite the dust ere the insurrection was quelled.

That confusion ensued amongst the whites goes without saying, for none knew exactly where the danger lay. Firm in his belief in his dark-skinned comrades the white-haired colonel mounted his horse and rode boldly into the midst of his regiment, which was assembled on

---

40 A tributary of the Ganges River.
41 A large covered boat used on the Ganges River.

the plain. He tried to harangue the men, but ere he had spoken many words there was a report, and a bullet shattered his arm. In a few seconds he fell from his horse riddled with bullets. It was the first blood. Then throwing off all reserve the black soldiers seemed to suddenly transform themselves to fiends. With hideous cries and shouts, and followed by a yelling rabble thirsting for the white men's lives, they rushed towards the town bent on slaughter.

And almost at the same moment a young and beautiful woman, mounted on a magnificent horse, her form concealed by a military cloak, crossed the plain, and, urging the animal to its wildest gallop, sped towards Delhi.

> To every man upon this earth
> Death cometh soon or late,
> And how can man die better
> Than facing fearful odds,
> For the ashes of his fathers
> And the temples of his gods.[42]

When the eighty-five condemned men were consigned to the gaol they were placed under the care of a native guard only, and the prisoners exclaimed to their guard: 'Are you countrymen of ours that you can calmly see us thus treated and disgraced by these accursed feringhees?' And the taunt was taken up and carried from man to man, and it ran like wildfire through the native regiments, and through the bazaars, and through the villages. And it was borne down the rivers and up the rivers, and over the dusty plain to Delhi men sped with the cry on their lips. And when the sinking sun was reddening the rolling waters of the Ganges, native eyes in Delhi were turning anxiously towards Meerut for the flaming signal in the sky, that should announce to them that fire and sword were doing their deadly work on the European residents in the great cantonment.

While the white men were sleeping the natives were acting. They surged to the prison, civilians and soldiers alike. Some of the latter were in uniform, some in their stable dress. Some were fully accoutred, and bestrode their chargers all ready for war. Others rode their steeds with only watering-rein and horse-cloth; but every soldier was armed with sabre and pistol, and hundreds of the rabble had pistols and guns

---

42 From Thomas Babington Macaulay, *Lays of Ancient Rome*, a collection of poems composed when Macaulay was working in India 1834–8.

of some sort. They met with no opposition at the prison. If the guard did not help they looked on passively. The cells were forced open, the prisoners brought forth, and native smiths were at hand to strike off the shackles. Then the erstwhile prisoners mounted behind their comrades and rode to the lines for more horses and arms, and Hindoos and Mohammedans, high caste and low caste, women and children, joined in one mighty shout, 'Death to the feringhees!'—'Deen, deen!'[43] which means 'Death'—and was to become their rallying cry throughout the great struggle. Forth they rushed like a destroying whirlwind. Wherever a white soldier was met he was mercilessly slaughtered. Such Europeans as were driving or riding were shot down, men, women, and children, without mercy, without pity. And from the dens of infamy, and the slums, and the bazaars, poured a stream of human beings pitiless as the fabled ghouls, and all bent on plundering and burning. As the moon rose it looked on an appallingly weird scene of horror and cruelty. The blazing bungalows of the English officers roared and hissed, and English women and English children, gashed and mutilated out of all recognition, lay dead in the streets. One of the first bungalows to be attacked was that of the colonel as he rode out to harangue his men. His wife fell, shot through the heart, as she tried to shield her child. Faithful to her trust, the old ayah endeavoured to carry the child off from its dead mother and place it in a place of safety, if there was such a place. But she was cut down with a sabre, and she and the sweet little girl were slashed to pieces. Then the house was looted and given to the flames.

Blanche Merton would have fallen a victim at that first outbreak of fury. But fearing the worst, she had not waited for the house to be attacked. She was moved by an impulse to die with her lover no less than to warn him and his comrades in Delhi, and, being a superb horsewoman, she rushed to the stables, having first seized the colonel's military cloak, which was hanging in the hall. With her own hands she saddled his favourite riding-horse, and, concealing her face with a black veil, she rode towards the river undetected, and having gained the highway beyond the Goomtee,[44] she gave her horse the rein.

That night was a night of horror in Meerut, the parallel for which could hardly be found in history. The whole town seemed to be a swirl-

---

43 A Muslim war cry. It appears that this was actually used as a contemporary commentator stated it showed the union of Hindus and Muslims against the British.
44 A settlement to the east of Meerut.

ing furnace of many-coloured flames. The air was sultry. There was not a breath of wind, and the stupendous column of smoke spread itself out over the doomed town like a funeral pall. The shrieks of horses and cattle as they were burned in their stables mingled with the gloating cries of the infuriated natives; while the roar of the musketry made itself heard above all, and proclaimed the carnage that was going on. Women and children and non-combatants cried to God for pity, and endeavoured to find shelter in the gardens, outhouses, stables, under the trees, but all without avail. The black demons searched them out, and shot them or hacked them to pieces. The streets were deluged with blood; the river ran red.

Many a heroic deed that has gone unrecorded was done that night by white men; and many a half-maddened mother, with a prayer on her lips, threw away her life in her fruitless endeavours to save the lives of her little ones.

But the scene of the story must shift. When the hellish work in Meerut had been finished the mutineers sped away to Delhi. But before they reached it the brave Blanche Merton had arrived. At such a pace had she ridden that her horse died soon after she had dismounted at Lieutenant Shelton's quarters, and she was so excited and so exhausted that she could scarcely speak. As soon as she got her voice she told them that mutiny had broken out in Meerut, and the English were being massacred. There was corroboration of her report in the flame-coloured sky away to the north-east where the bungalows were burning, but otherwise Shelton was disposed to think that her fears had led her to exaggerate the extent of the revolt. Glad he was to see her, and as he kissed her fondly he said:

'You are safe here, anyway, my darling, and I do not think there is any danger of the tide of mutiny flowing thus far.'

He was hopeful and sanguine, but it was different with others to whom the news was speedily communicated. They knew how weak the little force was in Delhi, and that they could offer but small resistance if the mutineers should get the upper hand in Meerut and attack Delhi.

The great magazine and fort, with its tremendous stores of war material, was no great distance from the palace; that superb home of the Moghul kings that lifted its proud domes and turrets above the Jumna. The entire place was under the charge of Willoughby, and he had with him two other lieutenants—officers of the Bengal Artillery, and six European conductors and commissariat sergeants, one of them being an Irishman named Scully. There were nine in all. Nine only to defend their precious charge! To us now it seems inconceivable that the authorities could have been so fatuous as to leave so important a place as Delhi unguarded. But so it was, save by a mere handful of men. Lieutenant Willoughby, however, was of the stuff that makes all Englishmen proud. Calling his little band together, he told them the news, and said that it was certain the mutineers would attempt a dash for the magazine, for they could do little without ammunition. But he added:

'We will hold the place, boys, against a host. The black devils may have a brief triumph in Meerut, and come here; but the garrison of Meerut, which is a strong one, will soon recover, and will send us succour; though, should the worst come to the worst, comrades, not a shell, not a gun, nor an ounce of powder, if we can help it, shall fall into the hands of the rebels, for we will blow the whole place into ruins, and find our graves beneath them.'

A tremendous cheer was the answer he received, and then the gallant band set to work to be prepared for whatever might happen. The outer gate was closed, and strongly barricaded. Guns were brought out and loaded with double charges of grape and canister, and placed in such a position that they commanded the approaches.

While these preparations were developing Shelton received orders to do all in his power to hold a house which had been used as a Government depot, and contained accoutrements and other stores, besides a number of rifles. He procured an ample supply of ammunition from the magazine, and he had with him a sergeant and a corporal. Blanche would have refused to have left him, even supposing he had wished it, but he knew there was nowhere he could send her to where she was likely to be safer than there. And so she insisted on being furnished with a revolver—which she had learned to use since her arrival in India—and she vowed that she would stand by his side to the death.

The morning sun was rising in a glory of crimson splendour when the mutineers, stained with blood and dust and grimed with powder, swarmed over the Jumna and clattered into Delhi. Under the windows of the palace they surged, and called for the king—that white-haired, treacherous old villain, who believed that his hour of triumph had struck, and that the house of Moghul would be restored to its ancient splendour. The rebels were admitted by the Mohammedan guard, and then they almost shook the wall with a thunderous shout of 'Glory to the Padishah and death to the feringhees!'

Swelled now by their comrades of the palace they swarmed into the town, cutting down every European they met, and a detachment rushed for the house held by Shelton and his sweetheart and his two other companions. The lower doors and windows had been barricaded; and from the upper windows a well-delivered fire checked for a moment the onrush of the mutineers. But it was only for a moment. Some of their number had gone down into the dust, but that only served to still further madden the survivors, who stormed the house, to be beaten back, however, once more by the defenders' fire. Recovering themselves, they fired a volley at the windows, and one of the bullets struck the corporal dead.

Shelton saw now that it would be impossible to hold the place for many minutes, and he turned with anxious gaze to the beloved woman at his side. Her face was pale as death, but she was calm, and in her hand she still grasped the smoking revolver. Every barrel was empty, and she had sent at least four of the rabble to their account.

'My beloved,' he exclaimed in a tone of despair, 'I fear that hope of saving you has passed.'

'Yes, darling,' she said, quietly. 'Hope for us in this world has gone; but we shall be united in the next. Load the revolver again.'

He quickly thrust a cartridge into each barrel, and returned it to her, and at the same moment he saw his brave and only remaining soldier companion go down, shot through the head. Then he kicked in the head of a barrel of powder he had taken the precaution to have brought up, and passing his arm round Blanche's waist he was about to fire his revolver into the powder, when he suddenly changed his mind, and said hurriedly:

'Darling, I believe we can escape and find safety in the fort.'

'Where you go, I will go,' she answered.

Hurriedly fixing a few feet of slow match to the powder barrel he lighted the loose end; then taking Blanche's hand they hurried down the stairs, revolvers in hand. They gained the back door, which led into the garden, and by almost superhuman effort they removed the barricading of the door and rushed out and cleared the garden before their escape was discovered. But at that moment there was a tremendous explosion, and the house they had just left crumbled to ruins. For some minutes the mutineers were scattered by the shock, and it seemed as if the brave Shelton and the equally brave Blanche would gain shelter. But they were seen, and a swarm of mounted soldiers sped after them. Placing Blanche against a wall Shelton stood in front of her, and emptied his revolver at the advancing horsemen, and two of their number pitched from their saddles, but the next moment the faithful lovers fell, clasped in each other's arms, and riddled with bullets. In life they had loved and hoped, and in death they were not divided; their hopes would become fruition in a better and a brighter world.

In the meantime how fared it with the brave defenders of the fort?

Baffled in their attempt to obtain possession of the house the mutineers rushed to the magazine with their rallying cry of 'Deen, deen!' Willoughby and his noble band were prepared for them. They had concentrated their nine-pounder guns, and behind them had piled up as much ammunition as they had had time to procure. A few yards away was a heap of powder, and a train carried from it into the magazine itself, where the heads had been knocked out of many of the barrels and the powder scattered, with loaded shells placed in it. There were tons of powder, shells, and explosives of all kinds; and when further defence was found to be impossible the train was to be fired.

While the howling troopers on horse and foot were speeding to the fort, mounted messengers were sent from the king to demand from Willoughby the surrender of the place.

'Back to your royal master, slaves,' was the haughty and defiant answer, 'and tell him to come himself and we will surrender the ruins, together with our corpses, to him.'

The messenger made known this defiant answer to the mutineers, who were now clamouring round in a surging, jostling mass, and a determined rush was made for the gate. But they fell back as a withering storm of grape shot tore through them. That storm was most destructive in its effects; but the soldiers and the rabble that had joined them from the slums and dens of the city were too strongly bent on slaying the Feringhees to allow themselves to be defeated by the slaughter of some of their number. So gathering themselves together again, they howled 'Deen, deen!' and made another rush, but once more they were hurled back by the blast of fire and shot.

Seldom in the annals of warfare has there been a more stubborn, more heroic, defence made by a handful of men against a host of trained soldiers than was made by Willoughby and his comrades; for, be it remembered that they were fighting regiments of soldiers who had been trained and drilled in the art of warfare by the English themselves, and, as often proved before and since, the sepoy makes almost as good a fighting-man as his white brother, although he perhaps lacks in that stubbornness and unconquerable determination which are peculiarly characteristic of the Englishman. But in the case we are dealing with the sepoys were stubborn enough. They knew, indeed, that it was death or victory with them. And they quite believed that if they could but obtain the immense accumulation of ammunition stored in the

Delhi arsenal, not only could they hold the city of the Moghuls against all the armies of England, but that they could actually conquer India. For it was big guns and shot and shell they wanted, and from nowhere else could they obtain them save Delhi. It was, therefore, their only hope, and it may safely be asserted that not one amongst them deemed it possible that the stores would not fall into their hands, as it was well known that only nine men held the fort. But what they did not know was that those nine men were unconquerable.

It is no disparagement of the rest to say that Willoughby, by his magnificent example, inspired the others to greater deeds of valour. When on the evening of the 1st of May, as he sat on the verandah of the colonel's bungalow at Meerut, he had stated that he would blow the magazine up rather than surrender it, he made no idle boast. But his belief was, as he and his noble companions worked the guns and kept the bowling foe at bay, that the necessity to destroy the magazine would not arise, since they would be able to hold out till succour reached them from Meerut. For not knowing the extent of the disaster which had overwhelmed that station, he naturally expected some portion of its strong garrison would immediately be despatched to Delhi's relief. But, alas! when the hoofs of the mutinous troopers' horses rung upon the bridge that spanned the Jumna before Delhi, they sounded the death-knell of every British resident in the city, with some three or four exceptions.

There is an expressive Hindostanee word, *lachar*, which means helpless and something more; and at this awful crisis in our Indian rule the English were certainly *lachar*. They might slay many of their foes, but they could not save their lives or property. Such as were soldiers knew that it was one of the risks attending their profession of arms that they might be called upon at any moment to fight for and lay down their lives. But it was hard, it was pitiable, it was maddening, that the clear women and sweet children should fall a prey to the brutal and tiger-like ferocity of the revolted soldiers, and there is no doubt that the thought of their loved ones nerved many an arm to fight with the heroism of desperate despair.

For five long hours did Willoughby keep the host at bay; and often and often during those dreadful hours did he rush to the bastion on the river face and turn his gaze in the direction of Meerut, hoping to see the succour he expected coming in the shape of a regiment of English soldiers speeding on with all the speed their chargers were capable of. But the plain was misty with dust and heat; and not a living thing was in sight beyond the river save some vultures that hovered lazily in the heated air as if waiting patiently for the feast they knew would soon be theirs.

And during those five hours the mutineers charged again and again at the gate which was so ably defended, but each time they recoiled, leaving a heap of their dead. No accurate record has come to us of the number of their slain on that awful day, but it has been computed at thousands, for mingling with the soldiers was an immense gathering of civilians who had armed themselves with all sorts of weapons, and poured forth to assist in massacring the English. But still the enormous number of their dead did not deter them. Indeed, the sight only served to frenzy them still more. Horses and men—soldiers and civilians—encumbered the ground, victims to the grape and canister belched forth by the nine-pounders. And the constantly accumulating heaps made it difficult for the living to reach the gate which they hoped to batter in. At last, however, they bethought themselves of ladders. The marvel is that they had not thought of them before. Scores of ladders were soon procured when once they had been suggested, and then with shouts and cries that rent the very air the mutineers began to swarm up the walls.

And now brave Willoughby felt that the supreme moment had come at last. Never had soldier more nobly, more devotedly, and more heroically done his duty. But he saw, alas! that his efforts were useless. For the last time he rushed to the bastion. One more look—a long, anxious look—over that great plain that was all a quiver with the fierce heat of the unchecked sun. But not a sign was there of the hoped-for succour. Meerut had failed them, and there was nothing left now but to die. Then the splendid hero went back to his guns.

'Comrades,' he said, 'we are abandoned to our fate. Meerut has not sent, perhaps could not send, us help. But though we are defeated we are not conquered. We have as soldiers done our duty, and defended to the last the stores committed to our care. Further defence is impossible, and there is but one more thing to do, and that is to die.'

He raised his sword as the prearranged sign, word was then passed by one of his lieutenants to Scully, who stood ready. Scully lit his match and fired the train.

There was an awful pause. The minarets and domes of the wonderful city glittered in the sunlight, and the face of heaven was without a cloud. Nature was peaceful and at rest; but men were striving to tear their fellow men to pieces, and there was a Babel of fierce, discordant cries. The walls of the fort were black with hundreds of soldiers and civilians who were struggling with each other as to who should be first to cut down the Englishmen. Between the sweltering crowds on the walls and the thousands below the scaling ladders formed a connecting link, and they were black, too, with the writhing masses of men trying to work their way up. Beyond the closely-wedged crowd that extended from the walls outwards for something like fifty yards was a fringe of rabble; the scouring of the gaols and the contributions of the places of infamy with which the city abounded. And in this fringe was a large percentage of women and young people of both sexes; though there wasn't one there but was athirst for the feringhees' blood. And when it was seen that the rebel sepoys had gained the summit of the surrounding walls of the fort there arose from thousands of lips an exultant roar, for it seemed that the Englishmen were at last in the power of the mob. But suddenly that roar ceased with a quick and paralysing accession of fear that struck the human mass dumb, for something had happened—a convulsion of nature, as it seemed. The sun was darkened; the firm earth rocked, and shook, and rose and fell, and concurrent with these things was a compact, sullen, solid boom, that expanded and stretched out as it were until it became a mighty and stupendous volume of sound. Where a few seconds before the walls had stood black with hundreds of fierce men on murder intent there was a heap of ruins; and all around not hundreds but thousands of human beings were hurled to the ground maimed, shattered, and slain. And of those who had presence of mind to turn and flee, some were overtaken and stricken senseless with flying masonry, masses of iron, or baulks of timbers; while others fell dead from fright, and others again went raving mad; and some rushed to the river and threw themselves in, desperate with despair, for it seemed as if their own god Shiva had turned upon his votaries and was bent on wiping them off the face of the earth. The effects of this great explosion were remarkable. The whole city was shaken. Ponderous houses reeled and tottered, and buildings miles away were rent and split. Every tree within a radius of a couple of hundred yards was blasted and withered. Huge masses of masonry were hurled high into the air. Heavy guns were tossed away as if they had been toys caught by a strong wind. The six feet walls of solid masonry were shattered to crumbling ruins, burying many hundreds of natives, while hundreds more were blown up into the air like wisps of straw. The destruction of the war material was complete. Not a pound of powder, not a shell, not a gun, remained for the natives to use against the white men. To that fact probably we owe our ultimate success over the rebels. For if all that ammunition and all those guns had fallen into the hands of the mutineers at that moment, there is no telling what they might have accomplished.

Willoughby had indeed nobly done his duty. To their disgrace, however, be it said, there were those at home—the fireside politicians, the little Englander and carpet-slipper travellers—who censured him for the act. But Englishmen at heart admire courage and devotion to duty. Generations yet unborn, when they read the pathetic story of Shelton and Blanche Merton, will draw a sigh of pity, while around the memory of Lieutenant George Willoughby will ever shine a halo of glory, and Englishmen will refer to him with a sense of swelling pride as the Hero of Delhi, who with fire and death helped to save India.

NOTE—Curiously enough Willoughby and a comrade, Lieutenant Forrest, escaped from the fiery blast that scattered such ruin and death around. Willoughby, however, was much burnt, and Forrest was severely wounded, having been shot in the arm. The brave Scully who fired the train must have been blown to atoms. It was estimated that 2,000 mutineers at least were killed by the explosion, and as many perhaps had been previously shot down by grape and canister which the heroic little garrison poured forth with such deadly effect.

IX
The Spectre of Rislip Abbey

[The particulars of this story have been supplied by a well-known Member of Parliament from his own experience. The story is told almost in his own words. He is the owner of a broad and fair estate in central England, and has gained an enviable reputation for his high intelligence, his administrative ability—which on more than one occasion has been of great advantage to his party—as well as for his princely hospitality.]

UP TO ABOUT TWENTY years ago I was a comparatively poor man, and had to supplement my income by literary work, which, being of a scientific character, had not a very wide market. However, at that time, I succeeded to a snug patrimony, which freed my mind at once from all anxiety about the future. I had been married for seventeen years, and had two daughters, Cynthia and Phyllis, aged thirteen and fifteen respectively. My wife was an invalid, and our medical attendant had frequently told me that her restoration to health depended to a large extent on her living in the country, and indulging in country pursuits. But want of adequate means had prevented our giving effect to this advice, for circumstances rendered it important that I should reside in London, and my wife resolutely refused to leave me. Consequently, we had been living in a modest flat, and made the best we could of its inconveniences and drawbacks.

It was not surprising, therefore, that one of my first cares as soon as I was in possession of my fortune was to seek for some suitable country residence. We were all fond of the country, and my tastes inclined to the life of a gentleman farmer. I therefore called one morning on my friend, the late Mr. George R——, the well-known West End auctioneer and estate agent. He had a connection all over Great Britain, and I knew that if anyone could find me the place I wanted he could. After we had chatted for some time, and I had made known my requirements, he began to discuss the pros and cons of several estates he had on his books, but against all there was some objection to urge as far as I was concerned, until at last he exclaimed with a chuckle:

'By Jove, I have it. Rislip Abbey, that's the place for you.' Then, calling his head clerk, he desired him to bring the printed particulars of Rislip, which were read out as follows:—

'Rislip—Containing about three thousand acres arable land, five hundred acres pasture, one thousand timber (mostly oak and beech), the rest park and ornamental grounds. The house is a quaint, old-fashioned, turreted mansion, believed to have been built about the end of the reign of Henry VIII. The place is without any historical interest. Most of the land lies well. The house stands high, and commands splendid views, but is in a dilapidated condition, not having had a tenant for the last thirty years. The property has been the subject of litigation, but the rightful ownership has now been determined.'

The foregoing were the crude particulars, so to speak, in outline, and having listened to them I questioned my friend further, and asked him if he had personally surveyed the property.

'I have,' he answered.

'And what is your opinion about it?'

'Well, at present it is a wilderness, and the house is well nigh a ruin. Chancery,[45] as you know, is like a blight and a curse—it ruins every property it has anything to do with, as well as breaks the hearts of men and women. Of course, the lawyers have done well while Rislip has been going to decay, and now the owners are too poor to spend any money on it, nor can they sell any portion of it for the next twenty-five years. But they would grant you a lease for that period for a merely nominal rent, and give you the option of purchase. It would want a good deal of money laid out on it in the first instance, but my opinion is you could soon bring the land under cultivation, and make it profitable. Anyway, go down and see the property. I'll go with you, if you like. You will soon see if it is likely to suit you, and, of course, you can get the ghost and all thrown in.'

'Ghost!' I exclaimed, with a laugh.

'Oh, yes. I understand there is a real, genuine ghost, according to local tradition. The yokels swear that the place is haunted. But I should say the only spirits you will find there are bats and owls.'

I laughed at the ghost idea. I was pleased to think myself a hardheaded man, and my disposition was to view most things from a severely critical and scientific point of view; while as for spiritualism, I had nothing but contempt for those who professed to believe in it.

Now, the result of my interview with my friend the auctioneer was that a week later we journeyed down to Rislip together, and spent three or four days in examining the estate. It was certainly not an exaggeration to call it a wilderness, while the house itself was crumbling to decay; but I saw at once the potentialities of the place, and as the situa-

---

45 The Court of Chancery would administer unclaimed estates.

tion of the house would have been hard to beat, while the rental asked was little more than nominal, I secured the refusal of the property for a fortnight. During that time I consulted my lawyers, took my wife and daughter down to Rislip, and as they confessed themselves charmed, and I found I could secure it almost on my own terms, I lost no time in closing, and at once proceeded to get estimates for putting the house in habitable condition.

As may be imagined, I was very busy for the next three months, and by means of a liberal expenditure and ample labour, a very different aspect was imparted to the erstwhile wilderness, and the house was ready for occupation by the early part of November. Though the prospect of moving at such a period wasn't very pleasant, we faced it boldly, and by the end of the month were comfortably installed in our new quarters. In carrying out the repairs and alterations in the house I had been careful not to interfere in any way with its structural arrangements, as its quaintness and rambling character appealed very forcibly to my antiquarian instincts. One of the features of the house was most certainly the dining-room. It was a room of really noble proportions, unusually lofty for a building of that date, with three straight windows on one side, and at one end a very deep bay, from which there was a view second to none in the country.

The floor, which had been laid with oak, was as level as a billiard table, and in a perfect state of preservation. The walls were all wainscoted from floor to ceiling, and as some of this had decayed, it had been found necessary to restore it during the process of renovating the house. In the course of this work the men discovered a sliding door so artfully let in as a panel that anyone unacquainted with its existence would never have found it out. Behind the sliding panel was a narrow passage, leading to a flight of stone steps that descended to a second passage, closed by a door. This door gave access to a short tunnel that had its exit in the grounds, near a lake of considerable dimensions.

Romantic no doubt as all this may seem, there was really nothing very remarkable in it, as very few country houses were built in Henry VIII's time, and, indeed, for long after his reign, without a secret passage, the object being to afford the occupants a means of escape in case of need. The contractor who carried out the work for me suggested that the passage should be blocked up. To this I would not give my consent, but insisted on its being left in its original state, and in this decision I was supported by my wife and daughters. I ought to add that running parallel with the dining-room, and communicating by a doorway, was another room of smaller dimensions, but so conveniently situated and well lighted that I at once appropriated it as a library, as I had a valuable collection of books.

By the middle of December we had quite settled down, and all felt charmed with our new home, then we began to send out invitations very freely to our friends and relatives for Christmas, as we were desirous of having a good house warming.

Of course, during the short time I had been in possession I had heard much gossip and gathered a good many interesting anecdotes about the property. The fact of its having at last changed hands aroused a great deal of interest and curiosity over a very extended area, for the history of Rislip was pretty well known, and the story of the Chancery suit and the ruin it had brought about had caused general regret, as it was regarded as a shame that so good a property should be allowed to run to waste. I found that there was a very curious belief that Rislip had its familiar spirit—in other words, that it was haunted. I tried to find out the foundation for this belief, but, as is usually the case, I was met with the reply—'Oh, I've never seen anything myself, but I've heard of people who have.'

When I tried to find out these people who, by common account, had had occular demonstration of the existence of disturbed spirits, I need scarcely say I failed. It is always so. Neither my wife nor I attached the slightest serious importance to the current stories. We were amused by them, and possibly there was just a tendency on our part to regard people who expressed belief in the supernatural as being far from what is generally termed 'strong minded,' to use a mild term.

But now, to come to the strangest part of my narrative. I had been dining one night with my family, and we had had a neighbouring gentleman and his wife as guests. They had departed, and my wife and the girls had retired. I had remained to indulge in a final cigar, and enjoy the comfort of the brightly burning fire and the warm room. Outside the weather was murky, cold, and dismal. My butler had been to inquire if I wished for anything more, and my wants having been attended to, he bade me good night and went to his room. After that I fell into a reverie. Possibly I may have dozed. Anyway, I was aroused to a sense of things mundane by a cold draught of air blowing upon me, and glancing round I saw, to my amazement, that the secret door or panel in the wall to which I have already alluded was wide open. Then I was still further amazed—I might almost say dumfounded—by *seeing a hand*, only a hand, slowly draw the panel into its place again.

It is almost impossible for me to describe the extraordinary sensation that crept over me. There was something so uncanny in the whole proceeding. Now, I have already said I was not a superstitious man, and I think I may also assert that I was by no means lacking in courage. Nevertheless, for the moment I was the prey to a feeling of absolute funk. Then suddenly I thought that a trick was being tried upon me, and anger got the better of my funk. I seized the poker from the fireplace, rushed to the panel, got it open with some little difficulty, and peered into the darkness, but saw nothing; listened intently, but heard nothing. Next I snatched a candle from the table and proceeded down the passage, but found no living thing, and the doors were properly fastened. Returning to the dining-room, I sat down to think, and came to the conclusion that I had been the victim of a trick of the brain, and laughed at my own folly. But when a quarter of an hour later I went upstairs to my bedroom I experienced an unaccountable and absolutely unusual feeling of nervousness. The next day my first impulse was to tell my wife of the remarkable incident of the night previous; my second to do nothing of the sort, but keep it a locked secret in my own breast. A week later my daughter Phyllis had been with me in the library. She was a clever shorthand writer, and had been taking some important letters down from my dictation. As the clock on the mantelpiece chimed out midnight I told her to cease work and go to her bed. She wished me good night, and trotted off.

A few minutes passed, then the door of the library was flung violently open, and Phyllis, half fainting, looking ghastly pale, and with a 'scared-to-death' appearance of face, rushed in and clung wildly to me.

'What's the matter, child; what's the matter?' I cried in alarm; but she remained speechless. Moments, perhaps minutes, slipped by, during which I kept urging her to speak. She found her voice at last sufficient to jerk out in a breathless way:

'Oh, pa, I've had such a fright. When I got up to the first landing such a strange-looking man was standing there. I was about to ask him what he was doing, when he raised his hand in a sort of warning way and disappeared.'

I laughed, but it wasn't a genuine laugh, and I pretended to speak lightly, as I said:

'My dear child, I've been overworking you and your poor tired brain has seen visions. Come, let me take you upstairs to your room. You must try and get a good night's rest. You will be all right to-morrow.'

She gave me a look that was full of meaning. She said with her eyes as plainly as possible, 'Don't try to turn it off in that way. I have seen what I have seen.' She had mastered her feelings by this time, and though she spoke no words, she went upstairs with me until we reached the first landing, which was lighted in the day time by a long stained glass window. Edging a little closer to me, she whispered, 'This was where I saw him.'

'Nonsense, nonsense,' I answered, though I was far from believing it was nonsense, but I wanted to reassure her. I escorted her to her door, saw that her lamp was burning, then kissed her good night and descended, and as I went down the last flight of stairs I turned suddenly, for I was sure I heard footsteps. And close behind me was a weird-looking man dressed in the costume of a gentleman of Charles II's reign. He appeared to be about sixty-five years of age. Long, grey, ringleted hair hung about his shoulders. His face wore an expression of awful anguish.

For a moment I experienced a shock, but I quickly recovered myself and tried to grasp him, but he was as unsubstantial as the air, and the uncanniness of the whole business made me involuntarily shrink back. Then he raised his hands, and drawing down the large lace collar from his neck, he bared his throat, showing me a tremendous gash that had severed the windpipe, and from which the blood seemed to pour in a stream. It was a fearsome sight, I must confess, and I had never before in the whole course of my existence experienced such an utterly 'gone' and helpless feeling as I did in the presence of that supernatural visitant, and before I had pulled myself together, as the saying is, the weird spectre raised his hand, pointed upward with an extended finger, and in an instant had disappeared.

I returned to my library and flung myself into a chair, and I asked myself seriously whether the incidents of the last quarter of an hour were not the result of some morbid condition of my own brain. That is to say, I was disposed to doubt whether my daughter had really rushed pale and fainting into the room, as I have described, or whether it wasn't a figment of my own imagination. But here let me say that I had always been regarded as an unimaginative person, with, as I have before said, a scientific mind, which required hard, stern facts to convince it. How was it then I had come to see visions?

I asked myself this question, and mentally argued the whole thing out, trying to explain away the vision; but, firstly, there were the mysterious hand and the sliding panel, and now here was a man of a bygone age who had horrified me by showing me his throat gashed, and rent, and bleeding.

I don't know really how long I sat revolving the problem in my brain, but I do know that I crept up to bed at last feeling terribly fagged mentally and physically.

I slept far beyond my usual hour the following morning. My family had already breakfasted, but Phyllis came and sat with me, and recounted her previous night's experiences. There was an unwonted paleness in her pretty face and a scared look in her eyes. I felt it wise not to say anything to her about what I myself had seen; but, moved by a sudden impulse, I said I was going up to London by the next train and would take her with me.

It was no unusual thing for me to be called away from home at a moment's notice, so that my wife was not surprised. Phyllis expressed her delight at going, and two hours later we were seated in the up express. On arriving at our destination, I quartered Phyllis at the house of my sister, while I went to a hotel where I was in the habit of staying when in town. The following day I called on an old and esteemed medical friend—a man not only eminent as a physician, but famous as an author of several erudite works dealing with all forms of mental disease. I detailed the experiences of myself and daughter to him, and he looked very grave and puzzled, but before venturing to express any opinion he said he would like to see Phyllis. So I drove off at once to my sister's, and took Phyllis back with me, and without entering into any particulars I simply remarked that I wanted the doctor to see her. She expressed surprise by her face, but remained silent. On arriving at the doctor's house I requested her to tell him what she had seen, which she did in a plain, intelligent way. My friend appeared more than ever puzzled, and, having sent Phyllis out of the room, he delivered himself somewhat as follows:

'Well, now, my dear fellow, the facts of the case are these. Both you and Phyllis are more impressionable than you imagine, and you have gone through a great deal of excitement lately in connection with your new quarters. Last night you overtaxed the girl's brain, and what she thought she saw was a pure fancy. Her sudden appearance in your room in a state of nervous agitation, her story, her manner, made a great impression on you, and what she told you she had seen suggested the same thing to you.'

'But how about the hand and the sliding panel?' I asked.

'The result also of a morbid condition of the mind,' he answered. 'Fancy, fancy, all fancy, my dear sir. Now you and Phyllis go and make a little journey somewhere. A trip to the South of France, a month at Monte Carlo, will do you all the good in the world.'

I left my friend's house far from satisfied. I knew he was sincere in his belief, but he was wrong in his diagnosis. Nevertheless, I began to think of carrying out his suggestion and visiting the Riviera. No doubt I should have done that if it hadn't been for the fact that three days later I received a telegram from home, summoning me back at once, as my wife had been taken ill.

I began to fear now that Rislip was to prove a curse instead of a blessing to me; and, depressed by an anxiety I had never known before, I caught the next train out. Phyllis, of course, accompanied me, and we reached Rislip about ten o'clock at night. I learnt that my wife had had a fit. The cause nobody knew, but she told me. She had been sitting in the dining-room alone, when she felt a draught as I had done. Then to her horror she saw a deathly-white hand sliding the panel back. Suddenly a quaintly dressed man, with a haggard, anguished face, appeared before her, and, baring his throat, displayed it gashed and bleeding as he had done to me. She was conscious of uttering a loud, shrill scream of terror. Then all was blank until she awoke to find a doctor attending her.

As she finished telling me her story, she expressed great anxiety lest her brain was giving way, and she only grew calm when I assured her that I had seen what she had seen, and that Phyllis had also met the ghostly man on the stairs. My medical friend's theory would not now hold water, because my wife had been ignorant of my own and Phyllis's experiences, so that she was not influenced by a recital which might have set up a morbid set of conditions in her own brain.

Up to this time I had always regarded spiritualism so-called as abominable quackery, and it always made me angry when I heard of the antics and silly pranks which the spirits called up at the *séances* of the professional humbugs indulged in. But now I myself had seen a spirit, my daughter had also seen it, and my wife had seen it. We all three claimed to be people of common sense, free from morbid taint, and not given to conjuring up bogeys out of every shadow that came in our path. And yet it seemed to me that the spirit that had made itself manifest unto us had behaved in a very idiotic way, for if it had a grievance why did it try to frighten us all to death? Of course, the matter was too serious to be pooh-poohed with a scornful laugh and a sceptical toss of the head. The statement of three persons, not quite fools, could not be ignored. I began to feel deeply interested in the psychological problem that was suggested to me, and after much cogitation I mentally asked myself whether the ghostly visitor had any particular reason for pointing upward. Anyway, I was prompted to try and find out, and made my way to the top of the house, where there was a range of garrets. Here I began to pry about in a very inquisitive way, and after long and patient searching for I knew not what, I chanced to strike a portion of the wall in a back garret with a stick I carried, and was rather astonished to find that it gave out a hollow sound. I rapped it again. The same sound; but a yard on either side and there was solidity.

I lost no time in getting the assistance of two of my men servants. I simply told them that I had accidentally discovered what I believed to be a door, and, prompted now more by curiosity than anything else, I, with their help, tore off the paper, then a lining of canvas, then more paper, till we got to some wood that had once been painted. Close examination revealed that it was a door, and not without considerable trouble we got it open, disclosing a deep recess. Lights were procured, and from out the recess we dragged a heavy mass of dusty and time-stained metal. It was apparently a bundle of lead rolled up. We unrolled it, and brought to light a quantity of human bones, including a singularly well preserved skull, to which a mass of hair still adhered.

What my feelings were I will not attempt to describe. Of course the servants were amazed. I sent them to their duties, again cautioning them to say nothing at present of our find. My next step was to lodge information with the county police, and in due course the inevitable coroner's inquiry was held, but elicited nothing beyond the medical opinion that the bones must have been where they were found for generations. Whose bones they were no one could even conjecture. Why they had been wrapped in lead, and hidden in the secret cupboard was no less inscrutable. The coroner's jury could return but one verdict. The remains were those of some person unknown, and how he had met his death it was impossible to say. The bones were ordered to be buried in consecrated ground, and with Christian burial, and that was done. At my own expense I placed a slab over the grave, bearing this line:

'Sacred to the memory of a stranger. Date of birth and death unknown.'

With the finding and burial of those bones the spectre of Rislip Abbey departed, and troubled us no more.

Now, the story I have told you is a true one. There is the independent testimony of my wife and daughter to corroborate mine. My theory is that in some far off time a brutal crime had been committed, and the murdered man's body had been rolled in a sheet of lead and thrust in the secret closet; but while the murderers could confine his body they could not confine his spirit. Though why, after so many generations had passed, I should have been selected to bring the matter to light I know not, and cannot even possibly suggest a theory, nor can the mystery of the crime be cleared up. Who the murdered man was, and why he was murdered, will never be known until the secrets of all hearts are revealed in the burning light of the Judgment Day.

X
The Cave of Blood

THE STORY OF A DOUBLE CRIME

O N THE SOUTH-WEST COAST of the Principality of Wales stands a romantic little village, inhabited chiefly by the poorer class of people, consisting of small farmers and oyster dredgers, whose estates are the wide ocean, and whose ploughs are the small craft in which they glide over its interminable fields in search of the treasures which they wring from its bosom. It is built on the very top of a hill, commanding on one side a view of an immense bay, and on the other of the peaceful green fields and valleys, cultivated by the greater number of its quiet inhabitants. At the period of this story distinctions were unknown in the village—every man was the equal of his neighbour.

But though rank and its unpolished distinctions were strange in the village, the superiority of talent was felt and acknowledged almost without a pause or a murmur. There was one who was as a king amongst them, by the mere force of a mightier spirit than those with whom he sojourned had been accustomed to feel among them. He was a dark and moody man—a stranger—evidently of a higher order than those around him, who had but a few months before, without any apparent object, settled among them. Where he came from no one knew. He was a mystery, and evidently knew how to keep his secrets to himself. He was not rich, but followed no occupation. He lived frugally, but quite alone, and his sole employments were to read during the day and wander out, unaccompanied, into the fields or by the beach during the night. He was a strange, silent, fearsome sort of man, with a certain uncanniness in his appearance that commanded respect no less than fear. It soon became a common belief that this man possessed miraculous powers, not only as a healer of human ailments, but as a prophet. It was, therefore, not to be wondered at that in that little community of simple fisher-folk he was looked up to as a superior being, who not only held the power of life and death in his hands, but was able to draw aside the veil that screened the future.

Sometimes he would relieve a suffering child or rheumatic old man by medicinal herbs, reprove idleness and drunkenness in the youth, and predict to all the good and evil consequences of their conduct. And in his success in some cases, his foresight in others, and his wisdom in all, won for him a high reputation among the cottagers, to which his taciturn habits contributed not a little, for, with the vulgar as with the educated, no talker was ever seriously taken for a magician, though a silent man is often decided to be a wise one.

There was but one person at all disposed to rebel against the despotic sovereignty which William Morgan—such was the name he chose to be known by—was silently establishing over the quiet village, and that was precisely the person most likely to effect a revolution. She was a beautiful young woman, the glory and boast of the village, who had been the favourite of, and to a certain degree educated by, the late lady of the manor; but the lady had died, and her *protégée*, with a full consciousness of her intellectual superiority, had returned to her native village, where she determined to have an empire of her own which no rival should dispute. She laughed at the girls and women folk who listened to the predictions of Morgan, and she refused her smiles to the young men who consulted him upon their affairs and their prospects; and as the beautiful Ruth was generally beloved, the silent Morgan was soon in danger of being abandoned by all save doting men and paralytic women, and feeling himself an outcast in the village.

But it was soon made clear that Morgan had no intention of allowing pretty Ruth to oust him from his position.

He had essayed to rule the village, and he was resolved to retain his hold over the people. He knew, too, that from another point of view this ascendency was necessary to his purposes, and as he had failed to establish it by wisdom and benevolence, he determined to try the effect of fear. The character of the people with whom he sojourned was admirably calculated to assist his projects. His predictions were now uttered more clearly, and his threats denounced in sterner tones and stronger and plainer words, and when he predicted that old William Williams, who had been stricken with the palsy, would die at the turn of the tide, three days from that on which he spoke, and that the light little boat of gay Griffy Morris, which sailed from the Bay on a bright winter's morning, would never again make the shore—the man died, and the storm arose, even as he said—men's hearts died within them, and they bowed down before his words, as if he had been their general fate and the individual destiny of each.

Ruth's beautiful face grew pale for a moment as she heard of these things; in the next her spirit returned, and she told some friend that she was going to Morgan to have her fortune told, and she would prove to every one that he was an impostor. She had no difficulty in getting up a party of young men and women to accompany her, and she set off for

Morgan's house with the avowed intention of 'unmasking and humiliating him.' It was rather remarkable, seeing that the man had never done her any harm, that she should have taken such a prejudice against him. When they reached his residence they made it very evident that they intended to insult him. They made jests at his expense, and rudely and satirically alluded to his professed powers of prophecy. Had Ruth been more observant and less self-conscious, she could not have failed to note that Morgan was far removed above the common-place, and was possessed of mental powers far above anyone else in the village. He was greatly annoyed by her insulting manner and intentional rudeness, but he concealed his feelings, though he silently resolved to humble her pride. 'I will make him tell my fortune,' she said. His credit was at stake; he must daunt his enemy, or surrender to her power; he foretold sorrows and joys to the listening throng, and he made one of the young men present and Ruth herself feel exceedingly uncomfortable by revealing a secret which they themselves thought no human soul knew beside themselves. Then for the first time Ruth began to think she had made a mistake, and had underrated her opponent. Nevertheless, her self-possession did not desert her, and in an easy, flippant manner, in which there was a challenge as well as a sneer, she bade him read her future. Morgan remained silent for some moments, and steadily gazed at her. He had a large book before him, which he opened, shut, opened again, and again looked sadly and fearfully upon her; she tried to smile, but felt startled—she knew not why; the bright, inquiring glance of her dark eye could not change Morgan's manner. Her smile could not melt, nor even temper, the hardness of his deep-seated malice; he again looked sternly, and then coldly uttered these slow, soul-withering words, 'Woman, you are doomed to be a murderess!' At first she sneered at his prediction, and then laughed at him; but with greater solemnity, and speaking as if he were inspired, he exclaimed, 'I tell you, Ruth, you will become a murderess! I see blood upon your hands and blood upon your face, and the black stain of awful guilt upon your immortal soul.'

Her arrogance was subdued, her haughty spirit overcome, and with something like a groan she hurried away. But from that day she found that she was a marked woman. The superstitious villagers shunned her, and she became, as it were, an outcast.

Abhorring Morgan, she yet felt drawn towards him, and while she sat by his side felt as if he alone could avert the evil destiny which he himself had foretold. With him only was she seen to smile; elsewhere, sad, silent, stern; it seemed as if she were ever occupied in nerving her mind for that which she had to do, and she grew melancholy and morbid.

But there were moments when her naturally strong spirit, not yet wholly subdued, struggled against her conviction, and endeavoured to find modes of averting her fate; it was in one of these, perhaps, that she gave her hand to a wooer, from a distant part of the country, a mariner, who either had not heard or did not regard the prediction, upon condition that he should remove her far from her native village to the home of his family and friends, for she sometimes felt as if the decree which had gone forth against her could not be fulfilled except upon the spot where she had heard it, and that her heart would be lighter if men's eyes would again look upon her in kindliness and she no longer sat beneath the glare of those that knew so well the secret of her soul. Thus thinking, she quitted the village with her husband; and the tormentor, who had poisoned her repose, soon after her departure, left the village as secretly and as suddenly as he had entered it.

But, though Ruth could depart from his corporeal presence, and look upon his cruel visage no more, yet the eye of her soul was fixed upon his shadow, and his airy form, the creation of her sorrow, still sat by her side; the blight that he had breathed upon her peace had withered her heart, and it was in vain that she sought to forget or banish the recollection from her brain. Men and women smiled upon her as before in the days of her joy, the friends of her husband welcomed her to their bosoms, but they could give no peace to her heart; she shrunk from their friendship, she shivered equally at their neglect, she dreaded any cause that might lead to that which, it had been said, she must do; nightly she sat alone and thought, she dwelt upon the characters of those around her, and shuddered that in some she saw violence and selfishness enough to cause injury, which she might be supposed to resent to blood. Against the use of actual violence she had disabled herself; she had never struck a blow—her small hand would have suffered injury in the attempt; she did not understand the use of fire-arms, she was ignorant of what were poisons, and a knife she never allowed herself, even for the most necessary purposes. How, then, could she slay? At times she took comfort from thoughts like these, and at others she was plunged in the darkness of despair.

Her husband went forth to and returned from the voyages which made up the avocation and felicity of his life, without noticing the deep-rooted sorrow of his wife. He was a common man, and of a common mind; his eye had not seen the awful beauty of her whom he had chosen; his spirit had not felt her power; and, if he had marked, he would not have understood her grief; so she ministered to him as a duty. She was a silent and obedient wife, but she saw him come home without joy, and witnessed his departure without regret; he neither added to nor diminished her sorrow. But destiny had one solitary blessing in store for the victim of its decrees—a child was born to the hapless Ruth, a lovely little girl soon slept upon her bosom, and, coming as it did, the one lone and lovely rosebud in her desolate garden, she welcomed it with a kindlier hope.

A few years went by unsoiled by the wretchedness which had marked the preceding; the joy of the mother softened the anguish of the condemned, and sometimes when she looked upon her daughter she ceased to despair; but destiny had not forgotten its claim, and soon its hand pressed heavily upon its victim; the giant ocean rolled over the body of her husband, poverty visited the cottage of the widow, and famine's gaunt figure was visible in the distance. Oppression came with these, arrears of rent were demanded, and the landlord was brutal in his anger and harsh in his language to the sufferer.

Thus goaded, she saw but one thing that could save her—she fled from her persecutor to the home of her youth, and, leading her little Rachel by the hand, threw herself into the arms of her people. They received her with distant kindness, and assured her that she should not want. In this they kept their promise, but it was all they did for Ruth and her daughter. A miserable subsistence was given to them, and that was embittered by distrust, and the knowledge that it was yielded unwillingly.

Among the villagers, although she was no longer shunned as formerly, her story was not forgotten. If it had been, her strange beauty, her sorrow-stamped face, the flashing of her eyes, her majestic stature and solemn movements, would have recalled it to their recollections. She was a marked being, and all believed (though each would have pitied her, had they not been afraid) that her evil destiny was not to be averted. They declared that she looked like one fated to do some dreadful deed. They saw she was not one of them, and though they did not directly avoid her, yet they never threw themselves in her way, and thus the hapless Ruth had ample leisure to contemplate and grieve over her fate. One night she sat alone in her little hovel, and, with many bitter ruminations, was watching the happy sleep of her child, who slumbered tranquilly on their only bed. Midnight had long passed, yet Ruth was not disposed to rest. She trimmed her dull light, and said mentally, 'Were I not poor such a temptation might not assail me, riches would procure me deference; but poverty, or the wrongs it brings, may drive me to this evil. Were I above want it would be less likely to be. Oh, my child, for your sake would I avoid this doom more than for mine own, for if it should bring death to me, what will it not bring to you?—infamy, agony, scorn.'

She wept aloud as she spoke, and scarcely seemed to notice the singularity (at that late hour) of someone without attempting to open the door. She heard, but the circumstance made little impression. She knew that as yet her doom was unfulfilled, and that, therefore, no danger could reach her. She was no coward at any time, but now despair had made her brave. She flung the door open, a stranger entered, without either alarming or disturbing her, and it was not till he had stood face to face with Ruth, and discovered his features to be those of William Morgan, that she sprung up from her seat and gazed wildly and earnestly upon him. He gave her no time to question.

'Ruth Tudor,' said he, 'behold I come to sue for your pity and mercy. I have embittered your existence, and doomed you to a terrible lot. What first was dictated by vengeance and malice became truth as I uttered it, for what I spoke I believed. Yet, take comfort, some of my predictions have failed, and why may not this one be false? In my own fate I have ever been deceived; perhaps I may be equally so in yours. In the meantime have pity upon him who was your enemy, but who, when his vengeance was uttered, instantly became your friend. I was poor, and your seem might have robbed me of subsistence in danger, and your contempt might have given me up. Beggared by some disastrous events, hunted by creditors, I fled from my wife and son because I could no longer bear to contemplate their suffering. I have sought fortune in many ways since we parted, and always has she eluded my grasp till last night, when she rather tempted than smiled upon me. At an idle fair I met the steward of this estate drunk and stupid, but loaded with gold. He travelled towards home alone. I could not, did not, wrestle with the fiend that possessed me, but hastened to overtake him in his lonely ride. Start not! No hair of his head was harmed by me. Of his gold I robbed him, but not of his life, though, had I been the greater villain, I should now be in less danger, since he saw and marked my person. Three hundred pounds is the result of my deed, but I must keep it now or die. Ruth, you, too, are poor and forsaken, but you are faithful and kind, and will not betray me to justice. Save me, and I will not enjoy my riches alone. You know all the caves in the rocks, those hideous hiding places, where no foot, save yours, has dared to tread. Conceal me in one of these till the pursuit be passed, and I will give you one half my wealth, and return with the other to gladden my wife and son.'

The hand of Ruth was already opened, and in imagination she grasped the wealth he promised. Oppression and poverty had somewhat clouded the nobleness, but not the fierceness of her spirit. She saw that riches would save her from wrath, perhaps from blood, and as the means to escape from so mighty an evil she was not unscrupulous respecting a lesser. Independently of this, she felt a great interest in the safety of Morgan. Her own fate seemed to hang upon his. She hid the ruffian in a cave which she had known from her youth, and supplied him with light and food.

There was a happiness now in the heart of Ruth, a joy in her thoughts as she sat all the long day upon the deserted settle of her wretched fireside, to which they had, for many years, been strangers. Many times during the past years of her sorrow she had thought of Morgan, and longed to look upon his face, and sit under his shadow, as one whose presence could preserve her from the evil fate which he himself had predicted. She had long since forgiven him his prophecy. She believed he had spoken truth, and this gave her a wild confidence in his power— a confidence that sometimes thought, 'If he can foreknow, can he not also avert?'

And she thought she would deserve his confidence, and support him in his suffering. She had concealed him in a deep dark cave, hewn far in the rock, to which she alone knew the entrance from the beach. There was another (if a huge aperture in the top of the rock might be so called) which, far from attempting to descend, the peasants and seekers for the culprit had scarcely dared to look into, so perpendicular, dark, and uncertain was the hideous descent into what justly appeared to them a bottomless abyss. They passed over his head in their search through the fields above, and before the mouth of his den upon the beach below, yet they left him in safety, though incertitude and fear.

It was less wonderful, the suspicionless conduct of the villagers towards Ruth, than the calm prudence with which she conducted all the details relating to her secret. Her poverty was well known, yet she daily procured a double portion of food, which was won by double labour. She toiled in the fields for the meed[46] of oaten cake and potatoes, or she dashed out in a crazy boat on the wide ocean, to win with the dredgers the spoils of the oyster beds that lie on its bosom. The daintier fare was for the unhappy guest, and daily did she wander among the rocks, when the tides were retiring, for the shellfish which they had

46 An archaic word for reward.

flung among the fissures in their retreat, which she bore, exhausted with fatigue, to her home, and which her lovely child, now rising into womanhood, prepared for the luxurious meal. It was wonderful, too, the settled prudence of the young girl, who made no comment about the food with which she was daily supplied. If she suspected the secret of her mother she respected it too much to allow others to discover that she did so.

Many sad hours did Ruth pass in that dark cave, where the man who had blighted her life lay in hiding; and many times, by conversing with him upon the subject of her destiny, did she seek to alleviate the pangs its recollection gave her. But the result of such discussions were by no means favourable to her hopes. Morgan had acknowledged that his threat had originated in malice, and that he intended to alarm and subdue, but not to the extent that he had effected. 'I know well,' said he, 'that disgrace alone would operate upon you as I wished, for I fore-saw you would glory in the thought of nobly sustaining misfortune. I meant to degrade you with the lowest. I meant to attribute to you what I now painfully experience to be the vilest of vices. I intended to tell you that you were destined to be a thief, but I could not utter the words I had intended, and I was struck with horror at those I heard involun-tarily proceeding from my lips. I would have recalled them, but I could not. I would have said, "Ruth, I did but jest," but there was something which seemed to withhold my speech and press upon my soul, and a dumb voice whispered in my ears, "As thou hast said shall this thing be." But take comfort, Ruth. My own fortunes have ever deceived me, and doubtlessly ever will, for I feel as if I should one day return to this cave, and make it my final home.'

He spoke solemnly, and wept; but his companion was unmoved as she looked on in wonder and contempt at his grief. 'You know not how to endure,' said she to him, 'and as soon as night shall again fall upon our mountains I will lead you forth to freedom. The danger of pursuit is now past. At midnight be ready for the journey, leave the cave, and ascend the rocks by the path I showed you, to the field in which its mouth is situated. Wait me there a few moments, and I will bring you a fleet horse, ready saddled for the journey, for which you must pay, since I must declare to the owner that I have sold it at a distance, and for more than its rated value.'

Midnight came, and Morgan waited with trembling anxiety for the welcome step of Ruth. At length he saw her, and hastily speaking as she descended the rock:

'You must be speedy in your movements,' said she. 'When you leave me your horse waits on the other side of this field, and I would have you hasten, lest something should betray your purpose. But, before you depart, there is an account to be settled between us. I have dared danger and privation for you, that the temptations of the poor may not assail me. Give me my reward, and go.'

Morgan pressed his leather bag containing his gold to his bosom, but answered nothing. He seemed to be studying some evasion, for he looked upon the ground, and there was trouble in the working of his lip. At length he said cautiously, 'I have it not with me. I buried it, lest it should betray me, in a field some miles distant. When I leave here I will dig it up, for I know the exact spot, and send you your portion as soon as I reach a place of safety.'

Ruth gave him a glance of scorn. She had detected his meanness, and smiled at his incapacity to deceive. 'What do you press to your bosom so earnestly,' she demanded. 'Surely you are not the wise man I deemed you, thus to defraud me. Your friend alone you might cheat, and safely; but I have been made wretched by you, guilty by you, and your life is in my power. I could, as you know, easily raise the village, and win half your wealth by giving you up to justice. But I prefer reward. Give me my due, therefore, and be gone.'

But Morgan knew too well the value of the metal of sin to yield one half of it to Ruth. He tried many miserable shifts and lies, and at last, baffled by the calm penetration of his antagonist, boldly avowed his intention of keeping all the spoil he had won with so much hazard. Ruth looked at him with withering contempt. 'Keep your gold,' she said. 'If it can thus harden hearts, I covet not its possession; but there is one thing you must do, and that before you move a foot. I have supported you with hard-earned industry—that I give you; more proud, it would seem, in bestowing than I could be in receiving from such as you. But the horse that is to bear you hence to-night I borrowed for a distant journey. I must return with it, or its value. Open your bag, pay me for it, and go.'

But Morgan seemed afraid to open his bag in the presence of her he had wronged. Ruth understood his fears; but, scorning vindication of her principles, contented herself with entreating him to be honest. 'Be more just to yourself and me,' she persisted, 'the debt of gratitude I pardon; but, I beseech you, leave me not to encounter the consequence of having stolen from my friend the animal which is his only means of subsistence. I pray you not to condemn me to scorn.'

It was of no avail that Ruth humbled herself to entreaties. Morgan answered not, and while she was yet speaking cast sidelong looks towards the spot where the horse was waiting, and seemed meditating whether he should not dart from Ruth and escape her entreaties and demands by dint of speed. Her stern eye detected this purpose, and, indignant at his baseness, and ashamed of her own degradation, she sprung suddenly towards him, made a desperate clutch at the leathern bag, and tore it from his grasp. He made an attempt to recover it, and a fierce struggle ensued, which drove them both back towards the yawning mouth of the cave from which he had just ascended to the world. On its very verge, on its very extreme edge, the demon who had so long ruled his spirit, now instigated him to mischief, and abandoned him to his natural brutality. He struck the unhappy Ruth a revengeful and tremendous blow. At that moment a horrible thought glanced like lightning through her soul. He was to her no longer what he had been. He was a robber, ruffian, liar—one whom to destroy was justice, and perhaps it was he——

'Villain!' she cried, 'you predicted that I was doomed to be a murderess; are you destined to be my victim?' She flung him from her with terrific force, as he stood close to the abyss, and the next instant heard him dash against its sides, as he was whirled headlong into the darkness.

It was an awful feeling, the next that passed over the soul of Ruth Tudor, as she stood alone in the pale, sorrowful moonlight, endeavouring to remember what had chanced. She gazed on the purse, on the chasm, wiped the drops of agony from her heated brow, and then, with a sudden pang of recollection, rushed down to the cavern. The light was still burning, as Morgan had left it, and served to show her the wretch extended helpless beneath the chasm. Though his body was crushed, the bones splintered, and his blood was on the cavern's sides, he was yet living, and raised his head to look upon her as she darkened the narrow entrance in her passage. He glared upon her with the visage of a demon, and spoke like a fiend in pain. 'You have murdered me!' he said, 'but I shall be avenged in all your life to come. Deem not that your doom is fulfilled, that the deed to which you are fated is done. In my dying hour I know, I feel, what is to come upon you. You are yet again to do a deed of blood!'

'Liar!' shrieked the infuriated victim.

'I tell you,' he gasped, 'your destiny is not yet fulfilled. You will yet commit another deed of horror. You will slay your own daughter. You are yet doomed to be a double murderess!'

She rushed to him, but he was dead.

Ruth Tudor stood for a moment by the corpse, blind, stupefied, deaf, and dumb. In the next she laughed aloud, till the cavern rang with her ghastly mirth, and many voices mingled with and answered it. But the voices scared her, and in an instant she became stolidly grave. She threw back her dark locks with an air of offended dignity, and walked forth majestically from the cave. She took the horse by his rein, and led him back to the stable. With the same unvarying calmness she entered her cottage, and listened to the quiet breathings of her sleeping daughter. She longed to approach her nearer, but some new and horrid fear restrained her, and held her in check. Suddenly, remembrance and reason returned, and she uttered a shriek so loud and shrill that her daughter sprung from her bed, and threw herself into her arms.

It was in vain that the gentle Rachel supplicated her mother to find rest in sleep.

'Not here,' she muttered, 'it must not be here; the deep cave and the hard rock, these shall be my resting place; and the bedfellow, lo! now he awaits my coming.' Then she would cry aloud, clasp her Rachel to her beating heart, and as suddenly, in horror, thrust her from it.

The next midnight beheld Ruth Tudor in the cave, seated upon a point of rock, at the head of the corpse, her chin resting upon her hands, gazing earnestly upon the distorted face. Decay had already begun its work, and Ruth sat there watching the progress of mortality, as if she intended that her stern eye should quicken and facilitate its operation. The next night also beheld her there, but the current of her thoughts had changed, and the dismal interval which had passed appeared to be forgotten. She stood with her basket of food.

'Will you not eat!' she demanded; 'arise, strengthen yourself for your journey; eat, eat, sleeper; will you never awaken? Look, here is the meat you love'; and as she raised his head and put the food to his lips the frail remnant of mortality remained dumb and rigid, and again she knew that he was dead.

It was evident to all that a shadow and a change was over the senses of Ruth; till this period she had been only wretched, but now madness was mingled with her grief. It was in no instance more apparent than in her conduct towards her beloved child; indulgent to all her wishes, ministering to all her wants with a liberal hand, till men wondered from whence she derived the means of indulgence, she yet seized every opportunity to send her from her presence. The gentle-hearted Rachel wept at her conduct, yet did not complain, for she believed it the effect of the disease that had for so many years been preying upon her soul. Ruth's nights were passed in roaming abroad, her days in the solitude of her hut; and even this became painful when the step of her child broke upon it. At length she signified that a relative of her husband had died and left her wealth, and that it would enable her to dispose of herself as she had long wished; so, leaving Rachel with her relatives, she retired to a hut upon a lonely heath, where she was less wretched, because there were none to observe her awful grief.

In many of her ravings she had frequently spoken darkly of her crime, and her nightly visits to the cave; and more frequently still she addressed some unseen thing, which she asserted was forever at her side. But few heard these horrors, and those who did called to mind the early prophecy and deemed them the workings of insanity in a fierce and imaginative mind. So thought also the beloved Rachel, who hastened daily to visit her mother, but not now alone, as formerly. A youth of the village was her companion and protector, one who had offered her worth and love, and whose gentle offers were not rejected. Ruth, with a hurried gladness, gave her consent, and a blessing to her child; and it was remarked that she received her daughter more kindly and detained her longer at the cottage when Evan was by her side than when she went to the gloomy heath alone. Rachel herself soon made this observation, and as she could depend upon the honesty and prudence of him she loved, she felt less fear at his being a frequent witness of her mother's terrific ravings. Thus all that human consolation was capable to afford was offered to the sufferer by her sympathizing children.

But the delirium of Ruth Tudor appeared to increase with every nightly visit to the secret cave of blood; some hideous shadow seemed to follow her steps in the darkness and sit by her side in the light. Sometimes she held strange parley with this creation of her frenzy, and at others smiled upon it in scornful silence; now her language was in the tones of entreaty, pity, and forgiveness; anon it was the burst of execration, curses, and scorn. To the gentle listeners her words were blasphemy; and, shuddering at her boldness, they deemed, in the simple holiness of their own hearts, that the Evil One was besetting her, and that religion alone could banish him. Possessed by this idea, Evan one day suddenly interrupted her tremendous denunciations upon her fate and him who, she said, stood over her to fulfil it, with imploring her to open the book which he held in his hand, and seek consolation from its words and its promises. She listened, and grew calm in a moment; with an awful smile she bade him open and read at the first place which should meet his eye: 'From that, the word of truth, as thou sayest, I shall know my fate; what is there written I will believe.' He opened the book and read:

' "Whither shall I go from Thy spirit, or whither shall I flee from Thy presence? If I go up into heaven, Thou art there; if I make my bed in hell, Thou art there; if I take the wings of the morning, and dwell in the uttermost parts of the sea, even there shall Thy hand lead me, and Thy right hand shall hold me." '

Ruth laid her hand upon the book. 'It is enough; its words are truth; it has said there is no hope, and I find comfort in my despair. I have already spoken thus in the secrecy of my heart, and I know that He will be obeyed; the unnamed sin must be——'

Evan knew not how to comfort, so he shut up his Bible and retired; and Rachel kissed the cheek of her mother as she bade her a tender good-night. Another month, and she was to be the bride of Evan, and she passed over the heath with a light step, for the thought of her bridal seemed to give joy to her mother. 'We shall all be happy then,' said the smiling girl, as the youth of her heart parted from her hand for the night; 'and heaven kindly grant that happiness may last.'

The time appointed for the marriage of Rachel Tudor and Evan Edwards had long passed away, and winter had set in with unusual sternness, even on that stormy coast, when, during a land tempest, on a dark November afternoon, a stranger to the country, journeying on foot, lost his way in endeavouring to find a short route to his destination, over stubble fields and meadow lands, by following the footmarks of those who had preceded him. The stranger was a young man, of a bright eye and a hardy look, and he went on buffeting the elements, and buffeted by them, without a thought of weariness or a single expression of impatience. Night descended upon him as he walked, and the snowstorm came down with unusual violence, as if to try the temper of his mind, a mind cultivated and enlightened, though cased in a frame accustomed to hardships, and veiled by a plain, almost rustic exterior. The storm roared loudly above him, the wind blowing tremendously, raising the new-fallen snow from the earth, which mingling with that which fell, raised a shroud about his head which bewildered and blinded the traveller, who, finding himself near some leafless brambles and a few clustered bushes of the mountain broom, took shelter under them to recover his senses and reconnoitre his position. 'This storm cannot last long,' he mused, 'and when it slackens I shall hope to find my way to shelter and comfort.' In this hope he was not mistaken. The tempest abated, and, starting once more on his journey, he saw some distance ahead what looked like a white-washed cottage, standing solitary and alone on the miserable heath which he was now traversing. Full of hope of a shelter from the storm, and lit onwards by a light that gleamed like a beacon from the cottage window, the stranger trod cheerily forwards, and in less than half an hour arrived at the white cottage, which, from the low wall of loose lime-stones by which it was surrounded, he judged to be, as he had already imagined, the humble residence of some poor tenant of the manor. He opened the little gate, and was proceeding to knock at the door, when his steps were arrested by a singular and unexpected sound. It was a choral burst of many voices, singing slowly and solemnly that magnificent dirge of the Church of England, the 104th Psalm. The stranger loved music, and the touching melody of that beautiful air had an instant effect upon his feelings. He lingered in solemn and silent admiration till the strains had ceased; he then knocked gently at the door, which was instantly and courteously opened to his inquiry.

On entering, he found himself in a cottage of a more respectable interior than from its outward appearance he had been led to expect; but he had little leisure or inclination for the survey of its effects, for his senses and imagination were immediately and entirely occupied by the scene which presented itself on his entrance. In the centre of the room into which he had been so readily admitted stood, on its trestles, an open coffin; lights were at its head and foot, and on each side sat many persons of both sexes, who appeared to be engaged in the customary ceremony of watching the corpse previous to its interment in the morning. There were many who appeared to the stranger to be watchers, but there were but two who, in his eye, bore the appearance of mourners, and they had faces of grief which spoke too plainly of the anguish that was reigning within. At the foot of the coffin was a pale youth just blooming into manhood, who covered his eyes with trembling fingers that ill-concealed the tears which trickled down his wan cheeks; the other—but why should we again describe that still unbowed and lofty form? The awful marble brow upon which the stranger gazed was that of Ruth Tudor.

There was much whispering and quiet talk among the people while refreshments were handed to them; and so little curiosity was excited by the appearance of the traveller that he naturally concluded that it must be no common loss that could deaden a feeling usually so intense in the bosoms of Welsh peasants. He was even checked from an attempt to question; but one man—he who had given him admittance, and seemed to possess authority in the circle—informed the traveller that he would answer his questions when the guests should depart, but till then he must keep silence. The traveller endeavoured to obey, and sat down in quiet contemplation of the figure who most interested his attention, and who sat at the coffin's head. Ruth Tudor spoke nothing, nor did she appear to heed aught of the business that was passing around her. Absorbed by reflection, her eyes were generally cast to the ground; but when they were raised, the traveller looked in vain for that expression of grief which had struck him so forcibly on his entrance; there was something wonderfully strange in the character of her perfect features. Could he have found words for his thoughts, and might have been permitted the expression, he would have called it triumphant despair, so deeply agonized, so proudly stern, looked the mourner who sat by the dead.

The interest which the traveller took in the scene became more intense the longer he gazed upon its action; unable to resist the anxiety which had begun to prey upon his spirit, he arose and walked towards the coffin, with the purpose of contemplating its occupant. A sad explanation was given, by its appearance, of the grief and the anguish he had witnessed. A beautiful girl was reposing in the narrow box, with a face as calm and lovely as if she was sleeping a deep and refreshing sleep, and the morning sun would again smile upon her awakening; salt, the emblem of an immortal soul, was placed upon her breast; and in her pale and perishing fingers a branch of living flowers were struggling for life in the grasp of death, and diffusing their sweet and gracious fragrance over the cold odour of mortality. These images, so opposite, yet so alike, affected the spirit of the gazer, and he almost wept as he continued looking upon them, till he was aroused from his trance by the strange conduct of Ruth Tudor, who had caught a glimpse of his face as be bent in sorrow over the coffin. She sprang up from her seat, and, darting at him a terrible glance of recognition, pointed down to the corpse, and then, with a hollow burst of frantic laughter, shouted:

'Behold, you double-dyed liar!'

The startled stranger was relieved from the necessity of speaking by some one taking his arm and gently leading him to the farther end of the cottage. The eyes of Ruth followed him, and it was not till he had done violence to himself in turning from her to his conductor that he could escape their singular fascination. When he did so, he beheld a venerable man, the pastor of a distant village, who had come that night to speak comfort to the mourners, and perform the last sad duty to the dead on the morrow.

'Be not alarmed at what you have witnessed, my young friend,' said he; 'these ravings are not uncommon. This unhappy woman, at an early period of her life, gave ear to the miserable superstitions of her country, and a wretched pretender to wisdom predicted that she should become a shedder of blood. Madness has been the inevitable consequence in an ardent spirit, and in its ravings she dreams she has committed one sin, and is still tempted to add to it another.'

'You may say what you please, parson,' said the old man who had given admittance to the stranger, and who now, after dismissing all the guests save the youth, joined the talkers, and seated himself on the settle by their side. 'You may say what you please about madness and superstition, but I know Ruth Tudor was a fated woman, and the deed that was to be I believe she has done. Aye, aye, her madness is conscience; and if the deep sea and the jagged rocks could speak, they might tell us a tale of other things than that. But she is judged now; her only child is gone—her pretty Rachel. Poor Evan! he was her suitor. Ah! he little thought two months ago, when he was preparing for a gay bridal, that her slight sickness would end thus. He does not deserve it; but for her—God forgive me if I do her wrong, but I think it is the hand of God, and it lies heavy, as it should.' And the grey-haired old man hobbled away, satisfied that in thus thinking he was showing his zeal for virtue.

'Alas! that so white a head should acknowledge so hard a heart!' said the pastor. 'Ruth is condemned, according to his system, for committing that which a mightier hand compelled her to do. How harsh and misjudging is age! But we must not speak so loud,' continued he; 'for see, the youth Evan is retiring for the night, and the miserable mother has thrown herself on the floor to sleep. The sole domestic is rocking on her stool, and therefore I will do the honours of this poor cottage to you. There is a chamber above this containing the only bed in the hut; thither you may go and rest, for otherwise it will certainly be vacant to-night. I shall find a bed in the village, and Evan sleeps near you with some of the guests in the barn. But, before I go, if my question be not unwelcome and intrusive, tell me who you are, and whither you are bound.'

'I was ever somewhat of a subscriber to the old man's creed of fatalism,' said the stranger, smiling, 'and I believe I am more confirmed in it by the singular events of this day. My father was of a certain rank in society, but of selfish and disorderly habits. A course of extravagance and idleness was succeeded by difficulties and distress. Instead of exertion, he had recourse to flight, and left us to face the difficulties from which he shrunk. He was absent for years, while his family toiled and struggled with success. Suddenly we heard that he was concealed in this part of the coast. The cause which made that concealment necessary I forbear to mention; but he suddenly disappeared from the eyes of men, though we never could trace him beyond this part of the country. I have always believed that I should one day find my father, and have lately, though with difficulty, prevailed upon my mother to allow me to make my residence in this neighbourhood. But my search is at an end today. I believe that I have found my father. Roaming along the beach, I penetrated into several of those dark caverns. Through the fissures of one I discovered, in the interior, a light. Surprised, I penetrated to its concealment, and discovered a man sleeping on the ground. I advanced to awake him, and found but a fleshless skeleton, cased in tattered and decaying garments. He had probably met his death by accident, for exactly over the corpse I observed, at a great height, the daylight, as if streaming down from an aperture above. Thus the wretched man must have fallen, but how long since, or who had discovered his body, and left the light which I beheld, I knew not, though I cannot help cherishing a strong conviction that it was the body of William Morgan that I saw.'

'Who talks of William Morgan?' demanded a stern voice near the coffin, 'and of the cave where the outcast rots?' They turned quickly at the sound, and beheld Ruth Tudor standing up, as if she had been intently listening to the story.

'It was I who spoke,' said the stranger, gently, 'and I spoke of my father—of William Morgan. I am Owen, his son.'

'Son! Owen Morgan!' said the bewildered Ruth, passing her hand over her forehead, as if to enable her to recover the combination of these names. 'Why speak you of living things as pertaining to the dead? Father! He is father to nought save sin, and murder is his only begotten!'

She advanced to the traveller as she spoke, and again caught a view of his face. Again he saw the wild look of recognition, and an unearthly shriek followed the convulsive horror of her face. 'There! there!' she said, 'I knew it must be. Once before to-night have I beheld you. Yet what can your coming bode? Back with you, ruffian, for is not your dark work done!'

'Let us leave her,' said the good pastor, 'to the care of her attendant. 'Do not continue to meet her gaze. Your presence may increase, but cannot allay her malady. Go up to your bed and rest.'

He retired as he spoke, and Owen, in compliance with his wish, ascended the rickety stair which led to his chamber, after he had beheld Ruth Tudor quietly place herself in her seat at the open coffin's head. The room to which he mounted was not of the most cheering aspect, yet he felt he had often slept soundly in a worse. It was a gloomy, unfinished chamber, and the wind was whistling coldly and drearily through the uncovered rafters above his head. Like many of the cottages in that part of the country, it appeared to have grown old and ruinous before it had been finished, for the flooring was so crazy as scarcely to support the huge wooden bedstead, and in many instances the boards were entirely separated from each other; and in the centre, time, or the rot, had so completely devoured the larger half of one that through the gaping aperture Owen had an entire command of the room and the party below, looking down immediately above the coffin. Ruth was in the same attitude as when he left her. Owen threw himself upon his hard couch, and endeavoured to compose himself to rest for the night. His thoughts, however, still wandered to the events of the day, and he felt there was some strange connection between the scene he had just witnessed and the darker one of the secret cave. He grew restless, and watched, and amidst the tossings of impatient anxiety fatigue overpowered him, and he sunk into a perturbed and heated sleep. His slumber was broken by dreams that might well be the shadows of his waking reveries. He was alone—as in reality—upon his humble bed, when imagination brought to his ear the sound of many voices again singing the slow and monotonous psalm. It was interrupted by the outcries of some unseen things who attempted to enter his chamber, and, amid yells of fear and execrations of anger, bade him 'Arise, and come forth, and aid.' Then the coffined form which slept so quietly below stood by his side, and, in beseeching accents, bade him 'Arise and save her.' In his sleep he attempted to spring up, but a horrid fear restrained him, a fear that he should be too late. Then he crouched like a coward beneath his coverings, to hide from the reproaches of the spectre, while shouts of laughter and shrieks of agony were poured like a tempest around him. He sprung from his bed, and awoke.

It was some moments before he could recover himself, or shake off the horror which had seized upon his soul. He listened, and with infinite satisfaction observed an unbroken silence throughout the house. He smiled at his own terrors, attributed them to the events of the day or the presence of the corpse, and determined not to look down into the lower room till he should be summoned thither in the morning. He walked to the casement, and peered through at the night. The clouds were many, black, and lowering, and the face of the sky looked angry, while the wind moaned with a strange and eerie sound. He turned from the window, with the intention of again trying to sleep, but the light from below attracted his eye, and he could not pass the aperture without taking one glance at the coffin and its lonely watcher.

Ruth was earnestly gazing at the lower end of the room upon something without the sight of Owen. His attention was next fixed upon the corpse, and he thought he had never seen any living thing so lovely; and so calm was the aspect of her repose that it more resembled a temporary suspension of the faculties than the eternal stupor of death. Her features were pale, but not distorted, and there was none of the livid hue of death in her beautiful mouth and lips; but the flowers in her hand gave stronger demonstration of the presence of the power before whose potency their little strength was fading—drooping with a mortal sickness, they bowed down their heads in submission, as one by one they dropped from her pale and perishing fingers. Owen gazed till he thought he saw the grasp of her hand relapse, and a convulsive smile pass over her cold and rigid features. He looked again. The eyelids shook and vibrated like the string of some fine-strung instrument; the hair rose, and the head cloth moved. He started up ashamed.

'Does the madness of this woman affect all who would sleep beneath her roof?' he thought. 'What is this that disturbs me, or am I yet in a dream? Hark!' he muttered aloud. 'What is that!'

It was the voice of Ruth. She had risen from her seat, and was standing near the coffin, apparently addressing some one who stood at the lower end of the room.

'To what purpose is your coming now!' she asked in a low and melancholy voice, 'and at what do you laugh and gibe? Lo! behold. She is here, and the sin you know of cannot be. How can I take the life which another has already withdrawn? Go, go, hence, to your cave of night, for this is no place of safety for you.' Her thoughts now took another turn. She seemed as if trying to hide some one from the pursuit of others. 'Lie still! Lie still!' she whispered. 'Put out your light! So, so, they pass by, and do not see you. You are safe; good night, good night. Now will I home to sleep,' and she seated herself in her chair, as if composing her senses to rest.

Owen was again bewildered in the chaos of thought, but for the time he determined to subdue his imagination, and, throwing himself upon his bed, again gave himself up to sleep. But the images of his former dreams still haunted him, and their hideous phantasms were more powerfully renewed. Again he heard the solemn psalm of death, but unsung by mortals. It was pealed through earth up to the high heaven by myriads of the viewless and the mighty. Again he heard the execrations of millions for some unremembered sin, and the wrath and hatred of a world was rushing upon him.

'Come forth! Come forth!' was the cry, and amid yells and howls they were darting upon him, when the pale form of the beautiful dead arose between them and shielded him from their malice. But he heard her say aloud:

'It is for this that thou wilt not save me. Arise, arise, and help!'

He sprang up as he was commanded. Sleeping or waking he never knew, but he started from his bed to look down into the chamber, as he heard the voice of Ruth loud in terrific denunciation. He looked. She was standing, uttering yells of madness and rage, and close to her was a well-known form of appalling recollection—his father, as he had seen him last. He darted to the door.

'I am mad!' said he. 'I am surely mad, or this is still a continuation of my dream.'

Some strange and unholy fascination drew him back again to the aperture, and he looked down once more. Ruth was still there, though alone.

But though no visible form stood by the maniac, some fiend had entered her soul and mastered her spirit. She had armed herself with an axe, and, shouting, 'Liar! liar! hence!' pursued an imaginary foe to the darker side of the cottage. Owen strove hard to trace her motions, but as she had retreated to the space occupied by his bed he could no longer see her, and his eyes involuntarily fastened themselves upon the coffin. There a new horror met them. The corpse had risen, and with wild and glaring eyes was watching the scene before her. Owen distrusted his senses till he heard the terrific voice of Ruth, as she marked the miracle he had witnessed.

'The fiend, the robber!' she yelled, 'it is he who hath entered the pure body of my child. Back to your cave of blood, you lost one! Back to your own dark hell!'

Owen flew to the door. It was too late. He heard the shriek, the blow. He rushed into the room, but only in time to hear the second blow, and see the cleft head of the hapless Rachel fall back upon its bloody pillow. His terrible cries brought in the sleepers from the barn, headed by the wretched Evan, and for a time the roar of the storm was drowned in the clamorous grief of those present. No one dared to approach the miserable Ruth, who now, in utter frenzy, strode round the room, brandishing, with diabolical laughter, the bloody axe. Then she broke into a wild song of triumph and fierce joy. All fell back, appalled with horror, and the wild screeching of the wind was like the exultant cry of the damned. Then an extraordinary thing happened—a blinding flash of lightning, as if the heavens themselves had burst into flame, illuminated every nook and cranny, and imparted an awful, ghastly, and weird effect to the dramatic scene. In a few seconds the lightning was followed by a terrific peal of thunder. The house seemed to rock to its foundations. The inmates were blinded and stunned, and, moved by some strange impulse, they all fell upon their knees and murmured a prayer. Presently, as their self-possession returned, they rose one by one, and then a feeling of unutterable horror held them spellbound. Ruth Tudor lay stretched upon the floor, half of her body under the coffin, her face distorted and horrible, while hanging half out of the coffin was the now dead body of her resuscitated daughter, a stream of hot blood flowing from an awful wound in the skull. Ruth Tudor was also stone dead, and in her hand she still grasped the axe with which she had battered out the life of her child, who had awakened from a trance to meet death at the hands of her maniac mother.

The predictions of William Morgan had been literally fulfilled.

XI

A Night of Horror

Bleak Hill Castle.

My dear old chum,—Before you leave England for the East I claim the redemption of a promise you made to me some time ago that you would give me the pleasure of a week or two of your company. Besides, as you may have already guessed, I have given up the folly of my bachelor days, and have taken unto myself the sweetest, dearest little woman that ever walked the face of the earth. We have been married just six months, and are as happy as the day is long. And then, this place is entirely after your own heart. It will excite all your artistic faculties, and appeal with irresistible force to your romantic nature. To call the building a castle is somewhat pretentious, but I believe it has been known as the Castle ever since it was built, more than two hundred years ago. Hester—need I say that Hester is my better half!—is just delighted with it, and if either of us was in the least degree superstitious, we might see or hear ghosts every hour of the day. Of course, as becomes a castle, we have a haunted room, though my own impression is that it is haunted by nothing more fearsome than rats. Anyway, it is such a picturesque, curious sort of chamber that if it hasn't a ghost it ought to have. But I have no doubt, old chap, that you will make one of us, for, as I remember, you have always had a love for the eerie and creepy, and you cannot forget how angry you used to get with me sometimes for chaffing you about your avowed belief in the occult and supernatural, and what you were pleased to term the 'unexplainable phenomena of psychomancy.' [47] However, it is possible you have got over some of the errors of your youth; but whether or not, come down, dear boy, and rest assured that you will meet with the heartiest of welcomes.

Your old pal,
DICK DIRCKMAN.

❧

THE ABOVE LETTER WAS from my old friend and college chum, who, having inherited a substantial fortune, and being passionately fond of the country and country pursuits, had thus the means of gratifying his tastes to their fullest bent. Although Dick and I were very differently constituted, we had always been greatly attached to each other. In the best sense of the term he was what is generally

---

47 Communicating with spirits.

called a hard-headed, practical man. He was fond of saying he never believed in anything he couldn't see, and even that which he could see he was not prepared to accept as truth without due investigation. In short, Dick was neither romantic, poetical, nor, I am afraid, artistic, in the literal sense. He preferred facts to fancies, and was possessed of what the world generally calls 'an unimpressionable nature.' For nearly four years I had lost sight of my friend, as I had been wandering about Europe as tutor and companion to a delicate young nobleman. His death had set me free; but I had no sooner returned to England than I was offered and accepted a lucrative appointment in the service of his Highness the Nyzam of Chundlepore, in northern India, and there was every probability of my being absent for a number of years.

On returning home I had written to Dick to the chambers he had formerly occupied, telling him of my appointment, and expressing a fear that unless we could snatch a day or two in town I might not be able to see him, as I had so many things to do. It was true I had promised that when opportunity occurred I should do myself the pleasure of accepting his oft-proffered hospitality, which I knew to be lavish and generous. I had not heard of his marriage; his letter gave me the first intimation of that fact, and I confess that when I got his missive I experienced some curiosity to know the kind of lady he had succeeded in captivating. I had always had an idea that Dick was cut out for a bachelor, for there was nothing of the ladies' man about him, and he used at one time to speak of the gentler sex with a certain levity and brusqueness of manner that by no means found favour with the majority of his friends. And now Dick was actually married, and living in a remote region, where most town-bred people would die of ennui.

It will be gathered from the foregoing remarks that I did not hesitate about accepting Dick's cordial invitation. I determined to spare a few days at least of my somewhat limited time, and duly notified Dick to that effect, giving him the date of my departure from London, and the hour at which I should arrive at the station nearest to his residence.

Bleak Hill Castle was situated in one of the most picturesque parts of Wales; consequently, on the day appointed I found myself comfortably ensconced in a smoking carriage of a London and North-Western train. And towards the close of the day—the time of the year was May—I was the sole passenger to alight at the wayside station, where Dick awaited me with a smart dog-cart. His greeting was hearty and robust, and when his man had packed in my traps he gave the handsome little mare that drew the cart the reins, and we spanked along the country roads in rare style. Dick always prided himself on his knowledge of horseflesh, and with a sense of keen satisfaction he drew my attention to the points of the skittish little mare which bowled along as if we had been merely featherweights.

A drive of eight miles through the bracing Welsh air so sharpened our appetites that the smell of dinner was peculiarly welcome; and telling me to make a hurried toilet, as his cook would not risk her reputation by keeping a dinner waiting, Dick handed me over to the guidance of a natty[48] chambermaid. As it was dark when we arrived I had no opportunity of observing the external characteristics of Bleak Hill Castle; but there was nothing in the interior that suggested bleakness. Warmth, comfort, light, held forth promise of carnal delights.

Following my guide up a broad flight of stairs, and along a lofty and echoing corridor, I found myself in a large and comfortably-furnished bedroom. A bright wood fire burned upon the hearthstone, for although it was May the temperature was still very low on the Welsh hills. Hastily changing my clothes, I made my way to the dining-room, where Mrs. Dirckman emphasized the welcome her husband had already given me. She was an exceedingly pretty and rather delicate-looking little woman, in striking contrast to her great, bluff, burly husband. A few neighbours had been gathered together to meet me, and we sat down, a dozen all told, to a dinner that from a gastronomic point of view left nothing to be desired. The viands were appetizing, the wines perfect, and all the appointments were in perfect consonance with the good things that were placed before us.

It was perhaps natural, when the coffee and cigar stage had arrived, that conversation should turn upon our host's residence, by way of affording me—a stranger to the district—some information. Of course, the information was conveyed to me in a scrappy way, but I gathered in substance that Bleak Hill Castle had originally belonged to a Welsh family, which was chiefly distinguished by the extravagance and gambling propensities of its male members. It had gone through some exciting times, and numerous strange and startling stories had come to centre round it. There were stories of wrong, and shame, and death, and more than a suggestion of dark crimes. One of these stories turned upon the mysterious disappearance of the wife and daughter of a young scion of the house, whose career had been somewhat shady. His wife was considerably older than he, and it was generally supposed that he had married her for money. His daughter, a girl of about twelve,

---

48 Probably the older meaning of 'neat' rather than 'fashionable'.

was an epileptic patient, while the husband and father was a gloomy, disappointed man. Suddenly the wife and daughter disappeared. At first no surprise was felt; but, then, some curiosity was expressed to know where they had gone to; and curiosity led to wonderment, and wonderment to rumour—for people will gossip, especially in a country district. Of course, Mr. Greeta Jones, the husband, had to submit to much questioning as to where his wife and child were staying. But being sullen and morose of temperament he contented himself by brusquely and tersely saying, 'They had gone to London.' But as no one had seen them go, and no one had heard of their going, the statement was accepted as a perversion of fact. Nevertheless, incredible as it may seem, no one thought it worth his while to insist upon an investigation, and a few weeks later Mr. Greeta Jones himself went away—and to London, as was placed beyond doubt. For a long time Bleak Hill Castle was shut up, and throughout the country side it began to be whispered that sights and sounds had been seen and heard at the castle which were suggestive of things unnatural, and soon it became a crystallized belief in men's minds that the place was haunted.

On the principle of giving a dog a bad name you have only to couple ghosts with the name of an old country residence like this castle for it to fall into disfavour, and to be generally shunned. As might have been expected in such a region the castle *was* shunned; no tenant could be found for it. It was allowed to go to ruin, and for a long time was the haunt of smugglers. They were cleared out in the process of time, and at last hard-headed, practical Dick Dirckman heard of the place through a London agent, went down to see it, took a fancy to it, bought it for an old song, and, having taste and money, he soon converted the half ruined building into a country gentleman's home, and thither he carried his bride.

Such was the history of Bleak Hill Castle as I gathered it in outline during the post-prandial chat on that memorable evening.

On the following day I found the place all that my host had described it in his letter to me. Its situation was beautiful in the extreme; and there wasn't one of its windows that didn't command a magnificent view of landscape and sea. He and I rambled about the house, he evinced a keen delight in showing me every nook and corner, in expatiating on the beauties of the locality generally, and of the advantages of his dwelling-place in particular. Why he reserved taking me to the so-called haunted chamber until the last I never have known; but so it was; and as he threw open the heavy door and ushered me into the apartment he smiled ironically and remarked:

'Well, old man, this is the ghost's den; and as I consider that a country mansion of this kind should, in the interests of all tradition and of fiction writers, who, under the guise of truth, lie like Ananias, have its haunted room, I have let this place go untouched, except that I have made it a sort of lumber closet for some antique and mouldering old furniture which I picked up a bargain in Wardour Street, London. But I needn't tell you that I regard the ghost stories as rot.'

I did not reply to my friend at once, for the room absorbed my attention. It was unquestionably the largest of the bedrooms in the house, and, while in keeping with the rest of the house, had characteristics of its own. The walls were panelled with dark oak, the floor was oak, polished. There was a deep V-shaped bay, formed by an angle of the castle, and in each side of the bay was a diamond-paned window, and under each window an oak seat, which was also a chest with an ancient iron lock. A large wooden bedstead with massive hangings stood in one corner, and the rest of the furniture was of a very nondescript character, and calls for no special mention. In a word, the room was picturesque, and to me it at once suggested the *mise-en-scène*[49] for all sorts of dramatic situations of a weird and eerie character. I ought to add that there was a very large fireplace with a most capacious hearthstone, on which stood a pair of ponderous and rusty steel dogs. Finally, the window commanded superb views, and altogether my fancy was pleased, and my artistic susceptibilities appealed to in an irresistible manner, so that I replied to my friend thus:

'I like this room, Dick, awfully. Let me occupy it, will you?'

He laughed.

'Well, upon my word, you are an eccentric fellow to want to give up the comfortable den which I have assigned to you for this mouldy, draughty, dingy old lumber room. However'—here he shrugged his shoulders—'there is no accounting for tastes, and as this is liberty hall, my friends do as they like; so I'll tell the servants to put the bed in order, light a fire, and cart your traps from the other room.'

I was glad I had carried my point, for I frankly confess to having romantic tendencies. I was fond of old things, old stories and legends, old furniture, and anything that was removed above the dull level of commonplaceness. This room, in a certain sense, was unique, and I was charmed with it.

---

49 The scenery, props and so on for a theatre production.

When pretty little Mrs. Dirckman heard of the arrangements she said, with a laugh that did not conceal a certain nervousness, 'I am sorry you are going to sleep in that wretched room. It always makes me shudder, for it seems so uncomfortable. Besides, you know, although Dick laughs at me and calls me a little goose, I am inclined to believe there may be some foundation for the current stories. Anyway, I wouldn't sleep in the room for a crown of gold. I do hope you will be comfortable, and not be frightened to death or into insanity by gruesome apparitions.'

I hastened to assure my hostess that I should be comfortable enough, while as for apparitions, I was not likely to be frightened by them.

The rest of the day was spent in exploring the country round about, and after a *recherché*[50] dinner Dick and I played billiards until one o'clock, and then, having drained a final 'peg,' I retired to rest. When I reached the haunted chamber I found that much had been done to give an air of cheerfulness and comfort to the place. Some rugs had been laid about the floor, a modern chair or two introduced, a wood fire blazed on the earth. On a little 'occasional table' that stood near the fire was a silver jug, filled with hot water, and an antique decanter containing spirits, together with lemon and sugar, in case I wanted a final brew. I could not but feel grateful for my host and hostess's thoughtfulness, and, having donned my dressing-gown and slippers, I drew a chair within the radius of the wood fire's glow, and proceeded to fill my pipe for a few whiffs previous to tumbling into bed. This was a habit of mine—a habit of years and years of growth, and, while perhaps an objectionable one in some respects, it afforded me solace and conduced to restful sleep. So I lit my pipe, and fell to pondering and trying to see if I could draw any suggestiveness as to my future from the glowing embers. Suddenly a remarkable thing happened. My pipe was drawn gently from my lips and laid upon the table, and at the same moment I heard what seemed to me to be a sigh. For a moment or two I felt confused, and wondered whether I was awake or dreaming. But there was the pipe on the table, and I could have taken the most solemn oath that to the best of my belief it had been placed there by unseen hands.

My feelings, as may be imagined, were peculiar. It was the first time in my life that I had ever been the subject of a phenomenon which was capable of being attributed to supernatural agency. After a little reflection, and some reasoning with myself, however, I tried to believe that

---

50 Exotic.

my own senses had made a fool of me, and that in a half-somnolent and dreamy condition I had removed the pipe myself, and placed it on the table. Having come to this conclusion I divested myself of my clothing, extinguished the two tall candles, and jumped into bed. Although usually a good sleeper, I did not go to sleep at once, as was my wont, but lay thinking of many things, and mingling with my changing thoughts was a low, monotonous undertone—nature's symphony—of booming sea on the distant beach, and a bass piping—rising occasionally to a shrill and weird upper note—of the wind. From its situation the house was exposed to every wind that blew, hence its name 'Bleak Hill Castle,' and probably a south-east gale would have made itself felt to an uncomfortable degree in this room, which was in the south-east angle of the building. But now the booming sea and wind had a lullaby effect, and my nerves sinking into restful repose I fell asleep. How long I slept I do not know, and never shall know; but I awoke suddenly, and with a start, for it seemed as if a stream of ice-cold water was pouring over my face. With an impulse of indefinable alarm I sprang up in bed, and then a strange, awful, ghastly sight met my view.

I don't know that I could be described as a nervous man in any sense of the word. Indeed, I think I may claim to be freer from nerves than the average man, nor would my worst enemy, if he had a regard for truth, accuse me of lacking courage. And yet I confess here, frankly, that the sight I gazed upon appalled me. Yet was I fascinated with a horrible fascination, that rendered it impossible for me to turn my eyes away. I seemed bound by some strange weird spell. My limbs appeared to have grown rigid; there was a sense of burning in my eyes; my mouth was parched and dry; my tongue swollen, so it seemed. Of course, these were mere sensations, but they were sensations I never wish to experience again. They were sensations that tested my sanity. And the sight that held me in the thrall was truly calculated to test the nerves of the strongest.

There, in mid-air, between floor and ceiling, surrounded or made visible by a trembling, nebulous light, that was weird beyond the power of any words to describe, was the head and bust of a woman. The face was paralysed into an unutterably awful expression of stony horror; the long black hair was tangled and dishevelled, and the eyes appeared to be bulging from the head. But this was not all. Two ghostly hands were visible. The fingers of one were twined savagely in the black hair, and the other grasped a long-bladed knife, and with it hacked, and gashed, and tore, and stabbed at the bare white throat of the woman, and the blood gushed forth from the jagged wounds, reddening the spectre hand and flowing in one continuous stream to the oak floor, where I heard it drip, drip, drip until my brain seemed as if it would burst, and I felt as if I was going raving mad. Then I saw with my strained eyes the unmistakable sign of death pass over the woman's face; and next, the devilish hands flung the mangled remnants away, and I *heard* a low chuckle of satisfaction—heard, I say, and swear it, as plainly as I have ever heard anything in this world. The light had faded; the vision of crime and death had gone, and yet the spell held me. Although the night was cold, I believe I was bathed in perspiration. I think I tried to cry out—nay, I am sure I did—but no sound came from my burning, parched lips; my tongue refused utterance; it clove to the roof of my mouth. Could I have moved so much as a joint of my little finger, I could have broken the spell; at least, such was the idea that occupied my half-stunned brain. It was a nightmare of waking horror, and I shudder now, and shrink within myself as I recall it all. But the revelation—for revelation it was—had not yet reached its final stage. Out of the darkness was once more evolved a faint, phosphorescent glow, and in the midst of it appeared the dead body of a beautiful girl with the throat all gashed and bleeding, the red blood flowing in a crimson flood over her night-robe, which only partially concealed her young limbs; and the cruel, spectral bands, dyed with her blood, appeared again, and grasped her, and lifted her, and bore her along. Then that vision faded, and a third appeared. This time I seemed to be looking into a gloomy, damp, arched cave or cellar, and the horror that froze me was intensified as I saw the hands busy preparing a hole in the wall at one end of the cave; and presently they lifted two bodies—the body of the woman, and the body of the young girl—all gory and besmirched; and the hands crushed them into the hole in the wall, and then proceeded to brick them up.

All these things I saw as I have described them, and this I solemnly swear to be the truth as I hope for mercy at the Supreme Judgment.

It was a vision of crime; a vision of merciless, pitiless, damnable murder. How long it all lasted I don't know. Science has told us that dreams which seem to embrace a long series of years, last but seconds; and in the few moments of consciousness that remain to the drowning man his life's scroll is unrolled before his eyes. This vision of mine, therefore, may only have lasted seconds, but it seemed to me hours, years, nay, an eternity. With that final stage in the ghostly drama of blood and death, the spell was broken, and flinging my arms wildly about, I know that I uttered a great cry as I sprang up in bed.

'Have I been in the throes of a ghastly nightmare?' I asked myself.

Every detail of the horrific vision I recalled, and yet somehow it seemed to me that I had been the victim of a hideous nightmare. I felt ill; strangely ill. I was wet and clammy with perspiration, and nervous to a degree that I had never before experienced in my existence. Nevertheless, I noted everything distinctly. On the hearthstone there was still a mass of glowing red embers. I heard the distant booming of the sea, and round the house the wind moaned with a peculiar, eerie, creepy sound.

Suddenly I sprang from the bed, impelled thereto by an impulse I was bound to obey, and by the same impulse I was drawn towards the door. I laid my hand on the handle. I turned it, opened the door, and gazed into the long dark corridor. A sigh fell upon my ears. An unmistakable human sigh, in which was expressed an intensity of suffering and sorrow that thrilled me to the heart. I shrank back, and was about to close the door, when out of the darkness was evolved the glowing figure of a woman clad in blood-stained garments and with dishevelled hair. She turned her white corpse-like face towards me, and her eyes pleaded with a pleading that was irresistible, while she pointed the index finger of her left hand downwards, and then beckoned me. Then I followed whither she led. I could no more resist than the unrestrained needle can resist the attracting magnet. Clad only in my night apparel, and with bare feet and legs, I followed the spectre along the corridor, down the broad oak stairs, traversing another passage to the rear of the building until I found myself standing before a heavy barred door. At that moment the spectre vanished, and I retraced my steps like one who walked in a dream. I got back to my bedroom, but how I don't quite know; nor have I any recollection of getting into bed. Hours afterwards I awoke. It was broad daylight. The horror of the night came back to me with overwhelming force, and made me faint and ill. I managed, however, to struggle through with my toilet, and hurried from that haunted room. It was a beautifully fine morning. The sun was shining brightly, and the birds carolled blithely in every tree and bush. I strolled out on to the lawn, and paced up and down. I was strangely agitated, and asked myself over and over again if what I had seen or dreamed about had any significance.

Presently my host came out. He visibly started as he saw me.

'Hullo, old chap. What's the matter with you?' he exclaimed. 'You look jolly queer; as though you had been having a bad night of it.'

'I have had a bad night.'

His manner became more serious and grave.

'What—seen anything?'

'Yes.'

'The deuce! You don't mean it, really!'

'Indeed I do. I have gone through a night of horror such as I could not live through again. But let us have breakfast first, and then I will try and make you understand what I have suffered, and you shall judge for yourself whether any significance is to be attached to my dream, or whatever you like to call it.'

We walked, without speaking, into the breakfast room, where my charming hostess greeted me cordially; but she, like her husband, noticed my changed appearance, and expressed alarm and anxiety. I reassured her by saying I had had a rather restless night, and didn't feel particularly well, but that it was a mere passing ailment. I was unable to partake of much breakfast, and both my good friend and his wife again showed some anxiety, and pressed me to state the cause of my distress. As I could not see any good cause that was to be gained by conceal-ment, and even at the risk of being laughed at by my host, I recounted the experience I had gone through during the night of terror.

So far from my host showing any disposition to ridicule me, as I quite expected he would have done, he became unusually thoughtful, and presently said:

'Either this is a wild phantasy of your own brain, or there is some-thing in it. The door that the ghost of the woman led you to is situated on the top of a flight of stone steps, leading to a vault below the build-ing, which I have never used, and have never even had the curiosity to enter, though I did once go to the bottom of the steps; but the place was so exceedingly suggestive of a tomb that I mentally exclaimed, "I've no use for this dungeon," and so I shut it up, bolted and barred the door, and have never opened it since.'

I answered that the time had come when he must once more descend into that cellar or vault, whatever it was. He asked me if I would accom-pany him, and, of course, I said I would. So he summoned his head gar-dener, and after much searching about, the key of the door was found; but even then the door was only opened with difficulty, as lock and key alike were foul with rust.

As we descended the slimy, slippery stone steps, each of us carrying a candle, a rank, mouldy smell greeted us, and a cold noisome atmos-phere pervaded the place. The steps led into a huge vault, that appar-ently extended under the greater part of the building. The roof was arched, and was supported by brick pillars. The floor was the natural earth, and was soft and oozy. The miasma was almost overpowering, notwithstanding that there were ventilating slits in the wall in various places.

We proceeded to explore this vast cellar, and found that there was an air shaft which apparently communicated with the roof of the house; but it was choked with rubbish, old boxes, and the like. The gardener cleared this away, and then, looking up, we could see the blue sky overhead.

Continuing our exploration, we noted that in a recess formed by the angle of the walls was a quantity of bricks and mortar. Under other circumstances this would not, perhaps, have aroused our curiosity or suspicions. But in this instance it did; and we examined the wall thereabouts with painful interest, until the conviction was forced upon us that a space of over a yard in width, and extending from floor to roof, had recently been filled in. I was drawn towards the new brickwork by some subtle magic, some weird fascination. I examined it with an eager, critical, curious interest, and the thoughts that passed through my brain were reflected in the faces of my companions. We looked at each other, and each knew by some unexplainable instinct what was passing in his fellow's mind.

'It seems to me we are face to face with some mystery,' remarked Dick, solemnly. Indeed, throughout all the years I had known him I had never before seen him so serious. Usually his expression was that of good-humoured cynicism, but now he might have been a judge about to pronounce the doom of death on a red-handed sinner.

'Yes,' I answered, 'there is a mystery, unless I have been tricked by my own fancy.'

'Umph! it is strange,' muttered Dick to himself.

'Well, sir,' chimed in the gardener, 'you know there have been some precious queer stories going about for a long time. And before you come and took the place plenty of folks round about used to say they'd seen some uncanny sights. I never had no faith in them stories myself; but, after all, maybe there's truth in 'em.'

Dick picked up half a brick and began to tap the wall with it where the new work was, and the taps gave forth a hollow sound, quite different from the sound produced when the other parts of the wall were struck.

'I say, old chap,' exclaimed my host, with a sorry attempt at a smile, 'upon my word, I begin to experience a sort of uncanny kind of feeling. I'll be hanged if I am not getting as superstitious as you are.'

'You may call me superstitious if you like, but either I have seen what I have seen, or my senses have played the fool with me. Anyway, let us put it to the test.'

'How?'

'By breaking away some of that new brickwork.'

Dick laughed a laugh that wasn't a laugh, as he asked:

'What do you expect to find?' I hesitated what to say, and he added the answer himself—'Mouldering bones, if your ghostly visitor hasn't deceived you.'

'Mouldering bones!' I echoed involuntarily.

'Gardener, have you got a crowbar amongst your tools?' Dick asked.

'Yes, sir.'

'Go up and get it.'

The man obeyed the command.

'This is a strange sort of business altogether,' Dick continued, after glancing round the vast and gloomy cellar. 'But, upon my word, to tell you the truth, I'm half ashamed of myself for yielding to anything like superstition. It strikes me that you'll find you are the victim of a trick of the imagination, and that these bogey fancies of yours have placed us in rather a ridiculous position.'

In answer to this I could not possibly resist reminding Dick that even scientists admitted that there were certain phenomena—they called them 'natural phenomena'—that could not be accounted for by ordinary laws.

Dick shrugged his shoulders and remarked with assumed indifference:

'Perhaps—perhaps it is so.' He proceeded to fill his pipe with tobacco, and having lit it he smoked with a nervous energy quite unusual with him.

The gardener was only away about ten minutes, but it seemed infinitely longer. He brought both a pickaxe and a crowbar with him, and in obedience to his master's orders he commenced to hack at the wall. A brick was soon dislodged. Then the crowbar was inserted in the hole, and a mass prized out. From the opening came forth a sickening odour, so that we all drew back instinctively, and I am sure we all shuddered, and I saw the pipe fall from Dick's lips; but he snatched it up quickly and puffed at it vigorously until a cloud of smoke hung in the foetid and stagnant air. Then, picking up a candle from the ground, where it had been placed, he approached the hole, holding the candle in such a position that its rays were thrown into the opening. In a few moments he started back with an exclamation:

'My God! the ghost hasn't lied,' he said, and I noticed that his face paled. I peered into the hole and so did the gardener, and we both drew back with a start, for sure enough in that recess were decaying human remains.

'This awful business must be investigated,' said Dick. 'Come, let us go.'

We needed no second bidding. We were only too glad to quit that place of horror, and get into the fresh air and bright sunlight. We verily felt that we had come up out of a tomb, and we knew that once more the adage, 'Murder will out,' had proved true.

Half an hour later Dick and I were driving to the nearest town to lay information of the awful discovery we had made, and the subsequent search carried out by the police brought two skeletons to light. Critical medical examination left not the shadow of a doubt that they were the remains of a woman and a girl, and each had been brutally murdered. Of course it became necessary to hold an inquest, and the police set to work to collect evidence as to the identity of the bodies hidden in the recess in the wall.

Naturally all the stories which had been current for so many years throughout the country were revived, and the gossips were busy in retailing all they had heard, with many additions of their own, of course. But the chief topic was that of the strange disappearance of the wife and daughter of the once owner of the castle, Greeta Jones. This story had been touched upon the previous night, during the after dinner chat in my host's smoking room. Morgan, as was remembered, had gambled his fortune away, and married a lady much older than himself, who bore him a daughter who was subject to epileptic fits. When this girl was about twelve she and her mother disappeared from the neighbourhood, and, according to the husband's account, they had gone to London.

Then he left, and people troubled themselves no more about him and his belongings. A quarter of a century had passed since that period, and Bleak Hill Castle had gone through many vicissitudes until it fell into the hands of my friend Dick Dirckman. The more the history of Greeta Jones was gone into the more it was made clear that the remains which had been bricked up in the cellar were those of his wife and daughter. That the unfortunate girl and woman had been brutally and barbarously murdered there wasn't a doubt. The question was, who murdered them? After leaving Wales Greeta Jones—as was brought to light—led a wild life in London. One night, while in a state of intoxication, he was knocked down by a cab, and so seriously injured that he died while being carried to the hospital; and with him his secret, for could there be any reasonable doubt that, even if he was not the actual murderer, he had connived at the crime? But there was reason to believe that he killed his wife and child with his own hand, and that with the aid of a navvy, whose services he bought, he bricked the bodies up in the cellar. It was remembered that a navvy named Howell Williams had been in the habit of going to the castle frequently, and that suddenly he became possessed of what was, for him, a considerable sum of money. For several weeks he drank hard; then, being a single man, he packed up his few belongings and gave out that he was going to California, and all efforts to trace him failed.

So much for this ghastly crime. As to the circumstances that led to its discovery, it was curious that I should have been selected as the medium for bringing it to light. Why it should have been so I cannot and do not pretend to explain. I have recorded facts as they occurred; I leave others to solve the mystery.

It was not a matter for surprise that Mrs. Dirckman should have been deeply affected by the terrible discovery, and she declared to her husband that if she were to remain at the castle she would either go mad or die. And so poor Dick, who was devoted to his charming little wife, got out as soon as he could, and once more Bleak Hill Castle fell into neglect and ultimate ruin, until at last it was razed to the ground and modern buildings reared on its site. As for myself, that night of horror I endured under Dick's roof affected me to such an extent that my hair became prematurely grey, and even now, when I think of the agony I endured, I shudder with an indefinable sense of fear.

XII

The Astrologer

THE BLACK FOREST IS rich in story and tradition of a weird and thrilling kind, but nothing can excel in ghastly horror that which is told of the sole heir of the once illustrious family of Di Venoni. For generations this family had held tyrannical sway over the district. Their power was tremendous; their word was law; they ruled with a hand of iron, and the peasants were their slaves. They were exceedingly wealthy. Their men were said to be brave, their women beautiful. But, as seems to be the fate of all powerful families sooner or later, they began to decay. The fatuous habit of intermarrying produced the usual result, and the curse of insanity fell upon them. Many were the tragedies that this led to; and the time came at last when there was but one sole remaining male representative. This was a youth, handsome and well proportioned, but of eccentric habits, and occasionally displaying those fatal signs which were only too well known. Nevertheless, it was believed that Reginald Di Venoni might escape the curse. The best medical advice was sought, and the opinion was that the chances were strongly in his favour, and he would escape.

Reginald was brought up under the care of his mother, who had been left a widow for some years. She was a haughty, austere, proud, and disdainful lady, who guarded her son with peculiar jealousy; for on him, as she knew, depended the existence of her house. If he failed, then indeed the power of the Di Venonis would be gone, and the family would crumble to decay.

The lady and her son lived in a large castle, which for generations had been the Di Venoni's stronghold, and had withstood and repelled many a determined attack. It was a gloomy pile, distinguished for its strength rather than its beauty, although internally much had been done for the comfort of the occupants. The castle was situated in Suabia,[51] just on the borders of the forest. It stood on elevated ground, and anyone standing on the turrets commanded an immense panorama of great beauty.

At some little distance rose the ruins of the once powerful castle of Rudstein. This had originally been the home of the Di Venoni; but an evil genius seemed to enter into it, and for two or three generations such ill-luck attended the family that they decided to desert their

---

51 An archaic spelling of Swabia, a region in the south-west of present-day Germany.

ancestral home. It was unroofed, and left to wind and weather and the evil things that haunt the great forest. One tower was left standing only, as a sort of landmark. In the meantime the new castle had risen, and here the family installed themselves. Here many of them paid the debt of nature, and here the last male representative was born. Here in lonely grandeur the widowed mother lived, surrounded by a retinue of servants and retainers, and having for companion her one sister—a much younger woman, of great beauty and lively disposition. She was known as the Lady Hilda, and it was said that she and her sister were by no means always in accord. She protested against the gloomy surroundings in which the scion of the noble house was being brought up, and she urged Madame Di Venoni to keep more company, and relieve the castle, if possible, of the air of brooding melancholy which seemed to envelope it. But madame had her own notions. She wanted to mould her son after her own fashion. She was afraid of exposing him to evil influences. She would not depart from the traditions of her race.

One day, when Reginald was about six years of age, a traveller came to the castle and begged for hospitality. It had been a terrible day— wild, stormy, and wet. The traveller was a mysterious looking man, who seemed to have travelled far on foot, and was weary, wet, and hungry. He was a foreigner, and spoke but little German. He was invited into the servants' great hall, where food and drink were set before him, and as night approached he was conducted to a chamber situated on the top of a tower. That night a very violent storm, which had been threatening all day, burst over the country and did enormous damage. The thunder was terrific; the lightning incessant; the rain descended in a deluge. During the time that the storm was at its height a female servant, happening to glance from her window, which commanded a full view of the tower where the traveller was lodged, averred that she saw him walking about on the flat roof of the tower, and exposed to the full fury of the storm. She declared that he had more the appearance of a fiend than a man; that occasionally he broke into wild eldritch[52] laughter, and ever and anon raised his hands aloft, as if daring the heavens and defying the lightning.

Frightened almost into a fit, and yet fascinated, the woman watched him for some time, and at last saw him conversing with the arch enemy of man himself. The following morning the servant hurried to her mistress, and told her this silly story, the outcome of ignorance,

---

52 Weird or sinister.

superstition, and fear; and she insisted that the traveller who had been entertained and lodged in the castle was an evil being, who held converse with the devil, and that unless he were put to death some terrible calamity would result from his visit.

The lady, who was only a degree or two less superstitious than the menial, was much impressed, for she lived in a district where superstition was very rife. People travelled very little in those days, and credence was given to the wildest and most outrageous stories; while a belief in the power of certain persons to hold communication with Satan was very common, especially in the Black Forest district. Indeed, even at the present day, when railways and telegraphs encircle the globe, natives of some of the remote districts in the forest still cling to this belief, and have all sorts of charms to protect themselves against the malignant influences of witches, warlocks, and forest demons.

Madame Di Venoni, having listened to the wild and weird story of the servant, summoned her major-domo,[53] and bade him bring the stranger to her. This was done, and when the stranger was ushered into her presence he bowed low and reverentially to the mistress of the castle, who, however, regarded him with something like awe, for truly enough he was a striking and remarkable man, and calculated to unfavourably impress anyone who was superstitious. He had a dark, swarthy face. His eyes were intensely black and piercing, his hair like jet.

'Whence come you?' demanded the lady, imperiously.

'From Rhenish Prussia,'[54] answered the man proudly, and drawing himself up as if by gesture he would resent the manner in which she addressed him.

'And whither go you?'

'To Russia.'

'With what object?'

'In search of knowledge.'

Madame was incensed by his proud air, and eyeing him suspiciously, said:

'Unless I am mistaken, you are a man of evil nature, and in communication with the enemies of the human race.'

The man laughed.

---

53 Chief servant.

54 The Rhine Province of present-day Germany. It is the eastern-most part of Germany bordering Luxembourg, Belgium and the Netherlands.

'No, madame,' he answered, 'unless the stars that shine so gloriously in the heavens above are enemies of the human race, for it is from the stars I derive my knowledge.'

This apparently mysterious answer appalled the lady, for she felt no doubt now that the man was a fiend, and she was about to summon her attendants and have him expelled when her little son burst into the room, followed by his aunt. The child was laughing merrily, and had come to show his mother some grotesque heads he had been drawing on a sheet of paper. But, catching sight of the stranger, he was instantly silenced and clung to his aunt's skirts, while the Lady Hilda regarded the man with intense interest.

'Is that your son?' he asked.

'No,' answered Lady Hilda, 'I am a single woman. He is the son of my sister there, the Lady Di Venoni.'

The man turned to madame, and speaking in a strange, far-away voice, and as if inspired by some strange prophetic instinct, he said:

'That boy is the hope and prop of your race. But have a care, have a care, for a curse is upon him. Take him from this gloomy dwelling. Show him the bright and fair scenes of the earth. Teach him charity and tolerance. Strengthen his body and broaden his mind, and watch his footsteps lest he stray. His life hangs by a thread only.'

Madame was horrified. She no longer doubted that this audacious stranger was an evil thing whose death would be a benefit to all men. As she caught her son up in her arms she screamed, and when her attendants rushed in she ordered them to beat the stranger and set the dogs upon him. Folding his arms he stood like a rock, and gazed at her with scorn and defiance. But he was dragged from the apartment and roughly hurried down the great stairs to the courtyard, where a call was made to let the dogs loose, but at that instant the Lady Hilda appeared upon the scene, and interposed to save the stranger from the fury and violence of the menials. She peremptorily ordered them to release him, and when that was done she bade him depart at once, saying:

'Your safety, your life, depends upon the speed with which you leave this castle behind you. You have spoken well and truly, and your advice is the advice of a wise man; but ignorance and tradition are powerful factors; they are difficult to counteract.'

The man bent his knee, and taking Lady Hilda's hand, kissed it gracefully, saying:

'I thank you, lady, and do not doubt that this generous act of yours will go unrewarded; but, I pray you let me have a word with you out of earshot of these human wolves, who seem panting to rend me to pieces.'

Unmindful of the angry looks darted at her, and the menacing attitude of the menials, she retired for a moment or two to a corner of the courtyard with the stranger, who, availing himself of the opportunity, said:

'Have you the courage to meet me alone in the forest, in order that I may give you some information!'

'Yes.'

'Good. Meet me, then, to-night at the tower of the ruins of Rudstein, as the moon rises. No harm shall befall you, but good will come out of it.'

She pledged herself to meet him. Then she ordered the gates to be thrown open, and the man departed, followed by the jeers and taunts of the people. Lady Hilda turned furiously upon them and upbraided them for their cowardice in attacking a defenceless man. She was not a favourite with them, but she had power, and they were silenced.

That night, as the moon was rising, Lady Hilda slipped out of the castle by a secret door, and hastily made her way to the ruins of Rudstein, where the stranger was waiting for her. For two hours they talked together, and, loving her nephew as she did, she anxiously inquired about his future.

'His hope lies in separating him from his mother,' said the stranger. 'It may seem unnatural and cruel, but she is too strongly influenced in the traditions of her race to see that the boy's welfare depends on every means being taken to save him from the curse of his ancestors.'

'But how know you all this?' she answered, somewhat awed, and yet recognizing the soundness of his advice.

'I read it in the stars,' he answered mysteriously. 'They are wondrous books in which the past and the future of men can be read for those who have eyes to see.'

Many more questions were asked and answered, and Lady Hilda returned to the castle deeply impressed by the strange man's manner. Again and again she visited him, and his influence over her became all-powerful. Of course, these visits were secret ones, and she kept her own counsel. The stranger took up his abode in the tower, where there was no fear of his being disturbed, for people had a dread of the ruins, as they said they were haunted. Lady Hilda procured him books and other things that he said he wanted, and she kept him supplied with food and money. During the time that this was taking place she was urging her sister to quit the castle, retire to the capital, and there bring up her son in the shadow of the court. But this the mother strenuously refused to do, while the ill-feeling between her and her sister increased. At last Lady Hilda disappeared, and with her nephew. She was ultimately traced to Cologne after some months' absence, and she and the boy were brought back. Within a week of her return she was found dead in her bed. She had been poisoned.

The burial of a dead Di Venoni was invariably an imposing sight, and there was no exception in Lady Hilda's case. None of the mummery and pomp and ceremony were omitted, and for three days the body lay in state in the great entrance hall, and those who were entrusted with watching the corpse at night averred that one night as the great bell of the castle was tolling the solemn midnight hours a peculiar dark-eyed man suddenly appeared. There was something so weird and strange in his appearance that they were dumbfounded with horror, and their horror was increased when they saw him lift the shrouded corpse from its coffin, press it to his breast, fondle it and kiss it, and lavish upon it all the manifestations of extreme love and affection. At last he replaced the body and disappeared as mysteriously as he came. This wonderful story soon spread from lip to lip, with additions and exaggerations, and great was the consternation when, as the unhappy lady was being borne to the burial vault of the Di Venoni in the neighbouring church, the remarkable stranger was recognized amongst the crowd. He seemed bowed in sorrow, but when an attempt was made to seize him be avoided it, and, as everyone declared, made himself invisible.

Years passed away. Reginald Di Venoni grew into manhood. He had become a self-willed, passionate, gloomy man, who avoided his mother—now an old and decrepit woman—and made no secret of the fact that he disliked her. For a long time he had abandoned himself to the pleasures of the chase, and he tried to give some colour and tone to his gloomy and monotonous life by riotous living.

One evening he had been out hunting, and having got separated from his followers, he was returning alone when, on reaching the ruins of Rudstein, his horse shied, and Reginald beheld a weird looking old man standing amidst the ruins. His hair was white, and he had a long, grey beard.

'Who are you?' demanded Reginald boldly, for he was courageous and daring to recklessness at times.

'One who has watched you from childhood, and who would now speak into your ear words of wisdom. Make your horse fast to that tree and follow me.'

Curiosity, no less than some spell which he seemed incapable of resisting, prompted him to do the bidding of the stranger, who led the way up the mouldering stairs of the tower. On arriving at the top he threw open a door and revealed an apartment, the floor of which was strewn with books written in strange characters. In one corner stood a large vase engraved with the signs of the Zodiac, and encircled by mysterious letters. A huge telescope was placed in the centre of the room, and pointed through a small aperture in the ceiling. As the old man entered he took up an ebony wand from a table near and with it drew circles in the air, then, turning to Reginald, said in a solemn and warning voice:

'Man of ill-starred fortune, you were born under an unlucky planet, and your future is involved in darkness. But for the sake of her whom I loved, your aunt, the Lady Hilda, I would save you from your doom.'

Reginald laughed somewhat scornfully. Although he was not without superstition he placed little faith in the wild stories which he had heard from his childhood, and he was in the habit of saying that there was little that was called supernatural that could not be explained by natural laws.

'Ah, now I remember you,' he exclaimed. 'Years ago, when I was a child, you came to my mother's castle. You frightened me then, and strangely impressed me.'

'And yet why should that have been?' asked the stranger. 'I was a simple student of the occult, and was travelling the world in quest of knowledge. I had heard something of your family. I knew the curse that rested upon your house, and even then I would have tried to avert it; but your mother would have set her dogs upon me as she set her menials. To your aunt I owed my life, and my love for her grew. By my advice she took you away to the capital, but that act cost her her life. For her sake I would now save you. Since her death I have made long journeys into different countries, but have always been drawn back here by some influence I could not resist. My days, nay, my hours are numbered now; but before I join the sweet Lady Hilda I would render you a service.'

Reginald was far from impressed, and laughed again, saying:

'It is kind of you, but suppose I decline your good offices. Indeed, I am capable of taking care of myself and my fortunes; and, frankly, do not desire any service at the hands of a half-witted imposter, as I believe you to be. For myself, I have no belief either in God or Devil, therefore am not likely to be frightened by anything you can tell me or anything you can do.'

The old man's face assumed a look of sorrow and distress, and, speaking in a voice that betrayed his emotion, he said:

'Sad indeed it is that you should lack reverence. But have a care, have a care! I warn you against infidelity, and against those sins which, if indulged in, will bring you to ruin. Listen, I say, and take heed. The star of your destiny already wanes in the heavens, and the fortunes of the proud family of Venoni must decline with it. When the stars shine to-night look to the west, and you will see your planet, distinguishable by its unusual brilliancy. Look to it, I say, and let your thoughts wander from it to the God who rules the universe, and to Him put up a prayer of repentance and a cry for light and guidance. But should you see a dull red meteor shoot across the face of your star of nativity, it will be a sign that a deed of blood will be done, and you will perpetrate it.'

For a moment or two Reginald was really impressed by the awe-inspiring tone and manner of the old man. But once more he broke into a scornful laugh, and said:

'If this is all you have brought me here for, you do but waste my time, and I will depart.'

'Go!' answered the old man. 'You pronounce your doom. But let me exact a promise from you. On the night of the third day from now return to this apartment, and, if you find me dead, give my body Christian burial.'

'Yes; you shall have burial, as one of my dogs should,' Reginald replied. 'But since you are an unwelcome tenant in this ruined tower, which is part of my property, I shall give instructions to have you driven away. However, as you confess to having liked my aunt, whom I loved better than I loved my mother, I will see that you do not want. You shall be furnished with means sufficiently ample to enable you to live where your inclinations prompt, only you must quit the tower.'

'This is my living place, as it is to be my death place,' exclaimed the old man. 'And again I charge you, return here in three days, or fail at your peril.'

Reginald was exasperated. His temper was aroused now, as he thought the old man was defying him, and he strode hastily from the room, hurried down the stairs, and, flinging himself on his horse, galloped to the castle, with the intention of giving orders to eject the strange old man from the tower at once. But by the time he reached the courtyard he had changed his mind, and he could not help confessing to himself that some indefinable sense of fear restrained him. At any rate, he would let the old fellow remain where he was for a few days longer.

Three days passed away, and the night came. Then Reginald remembered the man's request; at first he had no intention of returning to the ruins. As the evening wore on, however, he felt impelled by a feeling of overmastering curiosity to pay another visit to the wizard, if wizard he was. So, without making known his intention to anyone, he armed himself with a formidable spear used in boar hunting, and, calling his faithful boarhound Wanga to his side, he set off for the tower.

The night was beautifully fine. The air was still, the sky was cloudless, the stars shone with extraordinary brilliancy. As Reginald pursued his way he looked to the west, and saw an unusually bright star, and knew, according to what the old man had told him, that it was the star of his nativity. He reached the ruins in about half an hour's rapid walking. A weird silence seemed to pervade the place. No light was visible. There wasn't a sign of the old man's existence. Reginald told Wanga to precede him up the mouldering stairs, but the great hound whined and drew back and crouched at his master's feet, and remained unmoved even by the vigorous kick which his master gave him. So, with a muttered oath, Reginald mounted the stairs alone. He pushed open the door and peered in. The window of the chamber was screened by a curtain, on a shelf burned a small lamp, at the table sat the old man. He was dressed in a suit of black velvet embroidered with gold, while round his waist was a massive belt of silver. He wore a skull-cap on his head, in his thin white hand he grasped the ebony rod, while the index finger of the right hand was fixed on a passage in an open book that lay on the table before him.

Reginald spoke to him. There was no answer, no movement. For the first time he felt a sense of fear. He spoke again, but still no answer came. He advanced a few steps into the room.

'Do you not see I am here?' he exclaimed.

The old man rose up, not as a living being, but like a mechanical figure. The face was the face of a corpse. The eyes were dull and glazed, but for an instant they lighted up as they turned upon the speaker, though the light faded immediately, and without a sound the old man sank to the floor, dead.

The situation was so weird, so ghastly, so dramatic, that Reginald's fears were now fully aroused, and with a suppressed moan of horror he turned and fled. The dog was still crouching at the foot of the stairs, but rose with a cry of joy as his master appeared. As Reginald left the ruins he glanced at the west. His star of nativity was burning brilliantly, but suddenly a dull red meteor shot across it, and remembering then the old man's prophecy, he was so overcome that he dropped senseless to the ground in a faint. In a few minutes, finding that something was wrong, the faithful hound rushed back to the castle, and by his howling and barking attracted attention. When the servants hurried to the great gateway he indicated that something was wrong; so torches were procured and the dog was followed to where his master still lay insensible on the ground. He was raised up and carried back, but when he came to his senses he was in a raging fever. He frequently became delirious, and in the hour of his lunacy was accustomed to talk of an evil spirit that had visited him in his slumbers. His mother was shocked at such evident symptoms of derangement. She remembered the fate of her husband, and implored Reginald, as the last descendant of a great house, to recruit his health and raise his spirits by travel. Only with great difficulty was he induced to quit the home of his infancy. The expostulations of his mother, however, at last prevailed, and he left the Castle di Venoni for the sunny land of Italy.

Months passed, and a constant succession of novelty had produced so beneficial an effect, that scarcely any traces remained of the mysterious malady which had so suddenly overtaken him. Occasionally, however, his mind was disturbed and gloomy, but a perpetual recurrence of amusement diverted the influence of past recollection, and rendered him at least as tranquil as it was in the power of his nature to permit. He continued for years abroad, during which time he wrote frequently to his mother, who still continued at the Castle di Venoni, and at last announced his intention of settling at Venice. He had remained but a few months in the city, when, at the gay period of the Carnival, he was introduced, as a foreign nobleman, to the beautiful daughter of the Doge.[55] She was amiable, accomplished, and endowed with every requisite to ensure permanent felicity. Reginald was charmed with her beauty, and infatuated with the excelling qualities of her mind. After a time he confessed his attachment, and was informed with a blush that the affection was mutual. Nothing, therefore, remained but application to the Doge, who was instantly addressed on the subject, and implored to consummate the felicity of the young couple. The request was attended with success, and the happiness of the lovers was complete.

On the day fixed for the wedding, a brilliant assemblage of beauty thronged the ducal palace of St. Mark. All Venice crowded to the festival, and, in the presence of the gayest noblemen of Italy, Reginald Count di Venoni received the hand of Marcelia, the envied daughter of

---

55 The elected head of state of the Venetian Republic.

the Doge. In the evening, a masqued festival was given at the palace; but the young couple, anxious to be alone, escaped from the scene of revelry, and hurried in a gondola to the old palace that had been prepared for their reception on the Grand Canal.

It was a fine moonlight night. The stars were reflected in the silver bosom of the Adriatic. The sounds of music and sweet voices singing, mellowed and softened by distance, were wafted to them on the gentle breeze. Venice seemed to glitter with tens of thousands of lamps, and the gondoliers, as they passed and repassed, uttered their peculiar cries.

The young couple felt supremely happy, and they directed their boatman to propel the boat leisurely along, that they might enjoy the enrapturing beauty of the scene; for Venice—the sea set jewel—had never looked more beautiful, and the languid air of the summer night begot a delicious sense of dreaminess and a forgetfulness of the pain and misery of the world.

As Reginald lay back with his head pillowed in the lap of his bride he happened to turn his eyes to the west, and there beheld his star of nativity as brilliant as ever. Instantly his mind reverted to that awful night when the old wizard died, and he remembered the dull red meteor, and the weird prophecy. He became so agitated that his wife was alarmed, and inquired the reason of it; but he only laughed, said it was merely a passing memory that disturbed him, and soon her kisses and caresses restored him to serenity.

The succeeding six months were uninterrupted by a single untoward incident. He passionately loved Marcelia, and was beloved in return. His rough, uncouth nature had been smoothed down and refined by his wife and the society in which he moved. He felt supremely happy, and though at times a remembrance of the awful night in the ruins of Rudstein disturbed him, he managed to shake off the influence, and find a soothing balm in the caresses of his young bride.

One day, however, there came to him an urgent message to repair to his birthplace without delay, as his mother lay at the point of death. Although he had never borne her any very strong affection, he felt it was his duty to obey the summons, and so in company with his wife he journeyed with all speed to the Black Forest.

On reaching the castle he found that his mother was already in the throes of death, and delirious; as soon as he entered her presence she rose up in her bed, without seeming to recognize him, and cursed him for being an unnatural and unfilial son. It was an awful scene, and affected Reginald in an appalling manner. Without recanting a word, or, indeed, noticing him in any way, she fell back on her pillow and expired.

For some days Reginald was prostrated, and when his gentle and loving wife tried to soothe and comfort him he repulsed her furiously, until she was broken-hearted. But when he recovered his senses he lavished caresses upon her, and gave every manifestation that he loved her devotedly. A few days later, however, he was wandering with Marcelia through a very picturesque and beautiful part of the forest, when they seated themselves on a bank overlooking a stream. For some little time Reginald remained absorbed in thought, then he began to pick up handfuls of earth and scatter them in the water, and, with a wild glare in his eyes, he mumbled:

'This is a hateful world. All is dust and vanity. Nothing brings joy, or contentment, or peace. I am the last of my race. Why seek longer to support a rotten fabric? My kindred have squandered their substance, and destroyed the vitality of the family. Let us follow my mother through the gates of death. Come, give me your hand, Marcelia, and we will die together.'

His wife was horribly alarmed, and used every endeavour to soothe him; presently he grew calmer, and rose and allowed her to lead him away. They continued to wander further afield, at his request, until night closed, and the stars were burning. Brilliant above all the rest shone the fatal western planet, the star of Reginald's nativity. He gazed at it for some time with horror, and pointed it out to the notice of Marcelia.

'The hand of heaven is in it!' he mentally exclaimed, 'and the proud fortunes of Venoni hasten to a close.' At this instant the ruined tower of Rudstein appeared in sight, with the moon shining fully upon it. 'It is the place,' resumed the maniac, 'where a deed of blood must be done, and I am fated to perpetrate it! But fear not, my poor girl,' he added, in a milder tone, while the tears sprang to his eyes, 'your husband cannot harm you; he may be wretched, but he never shall be guilty!' Although Marcelia was dreadfully alarmed she concealed her feelings as much as possible, and induced him to hurry back. When he reached the castle he looked ghastly ill, and, going to bed, sank into a sort of coma.

Night waned, morning dawned on the upland hills of the scenery, and with it came a renewal of Reginald's disorder. The day was stormy, and in unison with the troubled feeling of his mind. He rose with the dawn, and, without a word to anyone, went off into the forest, nor did he return until the evening. Distressed beyond measure at his absence, she waited in dread suspense for his return, and sat at her casement gazing across the vast expanse of forest, which the westering sun was now flooding with a crimson light. Suddenly her door flew open, and Reginald made his appearance. His eyes were red and seemed to blaze with the light of madness, while his whole frame was convulsed as if he suffered from agonizing spasms of pain.

'It was not a dream,' he exclaimed, 'I have seen her, and she has beckoned us to follow.'

'Seen her, seen who?' asked Marcelia, alarmed at his frenzy.

'My mother,' replied the maniac. 'Listen while I tell you the strange story. I thought, as I was wandering in the forest, a sylph[56] of heaven approached, and revealed the countenance of my mother. I flew to join her, but was withheld by a wizard, who pointed to the western star. On a sudden loud shrieks were heard, and the sylph assumed the guise of a demon. Her figure towered to an awful height, and she pointed in scornful derision to you; yes, to you, my wife. With rage she drew you towards me. I seized—I murdered you, and strange cries and groans filled the air. I heard the voice of the fiendish astrologer shouting as from a charnel house, "Your destiny is accomplished, and the victim may retire with honour." Then, I thought, the fair front of heaven was obscured, and thick gouts of clotted clammy blood showered down in torrents from the blackened clouds of the west. The star shot through the air, and—the phantom of my mother again beckoned me to follow.'

The maniac ceased, and rushed in agony from the apartment. Marcelia followed, and discovered him leaning in a trance against the wainscot of the library. With gentlest motion she drew his hand in hers, and led him into the open air. They rambled on, heedless of the gathering storm, until they discovered themselves at the base of the tower of Rudstein. Suddenly the maniac paused. A horrid thought seemed flashing across his brain, as with giant grasp he seized Marcelia in his arms, and bore her to the fatal apartment. In vain she shrieked for help, for pity. 'Dear Reginald, it is Marcelia who speaks, you cannot surely harm her.' He heard—he heeded not, nor once staid his steps till he reached the room of death. On a sudden his countenance lost its wildness, and assumed a more fearful, but composed look of determined madness. He advanced to the window, dragged away the rotting curtain, and gazed on the stormy face of heaven. Dark clouds flitted across the horizon, and thunder echoed in the distance. To the west the fatal star was still visible, but shone with sickly lustre. At this instant a flash of lightning illumined the whole apartment, and threw a broad red glare

56 A mythological air spirit.

upon a skeleton that mouldered upon the floor. Reginald observed it with affright, and remembered the unburied astrologer. He advanced to Marcelia, and, pointing to the rising moon, 'A dark cloud is sailing by,' he shudderingly exclaimed, 'but ere the full orb again shines forth you shall die; I will accompany you in death, and hand in hand will we pass into the presence of our people.'

The poor girl shrieked for pity, but her voice was lost in the angry ravings of the storm.

The cloud in the meantime sailed on—it approached—the moon was dimmed, darkened, and finally buried in its gloom. The maniac marked the hour, and rushed with a fearful cry towards his victim. With murderous resolution he grasped her throat, while the helpless hand and half strangled articulation implored his compassion. After one final struggle the hollow death rattle announced that life was extinct, and that the murderer held a corpse in his arms. An interval of reason now occurred, and on the partial restoration of his mind Reginald discovered himself the unconscious murderer of Marcelia. Madness—deepest madness again took possession of his faculties. He laughed—he shouted aloud with the unearthly yellings of a fiend, and in the raging violence of his delirium he rushed out, climbed to the summit of the tower, and hurled himself headlong from it.

In the morning the bodies of the young couple were discovered, and buried in the same tomb. The fatal ruin of Rudstein still exists, but is now commonly avoided as the residence of the spirits of the departed. Day by day it slowly crumbles to earth, and affords a shelter for the night raven or the wild things of the forests. Superstition has consecrated it to herself, and the tradition of the country has invested it with all the awful appendages of a charnel house. The wanderer who passes at nightfall shudders while he surveys its utter desolation, and exclaims as he travels on:

'Surely this is a spot where guilt may thrive in safety, or bigotry weave a spell to enthral her misguided votaries.'[57]

---

57 A votary is someone who has made a vow to dedicate themselves to religious service.

XIII
The Dance of the Dead

FOUNDED ON A WELL-KNOWN GERMAN LEGEND

NEISSE[58] IS A SMALL town in Silesia.[59] At the period of this story it lay somewhat out of the beaten track, and its inhabitants led a simple, primitive sort of life, although bickerings and wranglings, cheating and knavery were not altogether unknown among them. On the whole, however, they were a fairly virtuous people, and the town earned an enviable reputation for hospitality, in spite of the fact that the mayor was far from being hospitable himself, but he did not hesitate to dispense hospitality with a lavish hand when he could do so out of the town funds.

This mayor, whose name was Hertzstein, was an exceedingly proud and ambitious man. He had been born in very humble circumstances indeed, his father having been a charcoal burner; but Rupert Hertzstein was endowed with more than average intelligence, though even as a lad be displayed a grasping, covetous disposition that made him many youthful enemies. As he grew in years he by no means changed, but he managed to make his way. Before he was fifteen he went to Saxony and apprenticed himself to a worker in precious metals, and showed so much intelligence that before he had completed the term of his apprenticeship he was master of his trade.

He was twenty-two when he returned to his native town, with a little money and a young wife. A daughter was born to him, and grew to be the most beautiful girl in Neisse. Her father prospered, made money, and became mayor. Indeed, he was a little king in his own way, but was tyrannical and exacting, and while everybody adored Brunhilda, his pretty daughter, he was far from being respected. When any of the young men of the village tried to win his favour in the hope of gaining the daughter's hand, he ordered them off with a peremptoriness that left no doubt about his determination.

---

58 A former German town, but since 1945 it is Nysa in Poland.
59 A region in central Europe. It is mostly in Poland but some parts in Germany and the Czech Republic.

'My girl,' he used to boast, 'shall marry a lord. My father was a charcoal burner, and in my youth I knew the curse of poverty. Now I am going to be the founder of a family, and rather than let Brunhilda marry a humble person I would carry her to her grave.'

Although he expressed himself thus forcibly and emphatically, he did not explain how he hoped to get a lord as a son-in-law, but that was a detail; and, being a deep, designing, and crafty man, he probably had some matured plan in his own mind.

Now it chanced that when Brunhilda was two-and-twenty a young artist came to Neisse, which was famed for a very ancient church and for marvellous views, which were to be obtained from different parts of the town, for it stood on an eminence in a very beautiful and fertile country. It was, therefore, no uncommon thing for artists to visit the place. This particular one became known as Robert Kuno, and he took up his quarters at the village inn. One day he was in the ancient church sketching a very picturesque archway, when Brunhilda entered with a number of other girls, laden with flowers, as they were going to decorate the church in honour of some festival.

Robert was at once attracted by Brunhilda's beauty, and, getting into conversation with her, he begged that she would pose for him while he made a drawing. She was by no means loth to do this. Indeed, she felt flattered, for she knew she was good-looking, and she would have been a strange woman if she had had no vanity. Robert placed her in the position he wanted near the archway, and produced a sketch, which he promised to turn into a painting, and he asked her to favour him again on the morrow, which she did, and the next day, and the day after that, and as a natural result the young artist began to talk to her in a way which by no means displeased her, although she knew that her father would be furious if he came to hear of it. And sure enough he did hear of it. Some envious jade went to him, and told him that Brunhilda was going day after day to the church to meet the artist.

The day following the mayor repaired to the church, and screened himself behind a pillar and witnessed the flirtation between Brunhilda and the artist, until at length, losing his self-control, he suddenly presented himself before them, and there was a scene. He used some very harsh terms to the young man, and, seizing the sketch he had been making of the girl, he stamped on it, and vowed if Robert did not leave Neisse within twelve hours he would have him arrested as a vagabond and confined in the stocks. Then he took his daughter home and lectured her on the monstrous wickedness of her conduct in allowing a 'vulgar, common artist fellow' to talk love to her.

As Robert failed to comply with the order to clear off, the mayor, true to his word, had him arrested as a vagabond, having no visible means of subsistence, and he was placed in the stocks which stood on the green opposite the mayor's house. The tyrannical magistrate thought that when his daughter saw her admirer in such an undignified position she would be disgusted, and think no more of him. But herein he was mistaken, for he caught her kissing her hand to him from her window, and manifesting every sign of sympathy. So Robert was at once set at liberty, on condition that he immediately left the place, which he consented to do, much to the joy and comfort of the mayor.

It was nearly a year after that an old bag-piper one day entered the town of Neisse. He was a strange, weird-looking old man, with great masses of white hair hanging about his shoulders, and heavy, beetling eyebrows screening his keen, grey eyes. His pipes, which seemed older than himself, were unlike any that had been seen before, and when the old piper tuned them up he awoke the most marvellous melody. Whence he came and whither he was going no one knew, and being by no means communicative, they were left in ignorance. But one thing he made clear—he did not lack money, and as there happened to be a very pretty little cottage to let, whose owner had recently died, the piper bargained for it and bought it, and soon after a young man came to live with him, and rumour soon had it that this young man was the strange piper's foster-son. Apparently the son was nearly blind, for he wore large blue goggle glasses, and always went about with a stick.

The son was very reserved and would not mix with the people, but the old piper became such a favourite owing to the sweet music he was able to discourse, that he was invited every evening, when the weather was fine, to repair to the village green, where the people were wont to dance. He was so wonderfully well-informed, too, and seemed to have travelled so extensively, that the old citizens invited him to their dinners, and he was petted and flattered. He played his pipes at christenings and wedding feasts, as well as pathetic and solemn airs when the dead were committed to the earth.

One marvellous tune that he played was known as 'Grandfather's Dance,' and so inspiriting was this, such a wild, mad, rhythmical jingle, that even the oldest of men and women who could move their limbs at all could not resist its strains, and fell to dancing. Indeed, the strains, it was averred, restored youth to the old, and even the paralytic and the rheumatic threw away their crutches when they heard them.

Now, strangely enough, the effect of the old man's art on his foster son was *nil*. He remained silent and mournful at the most mirth-inspiring tunes the piper played to him; and at the balls, to which he was often invited, he rarely mingled with the gay, but would retire into a corner, and fix his eyes on the loveliest fair one that graced the room, neither daring to address, nor to offer her his hand. This one was Brunhilda, and occasionally he managed to get speech with her, and it was noted that she was by no means averse to talk to him. And at such times she easily read in his brightening face the eloquent gratitude of his heart; and although she turned blushingly away, the fire on her cheeks, and the sparkling in her eyes, kindled new flames of love and hope in her lover's bosom, for this young man was none other than the artist who had resorted to this stratagem to woo her. And he was neither blind nor near sighted, but the goggles afforded him a disguise.

Willibald, such was the name of the piper, had for a long time promised to assist the love-sick youth in obtaining his soul's dearest object. Sometimes he intended, like the wizards of yore, to torment the mayor with an enchanted dance, and compel him by exhaustion to grant everything; sometimes, like a second Orpheus,[60] he proposed to carry away, by the power of his harmony, the sweet bride from the tartarian[61] abode of her father. But Robert always had objections: he never would allow the parent of his fair one to be harmed by the slightest offence, and hoped to win him by perseverance and complacency.

Willibald said to him one day, 'You are an idiot, if you hope to win, by an open and honourable sentiment, the approbation of a rich and proud old fool. He will not surrender without some of the plagues of Egypt[62] are put in force against him. When once Brunhilda is yours, and he no more can change what has happened, then you will find him friendly and kind. He will bow to the inevitable. I blame myself for having promised to do nothing against your will, but death acquits every death, and still I shall help you in my own way.'

Poor Robert was not the only one on the path of whose life the mayor strewed thorns and briars. The whole town had very little affection for their chief, and delighted to oppose him at every opportunity; for he was harsh and cruel, and punished severely the citizens for trifling and innocent mirth, unless they purchased pardon by the means of heavy penalties and bribes. After the yearly wine-fair in the month of

---

60 In Ancient Greek myths, Orpheus was able to charm all things with his music.
61 The father was a tartar, i.e. strict and forbidding.
62 A reference to the plagues described in the Old Testament showing God's demonstration of his power.

January he was in the habit of obliging them to pay all their earnings into his treasury, to make amends for their past merriments. One day the tyrant of Neisse had put their patience to too hard a trial, and broken the last tie of obedience from his oppressed townsmen. The malcontents had created a riot, and filled their persecutor with deadly fear; for they threatened nothing less than to set fire to his house, and to burn him, together with all the riches he had gathered by oppressing them.

At this critical moment, Robert went to Willibald, and said to him, 'Now, my old friend, is the time when you may help me with your art, as you frequently have offered to do. If your music be really so powerful as you say it is, go then and deliver the mayor by softening the enraged mob. As a reward he certainly will grant you anything you may request. Speak then a word for me and my love, and demand my beloved Brunhilda as the price of your assistance.'

The bag-piper laughed at this speech, and replied:

'We must satisfy the follies of children in order to prevent them crying.' And so he took his bag-pipe and walked slowly down to the townhouse square, where the rioters, armed with pikes, lances, and lighted torches, were laying waste the mansion of the worshipful head of the town.

Willibald placed himself near a pillar, and began to play his 'Grandfather's Dance.' Scarcely were the first notes of this favourite tune heard, when the rage-distorted countenances became smiling and cheerful, the frowning brows lost their dark expression, pikes and torches fell out of the threatening fists, and the enraged assailants moved about marking with their steps the measure of the music. At last, the whole multitude began to dance, and the square, that was lately the scene of riot and confusion, bore now the appearance of a gay dancing assembly. The piper, with his magic bag-pipe, led on through the streets, all the people danced behind him, and each citizen returned jumping to his home, which shortly before he had left with very different feelings.

The mayor, saved from this imminent danger, knew not how to express his gratitude; he promised to Willibald everything he might demand, even were it half his property. But the bag-piper replied, smiling, saying his expectations were not so lofty, and that for himself he wanted no temporal goods whatever; but since his lordship, the mayor, had pledged his word to grant to him everything he might demand, so he beseeched him, with due respect, to grant fair Brunhilda's hand for his foster-son.

The haughty mayor was highly displeased at this proposal. He made every possible excuse; and as Willibald repeatedly reminded him of his promise, he did what the despots of those dark times were in the habit of doing, and which those of our enlightened days still practise, he declared his dignity offended, pronounced Willibald to be a disturber of the peace, an enemy of the public security, and allowed him to forget in a prison the promises of his lord, the mayor. Not satisfied herewith, he accused him of witchcraft, caused him to be tried by pretending he was the very bag-piper and rat-catcher of Hamelin, who was, at that time, and is still in so bad a repute in the German provinces, for having carried off by his infernal art all the children of that ill-fated town.

The only difference, said the wise mayor, between the two cases was, that at Hamelin only the children had been made to dance to his pipe, but here young and old seemed under the same magical influence. By such artful delusions, the mayor turned every merciful heart from the prisoner. The dread of necromancy, and the example of the children of Hamelin, worked so strongly, that sheriffs and clerks were writing day and night. The secretary calculated already the expense of the funeral pile, for necromancers,[63] witches and wizards were burnt in those days; the sexton[64] petitioned for a new rope to toll the dead-bell for the poor sinner; the carpenters prepared scaffolds for the spectators of the expected execution; and the judges rehearsed the grand scene, which they prepared to play at the condemnation of the famous bag-piper. But although justice was sharp, Willibald was still sharper; for as he laughed very heartily over the important preparations for his end, he now laid himself down upon his straw and died!

Shortly before his death, he sent for his beloved Robert, and addressed him for the last time.

'Young man,' said he, 'you seest that in your way of viewing mankind and the world I can render you no assistance. I am tired of the whims your folly has obliged me to perform. You have now acquired experience enough fully to comprehend that nobody should calculate, or at least ground, his designs on the goodness of human nature, even if he himself should be too good to lose entirely his belief in the goodness of others. I, for my own part, would not rely upon the fulfilment of my last request to you, if your own interest would not induce you to its performance. When I am dead, be careful to see that my old bag-pipe

---

63 Someone who practises magic.
64 The person who looks after a church.

is buried with me. To detain it would be of no use to you, but it may be the cause of your happiness, if it is laid underground with me.'

Robert promised to observe strictly the last commands of his old friend, who shortly after closed his eyes. Scarcely had the report of Willibald's sudden death spread, when old and young came to ascertain the truth. The mayor was more pleased with this turn of the affair than any other; for the indifference with which the prisoner had received the news of his approaching promotion to the funeral pile, induced his worship to suppose the old bag-piper might some fine day be found invisible in his prison, or rather be found not there at all; or the cunning wizard, being at the stake, might have caused a wisp of straw to burn instead of his person, to the eternal shame of the court of Neisse. He therefore ordered the corpse to be buried as speedily as possible, as no sentence to burn the body had yet been pronounced. An unhallowed corner of the churchyard, close to the wall, was the place assigned for poor Willibald's resting-place. The jailor, as the lawful heir of the deceased prisoner, having examined his property, asked what should become of the bag-pipe, as a *corpus delicti*.[65]

Robert, who was present, was on the point to make his request, when the mayor, full of zeal, thus pronounced his sentence:

'To avoid every possible mischief, this wicked, worthless tool shall be buried together with its master.' So they put it into the coffin at the side of the corpse, and early in the morning pipe and piper were carried away and buried.

But strange things happened in the following night. The watchmen on the tower were looking out, according to the custom of the age, to give the alarm in case of fire in the surrounding country, when about midnight they saw, by the light of the moon, Willibald rising out of his tomb near the churchyard wall. He held his bag-pipe under his arm, and leaning against a high tombstone upon which the moon shed her brightest rays he began to blow, and fingered the pipes just as he was accustomed to do when he was alive.

While the watchmen, astonished at this sight, gazed wisely on one another, many other graves opened; their skeleton-inhabitants peeped out with their bare skulls, looked about, nodded to the measure, rose afterwards wholly out of their coffins, and moved their rattling limbs into a nimble dance. At the church windows, and the grates of the vaults, other empty eye-holes stared on the dancing place: the withered

---

65 'Body of the crime', in this sense though, the evidence.

arms began to shake the iron gates, till locks and bolts sprung off, and out came the skeletons, eager to mingle in the dance of the dead. Now the light dancers stilted about, over the hillocks and tombstones, and whirled around in a merry waltz, that the shrouds waved in the wind about the fleshless limbs, until the church clock struck twelve, when all the dancers, great and small, returned to their narrow cells; the player took his bag-pipe under his arm, and likewise returned to his vacant coffin.

Long before the dawn of the day, the watchmen awoke the mayor, and made to him, with trembling lips and knocking knees, the awful report of the horrid night scene. He enjoined strict secrecy on them, and promised to watch with them the following night on the tower. Nevertheless, the news soon spread through the town, and at the close of the evening, all the surrounding windows and roofs were lined with virtuosi and cognoscenti of the dark fine arts, who all beforehand were engaged in discussions on the possibility or impossibility of the events they expected to witness before midnight.

The bag-piper was not behind his time. At the first sound of the bell announcing the eleventh hour, he rose slowly, leaned against the tomb-stone, and began his tune. The ball guests seemed to have been waiting for the music, for at the very first notes they rushed forth out of the graves and vaults, through grass hills and heavy stones. Corpses and skeletons shrouded and bare, tall and small, men and women, all run-ning to and fro, dancing and turning, wheedling and whirling round the player, quicker or more slowly according to the measure he played, till the clock tolled the hour of midnight. Then dancers and piper with-drew again to rest.

The living spectators, at their windows and on their roofs, now con-fessed that 'there are more things in heaven and earth than are dreamt of in our philosophy.' [66] The mayor had no sooner retired from the tow-er, than he ordered Robert to be cast into prison that very night, hop-ing to learn from his examination, or perhaps by putting him to the torture, how the magic nuisance of his foster-father might be removed.

Robert did not fail to remind the mayor of his ingratitude towards Willibald, and maintained that the deceased troubled the town, bereft the dead of their rest and the living of their sleep, only because he had received, instead of the promised reward for the liberation of the

66 A quote from Shakespeare's *Hamlet*: 'There are more things in heaven and earth, Horatio, than are dreamt of in your philosophy.'

mayor, a scornful refusal, and moreover had been thrown into prison most unjustly, and buried in a degrading manner. This speech made a very deep impression upon the minds of the magistrates; they instantly ordered the body of Willibald to be taken out of his tomb, and laid in a more respectable place.

The sexton, to show his penetration on the occasion, took the bag-pipe out of the coffin, and hung it over his bed. For he reasoned thus: if the enchanting or enchanted musician could not help following his profession even in the tomb, he at least would not be able to play to the dancers without his instrument.

But at night, after the clock had struck eleven, he heard distinctly a knock at his door; and when he opened it, with the expectation of some deadly and lucrative accident requiring his skill, he beheld the buried Willibald *in propria persona.*[67]

'My bag-pipe,' said he, very composedly, and passing by the trembling sexton, he took it from the wall where it was hung up; then he returned to his tombstone, and began to blow. The guests, invited by the tune, came like the preceding night, and were preparing for their midnight dance in the churchyard. But this time the musician began to march forward, and proceeded with his numerous and ghastly suite through the gate of the churchyard to the town, and led his nightly parade through all the streets, till the clock struck twelve, when all returned again to their dark abodes.

The inhabitants of Neisse now began to fear lest the awful night wanderers might shortly enter their own houses. Some of the chief magistrates earnestly entreated the mayor to lay the charm by making good his word to the bag-piper. But the mayor would not listen to it; he even pretended that Robert shared in the infernal arts of the old piper, and added, 'The son deserves rather the funeral pile than the bridal bed.'

But in the following night the dancing spectres came again into the town, and although no music was heard, yet it was easily seen by their motions that the dancers went through the figure of the 'Grandfather's Dance.' This night they behaved much worse than before, for they stopped at the house wherein a betrothed damsel lived, and here they turned in a wild whirling dance round a shadow, which resembled perfectly the spinster in whose honour they moved the nightly bridal dance. Next day the whole town was filled with mourning, for all the damsels whose shadows were seen dancing with the spectres had died

---

67 The person himself.

suddenly. The same thing happened again the following night. The dancing skeletons turned before the houses, and wherever they had been, there was, next morning, a dead bride lying on the bier.

The citizens were determined no longer to expose their daughters and mistresses to such an imminent danger. They threatened the mayor to carry Brunhilda away by force and to lead her to Robert, unless the mayor would permit their union to be celebrated before the beginning of the night. The choice was a difficult one, for the mayor disliked the one just as much as the other, but as he found himself in the uncommon situation where a man may choose with perfect freedom, he, as a free being, declared freely his daughter to be Robert's bride.

Long before the spectre hour the guests sat at the wedding table. The first stroke of the bell sounded, and immediately the favourite tune of the well-known bridal dance was heard. The guests, frightened to death, and fearing the spell might still continue to work, hastened to the windows, and beheld the bag-piper, followed by a long row of figures in white shrouds, moving to the wedding-house. He remained at the door and played, but the procession went on slowly, and proceeded even to the festive hall. Here the strange pale guests rubbed their eyes, and looked about them full of astonishment, like sleep walkers just awakened. The wedding guests fled behind the chairs and tables; but soon the cheeks of the phantoms began to colour, their white lips became blooming like young rosebuds; they gazed at each other full of wonder and joy, and well-known voices called friendly names. They were soon known as revived corpses, now blooming in all the brightness of youth and health: and who should they be but the brides whose sudden death had filled the whole town with mourning, and who, now recovered from their enchanted slumber, had been led by Willibald with his magic pipe out of their graves to the merry wedding feast. The wonderful old man blew a last and cheerful farewell tune, and disappeared. He was never seen again.

Robert was of opinion, the bag-piper was no other than the famous Spirit of the Silesian Mountains.[68] The young painter had originally met him once when he travelled through the hills, and acquired his good-

---

68 The Spirit of the Silesian Mountains plays a great part in the German popular tales. He always appears full of mirth and whims. The people know him best by his nickname Rübezahl, the turnip counter. The accident which gave rise to this nickname has been related in a masterly manner in Musäus's *German Popular Tales*. [Author's note.]

will by rendering him some service, for the old man was, or pretended to be, in great distress, and Robert gave him wine and food, and housed him for many days. Then suddenly the strange piper disappeared, but shortly returned and promised the youth he would grant him anything he wished if he could, and he declared that with his magic pipes he could subdue anyone to his will. Then it was that Robert beseeched him to help him to win the consent of the Mayor of Neisse to wed his daughter. Willibald promised the youth to assist him in his love-suit, and he kept his word, although after his own jesting fashion.

Robert remained all his lifetime a favourite with the Spirit of the Mountains. He grew rich, and became celebrated. His dear wife brought him every year a handsome child, his pictures were sought after even in Italy and England; and the 'Dance of the Dead,'[69] of which Basel, Antwerp, Dresden, Lübeck, and many other places boast, are only copies or imitations of Robert's original painting, which he had executed in memory of the real 'Dance of the Dead at Neisse!' But, alas! this picture is lost, and no collector of paintings has yet been able to discover it, for the gratification of the cognoscenti, and the benefit of the history of the art.

---

69 There is a genre of painting known as *Danse Macabre* or *Dance of Death*.

XIV
The Mystic Spell

A WEIRD STORY OF BRAZIL. TOLD BY SIGNOR DON ALONZO
RODERICK, SPANISH CONSUL AT RIO DE JANEIRO

RIO AND ITS NEIGHBOURHOOD is perhaps one of the most beautiful spots on the face of the globe. Indeed, I am not sure but what
it may claim to be absolutely without a rival, for it has features that
are unique. Nature would almost seem to have exhausted her efforts
to build up a scene which lacks no single detail necessary for imposing
pictorial effect, though, as most people know, hidden beneath all this
entrancing beauty death lurks in a hundred forms; and he who is not
wary and ever on his guard is liable to be struck down with appalling
suddenness.

My predecessor had suffered much in his health, and succumbed at
last to the scourge of yellow fever. When I arrived to take up his work
I found everything in such confusion that I had to labour very hard
to reduce chaos to order and put the consular business shipshape. It
thus came about that for many months I was unable to leave my post
in Rio, and as a consequence my health began to suffer. Soon after my
arrival I made the acquaintance of a Portuguese gentleman named
Azevedo Souza, a merchant of high standing in Rio. His business was
of a very mixed character, and amongst other things he was an orchid
exporter. In this branch of his trading he had been exceptionally successful. Through his instrumentality collectors had had brought under
their notice some wonderful and hitherto unknown specimens of these
marvels of nature. His collecting station was far up north in the interior. He spoke of it enthusiastically as an earthly paradise, and gave me
many pressing invitations to be his guest, when he paid his periodical
visits to look after his affairs in that region.

Senhor Souza was an estimable gentleman, and very highly respected. He had a charming family, amongst them being a daughter, Juliette
by name, and one of the sweetest young ladies I have ever had the pleasure of associating with. At this period Juliette was about seven-and-
twenty, and as the apple of his eye to her father. She was invaluable to
him in his business, at any rate to the orchid branch of it; for not only
had she an all-round cleverness, but probably she knew more about
orchids than any living woman. She herself was the means of introduc-

ing to the scientific world an entirely new orchid, the flower of which was of such transcendent beauty that the Brazilians, used as they are to floral glories, said that this particular bloom must have been 'specially cultivated in God's own garden.' Juliette made a most arduous and hazardous journey into the depths of virgin forests in search of this plant, and narrowly escaped losing her life.

Perhaps, when I say that I was a bachelor the reader will readily guess that my acquaintance with Juliette aroused in me an admiration which I devoutly hoped would find its consummation in a happy union, for she was by no means indifferent to my attentions. Not only was she highly cultivated, but had astonishing linguistic powers, and spoke many languages fluently. She was perfectly acquainted with Spanish, and had read the beautiful literature of Spain extensively. Senhor Souza encouraged my suit, and at last the time came when I was emboldened to tell Juliette she was the one woman in the world who could make me happy. Ah, I shall never forget that night until the grave closes over me. We were seated in the veranda of Senhor Souza's splendid villa, situated just on the outskirts of the town, and commanding an enchanting view of the bay of Rio, with its remarkable Sugar Loaf Mountain and the marvellous range beyond it. And what a night it was! The glory of the stars, shining as they can only shine in the tropics; the sparkling moonlit sea; the soft, flower-perfumed breeze that stirred the foliage to a languorous susurrus;[70] the fireflies that like living jewels filled the air, begot in one a feeling of reverence, and strengthened one's faith in the Great God who created such a world of beauty. Those who have never experienced such a night under a tropical sky know nothing of what the true poetry of nature means. It stirs one with a ravishing, ecstatic feeling of delight which is a foretaste of the joys of heaven.

I had been sitting for some time with Juliette's hand in mine. We were silent, being deeply impressed with the magical beauty of the night, for we both had poetical instincts; indeed, Juliette's was a highly strung romantic temperament, and she was able to express her thoughts in language that could stir the pulses and move to tears.

But this night of all nights was a night for love, and as I pressed her hand I asked her to crown my happiness by becoming my wife. To my astonishment she shuddered, sighed deeply, and then in a tone of the most touching pathos exclaimed:

'Oh, why—oh, why have you asked me that?'

---

70 Murmuring or rustling.

'Juliette,' I answered in amazement, 'is it not a natural question for a man to ask a woman sooner or later, when every beat of his heart tells him that he loves her?'

'Yes, yes,' she replied in distressful tones, and shuddering again violently, 'but, but——'

'But what?' I asked as she paused.

'I pray you press me not for an answer.'

'This is extraordinary!' I remarked, feeling distressed beyond the power of words to express; and yet, distressed as I was, she was infinitely more troubled; she sobbed like one whose heart was rent. 'You know that I love you, Juliette,' I went on. 'You have encouraged me. You have tacitly bidden me to hope; and now——'

'Oh, yes, yes,' she cried with a catching of her breath, and a spasmodic closing of her fingers round mine. 'And I love you, I love you. But I have been living in a fool's paradise. I have been dreaming dreams. I thought that the sweet delicious time would go on indefinitely. You waken me now abruptly, and I no longer dream. I must not, cannot be your wife.'

'Juliette, what is this mystery?' I exclaimed, growing excited, for I was sure some extraordinary influence was at work, and that she was under a spell.

She laughed, though it wasn't the light laugh of joy peculiar to her, but a little forced spasmodic laugh of bitterness and despair.

'I will tell you,' she answered, trying to master her emotions by a mighty effort of will. 'It is better that you should know, otherwise you may deem me fickle, and think that I have trifled with your feelings. Years ago, when I was a little girl, I had a nurse, a strange old Brazilian crone who had been in the family service for many years. She was very fond of all my brothers and sisters, but for some reason I could never understand took a strong dislike to me. I think this dislike was mutual, for I remember that she used to make me shudder at times, and fill me with a nameless dread. This, perhaps, was hardly to be wondered at, for she treated me roughly and unkindly, and many a time I complained to my father. He, however, shared my mother's belief in the old woman's fidelity and gentleness, and would chide me for what he termed my unfounded, childish fears. Consequently I ceased to complain, and kept my little sorrows to myself.

'The name of this old nurse was Joanna Maria. One day she and I and an elder sister who was about two years my senior had been down to the bay, and wandering about the seashore in search of the beautiful shells which are often thrown up after a storm. Old Joanna was peculiarly irritable and fretful that morning. Once, when I stumbled over a rock and fell into a pool of seawater, she snatched me up fiercely, and shook me until nearly all the life was frightened out of me. Then she sat down, made me sit beside her, and, looking at me fixedly with her bleared eyes, said:

'"I am going to tell you your future. It grows dark, very dark; a foreigner will come from over the sea and will talk love to you, but if you listen to him and become his wife, a sudden and awful death will overtake you; you will leave him a widow while yet he is a bridegroom. Love and wifedom are not for you. I put a curse upon you."'

In spite of the fact that dear Juliette told me this with moving solemnity and gravity, I burst into laughter, and taking her in my arms said:

'Juliette, my beloved, what nonsense all this is! Surely you, with your high intelligence and great learning, do not attach the slightest importance to the malicious and spiteful utterances of an ignorant old crone. No, no, I am sure you don't. You are too sensible. Put these phantom fears away, darling, and trust to my great love to shield you from all harm. Say you love me; say you will be my bride. Do not send me from you on this wonderful night of beauty with a great load of sorrow at my heart. Speak, Juliette, my love, my life—comfort me. Tell me you will link your fate with mine.'

She sighed in response to my appeal. Then pressing her soft, fair cheek against mine, she tightened her arms around my neck and murmured low and sweetly:

'Yes, beloved, you are right. I will put the foolish, superstitious fear behind me. Old Joanna has long been dead, and I ought never to have allowed her empty, spiteful words to have influenced me. Take me, dear, when you will. I am yours only. I will be your wife! I will be faithful unto death!'

Scarcely had she uttered the words when she broke from me, and uttering a shrill scream of terror, sank into her chair, and, pointing to the far end of the veranda like one distraught, cried:

'There she is, there she is! Take her away, take her away, for I am horrified!' Naturally my eyes turned to where she pointed, and though I was neither a nervous nor a superstitious man, I started with a feeling of horror, for I beheld the shadowy form of an old negress. The moonlight fell full upon her repulsive face, which was filled with a look of hatred, while her eyes, glowing like a wild cat's, glared at me with a spite that would be difficult to describe. In a few moments her lips parted, revealing the white teeth that glistened in the pale light, and distinctly and unmistakably I heard these words: 'Shun her, the curse is on her! She will die as I foretold.'

Juliette heard this too, and with a pitiable scream of fright she fell in a swoon on the floor. The scream brought the servants and her father rushing from the house, and as they raised the prostrate lady up, they directed angry glances at me, as though they thought that I had done some wrong.

I was confused and trembling. I glanced towards the end of the veranda to where I had seen the vision, but there was nothing in sight, and I was recalled to my senses by the voice of Senhor Souza, who somewhat peremptorily demanded to know what had caused his daughter's illness.

'Senhor Souza,' I answered, thinking it was better to be perfectly frank with him, 'as you know, Juliette and I love each other. To-night I have asked her to be my wife. She consented. Immediately afterwards we heard a sigh, and turning beheld a vision which so alarmed your daughter that she screamed and fainted.'

'This is a strange story, very strange,' he muttered; 'and it is ominous. Tell me more about it!' The Brazilians are all more or less superstitious, and Senhor Souza was no exception. Having seen his daughter borne into the house and attended to by her maid and the female servants, he returned to me and made me relate minutely all that had passed.

As I felt that I ought not to conceal anything I gave him a plain, straightforward statement of the facts. He was much impressed and evidently uneasy. Again and again he asked me if I had seen the vision. Of course I had no alternative but to assure him that I could not have been mistaken, although I had no explanation to offer. I told him I was not given to seeing visions, that up to that night I had always been very sceptical; but now I was either a victim of a trick of the brain or I had seen what I had described. Moreover, I was certain, I said, that Juliette had seen it too. Otherwise, why did she scream and faint?

Senhor Souza showed decided reluctance to discuss the subject further that night, for he was evidently deeply affected, and much concerned about his daughter. So when I had been assured that Juliette was recovering, and would probably be all right in the morning, I returned to the town. As I drove along in the moonlight, I recalled all that had transpired, and I confess to a feeling of decided uneasiness. The fact is, I was unnerved a little. I had received a shock and its effects were not easily shaken off.

I did not sleep very well that night, but with the coming day my fears dispelled, and I quite recovered my wonted buoyancy when a special messenger brought me a little note from my Juliette to say that she was much better. That cheered me, and I was inclined to rate myself for having been so weak. But, of course, we are always brave in the day. Darkness makes cowards of us.

As soon as my duties permitted I rode out to Senhor Souza's villa and was pleased at being met on the threshold by Juliette. She looked pale and anxious, and a trace of fear still lingered in her beautiful eyes. We wandered into the garden together, and when the psychological moment had arrived, as I thought, I renewed my love-vows, and again urged her to consent to become my wife. Something of the previous night's agitation affected her, and as she clung to my arm as though she was afraid an unseen force might attempt to pluck her from my side, she said:

'Are we justified, think you, in defying fate, and in linking our lives together in spite of the curse?'

'Yes, undoubtedly,' I answered. 'The curse is nonsense. We can afford to laugh at the curse of a human being.'

'You saw the vision last night!' she asked.

'Yes.'

'And heard it speak?'

'I did.'

'You know then that I am not the victim of a delusion. At least, if I am so are you.'

'Beloved,' I cried, 'we are both victims of a delusion. It is well that we should think so. Curses avail not, neither can the dead harm us. Our happiness is in each other's keeping. Why should we throw it away? Surely we are strong-minded enough to be indifferent to the meaningless croakings of a spiteful and imbecile old woman. Hesitate, therefore, no longer; say that you will be my wife.'

Although my argument evidently told with her, she could not quite make up her mind, and she murmured, like one who was still under the influence of a great fear:

'I should like to, I should like to, dear one; but supposing that dreadful prophecy *should* come true?'

'It won't, my own love,' I answered. 'We have nothing to fear from the living, and the dead—well, the dead are done with.'

'Ah, you don't know. Perhaps, perhaps not. Who knows, who can tell? It may be that those who have passed away may still have the power to injure us. The old nurse hated me, and I fear that she has carried her hate beyond the grave.'

I used every argument I could to comfort and calm her. I urged her again and again to speak the word that would make my happiness complete. I told her that I was then suffering in health as a result of the climate, and weakened as I was, her refusal to comply with my request would probably have a fatal effect.

This latter argument appealed so forcibly to her that even her superstitious fears were overcome, and she said at last that if her father offered no objection she would not. Speaking for myself, although the night previous I had been much impressed, I was no longer so; nor was I inclined to attach any importance to the supernatural incident which had so alarmed us, consequently I felt perfectly justified in leaving nothing undone to overcome Juliette's scruples and fears. And now, as I had gained her consent, I suggested that we should go at once to her father and get his sanction, for the time had come when the state of my health demanded imperatively that I should seek a change; that I should go away into the highlands to recoup. But I was resolved not to go alone.

By this time I had completely won her, and so we went to Senhor Souza and told him of our wishes and desires. I noticed that his olive cheeks blanched a little, and a look of ineffable love and tenderness filled his eyes as he gazed on his child, whose beauty at that moment seemed to me the beauty of heaven, not of earth. The Senhor appealed to her to speak her mind freely and candidly, holding nothing in reserve. So she turned to me, and laid both her soft white hands in mine, saying:

'Father, this man has my heart. My body, therefore, belongs to him. Give me to him with your blessing, for I love him.'

The Senhor was deeply affected, and his voice was broken by emotion as he spoke. He stepped towards us and placed one hand on my head and the other on hers, and looking at me with misty eyes, said:

'I give her to you; take her. Guard her, watch over her, for she is my life; she is the core of my heart, the apple of my eye. Be good to each other, be true, loyal, and upright; and may God in His infinite mercy and wisdom bless and prosper you, and give you long years of peace, joy, and contentment. God bless you, God bless you,' he repeated with great fervency.

The old man ceased. He could say no more, emotion choked him. Juliette and I muttered a fervent 'Amen, amen!' and then we were alone; the Senhor had hurried from the room. I took my affianced wife in my arms, and kissing her passionately, told her that every dark cloud had gone. She sighed a sigh of joy, and nestled to me; but instantly the joy was turned to a cry of horror and alarm, for a mocking, bitter, fiendish laugh broke on our ears, and turning from whence the sound came, we saw a nebulous form defined against a background of velvet curtain that hung as a *portiére*[71] before a door. It was impossible to recognize the figure, and it faded in a few moments like a passing shadow. The laugh, however, was unmistakable. We both heard it. It struck against our hearts; it beat in on our brains.

'My love, my love!' I whispered in Juliette's ear, as she seemed as if she would swoon in my arms; 'be strong, be brave. God will smile upon us. The saints will watch over us.'

'Ah, dear one,' she exclaimed; 'let me go from you for ever, for it is destined I shall bring you woe and life long sorrow.'

'Juliette, not all the fiends in the nether world shall part me from you,' I answered firmly. 'We are pledged to each other, and your father has blessed us. We will have no fear, but go on our way with light hearts, and put our trust in God.'

She seemed comforted, and I remained there until late. The morrow was to see the commencement of the preparations for our nuptials.

During the ensuing weeks Juliette quite recovered her spirits. Or, at any rate, whatever her feelings and thoughts were, she was at pains to conceal them. It was arranged that our honeymoon was to be spent in the highlands, at the Senhor's orchid station. I was looking forward to the time of my departure from Rio with intense joy, as I was terribly enervated, and yearned to breathe the pure and bracing air of the mountain lands.

At length our marriage morning came, as bright and brilliant a day as ever broke on the fair earth. A few fleecy clouds flecked the deep blue sky, and a fresh wind blowing in from the sea tempered the great heat of the sun. Surely no woman ever looked more divinely beautiful than did my sweet wife on that her bridal morn. It seemed to me that she was touched with a spiritual beauty that was not of the earth. The pure white lilies that lay upon her heaving bosom were not more wondrous fair than she. When the ceremony had ended, she expressed a wish to retire with me to a little chapel. There for a brief space we might offer up silent prayer, and commune with our hearts. Devoutly did she cross herself, and fervently did she pray that she might make me happy.

Ah, sweet Juliette, as I think, even at this far-off time, of that morning, my heart turns to lead, and my brain would give way, were it not

---

71 Normally used to describe a curtain that substitutes for a door.

that your sweet and gentle spirit is ever near me, and bids me be of good cheer.

When we had done justice to the sumptuous repast provided for us by my father-in-law at the principal Rio hotel, we left by the railway known as the *Estrada de Ferro Dom Pedro*, and travelled for many hours to the extreme northern limit of the line, a place called Carandahy.[72] My father-in-law was to follow us in a few days. He would have started with us, but was compelled to remain behind to settle up certain business matters. My love and I remained that night at Carandahy, at the house of Senhor Oliveira, a great friend of my wife's father, who had kindly placed his house at our disposal.

We spent three days in that bracing mountain station, where every breath I drew seemed to put new life into my enervated frame. And my dear wife had now quite recovered her spirits, and was as blithe and happy as a lark. Every one was so kind; the scenery was so wonderful; the air so invigorating, and we twain were so perfectly happy that we felt a thankfulness which could find no expression in mere words. But there is a dumb eloquence which is greater than speech; and there are moments of ecstasy when one can only express one's feelings by silence. Such moments were those we passed at the mountain station of Carandahy. The joy was great; alas! too great to last, as was soon to be proved.

As our destination was Paraúna,[73] on the banks of the river of the same name, we left Carandahy on horseback, with a number of servants and attendants, while our baggage was to be brought on by ox waggon.

At Paraúna Senhor Souza had one of his orchid collecting stations, and in due course we arrived at the place, which is magnificently situated, while the dense forests in the neighbourhood are the homes of some of the most beautiful orchids in the world. It is a small town, but of no small importance, as in the neighbouring mountains there are some mines of precious stones which, though worked in a very desultory and half-hearted way, produce considerable wealth.

The Senhor's station was situated a little distance from the town, in a rather lonely spot on the banks of the river. It was in charge of a foreman named Crispiniano Soares, and he had under him five or six Brazilian packers, and many orchid hunters, mostly Indians, who were

---

72 A town about 300 km north of Rio.
73 A town about 1000 km north-west of Carandahy.

intimately acquainted with the country round about for leagues and leagues.

My dear Juliette knew the place well also, as she had been there before; and now she displayed the greatest interest in the work that was being carried on, while her knowledge of the various species of plants brought in was wonderful. She could classify and name every plant.

Those were long delightful happy days. I was her willing, loving, devoted student, and she was my worshipped teacher. It made her so happy to explain to me the names and habits of the plants; and it filled me with happiness to see her happy. Neither of us ever reverted to the strange visitation in Rio, nor to the prophecy of the old nurse. Indeed, I don't think we thought of it—at least I didn't—our happiness was too great. No shadow fell upon it, and yet an awful, damnable shadow was creeping up. Oh, if I had only had some faint warning! Why was there no angel in heaven to give me some sign so that I might have saved my darling. But no sound came. No sign arose. It seemed as if all the people worshipped my sweet wife. She was so beautiful, so kind, so gentle, so womanly. But no one was possessed with prescience to utter a word of alarm to put me on my guard, so that I might have striven to avert the awful doom.

One day it chanced that a mule I was riding stumbled over a piece of timber and threw me, somewhat injuring my right leg, so that I had to lay up for a little while. I urged my dear one not to let my enforced imprisonment—which I was assured would only be of a few days' duration—prevent her from taking her accustomed exercise. She said that she should remain by my side; but, oh, poor blind being that I was, the fiend prompted me to insist that she should go out and enjoy herself. It was not the custom of the country for ladies to go out alone, but in Juliette's case the circumstances were somewhat different. Firstly, her father, who had travelled a good deal, had brought her up more in the English fashion, and she was accorded vastly more liberty than is generally accorded to Brazilian girls. And secondly, she had proved herself so useful in the orchid branch of her father's business that he had allowed her to do much as she liked; and she had on more than one occasion gone out with some of the hunters into the very depths of the virgin forests, braving all the terrible dangers incidental to the pursuit of the blooms, and braving the hardships inseparable from it. In many ways Juliette was a wonderful woman. She was as clever as she was beautiful, and I who pen these lines declare solemnly that she was without a fault. Of course you will say I speak with a lover's enthusiasm. Very well, let it be so. But I think of her, and I see her, as an angel of God, with the golden light of heaven upon her wings. In the first hours of my awful sorrow, when my heart was rent in twain and my poor brain was bursting, I think I cursed God, and called impiously upon Heaven to justify the act which plunged me suddenly from the happiest man on earth to the depths of a blank, maddening, damnable despair. But Heaven was silent, and God in His infinite wisdom let me suffer until the awful revelation was made to me which I shall presently record. Then I bowed my head and prayed to Him to smite me. But I lived. And it is only now, when long years have passed, and I draw nearer and nearer to the hour when I shall take my departure to my love, who waits for me with outstretched arms on heaven's frontiers, that I am able to write calmly and think calmly.

In this necessarily brief record I have shown no disposition to moralize; but I would venture to observe here that some lives are mysteries from their beginning to their end. The majority of people perhaps lead common, humdrum, vulgar, unemotional lives. And they die, never having known what it is to live; but few I fancy could be found who will venture to deny that in the words of the great English poet, 'There are more things in heaven and earth than are dreamt of in our philosophy.' We are after all but poor weak things, with but a limited vision, and to few only is it given to pierce the veil that screens us from Sheol.[74] But to return to the thread of my story.

Juliette yielded to my persuasions, and one morning she said, if I could spare her, she was going with an old and faithful attendant, one Jocelino who all his life had been in her father's employ, to a *fazenda* (farm), about a two leagues' ride,[75] to see a negro who, according to a report, had secured a specimen of an orchid not at that time classified. In my sweet love's interest, as I thought then, I bade her go. And so her dear lips pressed mine, and promising that before the sun was below the horizon she would be at my side again, she went from me, and I looked upon her living face for the last time.

The sun gradually declined, and sank in gold and blood-red glory, but my love came not. One by one the great stars defined themselves in the deep blue heavens, but my love came not. The moon climbed up and flooded the earth with a mystic silver sheen, and yet she who was my heart and soul was still absent. A deadly fear stole upon me, and a

---

74 The place of stillness and darkness to which the dead go, according to the Hebrew Bible.

75 A league was traditionally the distance someone could walk in an hour.

strange foreboding turned me cold. I summoned Crispiniano to my side and commanded him to get as many of his men together as he could, and, dividing them into parties, send them out to search for my missing love. He tried to reassure me that all was well. She had been benighted he said, and had found refuge at some *fazenda*. Old Jocelino, he declared, knew every inch of the country for scores of leagues, and was so devotedly attached to the young mistress that he would gladly yield up his life for her.

'Yes, Senhor,' continued Crispiniano, 'take my word for it. Your dear lady is safe with old Jocelino, and the morrow will be but young when your eyes will again be gladdened with the sight of your wife.'

I admit that the foreman's words did afford me some comfort. Juliette, I thought, had allowed her enthusiasm to make her forgetful of the flight of time; and as night travelling in that country is out of the question, owing to the hundred and one dangers that beset the traveller who ventures to go forth in the darkness, she had sought the shelter of some hospitable roof, and so I countermanded the order for the search parties. But I passed an awful, restless night. No sleep came to me, and when the morning dawned I uttered a fervent 'Thank God!' But that day was to prove worse than the preceding night—a day of awful, brain-corroding suspense. Instead of my love coming to me with the golden morn, no tidings of her were obtainable when the day was darkening to its close. Crippled as I was, I insisted on a horse being saddled, as I was determined to go and seek her; but when I attempted to mount into the saddle I found it to be physically impossible. So I had myself lifted up, but was unable to grip with my legs, and fell off again. I was therefore perforce compelled to desist in my attempt, but I sent into the town of Paraúna and offered a big reward to any one who would go in search of my dear one, and bring me tidings. In less than an hour a party of two dozen mounted men was formed, and, dividing into sixes, each set off in a different direction.

I will make no attempt to describe the horrible suspense of that night. When the sun began to glow again in the heavens it found me feverish and well-nigh distraught. The people at the station did their best to comfort me. They tried to cheer me; they spoke hopefully; they expressed themselves as certain that all would be well. But all their good-intentioned efforts were fruitless; some strange foreboding possessed me. If I looked up to the heavens it seemed to me as if I were looking through smoked glass; and during those heavy hours I fancied I heard a weird and hollow voice repeating in my ears these words:

'At last it is fulfilled! At last it is fulfilled!'

I had had myself placed on a couch in the veranda which commanded a view of the wood, and there I sat, and endured and suffered—not from the physical pain of my injured limb, for I felt nothing of it, but from mental torture.

As the afternoon waned I suddenly saw an Indian rushing down the road in an excited state. My heart leapt into my mouth, for I was sure he was the bearer of tidings. He tore up the steps of the veranda without any ceremony, and falling at my feet began to smite his breast, as is the custom of these people when they are the bearers of bad news. Then he wailed out his message:

'They have been found, and are being brought here; but they are both dead.' The words beat in upon my tortured brain like the blows from a sledge-hammer. I have only a vague, dream-like knowledge of what followed. In my frenzy I rose like a giant in wrath, and I hurled the poor Indian from me with such terrific force that concussion of the brain, as I understand, ensued, and for days his life was despaired of. But I knew naught of all this. A merciful Providence stunned me, and day after day went by and I lay like one entranced. During this blank, my sweet wife and old Jocelino were hidden from the sight of men for ever and ever, for quick burial in that climate is imperatively necessary.

Senhor Souza, my father-in-law, arrived in time to attend to the funeral of his child, but the poor old man's heart was broken. They aver that when he turned from the graveside he looked twenty years older. All the light had gone out of his eyes, his back was bent, and he tottered and reeled and staggered like one who had the palsy. But a strong will-power upheld him for a time, because he had a duty to fulfil, which was to endeavour to bring the murderer or murderers to justice, for my dear one and Jocelino were both barbarously done to death.

You who have never suffered a great wrong at the hands of your fellow man may preach against vengeance; but as it is no virtue for a man to be honest when he has well-filled coffers, so he who decries vengeance when he has not been wronged is but an idle preacher. Let someone rob you of your most precious inheritance, and see then if you can sit calmly and exclaim 'Kismet!' [76]

Now listen to the story as it was gradually revealed to me when, after lying stunned and dazed for nearly three weeks, I began to realize once more that I was in the world of the living. Listen to it, I say, and you will not be surprised that I thirsted for vengeance. Up above the valley

---

76 Fate, from a Arabic word.

of Paraúna was a wild, barren, sun-scorched plateau which, after some three leagues or so, dipped abruptly into a gorge of great extent filled with virgin forest. Just where the plateau joined this belt of vegetation, the searchers found the bodies of Juliette and Jocelino. They were lying on their backs, and between them was a huge dead coral snake, one of the most deadly reptiles found in the Brazils. It is not unusual for those who are bitten by this hideous creature to die almost immediately, so virulent and powerful is the venom it injects into the blood of its victims, so that it was not an unnatural thought that both Juliette and the old servant had been bitten by the reptile. But two things served to almost instantly dispel this belief. The head of the snake was crushed, and on the bosom of sweet Juliette's dress, as well as on the shirt of the man, was a great patch of blood. And when the bodies were brought down and examined by a doctor it was discovered that both had died by being stabbed to the heart with a long thin knife, and there was no sign or symptom of snake-bite.

The dead coral snake lying between them, therefore, only added to the mystery. The horses they had ridden returned after many days by themselves. They had evidently wandered far and suffered much, but they were dumb and could tell nothing of the awful tale. They still carried their saddles and trappings. Nothing had been stolen. The mystery deepened, but about the mode of death there was no mystery. It was murder. Murder, cruel, revolting, damnable. Where the bodies were found a diligent search was made for the weapon with which the crime was committed, but it was not discovered. Jocelino, like all Brazilians who live in the country, carried a hunting knife, but it was long and broad, and it was resting unstained in its sheath attached to his belt.

Again I say it was murder—cruel, fiendish, deliberate murder. A crime so foul that it must have made the angels weep, and yet no angel in heaven stretched forth his hand to save my beloved from her awful end.

Bowed and broken though he was, Senhor Souza thirsted for vengeance on the slayer of his child, whom he loved with a tenderness passing words, and he offered a lavish reward to any one who would track the murderer down. To any individual of the people of that region the reward would have been a fortune, and Brazilian and Indian alike were stimulated to almost superhuman exertion. But the mystery defied their solving. The bodies lying side by side and the dead snake between them were elements in the puzzle to which no brain in that community seemed capable of finding an answer. As days went by and there was no result the reward was increased. The authorities themselves, usually lethargic and indifferent in Brazil, bestirred themselves in an unusual manner; but nothing came of it all. And as I began to drift back slowly to the living world, the old Senhor took to his bed, for his heart was broken. And it was decreed that he should rise no more as a man amongst men, for after lingering helpless and imbecile for many months, they carried him forth one golden day amidst the lamentations of his people, and laid him to rest beside his daughter.

And now what of myself? I have that still to tell which, for ghastly horror, has scarcely any parallel.

When I was able to realize the full measure of my sorrow, I knew that my beloved wife had been foully slain, and the motive for the crime was hard to define. But it seemed to me as I examined into the matter that probably she and the old servant had fallen victims to some strange superstition, and that might account for the dead snake being found between them. But whatever the motive that led to this diabolical destruction of two human beings, it was exceedingly desirable that the criminal should be discovered, so that he might be made an example of, as a terror to others who were inclined to evil-doing. In Brazil, unhappily, crime is common, but detection rare; at least, it is so in the wilder parts of the country. Money, however, is so greedily coveted by Brazilian and Indian alike that I watched with feverish yet hopeful anxiety the result of my father-in-law's large reward. And when I found there were no results, I added to it considerably myself, and I sent to Rio for a man who bore a high reputation as a detective. He was a half-breed in the Government employ, but he was just as much a failure as any one else. He learnt nothing. The mystery remained a mystery.

After this it seemed to me that further effort would be useless, for weeks had passed since the commission of the deed, and every day that went by only served to increase the difficulty. Around us was an immense tract of country consisting of valley, mountain, and virgin forest. Most of the tract was sparsely populated. There were no telegraph wires, no railways.

As may be supposed, I felt reluctant to tear myself away from the spot where my sweet one slept—notwithstanding that the place was hateful to me, for it was associated with her mysterious death. But duty called, and I had already been too long absent from my post. Everything, however, seemed hateful to me. Life itself had lost its savour, for the light of my life had gone out. No man could have been happier than I when I arrived in Paraúna. A few short weeks and that happiness had been turned to a sorrow so deep, so overwhelming that I solemnly declare I would have faced death with the most perfect resignation, and with the sure and certain hope that I should meet my darling in a world where there is neither sorrow nor sighing. But my departure could no longer be delayed, and my preparations being completed I had arranged to start on the morrow.

That night, after my evening meal, I sat alone, feeling miserable, dejected, broken-hearted, when there came to me old José, one of the station hands. He had been born and brought up in the Paraúna district, and had never travelled fifty leagues away from his birthplace. He was intensely superstitious, intensely devout, and no less intensely bigoted; but he had been a faithful servitor, and though he was then bowed and frail he was still retained in the service.

'Senhor,' he began, making a profound obeisance, 'truly it is sad that the mystery of your sweet lady's and Jocelino's death has not been solved. But what money has failed to accomplish devilry may do.'

He looked so strange that I thought he must have been indulging too freely in the native wine, and I asked sharply, 'What do you mean?'

'Let not your anger fall on me, Senhor. I do not practise devilry myself; the saints guard me from it.' Here he shuddered and crossed himself. 'But I have heard some wonderful stories of Anita, though, God be praised, I have given her a wide berth.' He crossed himself again.

'Anita! who is Anita?' I exclaimed impatiently.

'The devil's agent, Senhor,' he answered, 'as all the country knows for miles round; but few can look upon her and live.'

'Do not befool me with this nonsense,' I said. 'I am sick at heart, and weary. Go. Leave me. I am in no mood to listen to silly stories.'

'Nay, Senhor, I have no desire to befool you. But Anita—may the Virgin guard us from evil—is a witch, and they do say she has power over life and death. Perhaps—I only say perhaps—she might help you to bring the murderer to justice.'

Although I was irritated and annoyed, and inclined to peremptorily order the old fellow out of my presence, I restrained myself, he seemed so earnest, so sincere. So I was induced to question him further, and I learnt that somewhere up in the mountains an old and withered woman dwelt in a cavern, and consorted with snakes and wild animals, but was shunned by human beings as a rule, for she was said to possess the evil eye, and it was generally believed that she could assume any shape, and drive men mad with fear. Any way she was accredited with superhuman powers, and could show you your future as well as read your past.

I suppose that the frame of mind I was then in, coupled with a remembrance of the extraordinary incidents in Rio, had something to do with my desire to know more of this witch woman, and I asked José if he could take me to her. But he seemed startled by the bare suggestion, and again made the sign of the cross on his breast and forehead. No, he could not, and would not, though I poured gold in sackfuls at his feet; but there was Torquato, the negro in the village, he might for a consideration conduct me to Anita. Torquato was a dissolute, drunken fellow; by calling, a hunter, and used to making long and lonely journeys over the prairies and into the depths of the virgin forests. He was daring withal, and he had boasted in his cups that he had often sat with Anita, and she had shown him wonders. But of course no one believed him. They called him braggart and liar. Anxious to test if there was any truth in José's wonderful stories of Anita's power, I bade him fetch Torquato to me. What I had witnessed in Rio and what had happened since had removed my scepticism, if ever I had been sceptical, and now I was disposed to clutch at any desperate chance that promised to solve the mystery. In about an hour Torquato was introduced to me. He was a pure negro of powerful build, but beyond that was not remarkable. He was ignorant, but intelligent, and had the instincts of the born hunter. I questioned him closely. Yes, he knew Anita, he assured me, and could guide me to her. She was undoubtedly in league with the Evil One, he averred, and could perform miracles. The only way I could propitiate her would be by taking her an offering of tobacco and rum, for which she had a great partiality. My curiosity being aroused, I resolved to postpone my journey, and start off at daybreak, with Torquato as guide, to visit Anita, for he undertook to guide me, and said that as he had always propitiated the witch-woman he did not fear her, but he would not be answerable for me. I must take all risk.

The weather, which up to then had been exceptionally fine, changed in the night, and the morning broke with a threatening and lowering sky. The natives predicted a great storm, but in that region a storm threatens long before it breaks, so I started off with Torquato, for I could not restrain my impatience; he carrying on his broad shoulders a knapsack containing, amongst other things, a quantity of rum and tobacco, in accordance with his advice. I had taken the precaution to fully arm myself. I had a double-barrelled hunting rifle, a six-chambered revolver, and a formidable hunting knife, as well as a plentiful supply of ammunition. Our road lay by a rough track that wound up precipitous slopes; then across a strip of prairie and forest; and finally we had to toil up a sun-smitten, weather-scarred mountain side. But during our journey we had caught no glimpse of the sun. The overcast sky had been growing blacker and blacker, and when we reached the mountain heavy drops of rain began to patter down, and from out the darkened heavens there leapt a blinding flash of fire that seemed to extend from horizon to horizon; it was followed instantly by a peal of thunder that crashed and reverberated until one could almost have imagined that the end of all things had come. So terrific are these storms in the highlands of Brazil that they are very alarming to any one unaccustomed to them; moreover, the deluge of rain that falls makes a shelter not only desirable but necessary. Fortunately, the rain was only spitting then, but Torquato began to look round anxiously for shelter, when, with quite startling suddenness, and as if she had risen from the earth, a woman stood before us, and demanded to know what we wanted there. She was the wildest, weirdest, strangest looking woman I have ever set eyes upon. She was almost a dwarf in stature, with misshapen limbs, and long skinny arms out of all proportion to the rest of her body. Her face—I declare it solemnly—was hardly human. It was more like a gargoyle from some old cathedral. A few scant grey hairs covered her head; and her chin and lips were also covered with a growth of wiry grey hair. Curiously enough, she had excellent teeth, which were in striking contrast to the rest of her appearance, and her eyes, deep sunk in their sockets and overhung with a pent-house fringe of wiry hair, were keen and brilliant as a hawk's, and seemed to look not at you but through you. The upper part of her body was clothed with a blanket, tied with a piece of rope at the waist, but her arms, legs, and feet were bare.

This singular-looking being was the woman we were seeking. Torquato recognized and saluted her, and spoke some words in the Indian language which I did not understand. She then addressed me in Portuguese, and as I marvelled at her perfect teeth and brilliant eyes, I marvelled still more at the clearness of her voice. Its tones were the dulcet tones of a young girl's. Indeed, I am not sure if that is a right description, for a girl's voice is often harsh, whereas Anita's was sweet and mellow. But in general appearance no more repulsive being could be imagined, and it was easy to understand how great an influence she could exert over the minds of superstitious people; nor am I ashamed to confess that I myself regarded her with a mixture of curiosity and fear.

'The Senhor seeks me!' she said.

'Yes.'

'Follow then, and I will give you shelter from the storm.'

She turned and led the way up the mountain. Although her feet were bare, the rocks made no impression upon her, and yet my feet were hurt, well shod as I was. Suddenly we came upon a sort of rocky platform before the entrance to a cave. It was on the very edge of a deep ravine—a rent in the earth, caused probably by an earthquake in the first instance, and gradually widened and deepened by the action of water. The sides of this ravine went down in broken precipices for thousands of feet, and were clothed with dense undergrowth and monstrous ferns, the home, as one could well imagine, of every reptile and loathsome insect to be found in Brazil. At the bottom of the ravine was a brawling river.

We had scarcely gained the shelter of the cave, at the mouth of which some wood ashes still smouldered, when the storm burst with appalling fury. We could see the lightning occasionally smite the rocks, tearing off great masses and hurling them into the dark depths of the ravine, where probably human foot had never yet trod; while the roll of the thunder was so awful that it seemed like the bursting up of the universe. Anita appeared to delight in the storm, and now and again she raised her long skinny arms straight up above her head and laughed like one demented. Presently she turned and motioned us to follow her, and led the way into the depths of the cavern, having first lighted a pine torch which she drew from a recess in the rocks, and plunged it into the glowing ashes. We went along a kind of corridor, but had to stoop low to avoid battering our skulls against the jagged roof. The floor was wet and soft, and Anita, in answer to my inquiries, said it was due to a natural spring of water which gave her a supply all the year round.

When we had traversed about a dozen yards, the root got higher in the passage, and after another few yards we found ourselves in a spacious chamber, with an almost perfectly level floor. Looking up, one could see nothing but darkness, so high was the roof, and beyond was what appeared to be another passage. The cavern, according to Anita, penetrated into the bowels of the mountains for more than a league, but she alone knew the secrets of those inner passages and chambers, and would reveal them to no one. I was led to inquire the cause of a strange rumbling noise I heard, and she told me it was due to a subterranean river.

In the chamber in which we found ourselves a hammock was stretched from two opposite points of rock, and afforded the witch good sleeping quarters, no doubt. There were also two or three wooden stools about, and on the floor, arranged on what appeared to be a square of carpet, was a miscellaneous collection of articles, including an old-fashioned sword, some peculiarly shaped goblets, a large wooden bowl, some human bones, several knives, including a hunting knife, an old gun, and various boxes. In another corner of the chamber I noticed a quantity of cooking utensils, which seemed to indicate that there was a good deal of the human about the old witch after all, and that if she loved solitude she also liked a certain amount of comfort. In such a country a woman of that kind was sure to get an evil reputation, whether she deserved it or not.

At my bidding Torquato unpacked his knapsack, and I presented my peace-offering of tobacco and rum, which the hag accepted with every sign of gratification, and filling a wooden cup with some of the rum, tossed it off at a draught. She had stuck the torch in a niche or hole in the rock, and its flickering, dancing flame threw a Rembrandt weirdness over the scene; and every time the woman's eyes caught the flame they glowed and glistened with such an unnatural light that I experienced a sense of creepiness which is hard to describe. The woman's whole appearance was so uncanny that while the hammock and the cooking utensils proclaimed her human, she seemed altogether unnatural, and, I am bound to add, devilish. She squatted on the floor while I and Torquato occupied stools. I told her the purpose of my errand; and the whole of the time while I was speaking she fixed her glowing eyes upon me, but they did not look at me, but through me. When I had finished my story she drew her knees up, rested her chin on them, and became very thoughtful; and though I spoke to her several times, she made no reply, and Torquato said she was in a trance. Whether that was really so or not I don't know. But when the silence had remained unbroken for nearly half an hour, she rose up slowly, and not without a certain dignity and grace, and turning her glowing eyes on me, said:

'In three days the Senhor will come here again when the sun is declining, and I will talk with him.'

'But why not now?' I asked, beginning to regard her as a humbug whose strange and uncouth appearance helped her to pass as a witch-woman.

'I have spoken. In three days,' she replied, in such a decisive, commanding manner that I felt further parley would be useless.

'And can Torquato come with me?' I asked.

'Yes. 'Tis well he should. Go.'

There was no mistaking that peremptory order to depart; and, led by the negro, I groped my way back along the corridor, and was thankful to get into the open air. The rain had ceased, but the thunder still growled, the lightning still flashed; the air was delightful and refreshing after the rain. We stood for a few minutes at the entrance to the cavern, drinking in pure draughts of the cool fresh air, when suddenly there issued from the cave an eldritch scream, so piercing, so agonizing that it seemed to indicate suffering beyond human endurance, so startling that I instinctively made a movement to rush back into the interior of the cavern with a view to ascertaining the cause of that awful cry. But Torquato gripped my arm like a vice, and drew me forcibly away. His eyes were filled with a scared expression, and his face told of deadly fear working within.

'Come away, come,' he whispered with suppressed excitement. 'Anita is quarrelling with her master the Devil, and he is scourging her.'

I could hardly refrain from bursting into laughter at this statement; but Torquato looked so serious, so terribly in earnest, and evidently so firmly believed in what he said that I refrained. He continued to drag me along for some distance before he released my arm. He was then breathless and agitated, and sat down on a rock, and removing his large grass hat, he scraped the beads of perspiration from his forehead.

I was sorry, when I came to think of it, that I had allowed myself to be baulked in my intention to learn the cause of the strange wild cry which presumably came from Anita's lips; and for an instant I was tempted to reascend the mountain and enter the cavern again. But a glance at Torquato's scared face caused me to alter my mind, and in a few minutes we recommenced the descent, and in due time got back to the station. I had then come to feel a conviction that Anita was a humbug, and the scream was part of her imposition.

It was with something like feverish anxiety that I waited for the three days to pass. I really had no faith at that time in Anita's powers to tell me what I wished to know; but she was a remarkable creature, so uncanny and weird and wild in her aspects, so interesting as a study of abnormity that I was anxious to know more of her. I think I may safely say curiosity prompted me more than anything else, though I thought there was a bare possibility she *might* be able to clear up the mystery. When the morning of the third day came I found that Torquato was reluctant to again visit Anita, but at last I overcame his reluctance and scruples by the medium of silver dollars liberally bestowed, and without making known the objects of our journey we set off, well armed as before, and well provided with food in case of need. We hadn't the advantage of a clouded sky as on the previous visit, and the sun beat down with pitiless rays from the clear blue heavens. The heat was intense and tried my powers of endurance very much, but Torquato, being a child of the sun, was indifferent to the heat. As I suffered a good deal our progress was necessarily slow. Moreover, we had to exercise extreme caution on account of the numerous deadly snakes that lay in our path basking in the broiling sun, amongst them being the brilliant dazzling coral snake, one of the most beautiful but most deadly of the serpent tribe. It is a very vicious brute, and is said to be the only snake in Brazil that will attack a man without provocation—though in some districts the same thing is said about the sorocotinga,[77] which is also terribly deadly, and with no beauty to fascinate as in the case of the coral.

So slow was our progress that the sun was far down towards the western horizon when we reached our destination. We were startled by suddenly and unexpectedly coming upon Anita squatted on her haunches before the entrance to the cavern, while round her right arm was coiled a coral snake, its head moving backwards and forwards with a rhythmical sway. Instinctively I drew back, for the sight was so repulsive, but Anita rose and told us to follow her, and when I expressed my dislike of the snake, she waved her left hand before it, and its head and neck dropped straight down as if it were dead. I was amazed, for this power over the deadly reptile proved in itself that she was no ordinary being, although she might be an impostor in other respects. Both Torquato and myself hesitated to follow the hag. When noticing this she turned angrily and cried:

'Why come you here if you are afraid? You seek knowledge which I alone can give you. If you are cowards, go at once and come here no more.'

The taunt had its effect. I did my best to overcome the repugnance and even horror that I felt and entered the cavern with boldness, or at any rate assumed boldness, and Torquato followed. We reached the inner chamber where we had been on the previous visit. A burning torch was stuck in the rock, and threw a blood-red glare over the scene. I noted that the carpet was no longer there, but in its place stood a peculiarly shaped brazier containing living charcoal that gave off unpleasant fumes.

The old woman uncoiled the snake from her arm. It offered no resistance. It appeared to be perfectly passive. Then she coiled it into the figure of 8 at her feet, and told us to sit cross-legged on the ground as she did.

'You seek to know the past,' she said, fixing her awful eyes upon me.

---

77 The local name for a species of venomous viper.

'Yes.'

'But not the future?'

'No.'

''Tis well.'

She began to make eccentric movements with both her hands before our eyes, and what followed was as a dream. I was conscious of a peculiar sense of languor stealing over me that was far from unpleasant. Presently I saw the woman snatch the burning torch from the niche in the rock and extinguish it, and we were plunged in Cimmerian gloom. A few minutes, as it seemed to me, passed, when a startling and peculiar light permeated the cavern. It proceeded from the brazier, from which rose a slender blue column of vapour that gave off apparently a phosphorescent glow. Anita was still standing, the snake was hanging from her neck, its head darting backwards and forwards viciously as if it were attacking its prey, while the woman with her long skinny arms described figures in the air. The blue, flowing column of smoke or vapour rose slowly, for it was dense and spread out mushroom shape until it filled every corner and crevice, and I seemed at last to be gazing through the medium of blue glass at a rolling prairieland over which the sun was shining brightly. The woman, the snake, the brazier, had faded away now, and only that vast stretch of sun-scorched prairie was visible. But presently, afar off, I saw two people on horseback. They gradually came nearer, and I recognized my sweet wife and Jocelino. Juliette was laughing merrily and seemed blithe and happy. They halted in the shadow of a rock, and hobbling their horses partook of their midday meal. That finished, and after a short siesta, they mounted their steeds and rode at a gallop towards a belt of virgin forest which they entered and were lost to my view. Presently they emerged, each bearing a mass of a peculiar orchid with flowers of the most brilliant colours. They dismounted again and knelt down on the ground to arrange the flowers in a more convenient way for carrying. From out of the forest, and all unobserved by them, a tall, powerful Indian hunter stole, and crept stealthily towards them. I wanted to cry out, to warn them, but I couldn't; I was spell-bound. The Indian reached them, and with an extraordinarily rapid sweep of his arm he plunged a long knife into my loved one's bosom. Jocelino half started up, but before he could offer resistance the arm swept round and the knife was plunged into his breast. With a grim sardonic grin on his features, the murderer wiped his dripping blade, and returned to the forest, reappearing after some lapse of time grasping a writhing coral snake, which he suddenly flung high into the air, and when it fell with a dull thud at his feet he struck it on the head with the handle of his knife.

He next dropped upon his knees and seemed to go through some form of incantation, throwing dirt upon his head, bowing his forehead to the ground, and raising his hand to heaven alternately, until at last he rose, laid the bodies side by side on their backs, and placed the snake at full length between them. Then the whole scene faded, and there was a blank.

Once more the same scene came before my eyes, but this time it was moonlight. The soft silver light threw a mysterious sheen over the landscape. I saw a man come out of the forest. It was the murderer. His face was filled with a look of concentrated horror, and he began to move slowly across the prairie, glancing about him in a nervous, agitated way. I became conscious at last that he was coming towards me, and I was filled with a fierce joy at the thought that when he came within reach I could strangle him where he stood. The strangeness of it all is I could not move; I appeared to be rooted to the spot, but the Indian ever approached nearer to me, drawn by some power which he tried to resist, but against which he was helpless. And so nearer and nearer he came, and all the while that expression of concentrated horror was on his face. Although I could not move from the spot where I seemed to be rooted, fiercer and fiercer grew my joy, and I waved my hands about in expectant eagerness at the thought of being able at last to crush the worthless life out of the murderer of my sainted wife. On he came. I got frantic, I tugged and strained, but could not break away from the power that held me; my eyes ached with the strain put upon them, my pulses beat with a loud, audible noise, so it seemed to me; there was a burring and buzzing in my ears, an awful burning sensation was in my brain. I felt as if I were going mad with the horror of suspense.

At length the murderer came within my reach. I flung out my hands to seize him, when suddenly the moonlight faded, and there was total darkness. How long this darkness lasted I know not, but gradually the light began to spread over the landscape again; the moon shone full once more. At my feet the Indian lay on his back. One knee was drawn up; one arm was bent under his body, the other was raised up as if he were appealing to Heaven; his face was twisted and contorted with agony. He made no motion; he was stark and dead. Some strange irresistible fascination caused me to fix my gaze upon him, and as I watched I saw the face wither, the eyes fall into the sockets. Then the flesh of the arm turned green, and blue, and yellow, and gradually dropped rotten from the bones. Next the rest of the body began to rot away leaving the bones bare. Loathsome crawling things fed upon the decaying flesh, and cobras twisted themselves round his legs and arms.

The maddening, ghastly, gruesome horror of the scene was more than human brain could stand; and when a huge vulture suddenly descended and tore out the entrails and began to gorge upon them the climax was reached. With a mighty effort I burst the spell that enthralled me; uttered a great cry, and fell prone upon the ground.

What happened after that I know not. What I do know is I seemed suddenly to awake from a deep sleep. Above me the stars and moon were shining. From somewhere, far below, came the sound of falling water. The air was deliciously cool. I was covered with the skin of an animal, and squatted near me was Anita waving a palm leaf to keep the insects from my face. I glanced round and recognized that I was lying at the entrance to the cave.

'What does all this mean?' I asked.

'You have dreamed dreams,' she answered. 'You have seen that which is. Seek to know no more. But sleep, sleep, sleep.' She repeated the word 'sleep' with a sort of drowsy croon that seemed to lull and soothe me.

There was another blank. When I next awoke it was broad daylight and the sun was already high. I was lying on a bed of skins at the entrance to the cave. I sat up, and the sound of the falling water far below in the ravine sounded pleasantly. I called 'Anita, Anita!' but there was no response. Presently I saw a figure crawling from the cavern. It was Torquato. He suddenly flung himself upon me, and wept and moaned like one distraught.

'Oh, master, master, what horrors!' he cried.

'Of what do you speak?' I asked. 'Tell me all.'

Gradually he regained control of himself. Then he recited to me all he had witnessed. It was identical with what I had seen. The murder, the mystery of the snake, the rotting corpse, the loathsome maggots, the vulture gnawing the entrails. Again I called Anita, but there was no response. I bade Torquato go into the cave and seek her, but he flatly refused. I struggled to my feet. I felt strangely ill and weak, and every now and then I shuddered as a remembrance of the horror came back. Still I was anxious to see Anita again and question her. I entered the cavern, but all was dark and silent. I groped my way forward for some distance and called once more. Only the echoes answered me. It was all so solemn, so awe inspiring, so mysterious that I was glad to return to the fresh air again and to hear the voice of my companion. It was evident Anita did not intend to come to us, and so we slowly made our way down the mountain and reached the station at midday. And

I had resolved by that time to make another visit to Anita. For several days, however, I had to keep my bed as I was feverish and ill. Then I summoned Torquato. He had also been ill, and when I asked him if he would go with me to Anita once more, he said, 'No, not for a ton of gold'; so I sent to the little town for a notary. When he came I requested Torquato to tell the notary his marvellous experience and what he had seen. The notary wrote it down; Torquato signed it, and I appended a note over my own signature to the effect that I had witnessed the same scene. We next went before the Mayor of Paraúna and testified on oath to the correctness of our narrative, and that done, the strange document was deposited in the municipal archives of the town, where no doubt it can still be seen by the curious. My next step was to send out a party of trained hunters to the place where the bodies had been found, with instructions to search for miles round for any indications of a human skeleton. They returned after many days, and reported that two leagues or so from the spot where the crime was committed, in a sandy sun-smitten waste, where only a few cacti grew, they came across the bleached skeleton of a man. The bones were falling apart, but it seemed as if one leg had been drawn up, one arm bent under the body, the other raised. Beside the body lay a long, rusty knife. Who the man was we never discovered. Even the knife was unlike those in use in that part of the country. That the skeleton was the skeleton of my wife's murderer I haven't a shadow of a doubt. Why he murdered her must remain a mystery until the secrets of all hearts be known. Who Anita was, and by what marvellous power she was able to show me the horrors she did, I have no knowledge. There are mysteries of the earth which the human brain cannot comprehend. It is given to only a few to see as I have seen and live.

For many years I have kept the awful secrets to myself, but the sands of my life are running low, and I resolved to give to the world the story of my strange experiences. To those who may be inclined to scoff I would repeat, 'There are more things in heaven and earth than are dreamt of in your philosophy.'

NOTE TO 'THE MYSTIC SPELL.'—Although Signor Roderick, who supplies the material for the foregoing remarkable story, suggests no theory for the murder of his wife and her attendant, any one who has travelled in the interior of Brazil will have no difficulty in doing so. The Indians are exceedingly superstitious, resentful, and blood thirsty, as they are in many parts of Mexico. In the case of the Brazilians who inhabit the wild parts of the country, they regard certain parts of the virgin forests as their own special domains. As mentioned in the story, it is very unusual for a lady of good social position to be seen abroad, and the freedom which Juliette enjoyed in this respect was an innovation. Now if the vision that Signor Roderick saw, and which was conjured up by the mystic power of the witch-woman, was an accurate representation of the crime, it is easy to understand that some savage Indian, who had seen Juliette and Joceline enter the forest and carry off the orchid bloom, resented it. Moreover, he may have regarded Juliette as an unnatural being, for probably he had never seen a white woman before. No women—save Indian women, and they but rarely—ever entered those deadly forests, the haunts and homes of the most venomous reptiles and the most savage animals, where there are plants exuding so virulent a poison that if but one drop falls on the flesh gangrene ensues; where loathsome insects fall upon the intruder from the trees and eat their way into his body; where the very air is deadly to those who breathe it, other than the native born. Juliette's presence, therefore, in such a place must have filled the Indian with dire alarm, and inflamed him with a desire to slay her. To him, no doubt, the crime would appear as a justifiable one. Anyway, with the stealth and cunning of his kind he crept after her, and his cruel knife drank her blood, and having killed her, it followed as a matter of course that he should kill her companion.

Now these Indians worship strange gods and sacrifice to them, and snake sacrifice is common, not only in the interior of Brazil, but in Mexico. The slaying of the coral snake was therefore a sacrifice on the part of the murderer. How he met his own death must ever remain a mystery. Probably he himself perished from snakebite, for though these Indians show an extraordinary fearlessness of poisonous reptiles, and will catch them and handle them in a way that makes a stranger shudder, they are not proof against their bites, although they boast that they possess infallible antidotes against the venom of the serpent. This, however, may be regarded as no more than a boast. In the forests of Brazil are to be found some of the most horrible snakes the world produces. Apart from the Cobra coral, or to give it its scientific name, *Elaps maregravii*,[78] rattlesnakes of the most virulent kind are found, and then there is the hideous Cascavel.[79] It is said that death follows the bite of this snake almost immediately. The victim goes suddenly blind,

---

78 Nowadays this is called *Micrurus ibiboboca*, the caatinga coral snake.
79 A region to the west of Paraná.

and the flesh commences to peel off his bones through gangrene even before the breath is out of his body. The annual death roll from snake-bite in all parts of South America is appalling; and, as might be supposed, the Indians who roam the forests and prairies, either as animal or orchid hunters, furnish a large percentage of the victims. It is a feasible theory, therefore, that the cruel murderer of Juliette and Joceline lost his life through snakebite, probably the bite of the Cascavel.

As regards Anita, one can only suppose that she was possessed of some strange mesmeric or hypnotic power; but even if that were so, one is puzzled to understand how she was able to show her subjects the scene and incidents of the crime unless she herself knew them. The theory that suggests itself here is that during the three days' interval between Signor Roderick consulting her and his second visit, she had learned the story of the crime from some of the wandering Indians. She herself was an Indian and would be regarded by her tribe as 'a wise woman.' But whatever theory one likes to accept, it is a well-known fact attested over and over again by travellers that some of the Indian women of South America, especially in the neighbourhood of the Amazon, are gifted with the power of second sight and of forecasting the future. Such women are held in veneration by their own people, but Christians believe that they have an unholy alliance with the common enemy of mankind.

XV

The Doomed Man

FROM THE PAPERS OF THE LATE MR. RICHARD JOHN
GIBLING, MERCHANT, OF THE CITY OF LONDON

A S TO WHETHER THIS story shall or shall not see the light of publicity I leave to the discretion of my executor. I am resolved that
in my time it shall remain my own secret. I am partly actuated to this
course by a peculiar and constitutional sensitiveness to anything like
ridicule; while for a man in my position, a sober, prosaic merchant,
engaged in trade in London, to confess to belief in the supernatural,
would not only subject me to a good deal of chaff, but might possibly,
indeed I think it is highly probable that it would do me a good deal
of injury in my business. City life is a hard, stern struggle for existence. The City man is governed by immutable conventional laws, and
woe betide any one who transgresses them. Men engaged in business
generally become slaves to custom. You must don a tall hat and frock
coat; you must assume a smug respectability; you must go to church
on Sunday; your name must appear occasionally in charitable lists;
you must speak deferentially of your mayor and corporation; you must
conform to all the traditions and customs of the City, as prescribed by
the unwritten laws; you must periodically be seen at Guild[80] dinners;
your holidays must be taken at a fixed time, and be of a specified duration. In a word, 'must' may be said to be the text of your life. You must
do this and mustn't do that. And if you have the hardihood and boldness to set your face against the stern and fast rules to which you tacitly
bind yourself when you become a City man, well then, all the worse
for you. Now with a knowledge of these facts, which cannot be gain-
said, it will be understood why I have been so reluctant to make known
the extraordinary incidents which I here note down for the interest of
those who are curious in such things. But extraordinary as they are, I
set them forth as matter of hard, solid, undeniable truth. Throughout
my life I have taken 'Truth' as my watchword, as my father and grand-

---

80 A group of people working in the same trade or profession might belong to a guild.
  Towns and cities often have a guildhall where guild meetings would have taken
  place.

father did before me. It has been my proud boast, warranted by facts, that my word has been as good as my bond. And in all my dealings with men of many complexions of mind, no one could or would have thought of impugning my honour, my *bona fides*,[81] or my veracity. The business in which I was brought up, after a course at a public school, and to which I succeeded on the death of my esteemed father, was a very old-established one, having been founded by my paternal grandfather and his brother at the beginning of the seventeenth century.

It was in the year 1847, as our business and trade were spreading, that I opened a branch of our London house in Cuba, and placed a trusted and experienced manager in charge. Unfortunately this gentleman died in 1850, after a few days' illness, of yellow fever, and it became imperatively necessary that I should proceed at once to Cuba to look into matters, and appoint a successor to the deceased manager. A City friend recommended me to take passage in a rather noted sailing vessel called the *Pride of the Ocean*, belonging to a Liverpool firm, and then loading in the Liverpool docks, being chartered to proceed direct to Cuba. I thereupon applied to the owners, and being informed by them that the ship would be ready to sail in a week at the latest, I engaged my passage in her. She was a full-rigged ship of about a thousand tons, and was reputed to be able to sail with a fair wind seventeen knots an hour, being clipper built.

I arrived in Liverpool on the very day that the ship was advertised to sail. I was informed that she would warp out of the dock at midnight, when it would be high-water, and that two tugs would at once take hold of her and tow her beyond Holyhead. I did not reach Liverpool until the evening, and drove at once from the railway station to the vessel and went on board. Of course, everything was in the wildest confusion, and the noise and hubbub deafening; so, on receiving an assurance from the mate that I still had three or four hours at my disposal, I drove to the Adelphi Hotel, dined, played a game of billiards with a London gentleman with whom I had a passing acquaintance, and at eleven o'clock once more drove down to the docks and got on board the ship as the dock gates were being opened. Being very tired I went straight to bed, and the next morning, as the sea was very rough, I could not get up, as I am a poor sailor, and generally ill for three or four days at the commencement of a voyage. On this occasion I was a full week before I found my sea legs and sea stomach, and one morning I took my place

---

81 Good faith, from the Latin.

at the breakfast table for the first time, and was welcomed and greeted by the captain, whom I had not seen before. We were a very small party, as there were only three passengers beside myself, one being a Spanish lady who had been transacting some business in England on behalf of her husband, who was a Cuban planter.

The captain's name was Jubal Tredegar, a native of Cornwall, as I gathered. He was about fifty years of age, and had been at sea for over thirty. He had a swarthy sunburnt face, very dark hair, and black eyes, with a full, rounded beard, but clean-shaven upper lip. In every respect he was a typical sailor, save in one thing—he was the most melancholy seaman I have ever come across. It is proverbial of sailors that they are a rollicking, jovial set; but this man was the exception to the rule, and he at once gave me the impression that he had something on his mind. My sympathies were in consequence of this aroused, and I mentally resolved that I would endeavour to win his confidence, in the hope that I might be of use to him.

At first, however, I found that he was inclined to be taciturn, and resent any attempt to draw him out; but I learnt from the mate, that Tredegar had commanded the ship for three voyages, and was highly respected by the owners. He was a thoroughly experienced navigator, and studied his owners' interests. There was one thing I could not fail to note; he showed a disposition to talk more to me than to any one else, and discovering that he played a good game at cribbage[82]—a game I was particularly partial to—I got into closer touch with him, as one evening he accepted my invitation to a game, and after that we played whenever opportunity offered. But still he became neither communicative nor talkative, and no subject I could start appeared to have any interest for him.

We were playing, as was now our wont, one night in the cuddy[83] after supper, when I noticed that he seemed more than usually depressed, and kept examining the barometer and casting an anxious eye up through the skylight.

'What does the glass say, captain?' I asked at last.

'Well,' he answered, 'I think we are going to have a blow. There is dirty weather about somewhere.'

When four bells (ten o'clock) struck we finished our game and he went into his cabin, while I mounted the companion-way to the poop,

---

82 A card game that uses a wooden board and small pegs to keep the score.
83 A small cabin.

intending to smoke my usual cigar before turning in. I had run short of cigars, and the captain had promised to let me have a box of good Havanas, but not until I reached the deck did I remember that I had not a single weed in my case, so I went below again, and to the skipper's room, intending to ask him for the cigars. Getting no response to my knock I pushed the door open and was surprised to see him seated at his table, so absorbed in gazing at the photograph of a lady that he had not heard my knock. On perceiving me, he hastily thrust the photograph into a drawer and jumped up. I noticed him pass his hands over his eyes and turn away as if ashamed, pretending to search for something on the top of a chest or drawers. I thought it was an opportunity not to be lost so I said to him:

'Pray excuse my intrusion; I knocked but you didn't hear me. I would also take the liberty of saying I respect your emotion. A man need not be ashamed of moist eyes when he gazes on the face of some loved one who is far away. It's human. It shows a kindly heart, an impressionable mind!'

He turned suddenly and, putting out his hand to me, said: 'Thank you, thank you, Mr. Gibling! You are a good sort. A little sympathy sometimes is not a bad thing, and, hardened old shellback as I am, I suppose I've got a soft spot somewhere. But, excuse me, I must go on deck.'

I made known my errand, and having procured the box of cigars for me from his locker, I carried them to my cabin, and he went on deck, and when I had opened the box and taken two or three cigars out I followed him. The night was very dark. Nearly all the sails were set. There was an unpleasant, lumpy sea, and the wind was blowing in fitful gusts.

The captain ordered the watch to shorten sail, but before the order was entirely carried out a squall struck us, and the vessel heeled over tremendously and commenced to fly through the water, churning the sea around her into white, flashing, phosphorescent froth. Anyone who has ever made a voyage in a sailing ship knows the apparent, and often real, confusion that ensues when a sudden squall strikes the vessel. At such times the wind will frequently blow for a few minutes with hurricane force, and it is no unusual thing for sails to be split to ribbons—even for spars to be carried away. Given a dark night, a heavy squall, a rough sea, rent sails, and the land lubber who is unmoved must be made of very stern stuff. The rifle-like report and cracking of the long shreds of the torn sail are alarming enough to the inexperienced; but when you add to this the rattling of the ropes, the banging of blocks, the groaning of the ship's timbers, the harsh creaking of the spars, the roar, swish and hiss of the waves, the great masses of boiling white foam that spread around, and the hoarse voices of men on deck to unseen men up above on the yard-arms in the mysterious darkness, there is at once a scene which tests the nerves of the landsman to a very considerable extent.

The squall that struck the *Pride of the Ocean* was a very heavy one, and the main topsail went to ribbons. The skipper, who was a perfect seaman, issued his orders rapidly, but with judgement and a display of self-possession, while his officers ably seconded him. Three or four times he came close to me as he shifted his position on the poop, the better to make his voice heard above the howling of the wind, and the noises incidental to the tossing ship. I did not attempt to address him, knowing full well that at such a moment he required to concentrate all his attention on his duties. Once, when he came near me, I heard him mutter to my intense astonishment—'My God, my God, have pity on me!' It may be imagined to what an extent I was affected by this utterance. Had he said, 'Have pity on *us*,' I should at once have jumped to the conclusion that we were all in danger, but the cry for pity was for himself alone. It set me pondering, and connecting it with his usual melancholy, and the sad and distressful expression of his face, I was not only puzzled but anxious. A few minutes later, as the ship did not pay off as rapidly as she should have done, Captain Tredegar ran to the wheel to help the helmsman to jam the rudder harder over, and as he glanced at the binnacle[84] and his features were illumined by the light from the lamp, I was perfectly startled by his ghastly pallor. To such an extent was I moved that I rushed to him and asked in an excited way if he was ill. With a powerful sweep of his right arm he moved me from before him, and in tones of terror exclaimed—'There it is again! There, out there on the crest of that wave!' I peered into the darkness, but could see nothing save the phosphorescent gleam of the tumbling sea.

By this time I was quite unnerved, for a dreadful thought took possession of me. I thought that the skipper was suffering from incipient madness.

In a few minutes, having got the wheel well over, he called one of the watch aft to assist the steersman, and he himself went forward to the break of the poop, and continued to give his orders. By this time the men had got the flying ropes and flapping sails under control, and, the dark scud in the heavens driving to leeward before the hurricane blast,

---

84 A waist-high structure for holding the ship's compass.

the moon peeped through the ragged film and threw a weird, ghostly gleam of shimmering light over the swirling waters, while the track of the squall could be followed as it drove down the heavens to strike some other wanderer on the deep.

As is often the case, at the tail of the great blast was a deluge. It was as if some huge door in the sky had been opened and the waters fell out in a cataract. I hurried below, as I had no desire to be soaked to the skin, and when I reached the cuddy I found the Spanish lady passenger seated at the table, looking very scared and unhappy.

'Oh, Mr. Gibling,' she exclaimed, 'is there any danger? What an awful storm!'

I assured her that all was well, and that the rain would probably bring a dead calm.

'Did you see the captain?' she asked, still displaying great agitation.

There was something in her manner and the tone of her voice that struck me as peculiar, and I replied:

'Yes. I saw him on deck.'

'Ah, but I mean here. He has just come down and gone to his room. I spoke to him, but he would not answer me. He looked awful. I am sure there is something queer about him. His eyes seemed bulging from his head, and if he had seen a ghost he couldn't have been whiter. He is either ill or going mad. Do go to him.'

The lady's words did not tend to allay my own fears and suspicions, but, anxious not to add to her alarm, I said with an air of assumed indifference:

'The fact is, I suppose, he is over-anxious. Not that there is anything to fear, I am sure. We are in the squall zone, you know, but there is every prospect of making a good passage. However, I will go and talk to the captain.'

So saying, I left her, and made my way to the skipper's state room. I knocked as usual, but again there was no response; so I pushed the door open, and found Captain Tredegar seated in his chair, half his body bent over the table, and his face hidden by his arms. His cap had fallen off his head and was lying on the table, and I noted that his hands were opening and shutting in a spasmodic, nervous way. It was no time for ceremony. I should have been dull indeed not to recognize that the man was suffering. I therefore went to his side, and laying my hand on his shoulder said sympathetically:

'Excuse me, Captain Tredegar, but you are not well. Can I do any-thing for you? Do make a confidant of me. Believe me I am not actuated by mere vulgar curiosity. Pray command my services if I can be of any use.'

He lifted his head up. I had never seen before in any human face such a pronounced look of nervous horror. His eyes wandered about the room; the corners of his mouth twitched, and he sobbed like a child that had cried itself into a state of physical exhaustion. I was positively alarmed, and my first impulse was to run for assistance. As if divining my thoughts he seized my wrist in his powerful hand, thereby detaining me, and said in a broken voice:

'Pardon me, sir, you are very good. I am suffering from an attack to which I am at rare intervals subject; but I shall be all right directly. Please don't make a scene. There is some rum there in that bottle, give me a little neat. It will set me up.'

Although I was doubtful whether neat rum was the proper remedy in such a case, I could not resist his appealing manner, and taking the bottle from the rack I poured into a glass about a tablespoonful.

'Oh, more than that, more than that,' he cried. 'Fill the glass nearly.'

Perhaps at any other time I should have argued against his request, but I let the rum run from the bottle until the tumbler was quite half-full. He clutched it with trembling hand, and poured the contents at one gulp down his throat.

'Thanks, thanks,' he said, as he recovered his breath and placed the glass on the table. 'That will put new life into me. I feel better already.'

He rose, shook with a shudder as he did so, and taking his sou'-wester and oilskin from a peg donned himself in them. He put a hand on each of my shoulders, and looking me in the face, said with an impressive earnestness:

'Mr. Gibling, I am more than obliged to you. Add to my obligation, will you, by promising not to mention to anyone that you have seen me in one of my strange moods.'

'Certainly I will,' I replied with perfect frankness. 'You may trust me. And, as I have said, if I can be of service command me.'

'Very well; some day I may put you to the test,' he answered; 'good-night, and God bless you.'

He left me, and I heard him clatter up the gangway in his great boots. As I crossed towards my own cabin the Spanish lady was still sitting at the cuddy table.

'Have you been with the captain?' she asked.

'I have,' I replied.

'How is he?'

'He is all right,' I answered lightly.

She glanced about the cuddy as if to make sure no one was listening, and then, bending towards me as if inviting confidence, she said in a half whisper:

'Do you know, Mr. Gibling, when the captain came down from the deck a little while ago there was such a peculiar look in his face that I could almost have fancied he——'

She stopped suddenly in her speech, visibly shuddered, and put her pretty white fingers before her eyes. After an awkward pause I broke the silence by saying:

'Almost fancied he—what?'

'He had seen some gruesome and unnatural sight.'

I laughed, though I had an inkling of her meaning, for strangely enough a vague, phantom-like thought had been troubling me; but I could not define it, could not give it shape; now at her words it was clear enough, and an uncontrollable impulse impelled me to give it utterance:

'Ghosts, you mean,' and I laughed at my own words, for the idea seemed to me—a prosy,[85] staid, unromantic, London citizen—so utterly ridiculous. But not so to the lady. Her face assumed a graver aspect, and her eyes betrayed that whatever my views might be her mind was made up.

'What I mean is, he has seen a vision,' she remarked, with awe in her voice.

'Oh, nonsense,' I exclaimed. 'Hobgoblins and bogeys belong to the period of our childhood. When we come to years of discretion we should cease to be childish.'

My remark annoyed her. She rose and curled her lip disdainfully. 'I am not childish and I don't talk nonsense,' she said, as she swept past me without so much as giving me a chance to apologize. I felt annoyed with myself for having been so tactless, but otherwise laughed mentally at what I considered the absurdity of the position.

A few minutes later I went on deck to finish my final smoke before turning in. The rain had ceased. The air was delightfully cool. The wind had gone, but cats-paws came up every now and then, bellying the sails out for a moment or two with a great jerk, but dropping suddenly the canvas fell back against the masts with a bang and rattle of blocks and creaking of sheaves. The sky was a mass of picturesque clouds with fantastic outlines. Here and there groups of stars were visible, and with

---

85 Dull and unimaginative.

chastened light, as if shining through gauze, the moon made a silver pathway over the face of the deep until it blended with the horizon in impenetrable blackness, which rounded off, so to speak, the weird scene. The captain had discarded his oilskins, which were lying on the top of a hencoop, and he himself was leaning on his elbows over the taffrail, complacently smoking a cigar, and absorbed apparently in the contemplation of the phosphoric display that flashed and glistened under the ship's counter as she fell and rose to the swell. I approached him. He straightened himself up, turned his back to the rail, folded his arms across his breast, and puffing at his cigar as he cast a scrutinizing eye aloft at the flapping sails, he said in a cheerful tone:

'Quite a contrast to a little while ago, isn't it, Mr. Gibling? But it's the sort of weather we must expect in these latitudes.'

I was struck by his changed manner. He seemed so cheerful and light-hearted. He wasn't like the same man I had seen down in the cabin half an hour ago.

'Yes, I suppose so,' I remarked, for the sake of saying something.

'It's not your first voyage to sea, is it?' he asked.

'No.'

'Have you been to Cuba before?'

'Oh yes.'

'Ah! then you will know pretty well what kind of voyage it is.'

I told him that I knew fairly well what one might expect on such a voyage at that time of the year, and we continued to chat pleasantly for a little while until six bells struck (eleven o'clock). 'All's well!' came in solemn tones from the look-out man on the fo'c'stle.

'Well, I think I shall turn in,' said the captain, as he threw the stump of his cigar overboard, glanced up aloft, then at the binnacle, and calling the second officer who was on watch, and telling him to keep the ship on the same course until the morning, he moved towards the companion way, and I followed. When we reached the saloon he put out his hand. As I took it he said 'Good-night,' and immediately added in lower tones, 'Don't forget your promise.'

I turned in and tried to sleep, but for a long time tossed about, thinking of what had passed, and trying to account for the captain's strange behaviour; but the more I thought the more I got puzzled, and I came to the conclusion there was some strange mystery about him. I saw through my port the sun beginning to redden the eastern horizon before sleep came to me. I did not waken until long after the usual breakfast hour, so I breakfasted alone. The steward had kept something hot for me.

When I went on deck I noticed the Spanish lady reclining in a deck chair, near the companion-way. She was reading a book, and perhaps that accounted for her taking no notice of me as I bowed and said 'Good morning.'

The sun was shining brilliantly. The sky was cloudless save on the horizon, where there were woolly banks. A steady little breeze just kept the sails full, and the short, choppy waves danced and flashed in the sunlight with a suggestiveness of joy and gladness. The captain was not on deck, and I was informed by the second mate, who had the morning watch, that he had not turned out yet. Wishing to propitiate the Spanish lady passenger, I carried a camp stool to where she was sitting, and in the most fascinating manner I was capable of commanding I asked if I could sit beside her. She smiled sweetly, and accorded her gracious permission. We said some commonplace things about the weather; she descanted on the tropical beauties of Cuba, and criticized rather severely the English climate; while as for London, she spoke of it with scorn and much shrugging of shoulders; and to my amusement, although I must admit the truth of some of her strictures, she described it as a grim and grimy city of revolting ugliness, a city without poetry, without music, without sun. A city where the people struggled and cursed and jostled each other for bare existence. A city where the rich disdained to sniff the same air as the poor. A city of gin palaces and churches, of hypocrisy and smug self-conceit. A city of leprous sores and devilish wickedness, of hateful shams and heartless indifference, where the poor debtor was regarded as a criminal, and the rich despoiler of the widow and orphan as a saint. A city of moans and groans. A joyless, dark city, where Mammon was the only god that was truly worshipped.

These things, and many more of the same kind, she gave free vent to; and as they seemed to afford her satisfaction and did me no harm, I made no attempt to stop her flow of invective. Nor should I have noted them down here were it not that they to some extent represent the opinions which the majority of foreigners hold with regard to London.

When at last she paused from sheer exhaustion, I embraced the opportunity to turn the trend of conversation by saying:

'I am afraid, do you know, that I was a little rude to you last night,' but I hardly expected such a blunt reply as she made.

'Yes, you were exceedingly rude, and I hate rude men.'

'I hope you don't hate me,' I cried, laughingly.

'Oh no, not quite. You're a Londoner, you see.'

This was very severe. I confess I was hardly prepared for it, and I was tempted to say something cutting in reply, but checked myself, bowed, and merely remarked:

'Which is not my fault. Therefore pity me rather than blame me.'

'Certainly I do that,' she replied, with an amusing seriousness. 'But look here; answer me this. Why should you have been rude last night when I said what I did about the captain?'

'Madame,' I said, as I laid my hand on my heart and bowed, 'believe me I had no intention of being rude; but the fact is, I am a somewhat commonplace, matter-of-fact man, and I have no belief in anything that is said to be due to supernatural causes.'

'Supernatural or not supernatural,' she retorted, 'there are things going on around us which certainly cannot be explained by any known laws.'

'Possibly, and yet I doubt it,' I replied, with a sceptical smile.

'Well, your obtuseness is your own affair,' she said, with a shrug of her shoulders; 'but now, look here, Mr. Gibling, permit me to make a little prophecy. Captain Tredegar has something awful on his mind. He sees visions, and will ultimately go mad.'

Her words startled me. For the first time I was inclined to regard her seriously, in one respect at least; that was the ultimate madness of the skipper. That thought had haunted me, but I had tried to put it away. Even to my somewhat dulled perception it had been made evident that a man who could act as Tredegar had acted on the previous night was a victim to some obscure form of mental disease which might ultimately destroy him. Now the lady spoke with such an absence of vagueness, such a cock-sureness, that I asked her if she had known the captain long, and if she was acquainted with his past history.

'Indeed, no,' she exclaimed. 'I never saw the man in my life until I joined the ship in Liverpool.'

'Then why do you speak with such an air of self-conviction?'

'I speak as I think. I think as I know.'

'But how do you know?'

'Well, you are stupid,' she exclaimed, with a show of exasperation. 'I know, because I have a sense you don't possess. You are a soot-sodden Londoner. I was born where the sun shines. I have beliefs, you have not. I believe that men who do evil in this world can be haunted into madness by the disembodied spirits of those they injure. Now you may laugh and sneer as much as you like, sir, but I tell you this: when Captain Tredegar came down to the cabin last night his face clearly indicated that he had been terrified by something not human, and I saw madness written large in his eyes.'

I should be wanting in common honesty if I failed to say that this woman's remarks, rude as they were to some extent, put certain rambling thoughts of my own into shape, impressed me in a way that a short time previously I should have been ashamed to own to. They set me pondering, and I tried to recall every act, word, look and gesture of the captain's, with the result that I had to admit there was something strange about him. At that moment Captain Tredegar himself came on deck, with his sextant in his hand, in order to take the noonday sights for the reckoning. His breezy, jovial manner, and smiling bronzed face, seemed to make the conversation about him ridiculous, and tended to confound the prophet who had talked of madness.

He bowed politely to the lady, and chatted to her pleasantly. He greeted me with a cheery 'Good-morning,' and expressed a hope that neither of us had been much alarmed by the squall of the previous evening. He said the passage was going to be a splendid one; one of the best he had ever made; and if, as he anticipated we should do, we picked up a good slant of wind when we had made a little more westing, we should reach Cuba several days before the time we were expected.

The mate now came on deck also with his sextant, and he and the captain walked to the break of the poop to take the sights. When he was out of earshot I turned to the lady and said:

'He doesn't look much like a man who is given to seeing visions and is doomed to madness, does he?'

'You cannot see beneath the mask,' she replied, with another contemptuous curl of her lip, and laying great stress on the 'you'; and she added somewhat mysteriously, 'Wait, wait, wait,' repeating the word three times, with a rising inflection on each repetition. Then she turned to her book again, as if she wished me to understand that she had said her say and would say no more. I took the hint, and making a show of stretching my limbs, I rose and began to pace up and down. The subject of the conversation between me and the lady continued to occupy my thoughts against my will and desire, and the more I thought the more like a riddle did the captain appear to me. I was really astonished to find myself taking so much interest in him. A passing interest in one with whom you happen to be a fellow voyager is easily understood. But if Captain Tredegar had been a relative of mine, my own brother, in fact, I could hardly have felt more anxious or more desirous to solve the mystery that seemed to surround him. His appearance that morning, and his appearance and behaviour of the night before, were in such violent contrast that to put it down to the merely varying moods to which we are all liable was not satisfactory enough. What puzzled me more than anything else was his behaviour during the storm. To suppose that he was a coward and lost his nerve in a passing squall was absurd on the face of it. In the very height of the storm he delivered his orders with coolness and judgment, as I could testify, but what did he mean by exclaiming: 'There it is again! There, out there on the crest of that wave'? Then again, why the appeal to God to pity him? Having perplexed and fretted myself until I felt quite confused, I found myself unable to alter the original opinion I had formed, which was that Captain Tredegar was liable to attacks of mental aberration, and that being so he was not a fitting person to have charge of a valuable vessel and her living freight.

Viewing the matter from this point, I came to the conclusion, rightly or wrongly, that it was my bounden duty as an honest man to make representations to his owners as to the skipper's state of mind; for surely no one would say that a man liable to attacks of temporary mania was the proper person to be in charge of a ship. As I came to this decision I heard the captain call out from the break of the poop:

'Make eight bells.'

The boatswain struck the hour on the bell, and 'eight bells' was roared out by the men about the decks, while from the galley came the smell of duff and pea soup as the cook put out the dinner for those now going off duty. I was recalled to a sense of my surroundings by these little matters, and as the skipper passed me as he was about to descend to work out his sights and prick the chart, he said cheerily:

'Well, Mr. Gibling. It's time to splice the main brace, isn't it?'

I may explain for the benefit of those who have not made a voyage to sea that it is customary in most passenger vessels for the passengers to partake of a glass of liquor of some kind at noon, eight bells. This, in nautical phraseology, is termed 'splicing the main brace.' It is the most interesting period of the twenty-four hours to lands-people, because the captain and his officers having taken their sights, as it is called, they proceed to work them out, in order to discover the position of the ship—that is, her latitude and longitude—and that being done, it is marked on the chart.

As I accompanied the skipper to the cuddy, I began to think that perhaps after all I was doing him a wrong, and it would be unfair to say anything to his owners until I had received stronger proof that my suspicions were well founded. Certainly, as he sat at the table making his calculations and working out the position, he not only seemed the perfection of physical fitness, but fully endowed with keen and sound intelligence. As I noted this I came to the conclusion that it was no less my duty to suspend my judgment—than to watch closely and wait patiently.

Should it come to pass that this paper is made public, I wish it to be distinctly understood that at this period of the voyage I was halting between two opinions. On the one hand, I considered Captain Tredegar peculiar in many respects—a man of mystery, in short—and on the other, I was painfully anxious not to do him an injustice. It will also be noted that the conclusions arrived at by the Spanish lady, who was an emotional and superstitious woman, were not in accordance with my own. For according to her views, the captain's strange behaviour was the result of seeing visions; according to mine, he suffered from intermittent mania, which was probably traceable to a too free indulgence in rum or other potent liquors. Not that I had ever seen him the worse for drink, but he took a good deal more than was good for him, in my opinion, though it did not affect him as it would have done others who were not so case-hardened.

For the next few days our progress was not very satisfactory, owing to the light, variable winds. For a steamer it would have been almost ideal weather, but dependent as we were on the winds entirely, it was very tantalizing. During this time the skipper continued in his bright, cheery mood, and every evening at a fixed hour we sat down in the cabin for a game of cribbage. I took to studying him very closely, and from many little signs I saw I felt pretty certain that a great deal of his lighthearted manner was assumed. Occasionally I noted a strange wild look came into his eyes, and his cheeks paled as though some deadly fear had seized upon him. A mere casual observer would have failed to have seen these signs, but my perception had been quickened. I was ever on the alert, on the watch, and there was not much that escaped me.

A change came at last. One evening when I expected the skipper to take part in the usual game at cribbage he brusquely and rudely refused, and I saw the half-sullen, half-terrified expression in his face again. I thought it very peculiar that his mood should synchronize with a change in the weather. The barometer had been falling all day, and it was only too evident that we were going to have a dirty night. As the sun got low in the heavens, heavy banks of clouds came up, and the wind rapidly strengthened, until we had to shorten sail to such an extent that very little canvas remained set. The captain seemed extremely anxious. He walked up and down the poop in a restless, nervous way. Occasionally he stopped to gaze windward, and sometimes he muttered to himself. I resolved at last to speak to him, anxious and preoccupied as he was. So I went boldly up to him and said:

'We are evidently in for a change, don't you think so?'

He turned upon me with a dark, lowering face, his brow knit, and his whole manner that of one straining under suppressed passion.

'Yes, I do,' he answered excitedly, 'and be d——d you. Anyway, I'm a doomed man.'

He walked rapidly away without another word, and I stood for some little time dumfounded. Anyone who could speak in such a manner was surely mad, and I seriously considered it was my business to take counsel with my fellow passengers, if not with the officers of the ship, for a mad captain ought to be relieved of his responsible duties in the interest of every soul on board. But before I could stir away the man himself came back to me, and said in a most pathetic and appealing way that went to my heart:

'Pray pardon my rudeness, Mr. Gibling. You don't know how I'm troubled. I am suffering dreadfully, and if you knew all you would pity rather than blame me.'

'Why not place me in possession of the information, then?' I asked. He put his hand to his eyes for a moment or two and shuddered.

'It is so dreadful, so horrible,' he muttered mysteriously, speaking rather to himself than me.

'All the more reason, then, why you should take me into your confidence,' I said.

'Yes—perhaps you are right. I will, I will. Come to my cabin in half an hour and I will tell you the awful story.'

Further conversation was interrupted by the bursting of a squall accompanied by heavy rain, while a long swell that came up from the S.W. was a sure precursor of the coming gales, of which the squalls were only the heralds.

I at once descended to the cabin to get out of the rain, but quite half an hour passed before the captain came down. He passed me without speaking, but called the steward and ordered some tea to be taken to his cabin. And when another half-hour had elapsed the steward brought me a message to the effect that Captain Tredegar wished to see me in his room. The weather had now become very bad and the ship was labouring heavily. I found the captain seated at his table with a small Bible open before him, but which he closed and tossed into his bunk as I entered. He looked pale, ill, and careworn. He asked me to sit down, and remarked:

'You have shown much interest in me, sir, and instinctively I feel I can place confidence in you. The time has now come for me to speak, or be dumb for evermore. I am a doomed man. My fate is sealed, and it is that fearful certainty that weighs upon me like a ton of lead.'

His words and manner seemed to me unmistakably to indicate insanity, and I could not repress a feeling of alarm. He must have guessed my thoughts, for he said quickly:

'Don't alarm yourself, and bear with me patiently; my brain is perfectly clear, and I know what I am doing, although a stranger might be disposed to think I was labouring under a distempered imagination. But it is not so. An awful fear takes possession of me and unmans me. It paralyses my faculties and renders life a curse instead of a blessing.'

'A fear of what?' I asked.

'Of the dead,' he answered solemnly.

I looked hard at him again. That surely was not the answer of a sane man.

'What nonsense,' I said a little sharply. 'What harm can the dead do to the living? I gave you credit for being stronger minded than that. It is clear to me now that you are allowing yourself to sink into a morbid, nervous condition, that must end disastrously. Why on earth should you embitter your existence by imaginary evils? Shake yourself free of morbid, gloomy forebodings; be a man, and if you are a just one you need fear nothing, not even the living, let alone the dead.'

He did not attempt to interrupt this little outburst on my part, which perhaps was hardly justified. But I could not restrain myself. I was compelled to give vent to my thoughts.

'You mean well, Mr. Gibling,' he remarked, with perfect self-possession, when I had finished speaking, 'and I understand your feelings; but before condemning me, before allowing your wrath to run away with your judgment, be patient, forbearing, and listen to me as you promised to do. This may be the only opportunity that will ever occur for me to tell you my story.'

'Pray proceed,' I remarked; 'perhaps I have been somewhat hasty; you will find, however, that I am a good listener, and under any circumstances you may count on my sympathy.'

He remained silent for some minutes, his elbows on the table, his hands clasping his face, his eyes seemingly fixed on vacancy. He started and came to himself again.

'Mr. Gibling,' he began, 'I have a very strange story to tell you if you care to listen to it. Whatever your feelings are now, however sceptical you may be, I fancy your views will undergo a change by the time I have done. I repeat that I am a doomed man. My sands have nearly run out, and I must say what I have to say now or never.'

'Please go on,' I said as he paused, evidently waiting for me to speak.

'Very well,' he continued, 'I'll begin at the beginning. As you know, I am a Cornishman; I come from a race of seamen; the salt of the sea flows in my veins. What education I received was got at a school in Devonshire, where I passed nearly nine years of my life. At that school I had a chum. We were inseparable. We were more like brothers. His name was Peter Gibson. He was three or four years my senior, and was a rough, wild, boorish sort of fellow; not good at picking up the routine knowledge of a school training, but as sharp as a needle, with an insatiable thirst for stories of fighting and adventure. In this line he would read everything he got hold of, and one day he said to me: "Jubal, I intend to go to sea, and I'm going to be a devil; will you stick to me?" he asked.

' "Yes," I answered in a moment of boyish enthusiasm. He had great influence over me. I looked up to him as my superior, and regarded him as a leader.

' "You swear it!" he demanded.

' "Yes," I said again.

'Whereupon he made me go down on my knees, hold both my hands up to heaven, and take a solemn oath that I would stick to him, go with him wherever he went, and do whatever he did.

'Now you must remember I was a youngster at this time, and what I did was only what a boy might be expected to do. Gibson certainly had a good deal of influence over me. He was a masterful sort of fellow, with a great, bulky, powerful frame, while his pluck won my admiration. He funked at nothing, and could lick every boy in the neighbourhood.

'We left school about the same time, and though his father, who was pretty well off, wanted to put him in business, Peter declared he would go to sea. I had been intended for a seafaring life from my cradle. The males of my family always went to sea. The result of his determination was that he and I found ourselves fellow apprentices on board a full-rigged vessel going out to the East Indies. She was a trader, and during a voyage of nearly four years we visited a great many places in the East; saw a great deal of the world, and experienced fair and foul weather from the very best to the very worst. As might have been expected, Peter picked up seamanship very rapidly, and became one of the smartest sailors on board. My regard for him and his liking for me had never altered, and when we returned to Liverpool, from whence we had sailed, we were as much chums as ever.

'We were only at home two months when we were transferred to another ship belonging to the same owners, and rated as A.B.'s.[86] This voyage we sailed to Vancouver round the Horn, and from there we came down in ballast to Montevideo,[87] and loaded up with a general cargo for home. At this time there was a civil war going on in the Argentine Republic, and of course at Montevideo we heard a great deal of talk about it. Gibson used to get very excited over the war news, and over and over again he tried to persuade me to clear out from the ship and go with him to do some fighting. He'd no sympathies with either one side or the other, and I don't think he even knew what the row was about, but he wanted some fighting; fight was in his blood, and he was pining for what he called fun. I preferred, however, to keep a straight course, as my people before me had done. I wanted to gradually mount the ladder until I reached the top, and I knew that the quixotic expedition he proposed would have defeated my object. I therefore declined to fall in with his views. It riled him for a time, but at last he admitted that he had no right to try and persuade me against my will; but as far as he was concerned he was going. And go he did, much to my regret, I must confess. Although it went somewhat against my grain, I helped him to secretly get his duds on shore, and some money that I had I handed over to him.

'We spent our last night together at a *café* in the town of Montevideo; and when the time came for us to part he wrung my hand, and I was cut up in a way I had never been before. After that I saw no more of him, nor did I hear anything of him for ten years, when we met again under very extraordinary circumstances.

'I was then mate of a splendid barque called the *Curlew*, hailing from Bristol. We had taken out a cargo of iron to Bilbao,[88] there the ship was chartered by the Spanish Government to convey five hundred soldiers and a quantity of specie to Havana. The *Curlew* was an exceptionally fine vessel, with unusually good 'tween deck space, and therefore very suitable as a transport. We made a good passage to Havana, landed the troops, but were told we should have to retain the specie for a few days until some grandee or other came to receive it. He happened then to be up the country, but was expected back in the course of a week. As we had made a quicker passage than was expected, it had thrown him

---

86 Able bodied, the lowest role on a ship.
87 The capital of Uruguay.
88 A port in northern Spain.

out in his calculations. Well, of course, it didn't matter to us much, as our charter provided for our return to Bilbao; and, equally of course, so long as we were employed by the Spanish authorities we sailed under the Spanish flag.

'The second night after our arrival I went on shore, and in strolling through the town my attention was arrested by a sign over the door of a drinking-place. It read, "Old England, kept by Will Bradshaw." This and the sound of English voices induced me to enter, and I found the place pretty well crowded with sailor men and Spanish women of a disreputable class. I saw at once the sort of house it was, and as I did not consider it advisable for me as chief mate of a Government vessel to be seen there, I was for clearing out again when I noticed a big, brawny, powerfully-built fellow mixing drinks behind the bar. He was unmistakably an Englishman. His face was burnt brown. He had a dark, bushy beard, and looked like a man who had a large spice of the devil in him. Despite the beard the face seemed familiar to me, and when I heard him call out an order to one of his waiters, the voice left me no longer in doubt. It was the voice of Peter Gibson. So I pushed my way through the crowd to the counter, for it was not likely I could leave without renewing acquaintance with my old chum, and I asked, "Isn't your name Peter Gibson?"

'"No, it isn't," he yelled. "I'm Will Bradshaw, the boss of this place." I was taken aback for a minute, for I was sure I couldn't be mistaken. Then it flashed on me that Peter had a reason for being known as Will Bradshaw; so I pulled out a pocket-book, wrote my name on a leaf, tore it out, and handed it to him. I saw a look of surprise come into his eyes and his face change colour. Then he grasped my hand and wrung it, told an assistant to look after the place, and asking me to follow him, he led the way by a side entrance to a large garden at the back of the house, where seats were placed under the palm trees, and a few coloured lamps were hung up. Nearly every seat was occupied by men and women, and negro waiters were attending to their wants.

'Peter took me to a remote corner of the garden, where there was a sort of summer-house on a knoll.

'"We can have a quiet yarn here," he said. Then he called one of the negroes and told him to bring a bottle of wine, and that done, he began in his old masterful way to ask me questions about my career during the past ten years. I told him straight; but when I questioned him he shirked my questions, simply saying, "Well, I've had a lot of roughing, old chap, and have been in some queer corners. I drifted down here about two years since, just as the former proprietor of this shanty went off the hooks with Yellow Jack. I made a bid for the place and got it, but had to give bills for the greater part of the purchase money, and I've still got a lot of millstones round my neck. I'm rather sick, and think of chucking it and going on the rampage again."

'We yarned away for two hours, when I had to go, and naturally I asked him to come and see me on board the vessel. He turned up the next day, and the day after that; and I told him as an item of news that my skipper was going into the country on the morrow for a few days to shoot with a party of friends, and that I should be in charge; and I invited him to come on board and have dinner with me in the evening, an invitation he readily accepted.

'When he turned up he had a friend with him, a Spaniard who spoke good English, and whom he introduced to me as Alonzo Gomez. He said he wanted me to know this man, as he was a good sort, and might be of use to me. He was described as a planter, but I couldn't help thinking there was a good deal more of the loafer than the planter about him. However, he was very polite, as most Spaniards are, and as he seemed to be rather an amusing cuss, I thought I had judged him too harshly. Of course, I gave my guests a good feed, and made the steward open some champagne. During the dinner Peter asked me a lot of questions about the ship, and how much Spanish money we had on board, and where it was kept. If it had been anyone else, and at any other time, I should have resented these questions, but I felt there was no harm in answering my old schoolfellow and shipmate.

'When the dinner was over Peter said that for old acquaintance sake we must have a jorum of rum punch, and that he would make it. So I told the steward to get the necessary ingredients, and Peter set to work to concoct the liquor. I don't remember much more after that. I didn't come to my senses until the next morning. I found on turning out that the steward was ill, and on my going to him he told me that my friends had given him some of the punch. It had made him sick at first, and afterwards he fell into a heavy sleep from which he had not long awakened, and that he was then suffering from a frightful headache and a heavy, drowsy feeling. That was precisely my condition; but I attributed it to not having drunk wisely, but too well. The second mate, who had been on shore the previous night, undertook to do certain work I had to attend to; and having given the steward some medicine from the medicine chest, I went and turned in once more, and slept pretty well the whole day. Anyway, I did not turn to again until the following morning.

'In the course of that day, the high official who was to receive the specie came on board with an escort, and commanded the strong room in the after part of the cabin to be opened, and the specie brought out. I at once procured the keys from a safe in the captain's cabin, and on going to the strong room, I was surprised and alarmed to find that the various seals put upon the door at Bilbao were broken, and they had been broken quite recently, as two or three days before I had examined them and found them all right. My alarm and confusion increased when, having got the door open, we discovered that two of the boxes, one containing Bank of Spain notes and the other gold dollars, had been burst open, and partly rifled of their contents. Altogether a sum in notes and gold equivalent to twenty thousand pounds had been stolen.

'The big-wig was in a great state, and at once sent on shore for a magistrate and a lot of military officers, and began an inquiry there and then; and I, having been in charge of the ship for some days, was practically put on trial.

'Perhaps I needn't tell you that I felt I could at once name the thief. His name was Peter Gibson, alias Will Bradshaw. He and his Spanish chum had drugged me and the steward; of that I had no doubt then, and as all the crew had gone on shore except the boatswain and the cook, and two of the hands who were on duty at the gangway, it was easy for the rascals to carry out their nefarious scheme of getting at the specie.[89]

'Now, I'm not talking mere words to you when I tell you that it went against my grain to denounce my old schoolfellow and shipmate, and at first I resolved that I wouldn't. But, after all, a chap's own interests have to be counted first, and as Gibson had been mean hound enough to drug me and carry off money under my care, I didn't see why I should screen him. So I denounced him, and in a very short time he was under arrest. But even then he might have escaped conviction had it not been for his stupidity in keeping the banknotes. His friend, who was also arrested, turned out to be a notorious character with a most evil reputation, and was looked upon as an expert in picking locks. The task they had set themselves of stealing the money was comparatively easy, as all the conditions were in their favour, and I fell a too easy victim to their cunning.

'Well, of course, I had to attend the trial and give evidence. The crime was considered very serious indeed, as Government property

---

89 Coins.

had been stolen and Government seals unlawfully broken. The offence was called a first-class one, and the penalty was death. No such sensation had been provided for Havana for many a long day. It was considered better than a bullfight.

'To make a long story short, the result of it all was that the two rascals were convicted and sentenced to be shot. The verdict cut me to the heart, and as only a short shrift was allowed the culprits, as the sentence was to be carried out in twenty-four hours, I obtained permission to visit Gibson. I found him in rather a dejected state, seated in a courtyard of the gaol which was guarded by soldiers. As soon as he saw me he seemed to go mad, reviled me in language that was of a pretty fiery character, then cursed me and swore that he would haunt me and drive me to madness by appearing to me on dark nights at sea. "You are a doomed man," he said, "and will come to a sudden and terrible end. I leave my curse to you."

'I tried to reason with him, but I might as well have tried to reason with an enraged wild cat in the jungle. He did nothing but utter curses on me, and recognizing how hopeless it was to try and appease him, I withdrew, and the next morning he and his pal were shot at daybreak.

'Although I was much cut up by the way he had treated me, I did not attach any importance to either his curses or his threats. I wasn't altogether free from superstition, what sailor is? but I quite believed that when a person was dead he was done with. I soon began to find out, however, that I was wrong, for some weeks later, when we were on our passage back to Bilbao, I had the middle watch one night, just as we got into the Bay of Biscay. It was a wild night, and we were close hauled under double reefed topsails. Suddenly out of the waves came a glowing figure. It was Gibson's spectre. He shrieked at me, and I heard his curses again, and again he told me I was doomed.

'Since then I've seen him often. He has kept his word. He has haunted me, and is driving me mad and hounding me to death. Yes, I am doomed. I feel it and know it. Nothing can avert the doom.

'You know my story now. Don't ridicule it; don't laugh at me; for to me it's a terribly serious business, and I feel that I shall never see the dear woman I love again.'

~

He ceased speaking, and I noticed the wild, scared look in his eyes which I had seen before. The perspiration was streaming down his face, he appeared to be suffering great mental agony. I tried to soothe him, but it was no use, and he kept on repeating that he was doomed.

Now let me say here at once that I did not believe the captain had seen any real supernatural appearance. I regarded him as a highly imaginative and sensitive man. On such a man Gibson's curses and threats would be sure to make a very deep impression. It could hardly be otherwise, seeing that the two men had practically grown up together. They had been schoolmates and shipmates, and Gibson's violent end must have affected his once friend in no ordinary degree. Long dwelling upon the dramatic scene in the prison at Havana, the day previous to the execution, had taken such a hold on the skipper's imagination that he had worried himself into a belief in a mere chimera of the brain. To him, no doubt, the visions were real enough, although they were nothing more than disturbed brain fancies.

Such was the theory I consoled myself with, and I determined there and then to use every possible endeavour to get the captain out of his morbid condition, and prove to him by gentle reasoning that he was simply a victim to his own gloomy fears. I was so far successful at that moment that I induced him to turn in, having first of all called the mate down and given him certain instructions; then I compounded him a simple soothing draught from ingredients in the medicine chest, and at his own request I sat by him and read certain passages in the Bible, until he fell into a sound sleep.

I was considerably exercised in my own mind as to the proper course I ought to adopt, and I was tempted at first to take the Spanish lady into my confidence, and discuss the matter with her. But this idea was put out of my head at once, for she was sitting in the cuddy, as she usually did in the evening, where she passed her time either reading or in doing needlework. She saw that I came from the captain's cabin, and tackled me.

'How is the skipper?' she asked.

'He is a little indisposed to-night, but will be all right to-morrow, no doubt,' I answered.

'Not he,' she exclaimed. 'I tell you that man's a haunted man, and will either go mad or commit suicide.'

Remembering how dogmatically she had expressed herself on a previous occasion on the subject of supernatural visitations, I deemed it desirable not to enter into any discussion, and I also made up my mind that it would be a fatal mistake to let her know the captain's story, so I merely said, in answer to her statement, 'I hope not,' and passed to my cabin.

Now I want to repeat here, and for very obvious reasons, what were the views I held at this stage. I considered that the captain was suffering from a distressing nervous illness, the result of long pondering over an incident which could not fail to make a tremendous impression on him. But not for a moment did I entertain any belief in the supernatural. Necessarily I was exceedingly anxious, for there was no doctor on board, I had no medical knowledge myself, and we could not hope to reach our destination for another three weeks. There was every prospect then of the prognostications about a fine and rapid passage being falsified. The barometer had been steadily falling for some time, and all the indications were for bad weather. I knew that in that latitude, at that time of year, heavy storms were not uncommon, and it seemed likely that we should experience them. The anxious state of my mind kept me awake for some time, revolving all sorts of schemes, but nothing that seemed to me satisfactory. Eight bells midnight sounded, and I heard the mate come out of his room and go on deck to take the watch. I slipped out of bed, put on my dressing-gown and slippers, and stole over to the captain's cabin. To my intense relief I found he was sleeping soundly.

As the motion of the vessel made it evident there was a heavy sea on, I went up the companion-way to see what the weather was like. It was a wild, weird night. A south-west gale was blowing and a tremendous sea running. There was no moon, but the stars shone with a superb lustre wherever the ragged, storm-driven scud allowed them to be seen. I passed a few words with the mate, and asked him what he thought of the weather.

'It's a bad wind for us,' he answered, 'and the heavy squalls that come up every now and then prevent our setting much sail. But if I were skipper, I would crack on and let things rip. I'd drive the ship even at the risk of losing canvas.'

'Why don't you do so, as it is?' I asked. 'You've got charge of the deck for the next four hours, and have practically a free hand.'

'No I haven't,' he answered. 'I've got to obey orders, though I think sometimes, between you and me, sir, that the old man's got a bee in his bonnet, as they say in Scotland.'

'What makes you think that?' I queried, my interest in the skipper making me anxious to hear what the mate had to say. I had not before had any conversation with him about the captain's condition. Indeed, he was not a very talkative or communicative person. He was what is termed a cautious Scotsman.

'Well, I think it's because he's given to seeing the devil, or something as bad.'

I laughed, although I was serious enough; and being anxious to draw the officer out, I remarked:

'Well, I shouldn't say it's quite as bad as that; but he is ill, there is no doubt about it, and wants looking after.'

'I should think he does,' was the reply, given with peculiar decisiveness. Then, bending his head towards me, the better to make himself heard without raising his voice too much, for the howling of the wind made it difficult to hear sometimes, he added, 'Look here, Mr. Gibling, will you give me your promise that, if I express an opinion, it won't go any farther?'

'Yes, I think you may trust me,' I answered.

'Well, look here, sir, if you have any influence with the old man, you should persuade him to keep his room for the rest of the passage. And if he won't, I say that in his own interest and the interest of everyone on board this craft, that he should be made to stay there.'

Never before had the mate been so outspoken to me, and it was further evidence, if I needed any, that the skipper's condition had not escaped the observation of others; and I seriously determined to act on the suggestion, and use every effort to induce the captain to keep his room.

As a slight shift in the wind here necessitated the mate ordering the watch to trim the yards, I went below, and, feeling thoroughly exhausted, I drank a glass of whisky, and turning in, fell asleep. I must have slept between three and four hours, when I awoke with a start, for overhead was a tremendous hubbub. The tramping of heavily-booted feet, the rattling of cordage, the shaking of sails; while the ship, which was heeled over at an unusual angle, was quivering. I hastily donned my dressing-gown, and rushed on deck. A very heavy squall had struck us, and had torn the main-sail out of the bolt ropes. 'All hands' had been called on deck, and what with the shrieking wind and roaring sea, and the hoarse voices of the sailors, the situation seemed alarming enough to a landsman like myself. A lurch of the ship drove me down to the lee rail against the mizzen shrouds, which I clung to for dear life. Suddenly I felt myself gripped round the waist, and a body seemed to fall at my feet. I realized in an instant that it was the captain. He had only his shirt and drawers on. His feet were bare, his head was bare. So much I was able to make out in the darkness that wasn't altogether darkness, for a few stars still shone.

'For the love of God, for the sake of the Christ that was crucified, save me!' shrieked the unhappy man, as he crouched on his knees and linked his hands round my body.

'Don't give way like this,' I said, feeling almost distracted myself. 'Come, let me lead you down to your cabin. The mate will look after the ship. She is in good hands.'

It seemed as if the unhappy man did not understand what I had said to him, for pointing to the sea, he cried in a voice of acute terror:

'There, there, don't you see it? There on that wave? Oh, my God, it's awful!'

Mechanically I turned my eyes to where he pointed, and to my astonishment I saw what appeared to me to be a pale, lambent flame, shapeless and blue and nebulous. But I am conscious of thinking to myself that this was some natural phenomenon, like the well-known St. Elmo's fire.[90] Slowly, however, even as I watched (for my eyes were riveted on that light by some strange fascination), I saw the shapeless mass grow brighter. Then for the first time it seemed to dawn upon me that I was gazing upon something unearthly. My heart leaped to my mouth at the conviction, and a cold shivering thrilled through my body. I tried to shut out the vision, but my eyes would not close; I was under some spell, against which I had no power of resistance.

As I gazed, the flame assumed shape; the shape of a human being. I distinguished a face, wan and ghastly. The eyes were lustreless and fixed, like those of a dead man. In the naked body were many wounds, and from these wounds blood spurted out in streams, and as it seemed to me made the sea around crimson. I shuddered with horror at this dreadful sight; my knees bent under me, and I was on the point of sinking down, when I made a supreme effort and rallied. For the skipper was still clinging to me. I felt his weight, I heard his groans, but I saw nothing save that spectral figure with the gory streams pouring from its body.

Panting and breathless, a cold perspiration bursting through every pore, and with a feeling as if the scalp of my head was shrinking to nothing, I continued to gaze. The figure remained motionless, but its dull, glazed, dead eyes riveted themselves upon me as I thought, and I could not endure their gaze. I felt my brain maddening with terror; driven to frenzy I made a supreme effort to lift the captain in my arms

---

90 St. Elmo's fire is a bright blue or violet glow from pointed structures such as ships' masts that occurs in particular stormy conditions.

and carry him bodily down to his room. But he broke from me. He made as it seemed a flying leap from the poop to the waist of the ship; then another flying leap over the rail into the dark seething waters. I heard the heavy splash his falling body made. One long, piercing shriek as he floated astern filled the air.

I remember little more. There was a cry of 'Man overboard!' a wild rush of feet; a hasty cutting away of lifebuoys; hoarse voices mingling with flapping sails. How I got below I don't know, but I found myself lying in my berth with the Spanish lady standing over me, putting eau de cologne on my temples.

'Do you feel better now?' she asked in a not unkindly way.

'Yes, thank you,' I answered, feeling confused; 'but tell me, what does it mean? What has happened?'

'Why, don't you know?' she exclaimed; 'the captain has jumped overboard. I told you what would happen. He was haunted and went mad, I suppose. Anyway the poor fellow's gone.'

'And how did I get here?' I asked, with a dreadful sinking sensation at the heart and a dazed numb feeling in the brain.

'Well, you tumbled down the companion-way and were insensible when the stewards picked you up. You fainted, I suppose, with fright, eh?'

'I don't know, I don't know,' I murmured. 'It's all a dream.'

'Now tell me and speak the truth!' she said, in a commanding tone. 'Did you see anything!'

'Yes.'

'What?'

'The vision of a bleeding man.'

'Ah!' she exclaimed triumphantly, 'how about your scepticism now, eh?'

I had to confess that, according to my belief, I had seen the spectre of a man bleeding from several wounds; but still I thought it was nothing more than a delusion.

'But the captain was with you?'

'Yes.'

'And he saw it?'

'I have reason to think so.'

'Then were you both deluded? Anyway, poor fellow, he was deluded to his death. For he has perished.'

I could not enter into any argument. I felt too ill and distressed. I thanked her for her attention, and begged that she would leave me, as I thought I could sleep. She complied with this request, but I tossed and dreamed nightmare dreams, and dreamed and tossed for hours. It took me several days to recover from that awful shock to the nerves; indeed, I don't think I have ever quite recovered, or that I ever shall. I need scarcely say that from the moment the poor demented captain took that flying leap into the sea nothing more was ever seen of him, and an entry of his suicide was made in the log-book, and I signed it. On our arrival at Havana an inquiry was held by the British Consul, and I was called upon to state what I knew. I confined myself to saying that the captain believed himself that he saw a vision occasionally. He was very greatly affected, and I presume his brain gave way. I did not attempt to speak of my own awful experience. It was not necessary. Even if I had done so how could I have hoped to be believed? And yet I had seen with my own eyes. I, a scoffer in such matters, had been convinced, and what I have written here I solemnly declare to be true. Perhaps somebody cleverer than I, and more learned than I, may be able to explain away the mystery, but for me it will remain an awful, appalling mystery until I cease to breathe. Then, perhaps—who knows?—I may be able to solve it.

THE END

www.ingramcontent.com/pod-product-compliance
Lightning Source LLC
Chambersburg PA
CBHW060909250626
47159CB00008B/2925